**I frowned and moved forward to lightly
tap her shoulder. "Aspen?"**

A sudden shriek echoed through the kitchen as she spun around. Belatedly, I noticed she had earbuds in her ears and was focused on the open laptop in front of her. Her injured ankle wasn't up for the sudden movement as she whirled around to face me. I watched as she started to topple over, her hand flailing around ineffectively in the air in front of her.

I jerked forward, hands reaching instinctively so she wouldn't hit the floor. "Whoa, there. Sorry, I didn't mean to scare you."

Her momentum pushed her against my chest, sending one of my hands sliding across her ribs and the other across her backside to keep her upright. My intentions were good, but my starved libido registered the way her curves felt pressed up against me.

Her nearly black eyes gazed up at me. Her breath was warm against the base of my throat, and I could feel her fingers trembling against my biceps where she caught me for balance. . . . I could feel her heart pounding against my chest, and when she curled her hand around the back of my neck, I really couldn't see her as the enemy any longer.

I would never be able to pinpoint if I kissed her or if she kissed me. Not that it mattered. One second, we were staring at each other as I held her like she was the most precious thing on the planet, the next my mouth was all over hers, and I was kissing her the way you kissed someone you loved and hated at the same time. A little sweet, a little mean, and with enough passion to make us both forget we had a long, twisted road paved with mistakes and memories running between us.

Praise for
JUSTIFIED

"With a red-hot hero and emotional, unforgettable storyline, Crownover delivers the goods."

—Lori Wilde, *New York Times* bestselling author

"Off the charts attraction, dramatic suspense, heartbreaking betrayal, deep emotion, and unforgettable romance will keep you turning the pages to the climactic end. Fans and new readers will devour this fantastic story. I couldn't put it down!"

—Jennifer Ryan, *New York Times* bestselling author

"Once again, Jay Crownover proves why her words are so addictive! Her characters bleed life so tangibly, you feel like you're drowning in the emotions: in the best way possible. Five big huge stars for *Justified*! Don't miss this page-turner!"

—Harper Sloan, *New York Times* bestselling author

JUSTIFIED

A LOVELESS, TEXAS NOVEL

JAY CROWNOVER

FOREVER

New York　Boston

Copyright © 2019 by Jennifer M. Voorhees
Excerpt from Loveless, Texas Book 2 © 2020 by Jennifer M. Voorhees
Bonus Novella It's All About That Cowboy © 2020 by Carly Bloom
Cover photography by Rob Lang
Cover copyright © 2019 by Hachette Book Group, Inc.

Forever
Hachette Book Group
1290 Avenue of the Americas, New York, NY 10104
read-forever.com
twitter.com/readforeverpub

First Edition: June 2019

Forever is an imprint of Grand Central Publishing. The Forever name and logo are trademarks of Hachette Book Group, Inc.

The publisher is not responsible for websites (or their content) that are not owned by the publisher.

The Hachette Speakers Bureau provides a wide range of authors for speaking events. To find out more, go to www.hachettespeakersbureau.com or call (866) 376-6591.

ISBNs: 978-1-5387-4633-2 (mass market), 978-1-5387-4632-5 (ebook)

Printed in the United States of America

OPM

10 9 8 7 6 5 4 3 2 1

Dedicated to all of you holding this book right now, who don't consider loving the act of reading romance a "guilty pleasure"! I picked up my first romance novel when I was thirteen or fourteen. I stole a Nora Roberts book from my mom and never looked back. I was always an avid reader, but when I started reading primarily romance, suddenly I wasn't spending my free time wisely. Screw that noise. Uh...no. Reading is reading is reading. The content doesn't matter, and if it makes you happy, if it distracts you from the real world and real worries for a few hours, no one else gets a vote! For those of you who have been PROUD romance readers from the start—the ones who share your favorites, suggest new books, proudly flash those covers and titles all over social media despite the Judgy McJudgersons—thank you. I see you, and I appreciate you!

This book is for you!

JUSTIFIED

PROLOGUE

∞

ASPEN

I feel it is in the best interest of the child if full custody of the juvenile goes to the mother. I also approve her request for the increase in child support. The father will be allowed supervised visits overseen by a representative of the court. We will revisit the issue in a year."

At that statement, an animalistic growl sounded from the table across from me.

The former Mrs. Lawton dug her manicured fingers into my forearm hard enough to draw blood, and I fought back a wince. I hated her more now than I did in high school. If that was even possible, because I really, really hated her back then.

"We won. Aspen, we actually won. You're amazing. Worth every penny." Becca's voice was breathy and high. It matched her very blond hair, huge blue eyes, and very fake breasts. She looked like a Barbie doll, but she was far from a plastic, useless toy. The woman was a viper. Cunning and poisonous. I loathed representing her, hadn't wanted to do it, but the alternative was so much worse. She was practically a lethal weapon where her ex-husband was concerned, and I seemed to be the only one willing to keep this woman from completely destroying him out of spite.

Unfortunately, her ex-husband and father of her child made a lot of mistakes in court. And I was very, very good at my job. So, while I'd managed to rein in Becca's thirst for vengeance for the most part, there was no denying her ex still got annihilated in the courtroom. I'd gotten everything my client asked for, which included her ex-husband losing all parental rights to their nine-year-old son. The reason I resented having to represent her was because it was obvious Becca Lawton wasn't the best parent in the world, or actually concerned about her kid in the slightest. The little boy was the only thing her ex had shown any interest in fighting for during their contentious split. So, she'd latched on and thrown everything into keeping father and son apart for revenge, plain and simple. Like I said, she was a snake, which I already knew, because I'd often been her target when we were younger. If my father-in-law and boss hadn't insisted I be the one to represent the woman, I would've told her to take a hike months ago.

Right now I was wondering if I was any better than she was. I felt dirty and guilty as hell. I cast a look out of the corner of my eye to the man silently seething on the other side of the courtroom. Our eyes met briefly, and I had to look away almost immediately. If looks could kill, he'd have to arrest himself for murder. His hatred for me was as crystal clear as my hatred for my client was.

The seething animosity shouldn't hurt, but it did.

Because Case Lawton had always been *that* guy.

The guy who was always taller, bigger, stronger, faster, smarter, and more handsome than any other. He was the guy who made it impossible to see all the other available, possibly interested guys. Well, he blinded my starry teenage eyes to any other possible option at least. As the new girl in high school, it'd been hard to fit in, but Case was the first one to welcome me and try to put me at ease. He was the one who showed me around the school, introduced me to his friends, and assured me people would warm up eventually. He invited me to a football game, even though it was beyond obvious I didn't know anything about sports. He extended an invitation to my first high school party, when everyone else acted like I was invisible or carrying some infectious disease. He was nice to everybody, but the fact he took time to be nice to *me*, when no one else had ever made that effort before, meant I was a goner from the first time he smiled at me. I could never get over the fact he seemed to genuinely like having me around.

He was witty, unfailingly polite, and full of good ole southern charm. He seemed utterly untouchable, unstoppable. He never had a problem getting whatever it was he wanted, be it a football championship, a nearly perfect score on his SATs, or the prettiest girl in the entire county. His constant good fortune and the ease with which he had the entire small town of Loveless, Texas, eating out of the palm of his hand should've been annoying. It should have built up loads of bitterness in the rest of us who didn't have the same kind of unwavering charm.

No one ever disliked Case Lawton, or let their jealousy of him turn them bitter. Because it was no secret that, as perfect as Case's life looked on the outside, on the inside, it was far from flawless. Case's father was the sheriff of Loveless. He was also a big bully who used his position and his badge to abuse the locals. He had a very loose definition of law and order. Rumors had floated around for years that Sheriff Lawton was a bigger criminal than half the people he put away. No one could miss how desperately Case tried to make up for all of his father's glaring shortcomings. It was almost as if he was trying to save the entire Lawton name from disgrace.

Everyone, including me, knew Case wanted to leave Loveless right after graduation. We were rooting for him. He had a football scholarship locked down for a Big Ten school up north, and he didn't hide he was ready to leave Texas, and his father's tainted legacy, far behind. Of course, I selfishly didn't want him to go but secretly hoped he made it out, because he deserved better than being known as Sheriff Lawton's son.

It was right before graduation when the precarious house of cards he had built came tumbling down around him. Case fell from grace in the way only idols and gods can.

His mother passed away suddenly. He broke his leg in two places during the last game of the season. His father lost all the restraint he pretended to have, and all the Lawton siblings started showing up to school with obvious bruises all over them. And last but not least, the prettiest girl in the county, the one who nagged him constantly and begged him not to leave after graduation, conviently ended up pregnant.

There would be no escape, no bigger and better things for Case Lawton. No avoiding the long, dark shadow his father cast in this town. He joined the military days after graduation and minutes after putting a ring on the finger of the girl who'd effectively trapped him. He served his four years and returned to Loveless harder, colder, and so much angrier than before. He was no longer nice, easygoing, charming, and thoughtful. He came back to a very young wife who was practically a stranger and to a son who hardly recognized him. The rushed marriage was not one anyone would call happy.

Instead of being the town's favored son and biggest

success story, he was no different from any of the other young men who couldn't find their way out of the city limits. Soon, Case gave up all pretense of ever wanting more for his life and went to work as a deputy for his father in the sheriff's department. And the townspeople who had always rooted for him suddenly saw him as a failure. Their collective "told you so" could be heard as far away as the moon.

I didn't have a logical reason, beyond Case being my first real crush, as to why his giving up on his dreams affected me so deeply. All I knew was that it did. I'd harbored a passionate infatuation for Case from the first moment I saw him. My family moved to Loveless from Chicago my freshman year of high school. To say I was a fish out of water in the small Texas town was an understatement. I stood out like a sore thumb, had trouble making friends and fitting in. I mostly kept to myself, watching the new people and the world around me. Case made himself impossible to miss by being friendly and kind, so he immediately became the center of all my focus. It didn't matter that he treated everyone as if they were his best friend. All I cared about was the way he welcomed me and made me feel like I belonged, when everyone else made sure to make me feel like I didn't.

Obviously, he never knew of or returned my infatuation, but I didn't mind as long as I got a smile or a wave when he passed me in the hall. I was so used to being ignored; his attention, no matter how minimal, meant everything.

After high school, while Case followed his father's footsteps, I moved away for college. I graduated from law school and decided to move back to Loveless, even though my parents had long since gotten tired of small-town life and moved to Florida. When I went away to college, my father fully expected me to go into environmental law, the way he had. But I wanted to help the less fortunate, families and kids in a tough spot, those who felt left behind and discarded. I planned to be a voice for the underdogs, not the winners.

However, much like Case Lawton, I eventually ended up lost inside my own status quo. Instead of being an altruistic do-gooder, I found myself working for a legal firm that operated as a business, not as a charity, getting married, and trying to start a family. It took marrying someone with the right last name and history with the town for me to finally be fully accepted by everyone in Loveless. No one ignored me or pretended like I didn't exist anymore, but I always remembered that Case went out of his way to include me before I married up. He liked me for me, not my new last name.

My return home and new life was all going pretty smoothly, if not boringly and predictably, until the day I happened to be at the wrong place at the right time.

I was walking into the sheriff's department to speak with one of my clients. She was a young woman who was a victim of domestic violence. Case's father had arrested her instead of her husband, even though she was the one with black eyes and a broken nose. It just so happened I was walking up the steps and Case was walking down when a process server shoved a set of familiar documents into a surprised Case's hands. I hadn't seen him up close in years. Occasionally our paths crossed in the courthouse or the sheriff's office, but he never acted like he remembered who I was, and all of his previous approachability was long gone. He was not the devastatingly handsome teenager I had a crush on anymore. No. He was a very angry, restless man now. One I tended to give a wide berth to because the changes in him made me nervous.

"You've been served, Deputy Lawton."

I knew they were divorce papers before Case did. I'd sent plenty of them out in my few years practicing family law. I should've kept moving, my client needed me, but I couldn't get my feet to cooperate. Instead, I was frozen on the spot as Case read through the pages and pages of documents, pale blue eyes widening as he learned exactly how done with him his wife was.

When he got to the last page, he lifted his head and looked right at me. I doubted he even realized I was there, but then he whispered, "She wants to take my boy."

I couldn't stop myself from reaching out and putting a hand on his tense forearm. It was the first time I'd ever been brave enough to touch him, even back when he acted like he was my friend, I was too shy to ever touch him.

"It'll be fine. Get a good lawyer." It was the advice I would give to anyone in his shoes. And, by a good lawyer, I obviously meant myself, but we didn't know each other well enough anymore for me to be that bold. If we'd stayed friendly, or even in touch after high school, I would've offered on the spot. But he still intimidated the hell out of me, and I had to admit I questioned his sincerity and trustworthiness, since he knowingly went to work for a blatant crook like his father.

In a split second, the man morphed from a confused spouse and scared father to a fire-breathing dragon. He shook my hand off his arm and glowered at me from underneath lowered, dark brows. This was the Case who'd had his entire life stolen and was looking at losing it all once again. The friendly congenial mask he wore when he was younger was nowhere to be found.

"Do I know you?" His tone was as icy as every line in his big body locked as if he was ready for a fight.

I fell back a step. He didn't even recognize me. It was like a physical blow to all my tender, youthful fantasies. Again, it shouldn't hurt to be so forgettable and unremarkable, but it did. Even more so coming from the one person who always made me feel like I was seen, like I mattered and deserved to be included. "I'm Aspen Barlow, used to be Aspen Keating. We went to high school together. We met my first day of school. You showed me around." And pretended to be my friend. I couldn't get those sour words out.

His eyebrows twitched, and his mouth shifted to an emotionless line. "The weird girl who moved here from New York?" His gaze raked over me, seemingly unimpressed.

I bristled and locked down any scrap of emotion that might betray how badly his words stung. I'd lived here for years, built up a solid reputation. I thought I was finally fitting in and had shaken the "weird girl" reputation his bitchy wife had helped spread around when we were younger.

"Yep. That's me, the weird girl, but I moved here from Chicago, not New York." I nodded to the papers in his hand. "Trust me. Don't fight her without a good attorney. Courts always tend to give mothers the benefit of the doubt." I was speaking from experience.

"What do you know about it?" Case sounded confused and pissed enough to spit nails. I felt for the guy, he was clueless, and that was bad, especially considering his marriage was about to implode.

"More than I want to. I practice family law. Divorces and custody agreements make up the about eighty percent of my case list." I jumped down a full step when he let out a bark of disbelieving laughter.

"People actually let *you* represent them?" His gaze raked over my tailored black pantsuit and spiked heels. He made a face and twisted the papers in his hands. "Most of the lawyers in town grew up here. I'll go with one of them. They have to know there's no way Becca is a better parent to Hayes than I am. Thanks for your advice, but I've got this." He rolled the papers into a tight tube and stuck them in the back pocket of his tan uniform. Face set in a scowl, he walked away without another word, dismissing me as inconsequential, and my advice as empty words.

He was going to regret that choice.

I forcibly pushed the encounter out of my mind. Occasionally, at night when it was dark and quiet, I would let embarrassment and disappointment over the encounter sneak past my defenses, but mostly I put Case firmly in a "do not touch" box in the back of my mind. I thought my run-in with him was all said and done until a senior partner at my practice, who also happened to be my father-in-law, walked into my office and informed me I would be representing Becca Lawton, Case's soon to be ex, in her divorce.

Before I could tell him there was a conflict of interest, and that I was not a good fit to represent my high school nemesis, Becca Lawton was sitting in front of me airing years of dirty laundry between her and Case. She wanted to bury the poor man. She wanted everything he had. And she really, really wanted to break his heart by taking away his son. She did have some valid points. Case worked too much. Drank too much. He had an unpredictable temper, and his immediate family was a volatile mess. She also insisted he was unfaithful, but there was no proof of it. Mostly, she was tired of pretending to be happily married when she was anything but. She claimed she wasted her youth on Case, and her resentment was evident.

It was on the tip of my tongue to tell her I couldn't represent her. Sure, Case had issues, but nothing worthy of separating a father and son permanently. But then she looked me dead in the eye and told me she was willing to ruin him in court. She was willing to tell the judge that one night after binge drinking, Case admitted to her that he knew for a fact his father manipulated evidence in many of the cases that passed through the sheriff's office. She claimed Case was racked with guilt over one particular case, involving a young married couple that eventually led to tragedy. The young wife came to the sheriff to report long-term abuse. She was battered, had a broken arm, and was terrified. Case arrested the husband, but his father let the man go the same day, claiming there wasn't enough evidence to hold him. Not long after his release, the husband, who also happened to be a highly visible member of the local church, went on to stalk his young wife. He kidnapped her, assaulted her, and then killed himself right in front of her, all because Sheriff Conrad Lawton didn't do right by her.

Becca claimed that everything that happened to the woman weighed heavily on Case. He was feeling helpless, angry at the world. But one night, when he was drunk, he admitted to knowing that his father "misplaced" the damning photos of the woman's injuries and the doctor's statement that her physical examination showed signs of long-term abuse. According to Becca, Case caught his father in the middle of manipulating the facts and evidence, and he knew Conrad accepted a payment in order to protect the churchgoing husband. But Case never said a word, never told the town or the young woman's family the truth.

The story made my blood run cold. I was almost sure she was lying, but she was vindictive, and the story sounded believable. Everyone knew Conrad Lawton was a dirty cop, and if what she said came out in court, Case would not only lose custody, but also his job and possibly his freedom. He would be guilty of being part of a cover-up. A less scrupulous attorney would take Becca and her story and run with it, because all an attorney needed was suspicion. Just the hint of Case doing something illegal would be enough to derail his custody plea. I couldn't let that happen. I remembered how much Case hated his father, and I knew deep down that Case would never cover for him, particularly in a case this horrific.

Reluctantly, I pushed every reservation I had down and promised Becca I would get her everything she wanted. I told myself I could do it without completely ruining Case's image and dragging his name through the mud, because without implacable proof, I refused to believe he was following in his father's footsteps. Becca agreed to keep Case's drunken confession quiet as long as I stripped Case of literally everything he held dear. I think she liked the idea of forcing me to ruin my former crush's life, almost as much as she delighted in watching him squirm before the judge.

By the time we went to trial, Case foolishly had hired an old football buddy, an attorney I knew relied more on charm and flashy theatrics, rather than on any actual skill. I almost felt sorry for him. *Almost.* If he hadn't smirked at me like his victory was guaranteed the first day. Instead, we battled it out for months and months, and in the end, it was Case's father who finally swayed the judge to give Becca everything she asked for.

It seemed Sheriff Lawton thought he could use his usual intimidation tactics on the presiding judge. Threats were made, weight was thrown around, and for once, the patriarch of the Lawton clan ran up against someone who wasn't scared of him. The judge was concerned about young Hayes being under the influence of such a morally questionable man. He advised Case to take a good hard look at his life choices over the next year, and the case was closed.

At least it was supposed to be.

I should've known a guy like Case Lawton wasn't going to let such a catastrophic loss go without a word.

When I noticed he was waiting in the hallway, I foolishly hoped it was for his former spouse. When Becca breezed by him with a tiny wave and a wink, his entire face flushed and his back went ramrod straight. I ordered myself to keep moving, my job here was done. He didn't remember me, and now I was sure he really wanted to forget all about me.

His massive arms crossed over his wide chest, and his eyes cut through me like twin lasers.

"Are you happy? Do you feel good about what just happened, weird girl?" His words were cutting and blunt. I wanted to kick him in the shins for once again throwing out the taunt Becca had used in high school to alienate me. Back then he had told her to knock it off, but now he was using the words as a weapon against me.

I cleared my throat, tightened my hand on the handle of my briefcase, and refused to flinch away from the absolutely murderous look in his eyes.

"I told you to get a *good* lawyer, Mr. Lawton." I kept my voice calm, but the sarcasm in my tone was unmistakable. In court I wasn't a woman prone to sass, but outside of the courthouse, I wasn't afraid to speak my mind, and I no longer let others' opinions make me feel badly about myself. He was the one who initially made me realize I should matter, and it was a lesson I had taken to heart.

Case growled an ugly string of swear words in my direction and leaned forward. With his towering height, he loomed over me, and I had to suppress a full body shiver and the urge to shrink away.

"You ruined my life, Aspen Barlow. Everything that matters to me you've just ripped away. I would give what little I have left for you to have never stepped foot in this town. You better hope to God our paths don't cross anytime soon." He gave me one last scathing look before marching off down the hall, rage evident in his stride, completely unfazed that he openly threatened me.

I obviously no longer knew who Case Lawton was, and I didn't want anything to do with the angry, shortsighted man who just stormed away from me. Because I was suddenly having no problem seeing him as a person who would look the other way while his father tampered with evidence—even though he wore a badge and claimed to hate everything his father stood for.

After that day, it was common knowledge that Case and I were enemies, adversaries, rivals. I went out of my way to avoid him, and he made it a point to make my life a living hell whenever the opportunity arose.

If there was anyone I didn't expect to lean on when my own house of cards went up in flames a few years later, it was the newly appointed sheriff of Loveless, Texas, Case Lawton.

CHAPTER 1

ASPEN

Nine years later

 D o you have any enemies who would do something like this?" The question was practically snarled at me as I repressed an eye roll.

My office was trashed. Every drawer in my desk was open and the contents flung from one wall to the next. Both of my filing cabinets were tipped over and had dents where it looked like someone had tried to pry them open. All the pictures and degrees that decorated the walls had the frames smashed and the inside contents shredded. My computer was now only a mangled husk of wires and broken glass, and there was scarlet red paint splattered all over the plush Berber carpet and white walls. Ugly words were scrawled across all the windows, and again I wondered how no one passing by on the street had noticed anything amiss when the destruction was occurring. My office was right in the middle of Main Street. Granted, Loveless was no bustling metropolis, but Main Street always had a steady flow of foot traffic coming and going, and I was pretty close with the young couple who ran the coffee shop across the street. How had no one seen anything?

I crossed my arms defensively over my chest and narrowed my eyes at Case Lawton. When it came time to elect a new sheriff, I didn't regret casting my vote for him—anyone was better than his father—until right this moment. In all the years following his explosive divorce, and rude, threatening behavior afterward, we'd managed to maintain a proprietary distance from one another. It was a delicate dance we both knew all the steps to, but tonight, he was the one who showed up when I hysterically called to report the break-in and vandalism. When I first caught sight of him, I wondered if he'd shown up just so he could gloat.

My heart and my head had always had a very complicated battle going on when it came to Case Lawton.

My head liked to remind me that he was the only person who'd ever made me waffle in my convictions—and look the other way when the law was possibly compromised. I'd never done anything with the information his ex-wife handed over, not just because I couldn't prove it, but also because deep down I didn't believe it. Since taking over the sheriff's job from his father, Case had been nothing but law abiding. He was a stern yet fair enforcer of the law.

But my heart—the squishy, too soft thing—begged for me to make the first move, to mend fences and shift the dynamic between us if he ever gave me an opening. My heart never seemed able to fully let go of the memory of the young man who made such a difference when I was so alone.

"Aside from you? No. I don't have any specific enemies I can think of off the top of my head." But I was an attorney, and I did handle a lot of divorces and custody cases. Unfortunately, that meant there were often spouses and parents who felt like they were getting a raw deal on the other side of the courtroom. Not unlike the large man prowling around my office. Why was it still hard to breathe when I was this close to him? Shouldn't I have shaken that particular quirk loose by now? It'd been almost a decade since we'd said a civil word to each other.

"What about your husband? I heard you were separated. Is it an amicable split?" Case moved toward a particularly large puddle of paint on the floor. Crouching down he touched it with a tip of his finger. His hand came away smeared with red. "It looks like you just missed whoever was in here. The paint didn't even have time to get tacky."

I huffed out a sigh that sent my dark fringe of bangs dancing across my forehead. Case was the last person on the planet I wanted to discuss my impending divorce with. In fact, I didn't want to talk about my failed relationship with him at all but realized my soon-to-be ex-husband was bound to be a suspect. Sadly, David was not a man prone to acts of passion or rage. He was unfailingly calm, wholeheartedly steady, endlessly kind, and the divorce had been all my idea, not his. He was still stalling over signing the papers, even though I'd filed for divorce over eight months ago and moved out of our shared home in Loveless's only gated community over a year ago. David was still holding out hope I'd have a change of heart, even though I knew all the way down to my bones I wouldn't. We were done, but that didn't mean he would trash my office.

"Yes, the split is amicable. David would never do anything like this." In the nearly twelve years we were together, the man had raised his voice to me only twice. Once when I told him I was done with the emotional turmoil of trying to conceive, and the second when I walked out our front door.

"You recently left the law firm he runs with his father and

uncle. Is there any bad blood there?" Case asked the question matter-of-factly, but I felt like he was digging, trying to find a sore spot to push on. I knew somewhere inside he was thrilled my first few steps of independence were being sabotaged in such a graphic, unmistakable way. When I failed, he considered it a win. He'd proven that fact over and over again when we'd clashed in court during the last several years.

I bit back another sigh and fought the urge to tap the toe of my pointy, high-heeled boot. "The Barlows didn't want me to leave. I'm good at my job, and starting my own practice means competition in court and a fight for clients' money. They know many of my clients are going to follow me to my new practice. But we're family. They supported my decision." Well my father-in-law did, even if he didn't fully understand it. David didn't want me to leave the practice any more than he wanted me to leave our marriage, but my choice wasn't about him.

Opening my own practice, taking on cases I wanted to handle, working with clients who really needed me—not just the ones who could afford me—were all steps I needed to take to no longer simply be known as David Barlow's wife. Somewhere along the line, well after I'd become a Barlow, I'd forgotten exactly who Aspen Keating was and all about the things she was determined to accomplish. I was desperate to find the old Aspen again.

Case grunted a noncomment and walked over to the window, where a collection of offensive slurs were painted. The red paint started to drip, making the glass look like something out of a horror movie. He cocked his head to the side, and I ordered my eyes not to trace over the broad lines of his back and the way his tight backside delightfully filled out his too-tight jeans. Now that he was the sheriff, he no longer had to wear the all-tan uniform. He still had on the ugly shirt, but the rest of his outfit was casual, jeans, black cowboy boots, and a black Stetson. He still managed to bleed authority and control in just a partial uniform, and I hated how he seemed to take up all the space in the room. It was completely illogical to still harbor an unkillable attraction to a man who made it abundantly clear he could barely stand the sight of me. In fact, David had cruelly thrown my fascination with Case in my face the day I left him. It was the one and only time he'd ever mentioned what I thought was my secret crush on the sheriff, but it was enough to make me double my efforts to keep Case out of sight and out of mind.

"These words have any merit? Were you seeing someone on the side? Does your husband have a reason to be jealous?" Case looked at me over his shoulder while waving a hand at the ugly words dripping garishly down the glass.

I arched an eyebrow in his direction and lost the fight to impatiently tap my foot. I also gave up on the battle to keep from rolling my eyes at his perpetually condescending tone. "Ex-husband. And no, our relationship didn't end because either of us was unfaithful." Though I had to silently admit there were occasions when I had no clue where David was. Those times had increased with frequency in the last few years, making my decision to leave even easier. "I told you, David has nothing to do with this. I have no idea who could be behind it."

"Why did you come back to the office so late tonight?" His turned and looked at the toppled filing cabinets. "It looks like you may have interrupted whoever was in here when you showed up."

I felt like he was accusing me of something, so I automatically bristled. "I told you, I forgot a file I wanted to go over before going in front of the judge tomorrow. My mother called when I was leaving for the day, and I got distracted.

I spoke with her, decided to make myself dinner, and when I sat down to go over my notes realized I had left the file in my office. When I got here, the front door was open, and I could smell the paint. I called your office and waited until you showed up before coming inside." I knew enough to not go inside. I didn't want to give Case, or any of his deputies, cause to accuse me of tampering with a crime scene.

Not that I believed Case was a dirty cop like his father. He may have been under Conrad Lawton's thumb for too many years to count, but after his father cost him the custody of his son, Case was done with everything having to do with Conrad Lawton. He'd made it his mission to get the patriarch of the Lawton clan out of office, a task that took several years, but Case had accomplished it. Now he was working his ass off, day in and day out, to undo all the damage his father had done while using the sheriff's office as his own personal playground. However, Case still resented me, loathed me, blamed me. He might believe wholeheartedly in justice and law, but I wouldn't put it past him to use whatever small mistake I made against me.

"I keep client files in there. I suppose someone could theoretically want them if I'm representing their spouse in a separation. Divorces can get ugly, especially in a small town." Everyone knew everyone else's business, which was why I wasn't surprised Case knew about my impending divorce and the fact that I'd left my previous practice. There were very few secrets in Loveless. Even fewer of them when you stood out like a sore thumb.

"Any of your current cases nastier than the others? Have you been getting threats? Or has anything unusual happened that you may have written off as part of the job?" He rubbed his thumb along the line of his chin and turned sharp, arctic blue eyes in my direction.

It wasn't fair. He really shouldn't have been allowed to age as well as he had. It would be much easier to hate him back if he'd ended up haggard and slightly thick around the middle like his father. Instead, I'd watched from afar as Case got better and better over time. He was harder, more rugged and masculine than he'd been in high school, and more broody and moody than when he'd returned from the military. He even looked good with the very faint hint of silver starting to thread through the stubble on his chin and in his neatly trimmed sideburns. The rest of his hair was thick and jet-black. It was a striking combination with those bright blue eyes of his. He'd always been a bit of a heartbreaker, but now he was something beyond that. A heart destroyer, or maybe even a heart annihilator. He crushed the delicate things without even trying. I knew it well. Mine had been one of his first victims.

I shook my head and tapped my toe impatiently once again. "Nothing too weird. And I don't have a case I can think of that would lead to such a volatile reaction." The only odd thing in my life recently was my mother calling me once a day to try and talk me out of leaving David.

She'd never been particularly interested in anything I was doing with my life until I left my husband. As soon as I told her I was asking for a divorce, she turned into a helicopter parent and couldn't be any more up in my business. She was driving me nuts. I wanted to believe she only cared about my well-being, but I knew there was more to it than that. The woman hadn't even pretended to be sympathetic during the years of struggle while David and I tried and failed to conceive.

I wasn't sure if my soon-to-be-ex had enlisted her help, or if she was being super annoying of her own volition. Either way, I was over it. If my mother tried to convince me I was going to die alone one more time, I was going to lose it. Tonight, I'd finally told her enough was enough. I couldn't listen to it anymore. She'd been irritated and hung up on me, but that was nothing new.

My father passed away a few years ago, and my mother almost immediately remarried. Her new husband was another cold, emotionally distant man, much like my father had been. Only this one liked to play around in the stock market and had varying degrees of success. My mother didn't hesitate to ask for money when he had a bad month, and I never hesitated to hand it over. I didn't doubt she was concerned that, without David's half of the income, her easy access to my cash would be much more limited.

I saw her briefly on the occasional holiday—which was plenty for both of us. The only thing I'd ever gotten right in my life as far as either of my parents were concerned was marrying into the Barlow family. Both my parents loved David and his parents. Well, they loved their money and the clout their name carried in Loveless. Once I had David's ring on my finger, I was finally living up to my potential, and I think they were shocked someone from old money was willing to take on the weird girl from the city who had a penchant for all-black clothing and an unending desire to fight for human rights. I was as far from a southern belle as any woman could get, but David loved me anyway. Which was why mother was berating me for letting such a good catch slip through my fingers. I would eat glass before telling her David wasn't as great as she believed him to be.

David was a nice guy, a decent lawyer, decent in bed, but he was predictable. Any given day I could map out exactly what our interactions were going to be like, the words we were going to say to each other. It had all become so comfortable and boring. I felt like I was suffocating on the expected.

Except tonight was anything but predictable and expected. I never would've believed Case and I could spend this much time in an enclosed space without bloodshed or tears. It was the longest I'd been this close to him in years, and the longest stretch of time he had tolerated me. It was weird and oddly thrilling. It'd been far too long since anything in my life had taken me by surprise.

Case turned around, so he was facing me, and I shook myself out of my thoughts. He cocked a dark eyebrow and laced his thumbs through a couple of belt loops on the front of his jeans. A muscle twitched in his tanned cheek, and his eyes flicked over me. Slowly, the usual irritation he showed when we clashed started to bleed into the blue of his gaze. I gave him credit for keeping his cool and being professional up until this point, but it seemed like he'd reached his limit of courtesy.

"You have to give me something to go on, Counselor. I find it hard to believe there's no one in this town you've pissed off enough to trash your new office. We both know you're a pit bull in court and will do whatever it takes to get your clients whatever it is they are asking for...no matter how unreasonable the request may be." His top lip curled up a tiny bit before he forcibly made his expression blank and unreadable once again. "You tend to piss people off without even trying. There has to be someone who's threatened you, tried to intimidate you. I need a name, Aspen."

I flinched when he said my name. He didn't use it often, and when he did, I was torn between being thrilled and annoyed at how he always made it sound like a dirty word.

Losing what little hold I had left on my temper, I threw my hands up in the air and scowled at the big man in front of me. "The only person in this entire town who I absolutely know has a grudge against me, and who regularly tries to intimidate me, is *you*, Sheriff." I waved a hand around the carnage that used to be my work space. "So, unless you want to start by investigating yourself, I don't know what to tell you." Frustration was evident in every word, but Case seemed totally unmoved by the outburst.

He reached up and tipped the brim of his cowboy hat back with his index finger. He shot one more look around the room and lifted his broad shoulders and let them fall in a careless shrug. "I'll send the tech team in to dust for prints, but I can't guarantee we'll get anything. I'll see if the coffee shop across the street managed to get their cameras fixed yet. Maybe they recorded whoever broke in. You're gonna have to take a few days off while we get things sorted."

I narrowed my eyes even further. "I have to have access to my case files. I have to be in court for the next few days." I looked at the smeared paint. It was going to be a bitch to clean once it dried, and I silently wondered if that was part of Case's plan. He would never pass up an opportunity to make my life more difficult than it already was.

"You can take what you need. See if you can figure out if anything is missing while you're at it. Get the locks changed when you get a chance and think really hard about who might be behind this. If you give me a name or two to chase down, it would be helpful."

He sounded totally disinterested in figuring out who had trashed my office, but at least he wasn't brushing me off. If I had a name to give him, I would. I honestly couldn't imagine anyone being this angry at me. I was going to have to look through my current cases and see if any one of the spouses on the opposing side stood out as a possible danger. I represented plenty of women, and the occasional man, trying to leave an abusive relationship, but mostly it was couples who simply grew tired of the work it required to keep a marriage together.

I hurried under Case's watchful eye, gathering what I'd need from the mess. I was careful to avoid the paint smeared everywhere, but the words painted across the window kept catching my attention. When I was younger, I'd gotten used to people labeling me. *Weirdo, freak, odd, strange, off, different*...they all were used more frequently than my actual name throughout high school. By everyone, aside from the man whose gaze I was currently avoiding. He always called me Aspen until that day on the stairs when he got the divorce papers. That was when things changed.

But it was strange to see such strong language staring back at me now. Harsher words that weren't even used to describe me in high school. The words were meant to wound and send a message, but they were so off base it was ridiculous.

I dated here and there through college, where the boys were more open-minded and accepting. Then I'd met David at a fund-raiser within months of coming back to Loveless. We were both in the field of law, both back in a small town after attending college in a big city, both looking for something serious and finding it within each other. He was the only person I was with for over a decade. Not that I would find those words appropriate in any occasion, even if my bedroom door was open to all comers.

Shaking my head at my wandering thoughts, I clutched the files to my chest as I followed Case out of the building. He was on his phone, ordering someone to come over and snap pictures and dust for fingerprints. I felt pretty dismissed, so I turned on the heel of my very expensive boot and started to walk to where my Audi was parked in front of the building. Everything in my arms nearly went flying all over Main Street when Case's heavy hand fell on my shoulder, stopping me in my tracks with a jolt.

"Hold on a second." He barked a few more orders into his

phone and pushed the brim of his hat back even more. His dark eyebrows were pulled into a V, and the tick in his cheek seemed to be fluttering even faster than it had been when we were in my office. "Since you have no clue who could be behind this, I'm advising you to keep your eyes open and put an ear to the ground. I'd bet good money the vandalism is related to one of your cases. Someone is trying to send you a message. You should take extra precautions over the next few days, and if anything seems out of sorts, you need to give my office a call."

I stiffened more because of his bossy tone and glare than anything he was saying. "I've been in this business a long time, Sheriff. I know how to watch my back. Thank you for hurrying out here and taking my complaint seriously."

It was his turn to roll his coolly expressive eyes. Obviously, he knew I doubted him taking my situation seriously, considering our history. However, Case proved he was a good cop, regardless of the foul, corrupt reputation his father had left behind and any doubts I may have had.

"I'm good at my job as well, Counselor." I couldn't miss the biting sarcasm laced throughout his tone.

I was about to walk away once more when a familiar luxury car pulled up next to mine. I barely bit back a groan as my soon-to-be ex-husband climbed out of his Lexus. David was still dressed in a suit—minus a tie—and his usually meticulously styled hair looked messy and was sticking out at odd angles. He gave Case a brief nod before his entire attention focused on me. His eyes were serious behind his expensive glasses, and I felt like he was about to interrogate me the way he did when he was examining a witness on the stand.

"What's going on? Why is the sheriff here? Why are you at your office so late?" The questions were fired one after another, and I wanted to throw myself in front of the window with the bloodred words painted on it. There was no hiding that particular act of vandalism, and I knew the graphic display was going to send David into an emotional tailspin. He'd always been protective, or overbearing, to be more accurate. After the night I'd had, I was in no mood to deal with the impending demands to move back home so he could take care of me. To make matters worse, I could feel Case watching my interaction with my estranged husband with harsh, judgmental eyes.

"There was a break-in. No big deal, it happens. My office is in a prime location. The sheriff took a look around and is handling things. Nothing for you to worry about." I plastered a smile on my face and reached out to pat David on the arm. He was incredibly tense, so much so I could feel him vibrating under the fabric when I touched him. "What are you doing out this late?" He was usually in bed by now if he wasn't out of town on business or entertaining a client. I could set my watch by his habits.

David raked his fingers through his hair and narrowed his eyes at me behind the lenses of his glasses. "I had a late meeting with Father and Uncle Keith at the country club. We were discussing hiring a new attorney to fill your spot."

He threw the words out pointedly. I think he expected them to wound, but all they did was send relief shooting through me. If they hired a new attorney, maybe he could finally realize it was time to move on. He really was a decent guy and deserved the kind of forever he thought he was getting when he proposed to me.

"I saw your car and the sheriff's SUV on my way home. I was worried. You know what I think about you living all the way across town on your own."

He hated it, but he didn't have any say in the matter. Luckily, I was saved from making a snarky reply by Case clearing his throat and muttering, "I'll be in touch sometime tomorrow after the tech team is done in your office. Think about what I said, Aspen." He inclined his dark head toward the window David had yet to notice. I glared at him as he dryly told David, "Be a gentleman and find some plywood to cover that window up for her. We don't need that kind of profanity right in the middle of Main Street."

He tipped his hat down over his eyes before he sauntered away, and I swore I could hear him chuckle under his breath. The asshole knew exactly what he was doing by pointing out the vulgar words to my soon-to-be ex. I heard David gasp and braced myself for the one million questions that I knew were going to come next. I was already tired and stressed-out, I didn't need a showdown with David on top of everything else.

Damn that Case Lawton.

CHAPTER 2

∞

CASE

I couldn't hide my smirk as I walked away from Aspen Barlow and her overbearing husband. I had vague recollections of David Barlow from back in the day. He was a couple of years older than I was, and we definitely didn't run in the same social circles, then or now, but I knew the man was entitled, pompous, and domineering. Unlike Aspen, David and the rest of the Barlows focused on criminal law, so our paths crossed in court rather frequently. I wasn't a fan of anyone who made their living off of freeing criminals from the consequences of their actions, but I would rather see anyone other than the dark-haired woman who torpedoed my life with almost no effort.

Aspen had made it crystal clear she didn't want her ex sticking his nose in her business, so obviously, I had to do my best to drag him right into the center of it. Few things made me happier than making the petite lawyer miserable. She was really good at keeping her distance, so the opportunity to ruin her day didn't come around as often as I wanted. I was petty and resentful enough to make the most of any open-ing she gave me. Satisfied that she was beyond frustrated at having to deal with her ex, I cast another look at the defaced window on the way to my city-issued SUV. I frowned at the words and wondered again how no one had noticed anything amiss.

It wasn't like Loveless was immune to crime. We had had our fair share of troublemakers, many of whom had thrived under my dad's tenure as sheriff. But most of the regular offenders tended to stay out of downtown. They kept their crimes out in the hill country, where it was much harder to track them. Someone vandalizing a huge window right in the center of town wasn't something I'd run across before. Sure, there was an occasional teenager who spray-painted the side of a building to try and gain street cred, but it was nothing like this. This level of destruction seemed brazen and bold. It also indicated a level of anger that was dangerous and possibly lethal. Trashing such an obvious target, and such a well-known figure in the community, felt as if the perpetrator had nothing to lose and cared very little about getting caught.

It also surprised me that someone else appeared to dislike the pretty, sharp-tonged attorney as much as I did.

Over the years it had become common knowledge that I held a grudge where Aspen Barlow was concerned. My di-vorce was already an ugly, heated mess, but when Aspen entered the fray, things got a hundred times worse. The weird goth girl from Chicago who never really fit in with small-town Texas life was a brilliant attorney. She was spectacular in court, charismatic and charming. She ran cir-cles around my good ole boy lawyer. She was more fully prepared, better organized, passionately compelling, and far more interested in the outcome than my old football buddy ever was. It was clear from the first moments in front of the judge that I had sorely misjudged the quiet, serious girl from high school. It still burned deep in my bones the way my shortsightedness, combined with Aspen's fierce dedication, had led to me losing the only thing in the whole world I really cared about.

My son, Hayes.

Thinking about Hayes was the one thing guaranteed to pull my mind away from work. I looked at the time on the radio inside the vehicle and sighed. I was supposed to be home in time for dinner, but Aspen's call had come through dispatch on my way out the door. I was man enough to admit I wanted to see the crime scene as much as I wanted to see her rattled. It was rare for Aspen Barlow's feathers to be ruffled, and I wasn't going to pass up an opportunity to bask in her finally not having the upper hand. Only, the damage to her office had been far more severe than she had made it seem on the phone, and her face was paler than usual. Her hands were shaking, and she refused to look me in the eye when she guided me into her destroyed office. Instead of gloating, I was worried... which pissed me off.

I didn't want to worry about Aspen Barlow.

But she was a member of my community, a citizen of the town I was sworn to protect, and I refused to pick and choose who was worthy of my protection and service the way Conrad Lawton had.

Flicking a finger over the screen of my cell I called my son. It blew my mind Hayes was more of a man these days than a teenager. He was almost as tall as me but had my younger brother's long, lanky build. Hayes had the usual Lawton black hair–blue eyes combo that both my brother and I had. He was already a ladies' man and had a flair on the football field just like his old man. Fortunately, he was also much smarter and more careful with his heart than I'd been back in those days. He was the single thing I'd gotten right in this world, and I couldn't love him more if I tried.

When his surprisingly deep voice answered my call, I couldn't hold back the smile that tugged at my face. Hayes was going to turn eighteen soon, and then he was headed off to college. He was at the start of creating a life of his own, so it always thrilled me when he made time for his old man. We grew very close when he got older and Becca could no longer pull the strings tied to our relationship. And I worked hard every day to make sure he and I stayed that way. I never wanted him to see me the way I saw my own father.

"Hey. Sorry I didn't call. I got caught up on a last-minute case. I should be home within the hour. I hope you ate without me." I rubbed a hand over my face and stared out into the darkness through the windshield. "Did you get your homework done?"

A low chuckle hit my ear, and it warmed me all the way down to my toes. He was such a good kid. I was lucky I got the chance to be his dad.

"Yeah, Dad. It's all done. I put your dinner in the oven so you can eat when you get home. Were you dealing with the vandalism of Mrs. Barlow's office on Main Street? Mrs. Clooney said she overheard some people talking about it at bingo tonight." There was a soft fondness for our eighty-year-old neighbor in his tone. The older woman had helped me out with Hayes regularly since he came to live with me full-time when he was fourteen years old. I wouldn't be surprised if he'd taken his homework over to her house and worked on it while keeping her company before taking her to the church for bingo like he did every week.

I grunted and tapped my fingers against the steering wheel. "Yeah. I got called out for the vandalism and break-in. The situation was a little messier than I anticipated. Took longer than I thought it would."

Hayes laughed again, and I heard him tsk-tsk me over the line. "It took longer because you probably spent a solid twenty minutes arguing with Mrs. Barlow. Like you always do. Doesn't seem right her new place got trashed. She didn't do anything to deserve that kind of treatment. She's a nice lady."

Hayes knew Aspen better than I did. For years, Becca fought me tooth and nail to keep me out of my son's life, and for most of that time, Aspen was the attorney representing my ex-wife. Aspen had endless meetings with my son and spent more time alone with him than I did until he was a teenager. When Hayes was finally old enough to speak for himself in court, he explained to the judge which parent he wanted to spend most of his time with—me. Becca was furious when she no longer had a leg to stand on. Our son flat out told the judge he wanted to live with me. For the first time in years I felt like I could breathe. Being the temperamental, high-strung woman she was, Becca fired Aspen on the spot and accused her of throwing the case. The look of relief on Aspen's face had only lasted a moment, but I remembered it, and it made it hard to ignore my son's insistence that she wasn't a bad person, just someone stuck doing her job even when it wasn't a pleasant situation.

"No, she didn't do anything to deserve it, but I bet she's made more than one person angry while in court. I'm pretty sure this was someone's idea of petty revenge." But I wished I could shake the feeling that the destruction and slurs went deeper than simple retaliation. "She'll be all right and back up and running in no time."

I started the SUV and slowly backed out of my parking spot. I flicked a glance over to the sidewalk where Aspen was still squared off against her estranged husband. Her arms were crossed defiantly over her chest. Her dainty chin tilted upward, and her dark eyes and eyebrows were scrunched together in a fierce scowl, giving the impression she was a split second away from losing it. It was the reaction I'd wanted when I dropped the bomb between them, only now, I was annoyed by the way her soon-to-be ex was looming over her and pointing his index finger in her face. I didn't like men who intimidated women with their size and strength.

David Barlow wasn't a huge guy. He was several inches shorter than me, and he was pretty soft, all things considered. However, he was still a lot bigger than Aspen. Most people were. The woman was barely an inch or two above five feet. She simply seemed taller because of all the attitude she packed into that small frame. Her only oversize feature were her wide, dark doe eyes. They were huge, prominent, and right now glaring at the man across from her like he had been the one to ruin her day.

Remembering my son on the other end of the phone I sighed and told him, "Hey, kiddo, I gotta go. I'll get home as quick as I can, but don't wait up for me." I could practically feel Hayes rolling his eyes somewhere on the other end of the call. "And don't spend all night on the phone." Hayes seemed to chat up a different girl every day of the week, and it was getting old dragging him out of bed in the morning so he wouldn't be late for class.

"Be safe, Dad." It was how he ended every call, and it never failed to get me right in the gut.

Swearing softly under my breath, I pulled alongside the arguing couple and rolled down the passenger window. David Barlow looked at me over the top of Aspen's head and scowled fiercely at the interruption.

"Can I help you?" The man didn't even have the decency to address me by my title.

I cocked a brow. "I was about to ask the same thing. Think it's time you move whatever conversation you're having from the sidewalk. You're going to draw attention to what happened here."

The man in the suit stiffened, and Aspen whipped around to glare at me. She opened her mouth to say something, but her jackass of a husband immediately talked right over her.

"Tell her she should come home with me. Tell her it isn't safe for her to be alone with stuff like this going on. Obviously, someone wishes Aspen harm, and the best place for her to be is where I can keep an eye on her." There was no question or cajoling in David's tone. He made his demands like a man who fully expected them to be followed without hesitation.

Unfortunately for him, I was the one used to giving orders. "Counselor, do you want me to escort you home? I'll make sure to have one of my patrol units swing by your place every few hours if you're concerned about whoever did this showing up at your place tonight."

I grinned when David's chest puffed up with indignation. I liked to ruffle Aspen's feathers, but it was just as much fun to push the rich boy's buttons.

The clearly aggravated woman threw her long, midnight-colored hair over her shoulder and turned her back on both of us. "I'm going home. I don't need an escort or a babysitter. I'll be fine, thank you both for your concern." She neatly evaded her husband's manicured hand as he once again reached for her. The feisty attorney was ensconced in her luxury sports car and gone in a flash.

David Barlow turned his attention to the window and back to me. "Shouldn't you be the one to cover the window up? You're a public servant, after all. My taxes pay your salary." He tugged on the front of his suit jacket and reached up to adjust his glasses. Pretentious son of a bitch. He probably didn't even know what plywood was. "I'm really worried about her. She doesn't always see the big picture."

I leaned back in my seat and inclined my head slightly. His concern was understandable. It was obvious he was still in love with the prickly woman. "I'll have patrol run by her house, and I'm going to see if I can track down any surveillance of the front of the building. Since it's on the main drag, I might get lucky. Aspen and I have bad blood between us, but I'm not going to drop the ball on her case." And I would get the damn window covered up if he wasn't going to do it. Mr. Manicure probably didn't even own a hammer.

David narrowed his eyes at me behind his lenses and put his hands on his hips in a gesture that I assumed was supposed to look intimidating. "You better not, Lawton. I know you're supposed to be an improvement over your old man, I'd like to see you prove it." With one last lingering glare he stormed to his Lexus and took off in a huff, much in the same way Aspen had.

They were an odd match. I remembered vaguely hearing about the country club king proposing to the bleeding-heart liberal right around the time my marriage really started to fall apart. I was so busy trying to make Becca happy and keep my family together I'd let the information roll in one ear and out the other. I'd never given much thought to the people in town with more money than sense, but I'd liked getting an update on Aspen. When I was younger I had a soft spot for the quirky girl from out of town who never fit in. She was so honest back then, so innocent. But when my marriage went up in flames, and with Aspen right in the center of the wreckage, it was hard not to wonder how someone who destroyed marriages for a living managed to have a happy and healthy one of her own. Watching the separated Barlows interact tonight, I understood a little better that no one's marriage was perfect behind closed doors. Some folks were just better at hiding the cracks and keeping the ugly out of sight.

Instead of heading home, I went back to the station, filled out a detailed report for the break-in, and left my notes for the tech crew. I also swung back by Aspen's office and tacked up a sheet of plywood over the ruined window. No one needed to be greeted by those derogatory words in the morning. They would scandalize the church ladies and send the teenagers into a hysterical tizzy. I didn't want my dispatcher to be fielding complaints for endless hours when I could cover up the worst of things.

I was pulling into the driveway of my modest ranch-style home when my phone went off once again. I groaned into the darkness when I heard my ex-wife's very specific ringtone fill the cab of the vehicle.

My split with Becca had never been easy or amicable. I would never forgive her for the years I missed with Hayes, and she would never forgive me for not being the golden goose she'd thought she landed back in high school. The years following my return from deployment had been anything but blissful. We fought constantly, and both of us went out of our way to be as mean to each other as possible. It was far from my finest hour, but everything was unraveling around me, and there hadn't been a port in the storm. Becca and I always pretended to play nice with each other in front of Hayes, but when he started getting old enough to realize it was strange his parents hardly spoke to each other and often spent the night in separate bedrooms, it was obvious there was nothing left of our relationship at that point. But I had no clue how evil Becca could be until we started the official divorce proceedings. She claimed I ruined her life, that I stole her very best years away from her, and she was determined to make me, and by extension my son, suffer for it.

When I finally got primary custody of Hayes, most of the communication I had with Becca passed between our lawyers. She occasionally called me directly to bitch about this and that, and remind me that I ruined her life. She would sometimes ask for money when she was between boyfriends, but that was about it. She didn't typically call out of the blue in what was quickly becoming the middle of the night.

Starting to wonder if my day was ever going to end and if I was ever going to get something to eat, I begrudgingly answered the phone. Becca was the one person in Loveless I liked even less than Aspen, so talking to both of them, at length on the same night, was my own personal version of hell.

"What do you want?" I didn't pretend to play nice with her any longer. It took up too much time and energy. I focused on Hayes. He was the only part of being with Becca I wanted to remember. The only part I still had a place in my heart for.

"Rude. I can't believe you still have the manners of a Neanderthal. No wonder you're still single after all of these years, Case. Lord knows the old biddies in this town have done their very best to marry you off every chance they get." She sounded snide, but it wasn't anything new. She always liked to poke at me until she got some sort of reaction. I'd learned to bite my tongue around her a long time ago. Everything I said was thrown back in my face when I was fighting to see my kid, so I refused to give her ammunition.

"It's been a long day, Beck. I'm tired and I'm hungry. Tell me what you want. I'm not in the mood to spar with you tonight." I was never in the mood, but my patience tonight was especially thin after dealing with Aspen.

"I hate it when you call me that." She sniffed and then

launched into a tirade. "I want Hayes for the weekend. He won't return any of my texts or calls. I want him to meet Kenny. We've been dating for six months now, and I think it's time they get to know one another."

"Is he the rodeo guy or the bartender?" Becca had a very specific type. Men who looked an awful lot like I did back in my twenties and who happened to be a whole lot younger than she was now. The last guy who she swore was "The One" was closer to Hayes's age than mine. I tried to stay out of all things related to Becca, including her love life, but when she tried to drag our kid into her shenanigans, I put my foot down.

"I've told you over and over that I'm not going to make Hayes respond to you if he doesn't want to. He's almost eighteen. He gets to decide who he wants to invest his time and energy into. If you want to be one of those people, maybe try and put some parental effort in. You blew off his last three football games, and you only remembered his birthday this year because I texted you." I tried to keep the censure out of my tone but failed miserably. She'd never been the mother of the year, never really went out of her way to make Hayes her first priority. Which was why it'd been such a slap in the face when the judge ruled she was a more fit guardian than I was. Hayes always came first in my world, no questions asked.

"I hate football. He knows that. This is important to me. I want to see my son." She sounded petulant and sullen. I had zero sympathy for her. I had begged, pleaded, and implored her not to take Hayes away from me. But Becca remained ice-cold, even as she knowingly broke our son's heart.

"Football is important to Hayes. It's a two-way street. Give a little, and you'll get something back. Hayes is a good kid. He loves you, but you need to show up for him every now and then." It was ridiculous I was still giving her parenting basics when our child was almost an adult. She was never going to outgrow being a selfish, spoiled brat.

"He listens to you. You're his hero. If you tell him to come and see me, he will. Why can't you ever do anything I ask of you, Case? You're so busy trying to clean up your father's mess and salvage the great Lawton name, you've lost sight of the people closest to you who need you." I heard her working up to one of her very practiced and very fake crying jags. I'd let the gigantic tears and heartbreaking sobs manipulate me for most of my formative years. I was immune to them now.

"Beck. If he wants to see you, he will. End of story. I'm not going to pressure him or coerce him into doing anything he isn't comfortable with. What I am going to do is remind you that Hayes is college bound in a very short time. You think getting him to drive across town is a challenge, wait until you have to get him to come halfway across the country. There is a very narrow window for you to prove to Hayes that he means something to you. If you let it close, there will be no prying it back open. Think about your son instead of yourself for once."

She shrieked in outrage on the other end of the phone. Knowing how quickly things would escalate, I told Becca I had to go and hung up on her midyell.

I grabbed my Stetson off the top of my head and wiped my forearm across my forehead. My feet dragged as I made my way toward my front door.

Complicated women were going to be the death of me, and they were absolutely the reason I was going gray so damn fast. No doubt about it.

CHAPTER 3

ASPEN

I was acutely aware of how dark and empty my house was when I shut the front door behind me. I toed my boots off and hit every light switch I passed on the way to the kitchen. Soon all of the lights in the place were blazing brightly, and the uneasy shiver running up and down my spine finally started to fade. I refused to let the events of tonight drive me back in David's direction, even if every little creek and moan of my old Craftsman had me jumping out of my skin. I loved my house because it was older and needed some TLC. Both floors of the home had needed some serious attention when I first moved in. The whole house needed a second chance on life, just like I did. I was fine on my own, and I was going to prove it. I started off the renovations by building my dream master suite on the second floor. It was my escape from the world and I loved everything from the baseboards to the light switches. I fully expected David to show up at some point demanding to check every lock and window, but he wasn't allowed in my sanctuary. I'd never been helpless or inept, and I especially didn't want him feeling like I was his responsibility when I was doing my best to cut all ties to him.

I wished he would learn to let go.

After pouring a very full glass of red wine, I changed into a stretchy pair of yoga pants and an oversize T-shirt with a faded logo of an old heavy metal band on it. Well, it was a normal size T-shirt, which just happened to be oversize on me. I was used to swimming in clothes and having to get everything tailored for it to fit properly. I'd long since grown accustomed to my particularly small stature, too big eyes, and overly pale skin. I tended to run closer to striking or unusual-looking rather than any form of conventional beauty. My features were too pronounced and dramatic to lend themselves to simple compliments. Staring at myself in the bathroom mirror I started to think back on all the things that had led to me to this moment.

When I was little, my father told me I looked like Snow White, which I always thought was sweet. But by the time I reached high school, I'd grown used to people asking me if I was trying to be Lydia from *Beetlejuice*, or Wednesday Addams. The frame of reference for seriously pale girls who tended to wear all-black at all times was limited in small-town Texas. But being called weird and being looked at like I crawled out of a gutter whenever Case wasn't around to play savior left lasting damage to my psyche. Each and every time it happened, I was reminded that I didn't really have a place in Loveless, and it stung. I was used to being alone, but being lonely, that was a feeling I never quite knew what to do with. Sometimes it felt bigger and more prominent than anything else I tried to feel, which was probably why I'd latched on to the simple kindness Case showed me.

Funnily enough, as soon as I started dating David Barlow,

no one called me a weird girl anymore. No one looked down their nose at me, and no one snidely asked how long I was staying in town. As soon as David and I were official, it was like the people of Loveless no longer had any choice but to accept me. I wished I could say I was no longer lonely, but it would be a lie. I was rarely alone after David entered my life, but sadly, I was still lonely.

David wasn't into any of my quirky hobbies or outside interests. He didn't care about cool vintage clothing or watching crime documentaries with me. He didn't get why I was obsessed with upcycling and scavenging funky antiques at flea markets. He laughed when I told him I wanted to learn how to swing dance, and he flat out refused to go with me when I told him I was going to a Women's March in D.C. He called me and my interests cute instead of weird, but I was still alone most of the time because he wasn't invested in the things that made me happy outside of our marriage.

I liked to think over the years I'd proven myself, that I deserved my office on Main Street and my roster full of clients. I was active in the community, even after my separation. I cared about my neighbors and the goings-on in my city. No one was happier to see Case's father leave his position than me. One of the reasons I'd been adamant about returning to Loveless after college was the memory of marginalized men and women being railroaded by an unjust system, headed by Conrad Lawton. I hated the way the former sheriff used his own biases in determining the guilt and innocence of offenders in Loveless.

In a bigger city, I knew my impact would be minimal. I would be one voice of many screaming into the wind. In Loveless, my voice was loud and impossible to ignore. I could stand out, rather than blend in. Something I'd always done anyway, but now I understood how to use my differ-

ences to my advantage. I desperately wanted—no needed—
to make a name for myself. I planned to fight hard for all
of my clients, regardless of what economic and social background they came from. I truly believed I could do a lot of
good for this community.

Instead, as soon as my feet hit the Texas dust, I was immediately swept up in the privilege and prestige of having the
Barlow name and was handed cases and clients I would have
preferred to skip over. Clients with too much money and an
ax to grind.

Clients like Becca Lawton.

When Becca fired me right there in the middle of the courtroom as soon as Hayes picked his father over her, I couldn't
stop the wave of relief that swept over me. Dealing with the
woman and her outrageous demands was exhausting. She was
at the top of the list of unreasonable clients, and she just kept
asking for more. Always threatening to disclose Case's supposed secret when she didn't get her way. I had no clue how
Case continued to meet her demands, but he did each and
every time as long as it meant he was allowed access to his
son. When the time came for Hayes Lawton to choose which
parent he wanted to be his primary caregiver, I had no doubt
he was going to pick his father. I think Case and I were the
only adults in the hearing not surprised that the now-teenager
picked his father over his mother.

When David and his father heard about Becca firing me, it
had been a major turning point in my professional and personal
relationship with them both. My father-in-law wanted his client
back. My husband wanted to make his father happy. Neither
of them cared that Hayes was better off with Case and that I
felt awful about my role in keeping them apart for so long. It
was in those moments and in the center of those conversations
I realized I'd lost my drive, my purpose. I planned on coming

back to Loveless to make a difference, but all I'd done was slide into the comfortable role of being David Barlow's wife. I'd planned to scream about injustice and had ended up whispering meekly instead.

I tried to talk to David about how unfulfilled and empty I felt, but all I got was a kiss on the forehead and a promise I would feel better about things after a good night's sleep. He handled our endless debate about continuing to try for children in the same way. He didn't take my complaints or steadily growing melancholy seriously. In the end, I'd had no choice but to walk away. It was the best decision for both of us, even if David still couldn't see it.

Now that I'd had space and time to process the way everything broke down, I knew I had to take responsibility for allowing myself to become complacent. Being with David and being a part of the Barlow family was easy. I had status. I had friends. I had a guaranteed job. Going back to being the awkward and admittedly strange girl, Aspen Keating from Chicago, was much harder. She didn't have any of the things Aspen Barlow did. Things that were surprisingly easy to give up when push came to shove.

As it turned out, I didn't really like the so-called friends I'd made through my association with David. The contacts didn't matter when it came time to represent the people who really needed my help. And status, well status was nice, but I'd survived without it when I was younger, and I wasn't exactly missing out on it now. I was too busy trying to make an actual difference in people's lives to wonder whether or not they were talking about me behind my back. I'd considered getting a cat to combat the lingering loneliness, but I worked too much and my hours were too unpredictable. I didn't want a pet to feel abandoned while I tried to figure out once again who I was supposed to be.

Shaking myself out of those thoughts, I leaned back against the headboard of my bed and opened my laptop. I wanted to look over my most difficult, volatile cases to see if a name or two popped out. I was sure the break-in at my office was tied to my work. Taking up for the abused and neglected meant there was a monster sitting on the other side of the aisle. I was no stranger to just how awful humans could treat one another.

At the top of the list was a husband currently out on bail after breaking his wife's jaw and putting both of their children in the ER. I was representing the wife in the divorce and petitioning the court for protection orders for the entire family against him. He was a bully with a hot temper, and I could easily see him scrawling those ugly, libelous words across my office window. He'd screamed them at me in court. I'd have to check when his attorney got him sprung from lockup to make sure the times lined up, but he was definitely a suspect.

There was also a teenager I was trying to get emancipated from his neglectful mother. The DA had asked me to take on the case after a neighbor called to report a foul smell coming from the property next door. When the police responded they found a woman hoarding not only pets but also keeping her children in squalor and filth. Social Services intervened for the younger ones, but there was a teenaged boy who hovered on the edge of being an adult. He wanted to be emancipated so he could gain custody of his younger siblings. It was a tricky, complicated case, made even more so by the sheer insanity of the mother. She was also currently out on bail awaiting her trial for several counts of child abuse. I didn't hesitate to add her name to the list.

I jotted down a few more generally disgruntled former clients, like Becca Lawton. I couldn't really imagine the woman holding such a massive grudge after all these years, but she had been pretty pissed when her son walked away from her... taking her monthly check from Case with him.

The list, along with the thought of the mess waiting for me tomorrow, was starting to make my head hurt. I shut the computer down, chugged the rest of my wine, and toyed with the idea of getting up and turning off the lights. Deciding I was too tired and still too freaked out, I closed the door and locked it when I entered the room, crawled under the covers, threw my arm over my eyes, and went to bed with nearly every light in the house left on. Sleep came easily after the wine and the long day, but my dreams were anything but sweet.

I kept seeing red words dripping like blood down snowy white walls. The letters mixed together to form every insult, affront, and slur that had been hurled my way since I was young. I kept trying to escape the room, but there was no way out. The taunts and jeers kept chasing me, and I was sad, even in my sleep, that I didn't have a younger version of Case Lawton there to act as a buffer from all the ugliness. I'd had a bit of hero worship going on back then, and apparently, I still saw him as some kind of savior. Soon, dream-me had red smeared all over her hands. It was all very disturbing, even more so when the room started to get suffocatingly hot. I tried to wipe sweat away from my brow but only ended up dragging paint across my face. I told myself to wake up, screamed silently in my head it was time to open my eyes, but the red words and the heat continued to swirl around me in a confusing mess. The acrid smell of smoke obliterated my senses, and I started to wonder if I was dreaming of being in hell.

I kicked the covers off, thinking it would cool me down, but as soon as I moved I started to cough and choke. Suddenly it felt like I was trying to escape my bedding. I couldn't breathe and came awake with a jerk when I realized the smell of smoke wasn't something I was merely dreaming about. Kicking the comforter to the floor, I blinked burning eyes into the haze slowly and steadily filling my room.

"What in the hell?" I scrambled out of bed, head cocked, listening for the wail of my smoke detectors. I immediately regretted opening my mouth as the taste of smoke and char coated my tongue and sent my entire system into fight-or-flight mode.

The house was eerily quiet aside from a very distinct pop and crackle right outside of my bedroom door. Coughing and wheezing, with tears rolling down my cheeks, I rushed over to the door. I was reaching for the brass knob when all the fire safety reminders from elementary school suddenly resurfaced. Instead of touching the metal with my bare hand, I wrapped the loose fabric at the bottom of my shirt around my palm and cautiously reached out. I immediately jerked back with a hiss. My palm burned with pain, and I could hardly move my fingers. The metal was hot enough to scald, and I could feel heat on the other side doing its best to push through the heavy wooden door.

Stumbling, I wiped at my sweaty face and did my best not to cough up a lung as the haze in my room thickened and made it even harder to breathe. Almost blind from tears and smoke, I felt my way along one of the walls to where my en suite bathroom was located. It was the one room where I hadn't turned on a light before going to bed. I had to grope around for a washcloth, but eventually, my fingers touched soft fabric. I ran it under the faucet for a brief minute before slapping the soaked wetness over my mouth. If I wasn't going out through my door that meant my bedroom window was my only option, but I needed to be able to breathe and think clearly enough to pry it open and climb out onto the roof.

The heat in my room was nearly unbearable, and I could now see a bright red-and-orange glow along the line at the base of the door. The fire was very real. This wasn't a dream. It was a nightmare. I was struggling to take a full breath through my makeshift mask, and I was starting to get very light-headed.

My heart was racing so fast I was worried it might give out, and I could hear the rush of blood between my ears. I was doing my best to keep a level head, but my body was betraying me.

Once I reached the window, it took a solid minute to get my limbs to cooperate and get the little latch and the lock to release. By that time the smoke was so thick, I couldn't even see my hands in front of my face, and my eyes were burning so badly all I wanted to do was keep them squeezed shut. I banged my forehead against the glass and ordered myself to focus. There was only one way out of this room, and I was staring right at it.

The bedroom door gave way with a sudden crack. Flames leaped into the room impatiently and immediately started to race across the floor. I'd been afraid before, but coming face-to-face with the fire was horrifying. It was eating up my entire bedroom, and I knew it wouldn't be long before the flames were reaching for me as well.

Focus. Focus. Focus. I chanted the words inside my head repeatedly as I finally maneuvered the lock open. My fingers were covered with soot by the time I got the window jerked up wide enough for me to slip through.

With the sudden influx of oxygen the fire behind me roared even louder and burned even brighter. I stumbled across the rough shingles in bare feet, still struggling to see and breathe as I made my way to the edge of the roof.

My house wasn't huge, but standing over the drop-off,

looking down at my small lawn, it suddenly seemed gigantic. A particularly violent coughing fit hit me, and I nearly toppled off my precarious perch. The night sky and the grass below sort of blended together as vertigo threatened to take my legs out from underneath me. I blinked away the tears that were still obliterating my vision and tried to reassure myself if I jumped, a broken leg was the lesser of two evils.

Vaguely I thought I heard sirens somewhere off in the distance, but maybe it was wishful thinking.

"Aspen. What's going on? Are you all right?" Captain Idiot asking the obvious was my neighbor. I didn't usually run into the people who lived on either side of me, but occasionally the husband who was now standing in my yard in a bathrobe and flip-flops would wave to me when he was taking his kids to school. Suddenly he seemed like the best neighbor in the whole world. I was so happy to see him.

"I need a way to get down." The words were hard to get out, and I wasn't sure they were loud enough to hear. My throat felt like it was made of sandpaper and my lungs were barely working.

"I called nine-one-one. Help is on the way."

There was a long pause where I sat down on the side of my roof and let my legs dangle over the edge. I could feel the heat building at my back. The fire was getting louder and louder. I was going to have to jump. There wasn't going to be enough time for help to arrive. I was going to pass out. I could feel unconsciousness pulling hard at me. My vision narrowed to pinpoints, and my lungs screamed in agony with every breath.

"How on earth did your house catch on fire? Didn't you update the wiring when you moved in?" Okay. The dad next door was starting to seem less helpful. Couldn't he see I was about to break my damn neck by jumping off my roof?

Taking as big a breath as my injured lungs would allow, I put my hands next to my hips and scooted as close to the edge as I could manage. I squeezed my eyes shut and prayed to whatever god might be listening that my landing wouldn't hurt too badly. And then I pushed myself off the ledge.

I hit the ground with a thump that rattled every bone in my body. Both my elbows smacked into the lawn with enough force to make my head spin, and I felt one of my ankles pop in a totally unnatural way. My spine shook so hard I felt the impact in my teeth, and the little air in my lungs was forced out in a whoosh.

I couldn't pry my eyes open, but I could feel tears of pain mixing with the tears from the smoke. The unhelpful neighbor was yelling something at someone, but I hurt too much, and my head was spinning too fast to care what was going on beyond the agony radiating throughout my body.

"Aspen. Open your eyes." The familiar voice managed to thread through the fireworks of anguish exploding behind my eyes. "Look at me." Normally I hated how bossy and rude Case Lawton was, but at this very moment, all I wanted to do was obey him. And hug him. Yeah, I kinda always wanted to do that, but even more so right now.

The sound of sirens became louder, but so did the sound of the fire. I tried as hard as I could to get my eyes open, but they didn't want to cooperate. I painfully rolled to my side as another fit of body-racking coughs rattled me. I felt a hand slide through my hair and something cold was pressed to my forehead. It felt so good a sigh escaped my injured throat.

"You really jumped off the damn roof?" Case's deep voice was both soothing and irritating at the same time, but I didn't want to move away from that hand in my hair. "Not sure if I'm impressed or pissed off, Counselor."

How he felt didn't matter. I didn't have a choice, and once

the fire was done devouring my home, I wasn't going to have anything left to my name.

It was a terrifying thought. Almost as scary as jumping off the roof into the darkness. Adrenaline tried to get me to open my eyes once again, but I had nothing left to give. When the blackness overtook me, it didn't come softly and quietly, it pushed its way into my head and swept me away with the force of a hurricane. I free-fell into the darkness with the same rush I felt when I jumped off of my house, only this landing was much softer.

CHAPTER 4

∞

CASE

So glad I didn't go through with the urge to get a cat."
Aspen's voice was barely recognizable under the wheeze
from her ravaged throat.

I kept my hand on her head as her eyelids stopped fluttering behind her tightly closed lids. Her black eyelashes were
an inky fan casting shadows over white cheeks. Her skin was
several shades paler than normal and streaked with varying
shades of black and gray soot. Her breathing was slow and
shallow, her chest barely moving. I could see that her ankle was already puffy and turning an ugly shade of purple
and black. The hand she had lying limp and lifeless across
her stomach was also red and irritated-looking, the fingers
slightly blistered. And when I moved my hand through her
dark hair, they came away wet and sticky with blood. I
decided I was fully pissed and no part impressed that the
crazy woman had jumped off her roof instead of waiting for
help to arrive.

"Is she going to be okay? I can't believe she jumped off

the roof!" The man hovering over my shoulder dressed in a bathrobe and very little else was starting to get on my nerves.

"If you saw her standing on the roof and knew the house was on fire, why didn't you run and grab a ladder or something and help her down?" I couldn't keep the snap of anger out of my voice when I asked the question. I understood the guy was just a concerned neighbor, but seeing Aspen laid out on the grass so quiet and still, the opposite of how she normally was, had unreasonable anger pushing against my skin.

Bathrobe Guy crossed his arms over his chest and looked down his nose at me. "Everything happened really fast. We smelled the smoke, I called nine-one-one on my way out the door, but by the time I got into Aspen's yard she was already on the roof." The man huffed a little and mumbled, "She didn't scream for help. We didn't hear smoke detectors go off. The only indication anything was wrong was the smell of the smoke. I didn't know how bad the fire was until I got in front of the house. I could see the flames shooting out of the upper windows once I reached the sidewalk. She had no choice but to go out onto the roof."

But she didn't have to jump.

Less than ten minutes ago I was woken up by the call that there was an emergency on Aspen's block. I was out the door and on my way to her house in under two minutes, knowing the fire and rescue team would beat me to the scene. I'd pulled into her small neighborhood just as the fire truck was coming to a stop in front of her house. We all watched in horrified captivation as the small, dark-haired woman pushed herself off of the roof and landed with a heavy thud in the grass. I couldn't even begin to imagine the fear and desperation that had driven Aspen onto her precarious perch in the first place. But watching her flail in the air and land like a broken doll in a limp heap, I had to believe there was a better solution.

I was jostled out of the way as paramedics quickly surrounded the tiny form I was kneeling over. I watched closely as they took Aspen's vitals, and all of us jumped as a loud crack suddenly filled the quiet night air. Several heads swiveled and watched in stunned silence as the entire upper level of the Craftsman caved in and collapsed in on itself. Fire shot into the sky, the red and orange glow illuminating the scene. I sucked in a breath as I watched the spot where the woman at my feet had been balanced mere moments ago turned into nothing but fuel for the hungry flames. It looked like taking a leap of faith might've been Aspen's best bet after all. And I was back to being impressed by her quick thinking instead of being angry at her risky behavior.

The noise and the heat from the reinvigorated blaze were enough to get the nosy neighbor to finally back off. He muttered something about being worried about his own home and family, scuttling across the lawn with the ties of his robe dragging on the grass and flashing a pair of very unflattering pink boxer shorts. With a raised eyebrow, I watched him go, pondering his statement that there had been no warning signs that the house was on fire aside from the smoke.

I didn't know much about the unconscious woman in front of me, but I did know Aspen Barlow was diligent, precise, and always prepared. She didn't strike me as the type of woman to let something like low batteries in a smoke detector slide. The entire neighborhood should've been woken up from the shriek and wail of the smoke alarms the minute the fire started. Not to mention Aspen should've had plenty of time to get out of her home. Combined with the earlier break-in, I had a really bad feeling. And not the normal kind I got when I had to deal with the feisty attorney.

I glanced at the paramedic closest to me and asked, "Is she going to be all right?"

The young guy looked over his shoulder at me and gave a half shrug. "She's definitely dealing with some severe smoke inhalation, but her lungs haven't collapsed. We all saw her take a header off the roof, so I'm sure she's probably got a concussion. Can't get a good look at the cut on the back of her head because of all her hair, but I imagine it needs to be stitched up. The ankle looks sprained, not broken. I would guess second-degree burns on her hand. She's not in great shape, but nothing fatal as far as I can tell. Her blood pressure is a little bit low, which could be an early sign shock is setting in. That's the most concerning thing going on right now. We're going to take her to the emergency room over at Memorial. You can call them for updates on her condition."

I nodded absently and looked back toward the now engulfed upper-level of Aspen's home. There were several fire hoses turned on the blaze, water knocking the flames back and keeping them safely out of the reach of the other homes nearby. I saw the fire captain talking into a handheld radio, directing several of his men around the nearly destroyed home.

Picking my way across the now soggy and torn-up lawn, I headed to where the captain was staring at the wreckage through narrowed eyes. I'd worked with Warwick Nelson on more than one case over the years. He'd studied to be an EMT around the same time I was in the police academy. He'd also been promoted to fire chief right when I'd taken over the office of sheriff from my father. His promotion was one my father tried and failed to sabotage, simply because Warwick was biracial. There was no end to my old man's prejudices.

I respected Wick. He was never one to look the other way when my father was running roughshod all over the citizens of Loveless. And I trusted him implicitly when it came to dealing with anything having to do with fires. Those that were intentionally set, and those that were not.

"The upper level is a total loss. I think my boys managed to save most of the main floor, minus the living room, where the master bedroom landed when it collapsed. She didn't have any pets, or anything in there did she?" He cocked his head to the side and gave a questioning look.

I rubbed a hand over my mouth and shook my head. "I don't think so. She said something about being glad she never got a cat right before she passed out, but the paramedics think she probably has a concussion." Who knew if she was making any sense or not?

"The boys smelled an accelerant as soon as they went through the front door. If they had to guess they would point the finger at common gasoline. We'll have to run some tests to be sure. I'm going to have to call in a fire investigator for this one, since it seems it was deliberately set." He frowned as he said the words. "Don't know who would want to hurt Aspen. She's a nice gal. A little high-strung, but she offered to help my cousin out for practically nothing when she found out his ex-girlfriend took their baby during a scheduled visit and ran off. Don't know if my family would've ever had a shot at seeing little Camilla again if it wasn't for her."

I grunted so I wouldn't have to comment on Aspen being nice. All that mattered was her being a victim of not one, but two serious crimes in such a short span of time and while under my watch. It was my job to protect her and make sure she received justice for the crimes commited against her. Whether I liked her or not was irrelevant. "Her office was broken into earlier tonight. She couldn't pinpoint a reason, but now I'm wondering if she kept a spare key to her house somewhere on the premises. Maybe they broke into her work space, so getting into her personal space wouldn't be as difficult."

"Can't believe she didn't hear the fire alarm. Jumping off the roof like that..." He shook his head and sighed. "She's lucky she didn't break her neck."

"The neighbor in the bathrobe said there was no noise. The smoke detectors didn't go off, so Aspen probably didn't have any warning until she smelled the smoke as well."

"Even if someone was moving around her house? They had to have doused the upper level. I mean soaked it down to the damn studs holding the house upright. That's where all the damage is located. The rest of the house is barely touched." Wick frowned and looked down at the radio in his hand as it squawked to life.

A disembodied voice declared, "We've got one hundred percent containment, Chief."

"That's good, Barnes. Get your crew out of there." His attention shifted back in my direction, but I barely noticed.

I was thinking about someone moving through Aspen's house with enough familiarity to know not only where her bedroom was located, but also where the smoke detectors were. The lady lawyer was in some deep shit. I could feel it.

I pushed a hand through my hair. It was rare I left the house without my Stetson, but the middle of the night emergency call, combined with an unwanted shot of panic when I heard who the victim was, meant I wasn't firing on all cylinders when I ran out the door. None of the patrol units I sent to check on her house earlier in the night reported anything out of place or amiss. So the late-night call was unexpected and jarring. Luckily I'd remembered to leave Hayes a note at the last minute just in case I didn't make it back before he had to get up and head to school.

I clapped a hand on Wick's beefy shoulder and inclined my head in the direction of where I'd parked my SUV. "I'm gonna swing by the hospital and check on Ms. Barlow.

Maybe she's awake and can give me more to go on than she did for the office break-in. Give your investigator my number. I'm gonna have questions after he goes over the scene." I was going to have lots of them.

"Case." I paused midstep and looked back at the fire chief. "The girl just lost everything. And I do mean everything. All her personal effects are ash. Maybe take it easy on her for once." Dark eyes assessed me knowingly, and I pushed down the urge to flinch. I'd been civil to Aspen all throughout the day, but our animosity toward each other was well known. "I don't think she had any family in town aside from her ex and former in-laws. She could use a friend when she wakes up."

I stiffened and narrowed my eyes. "I'm going to find out who's harassing her and I'm going to make sure she's safe. Both of those things are my job. But I will not be Aspen Barlow's friend." I barked the words with more force than necessary. However, there was a small, sneaky part of my brain trying to ask why I was so determined to keep on loathing her.

Wick chuckled and used his elbow to nudge me in my ribs. "Didn't say it had to be you. Give your sister a call. She's the nicest out of all you stubborn Lawtons. I'm sure Kody wouldn't mind taking a ride over to Memorial and giving the poor girl something to wear. I'm not kidding when I tell you everything she had in that upper level is gone."

I grunted again and nodded absently. Wick was wrong about my little sister being the nicest Lawton. She was wild, fierce, mouthy, bossy, and a total pain in the ass. She had to be while living under Conrad Lawton's roof. She was also unwaveringly loyal. My baby sister knew I put a lot of the blame on losing Hayes directly at Aspen's doorstep. She's always made it a point to dislike the woman on principle alone. Plus, they ran in very different circles. Aspen owned the courtroom while dressed in designer pantsuits and sky-high heels. My baby sister owned a dive bar and wore cutoffs and battered boots to work. I wasn't sure Aspen would appreciate the hand-me-downs, even if I could convince Kody to play nice.

"I'll try Kody first, and if she tells me to go to hell, I'll ask Crew if Della left anything at their place before she went to Paris."

My little sister was a wild card, but my younger brother's girlfriend was as predictable as they come. Della Deveaux was as far from the type of woman I'd ever expected my reckless, careless, slightly broken little brother to settle down with. The woman had class through and through. She was stunning in an expensive and practically untouchable way. She was also a bona fide city girl, one with a high-paying, high-class, high-profile job. She was often jetting off to places like Paris, London, and Milan, but for some reason, she was stuck on my kid brother and seemed happy enough to call Loveless home when she wasn't on the go.

Della was also much nicer than Kody, on any given day, even if she came across as ice-cold upon first impression. If my little sister didn't want to be charitable, I knew Della wouldn't mind sacrificing some of her stuff for the greater good.

Wick nudged me again and offered a lopsided grin. "You got a good family, Case. Don't know how you kids made it into decent human beings growing up under Conrad's thumb. But you did, and you should be proud. You might wanna remember how hard you worked to be seen as more than Conrad Lawton's boy. I think our local lawyer might know a little something about trying to be accepted." He walked away with a promise to put the fire investigator in touch.

Grumbling under my breath about never being able to

catch a break. I called my sister. It was a little past one in the morning, so I knew she would still be at the bar, getting ready to shut things down. Kody loved that dive more than she loved me and Crew half the time. When our mother passed away, she left each of us a small inheritance. Kody used her share to open the bar. She claimed it was the one thing she had that kept her close to our mom, since our dad had all but banished mom from the house as soon as her headstone went up.

"Hey, big brother. Why you callin' so late? I haven't broken any laws...today." Kody was always quick with a joke and with her temper. Sometimes I wondered if she had more of our father in her than she wanted to admit, but then she would do something totally selfless and kind, and remind me she was without a doubt our mother's carbon copy.

"I have a situation and I was hoping you could help me out." I wasn't one to reach out. I tended to believe I could handle anything coming my way on my own, but I had no idea how to handle Aspen Barlow. The damn woman had had the upper hand since I met her.

"Case Lawton asking for help? Has hell frozen over?" Kody pulled the phone away from her mouth before yelling, "Last call, losers. Drink 'em up!" There were groans and some complaints in the background, and I could perfectly picture my sister rolling her expressive green eyes. She was the only one who inherited our father's penetrating green gaze. When we were little, she begged our mom for blue contacts so she could match me and Crew. Now that we were all grown, I often wondered if her desire was more about not looking like Conrad than it was about looking like us. "What's going on, Case? You never call out of the blue asking for favors. That's much more Crew's thing."

I sighed and rubbed my tired eyes. "There was a fire

tonight. Aspen Barlow's house went up, and she lost everything. They sent her to the hospital unconscious and bruised from head to toe because she jumped off of the second story to escape. She could use a helping hand, and I was hoping that hand might be yours."

There was a moment of silence before Kody let loose with a long line of swear words. "Aspen Barlow? We hate her. She ruined your life. She took Hayes away from you. Why on God's green earth would you be worried about helping her out? She married rich. Let the Barlows figure it out, we have more important things to worry about than some rich bitch lawyer."

I sighed again and tried not to picture my very comfy bed and a full night's sleep. "I have my reasons to hate her. That doesn't mean you have to. Plenty of people in this town seem to have nothing but good things to say where she's concerned, and she sure as shit didn't do anything to deserve what happened to her house tonight." I climbed into the SUV and dropped my forehead down so I could rest it on the steering wheel. "And I worry about her because I want to be better than Dad was. Ignoring someone who lost everything just because we have bad blood in the past is exactly what Conrad Lawton would've done while wearing this badge. I refuse to be like him. I refuse to let you or Crew be like him."

Kody went quiet for a long minute. I really wasn't sure which way she was going to go. Sometimes her hotheaded stubbornness got the better of her, but I liked to believe her huge heart would always win out. Luckily my faith paid off because after another swearing jag Kody growled, "Fine. Let me kick the last few holdouts outta the bar, and I'll run home and throw together a bag to get her through a few days. I doubt anyone with the last name Barlow has ever worn clothing bought from Target, but beggars can't be choosers."

"She wasn't always a Barlow. I'm sure she'll be grateful for whatever you come up with. She might not even be awake yet. She smacked her head pretty good when she jumped. I'm not sure how badly she was injured. I'm on my way to the hospital now to check up on her and see if I can ask her some questions." There were so many questions. "Thanks, Kode. I knew I could count on you."

She snorted. "No, you didn't, which is why you pulled the 'don't be like dad' card. You've always been really good at playing dirty without anyone realizing it, Case. But I can see right through you."

She really could. Through both me and Crew. She was the only one who really understood either of us.

"I appreciate you playing nice. I'll see you in a few." I hung up the phone after a quick good-bye and started the SUV. I could feel exhaustion tugging at me, but I didn't have time for it. I was going to have to swing by the twenty-four-hour diner on the way to the ER and grab the biggest black coffee they made to go. The stuff at the hospital was only a step above the crap we made at the station. I had no idea how long I was going to be hanging around, waiting for Aspen to wake up, or even if she was going to be able to talk when she did. Smoke inhalation was a real bitch, and she'd barely been able to speak when she was mumbling about the cat.

It looked like I was in it for the long haul.

CHAPTER 5

∞

ASPEN

There you go. Get those eyes open, Sleeping Beauty." I wasn't sure why, but I wanted to obey the command. "In my experience, there are no princes wandering aimlessly around Loveless. And honestly, if some dude is trying to kiss you while you're unconscious, you should press charges, not fall madly in love with him."

I didn't recognize the voice. But that might be because my head felt like it was going to split into two. The second I tried to peel an eye open, a whimper of pain ripped out of my sore lungs. I hurt all over, my entire body aching. I was miserable and still didn't know who was in the room with me, but she was funny. I agreed with her about the lack of princes in Loveless. I could hear someone moving around, and there was a faint scent of wildflowers mixed with something darker and smoky, like expensive booze. I didn't know anyone who smelled that way, or who spoke in such a brash, flippant manner.

"Seriously, wake up. I don't think my brother has been home in over forty-eight hours. He looks like shit, and he's going to crash and burn any minute if you don't open your eyes and tell him you're okay so he can get back to his kid and regularly scheduled life. I get that having your house go up in flames while you're inside of it makes for a really shitty night, but sooner or later you're going to have to open your eyes and get to work on cleaning up the mess."

The voice got closer, and I felt the brush of cool fingertips against my forehead. "I think it's pretty badass you dived off the roof and saved yourself. I think I would've done the exact same thing in your shoes. Case insists there was a better way, one that wouldn't have landed you in a hospital bed, but he always thinks he knows best. I call it big brother syndrome. I'm surprised he's as worried about you as he is. I mean he's a good sheriff and gives his all to his job, but he really doesn't like you." A soft laugh tugged at my consciousness, and I struggled to look at the woman with the soft drawl who was currently my only link to reality. "Case likes everyone. He always has. I think he tries to make up for Dad pretty much hating everyone who was even slightly different. I guess that makes you pretty special."

Finally, I managed to pry my eyelids open a slit. The light burned its way into my skull and the pain radiating all over my body intensified by 100 percent. When I moaned in complaint, my throat felt like it was doused with acid. I was a mess, but eventually, the woman leaning over the bedrail swam into focus.

She was pretty in a wholesome, natural kind of way. She had a head full of wild, tawny curls, wide green eyes, and a cupid bow mouth that seemed quick to grin. She wasn't wearing any makeup, so the freckles that dotted the bridge of her nose and fanned across her cheeks stood out against her peaches-and-cream complexion. If she hadn't mentioned being Case's sister, I never would have guessed she was a

Lawton. She didn't look like her brothers or her nephew in the slightest, but she had that Lawton take-no-prisoners attitude practically oozing out of her pores.

"W-he-re..." I tried to ask where I was and what happened, but I barely got the first few syllables out before my throat closed up and fireballs of pain shot down through my lungs. Immediately tears filled my eyes, and my entire body tensed up.

"Wow, take it easy. You've been unconscious for nearly two days. You gave yourself a solid knock on the head when you jumped off the roof. You also sprained your ankle, gave yourself first- and second-degree burns on one of your hands, dislocated an elbow, and your lungs and throat are all jacked up from smoke inhalation. You're going to be hooked up to an oxygen tank for a least a week, and you probably won't be able to talk much for the next day or two."

I wanted to ask how she knew so much about my condition when she was a stranger, but I couldn't do more than blink against the tears pooling in my eyes.

"Let me call the nurse, now that you're awake. She's really nice. We went to high school together. I told her you and I were friends, so she may have filled me in on all your bumps and bruises when I asked why you weren't waking up. Don't be too mad at her. She was only trying to help. Is there anyone you want me to call for you? Your husband has been here every day to check up on you. He wanted to move you to a private room and pay some specialist to come in and evaluate you. He was really scared when you didn't wake up after the first night. He seems pretty worried. He'll be happy to hear you're awake."

This woman talked a mile a minute, and I was struggling to put a single thought together before she jumped onto the next subject.

"Case doesn't seem to like David very much, and man, you should've heard the two of them go at it when my brother pulled the sheriff card and asked David if he had a key to your house. I thought his head was going to explode. Your husband doesn't like answering to anyone."

"Ex." I coughed as soon as I wheezed out the word. "Ex-husband." I once again hated that he wouldn't just sign the damn paperwork. I didn't want David to be hovering in the hospital, making any kind of call on my behalf. Until the divorce was final, he still had too much hold over my life.

The pretty, talkative woman cocked her head to the side and narrowed her eyes at me. "Doesn't act like an ex. Lemme go let everyone know you're awake."

She dashed out of the room, leaving nothing but the sound of monitors beeping and the harsh sound of my labored breathing. Slowly, I cataloged the list of injuries she had tossed at me.

The lungs and throat were impossible to miss. Every breath in burned, every breath out felt raw. My head hurt. It was throbbing with a low, steady thrum. My ankle ached. I could feel it throb in time with my heartbeat, which was annoying and uncomfortable. My arm was immobilized, so I couldn't really feel my elbow, but looking down at the limb, I could see how bruised and swollen it was. The hand on the same arm was swaddled in white gauze, but I could see red, irritated skin around the edges. Of all my bumps and bruises, it was the burn on my palm that hurt the worst. I could feel my palm aching, and my fingers were overly sensitive and tender. Vaguely I recalled reaching for the brass doorknob on my bedroom door when I first realized the house was on fire. It looked like the T-shirt hadn't been enough protection against the hot metal.

The door to the room swung open and a flurry of scrubs-clad medical personnel suddenly surrounded my bed. I was poked and prodded. I answered questions with either a nod or shake of my head and tried not to move too much, since it sent spikes of agony through my brain. I begged as effectively as I could for a glass of water and was rewarded with a cup of ice chips instead. They helped the fire in my throat some, but I knew there was no way I was making words work for a while. Eventually, I was left alone with a doctor who gave me a more detailed rundown of everything I'd injured. Case's sister had left out the fact that the back of my head was stapled shut. Apparently, I had an appointment with a neurologist later that day, and the results from a CAT scan would determine how long I had to stay in the hospital. Without question, I was looking at a minimum of another forty hours for observation.

When the doctor left, all I wanted to do was go back to sleep, but the door didn't even shut behind him before Case was waltzing into the room like he owned the place. I looked past him, expecting to see his whirlwind of a sister following him. I found her assertive, honest personality and dry humor oddly comforting. She was a nice distraction from the pain that was consuming me.

I watched warily as Case lowered his large frame into a chair he pulled up next to the bed. He set a silver Thermos on the rolling table nearby and said, "My neighbor, Mrs. Clooney, made some potato soup and ordered me to bring it to you after lecturing me for an hour for not being home the last two days. She's a good cook and the only grandparent Hayes has ever really had." His gaze skimmed over me and darted over all the monitors giving away the fact my heart rate increased notably the closer he got.

"Your house isn't a total loss. You'll have to rebuild the entire top floor and do some extensive repairs on the main level, but less than thirty percent of it was damaged. It's a mess, and I'm sure dealing with insurance is going to be a nightmare, but you're still here, and the structure is salvageable, so I think it's a win." He turned his eyes back toward mine, and I swore I could practically feel the blue gaze burning my skin. "I asked my sister to bring you some stuff, since your bedroom was where the damage was concentrated. For once in her life, Kody decided to be agreeable. My brother's girlfriend also offered to pitch in when she heard what was going on. Not sure how you feel about hand-me-downs, but you've got enough to get you through a couple of days when the doctors spring you."

I nodded and tried to blink the fresh rush of tears out of my eyes. It was hard to get my head around the fact that this man who despised me had gone out of his way to be so thoughtful and considerate. I'd known Case Lawton was a good guy all along, and here he was proving it when I was at my most vulnerable and weak.

"I know you're tired and in pain, but I need to ask you some questions about the break-in and the fire, okay?" His bright gaze drilled into me, and it took a lot of concentrated effort not to squirm under the intensity of it.

I pointed to my throat with my good hand and winced as the small movement made my whole body throb. I gave my head a barely discernable shake, letting him know I couldn't speak.

"You don't have to talk to me. Just use thumbs-up and thumbs-down for yes or no. I'm going to keep the questions as simple as I can. We'll talk more when you get your voice back, and when you're not beat up and exhausted. Does that work?"

I flicked the thumb of my good hand up and watched as Case gave a responding grin. He took off his Stetson so I could see his face clearly. I took a moment to note he really did look as tired and worn-out as his sister mentioned. There were dark circles under his pale blue eyes, his stubble had bloomed into something closer to a light beard and the fine lines fanning out from the corners of his eyes seemed more pronounced than normal. I guessed there was a lot of pressure on him to figure out who was terrorizing his town. At the end of the day, the safety of all of the residents of Loveless fell on him, which explained why he was paying so much attention to what was happening to me. *Not* because he cared.

"Okay, good. I think this will work." He pulled the chair closer to the side of the bed and reached out to wrap his hand around the top rail. "Did you have a spare set of house keys in your office?"

I started to nod and hissed when I forgot that was a bad idea. I gulped and slowly lifted my thump up. I kept both a spare house and car key in my desk just in case. I also kept a spare key to my office at home. I liked to be prepared.

"Did you tell anyone about the spare keys? Your paralegal? Your secretary? A friend? Your husband?" Case was trying to keep his tone even and calm, but I could hear the bite in it when he asked the question.

I turned my thumb upright once again. My secretary and paralegal both had access to my office and desk. I'd willingly handed over the keys to both of them a time or two when I needed an errand handled. Which meant anyone who was in my office at the time I passed them off might know about their existence as well. And I was sure David probably knew about my backup keys. I'd kept a similar set in my desk when I worked at his firm.

Case nodded sharply. "Okay. The keys weren't a secret. I'll need a list of anyone you know for sure knew about them. I think the break-in was a way for whoever set your house on fire to get the keys so they could get inside your home undetected."

I felt my eyes widen, and I sucked in a breath. The action hurt, and I immediately started coughing and wheezing, which set my lungs on fire and turned my aching head inside out. Case pushed out of his chair and reached for the cup of ice chips. I watched with huge eyes as he started to gently press the cold relief against my lips.

"You didn't hear anyone in the house?" He asked the question as the melting water slid across my lips and tongue.

I turned my thumb downward. The house was quiet before I went to bed. I remembered my glass of wine and the list of possible suspects I'd been working on for him. I winced when I thought about the contents of my room, which was now a pile of ash. It was going to take forever to replace everything.

"The neighbor said they didn't hear anything. No smoke detectors going off. No screaming when you realized the house was on fire. Did you have working detectors in the house?"

I nodded, which surprised him and pushed his fingers against my lips. We both stilled for a moment at the contact. His fingertips were rough, but I liked the slight abrasion. Case cleared his throat and took his hand away.

"Had you checked them recently? You're sure they were working, and the batteries weren't dead?"

I pushed my thumb up. I checked the smoke detectors once a month like clockwork. The Craftsman was an older home, so I tried to be diligent with all the maintenance on it. I bought it because it spoke to me as a metaphor for where my life was right now. I was going to breathe new life into both.

Case lifted a hand and rubbed the back of his neck. "That means someone was in your house. They disabled the smoke detectors and then set the fire. I haven't talked to the investigator working the case yet, but I know an accelerant was used. If I had to wager a guess, I bet they're going to find your bedroom door was tampered with or barricaded shut. Someone wanted you trapped in that room when the house went up. No one would've guessed you were going to jump off the roof. The more I think about it, the clearer it becomes someone might want you dead, Counselor."

I recoiled from his words and started to shake all over. My foggy brain was having a hard time keeping up with what he was saying, and immediate denial flooded through me.

How could someone be trying to kill me? Why would anyone want me dead?

I wasn't that important or that special. Sure, I dealt with a variety of challenging clients and cases, but none of that equaled murder in my mind.

The heart monitor went erratic somewhere above my head, and Case looked panicked for a second. A nurse immediately entered the room and started fiddling around on the other side of my bed. She gave Case the stink eye and told him I was in no condition for anything stressful or strenuous. However, hearing someone might want me dead was both of those things.

Case grabbed his cowboy hat and gave me an unwavering look. "I think you're in serious danger, Aspen. I need to know where you're going and who you're going to be with once you get discharged. It's my job to keep you safe."

Right. His job. I needed to remember that.

Squeezing my eyes closed I offered him one last thumbs-up and hoped it would be enough to send him on his way, at least for a little while. It must have been sufficient because Case walked out of the room leaving his warning and the homemade soup behind.

The nurse didn't leave me alone until my heart rate was

back to normal. By the time she was satisfied I wasn't going into arrhythmia or having a heart attack, the neurologist came in and did another examination. He ran down the list of what I should be aware of moving forward after suffering such a severe concussion and asked if I had anyone I wanted the information passed along to. Maybe I should've filled my mother in, and I knew David was going to be pissed to be kept out of the loop, but I needed time to process what was happening before someone else came in and tried to take over while I was laid up.

After that, I quickly fell asleep after a potent cocktail of painkillers and a warning to expect a nurse to be checking on me several times throughout the rest of the day and night. It was a relief to drift away from the pain pounding along every nerve and to escape the multitude of questions swirling around my mind after Case's blunt revelation.

I got the hazy impression of people coming in and out of the room at random intervals. I guessed David was one of them because I felt a kiss on my forehead at one point and heard the familiar promise that things would be all right. I decided it was too much effort to open my eyes for him and let sleep suck me back under so I didn't have to deal with my stubborn ex.

It must've been much later when I gained awareness again. The lights in the room were dim, and I was hungry. My body still felt like one giant exposed nerve ending, but the headache had dulled, and my brain no longer felt like it was stuffed with cotton candy. My burned hand was still making itself known, and my injured ankle decided it would like to be acknowledged, but overall, I was feeling marginally less like I was going to die.

It took a minute for me to register I was also not alone in the room.

Hushed voices lifted out of the darkness. I instantly recognized Case's raspy growl, but it took longer to realize the woman he was speaking to was his sister.

"She doesn't seem so bad. The way you described her all these years, I was expecting a monster. She's a tiny little thing, isn't she?"

Case snorted. "Don't let her size fool you."

"You know that she's going to be okay. Go home, Case. Sleep in your own bed. Spend time with your son. She's not going anywhere for a few days, and I seriously doubt anything is going to happen to her while she's in the hospital. You can't stand guard over her twenty-four hours a day. You have other responsibilities, and I don't think her rich husband likes it." Kody Lawton's tone and attitude softened noticeably when she spoke to her brother. There was an unmistakable gentleness there, and I kind of wished I could see the two of them together to see if Case reciprocated the sentiment. I'd never witnessed him being docile. He was always all hard edges and unbreakable stone when we dealt with each other. I wanted to witness Case being someone other than my sworn enemy.

"Something feels really off with this whole situation. And she left Barlow." Case bit out the last part of the sentence begrudgingly.

A feminine sigh filled the dark space. "She left him, but he obviously hasn't left her. Don't get yourself tangled in that mess. The Barlows have more money than God, and you're an elected official. This entire town needs you because lord only knows who the rich and entitled would buy to replace you if you piss them off badly enough. What if it was someone worse than Dad? Where would we be then?"

"The only thing I'm tangled in is trying to figure out who might have it in for her and to make sure she doesn't get hurt again on my watch. That's my job, Kody."

Another sigh. "Fine. It's your job, so do it and go home. You aren't going to do anyone any good if you fall flat on your face. If it makes you feel better and gets you out of here, I'll stay with her. I can call Crew and ask him to watch the bar for me until they release her."

These Lawtons were something else. First, Case rallied the troops when he heard I lost all my personal belongings, and now his sister was offering to sit with me so I didn't have to be alone. I swallowed back against the rush of emotion that clogged my ravaged throat. There was something about support coming from an unexpected place that really got to me. I was an emotional mess.

I moved on the bed, which made the siblings aware I was awake. Kody's face and messy hair came into view first. She offered a lopsided smile.

"How you doing, Superwoman? Do you need anything?" I rolled my head to the side in a half "no" and pointed at the call button near my head. I could call the evening nurse in to help me. I was not the Lawtons' responsibility, and the last thing I wanted was to be indebted to a man who had held a grudge against me for so long.

I made a writing gesture in the air. I needed a way to communicate beyond yes and no.

After a few minutes of looking around, Kody came back with a shrug and her cell phone. She opened the note writing app before putting the device in my good hand.

"Can't find a pen or paper. Just type what you need." Case ambled over and stood by her shoulder, watching me with slightly narrowed eyes.

As quickly as I could with one hand, I thanked Kody for the provisions and assured her I would be fine on my own. She didn't need to stand vigil next to my bedside. I told Case to go home. I promised to keep him updated about my whereabouts but, again, maintained there was no point in keeping watch over me. I wasn't convinced he was accurate in his assessment of how serious my situation was. How could anyone want me dead? It just didn't make any sense.

The siblings exchanged a look, and finally, Kody shrugged in defeat. "All righty. I'm out if you don't need me. I'm going to leave my number though. Call me if you need me to get you any toiletries and whatnot. I'm sure you usually use expensive French products like Della, but I can get you stuff to get by in a pinch." She poked Case in the shoulder, which made him frown. "Listen to the woman and go home."

I nodded as vigorously as I could. The last thing this situation needed was for Case to blame me for stealing more time away from his son. He didn't need to watch me sleep when he could be home with Hayes.

After a few moments of obvious indecision, he dipped his chin in a gesture of reluctant agreement. "Fine. We'll get out of your hair, but I'll be back tomorrow to check on you."

It sounded like that was as much of a compromise as I was going to get, and frankly, I was too worn-out to argue. There were worse things in the world than being the focus of Case Lawton's concern. I just had to remind myself not to get used to it.

After all, he was only doing his job.

CHAPTER 6

∞

CASE

You're actually home. I wasn't expecting that. You have time to eat this morning?"

There was a hint of surprise but no censure or blame in my son's voice when I stumbled into the kitchen early the next day. The last few I'd been gone before the sun came up. I'd finally met with the fire investigator, and just like I predicted, someone tried to trap Aspen in the upper level of her home before setting it on fire. The burn pattern led right out her bedroom door. I'd also tracked down her paralegal and her secretary to ask about the spare keys in Aspen's office. Both women admitted to knowing right where they were, and both mentioned Aspen never kept the location much of a secret, which meant I needed to know who out of her current client list posed the biggest problem. Any number of clients who had been to the office could have seen the keys being exchanged or put away. But because of attorney-client privilege, I didn't get very far. Luckily Aspen's secretary kept an ear to the ground and gave me a

to know that someone who looked like she had the
at her feet was standing directly in the center of my
'pic of failures. Still, calling her "weird girl" was not a
moment for me.

:yes·pulled me out of the reminiscing as he continued to
.e about the new student. "She doesn't talk to me, or even
/ look at me. I've said hi a couple times, but she blows me
told a couple of the guys on the team to stop talking crap
it her, but you know how this town is. Everyone freaks out
n someone blows through who doesn't match with how
▪gs have always been. Mrs. Barlow's lived here a long time,
ried a local, does good work for the community, and peo-
still whisper about her behind her back. You should hear
stuff they're saying now that she's in the middle of your in-
▪tigation. I overheard one of my teachers saying she thinks
;. Barlow burned her own house down because she wants
Barlow back. It's so dumb." He huffed out a breath and
:hed for the plates he'd already set out. Dishing out the
◄d into two portions, he passed one to me, and I followed
▪ over to the dining room table.

▪ sighed heavily. "A lot of folks fear change. They get
ifortable, and anything that disrupts that comfort can be
a as unwelcome."

Eyes that were identical to my own gave me a level look.
at's why it took so long for you to take over the sher-
job from granddad. Everyone knew he wasn't doing his
ight, but they were scared to let someone else take over,
use it meant things were gonna change. Change isn't al-
; a bad thing. There's no moving forward if you stay
ling still in the same spot forever."

was sure he was talking about the new girl at school, but
; also clear he was talking about me and my unwilling-
:o see Aspen Barlow as anything other than the enemy.

couple of names to run down off the record. It seemed there
were quite a few disgruntled spouses who had threatened
harm and retribution after dealing with Aspen in court.

It'd been a busy, hectic few days and I hadn't been home
much. I winced remembering the way I was painted as an
ineffective parent and absentee father back when Hayes was
young because I was always working. It didn't matter that
Mrs. Clooney undoubtedly kept him fed and watched out for
him while I was working these days. Taking care of him was
my job, and it was just as important as tracking down whoever had it in for my arch nemesis.

"Sorry I haven't been around. This case I'm working on
is complicated." So were my feelings toward the woman at
the center of it.

Hayes shrugged his broad shoulders and cocked his head
to the side. He looked more and more like me the older he
got. I'd fought for so long to be a part of his life, it was hard
to imagine the house being empty once he left for college. I
wanted to be here, with him, making the most of the time we
had left together, not running around trying to pinpoint who
in my town hated Aspen more than I did.

"You've got a job to do, Dad. It's an important one. Plus,
I've been busy. We've had two-a-days, midterms are coming up, I've been dodging Mom, and there's this girl at
school..." He trailed off and turned back to the pan he was
stirring on the stove. It looked like it was scrambled eggs and
bacon for breakfast. I moved to the coffeepot and rolled my
head around, making my neck pop. I was getting too old for
sleepless nights.

I ruffled the back of my son's dark hair and propped
a hip on the counter next to the stove. There was always
some girl. He changed them so fast I'd stopped learning
their names a forever ago. As long as he was respectful and

honest with them, I didn't mind him dating his way through the teenage female population of Loveless. I may have even encouraged him to not settle down. I tried not to dwell on how different my life might have been if I hadn't fallen for the wrong girl in high school. If I weren't so smitten with Becca and convinced she was my one and only, who knew where my path would have led? Maybe there was a chance I would've seen new-to-town Aspen as more than a wounded bird who needed help learning to fly. It was good Hayes didn't have the same kind of anchor weighing him down. I wanted him to get out in the world and experience everything I'd missed out on.

"This girl, is she the same blonde you were telling me about last week? The quiet, smart one?" I tried to pay attention to the details when he bothered to share them, so he knew when I was home he was my sole focus and priority. I tried really hard to leave Sherriff Lawton at the office so I could just be Dad when I was with Hayes.

He pushed his messy hair out of his eyes and straightened. I blinked in silent surprise when I realized we were almost eye to eye. It was hard to see him as my little boy when he was nearly the same height as I was.

"Affton? No, we still hang out and stuff, but she's all about blowing out of town as soon as possible. She cares more about what's ahead of her than what's standing in front of her right now. We're still friends, and she's an awesome study partner, but I don't see anything more there." He flashed me a grin I swore he inherited from his uncle Crew. It was full of mischief and charm, same as my younger brother's. "Kind of a bummer, because she's really-really hot, but no, this girl is new. She just moved here from somewhere in California. She has purple hair and a tattoo. She wears combat boots and a leather jacket no matter how hot it

is outside. I have a couple of classes with [ ] some issues fitting in, and a few of the ki[ ] a hard time. She ignores it for the most [ ] wondering why she doesn't make more of a[ ] in. We're getting ready to graduate. Why ma[ ] months of high school miserable for yourself[ ] head a little shake and moved the pans around[ ] the stove.

I took a sip of the strong, black coffee and si[ ] as the caffeine hit my system. "Sounds familiar. [ ] was just like that girl back when I was your age.[ ] dressed like she was going to a funeral, spouted[ ] like it was regualr conversation, used big words[ ] derstood, refused to eat meat…in the middle o[ ] Texas. No one quite knew what to make of her, an[ ] seemed interested in trying to acclimate." I shrug[ ] different worked out for her in the long run. She[ ] ful, memorable, and found someone who appreci[ ] differences. I guess some people are made to stan[ ] than fit in." I lifted an eyebrow in his direction. [ ] kids giving her a hard time, you better not be o[ ] I know you were raised better than that." By me[ ] been the queen of the mean girls back in the d[ ] the one who started calling Aspen "weird girl" a[ ] until the nickname stuck. When I was younger[ ] gave a damn, I always told her to knock it off[ ] to let her throw the nickname around. When I [ ] the old, hurtful name on the stairs of the sheriff[ ] later, it was because I was blindsided by the d[ ] off-kilter from seeing her again after so lon[ ] rassed that she had a front-row seat to one[ ] moments of my life. It was a knee-jerk reac[ ] until she snottily told me to get a *good* lawy[ ]

It was the role I'd cast her in so long ago, even if the title may not fit anymore. I wasn't sure when my kid got smarter than me, but I was proud of him. Nothing was going to hold Hayes back. He was meant for so much more than this town and carrying the endless burden of the Lawton name.

I snagged a piece of bacon off the plate and used it to point at Hayes. "Sometimes it just takes a little shove from the right person to get things moving. Usually, where one goes in this town, the rest follow. You lead the way by example, kiddo, the rest will follow along."

He nodded solemnly and snatched the piece of bacon out of my hand. "I will. I've never really had a girl completely ignore me before. I kinda want to know what her deal is."

I grunted and shoveled eggs into my mouth. After chewing and chasing breakfast down with more high-octane coffee, I got to my feet to take my dirty dishes to the sink and clapped a hand on my son's broad shoulder. "Don't get distracted, Hayes. You've got the big picture to think about. Being nice to a new girl at school is one thing, but don't make her a project." I refused to let him fail in any of the same ways I had. "You have to stay focused on your future."

It was Hayes's turn to heave a weighty sigh. "I know, Dad."

I squeezed again and felt him tense under the gesture. "As for you actively avoiding your mother, maybe you should hear her out. You know I do my best to let you handle her however you see fit, but the time you have to see her and spend with her is limited. You never know what's waiting around the corner. Don't write her off without thinking through *all* of the implications of your actions."

My son growled under his breath and angrily pushed his plate away from him. He shook my hand off his shoulder and rose to his feet. "Do you think she thought of *any* of the implications of her actions when she refused to let me see you when I was little? Do you think she cares about anyone but herself? She doesn't care that it makes me uncomfortable to see her with guys who are only a few years older than me. She doesn't listen to me when I tell her I don't want to hear her talk shit about what a crappy husband and father you were. She doesn't show up for a single thing that matters to me. She doesn't have the first clue as to who I am or what makes me happy, so why should I go out of my way to be there for her when she decides she's bored and wants company? I'm her son, not a pet."

I lifted my hands in front of me in a gesture of surrender. "Whoa, I'm not telling you what to do, or how to do it where your mom is concerned. My relationship with her has always been complicated. I can't imagine how much harder it would be if she actually wanted me around. I trust you to do the right thing, and I believe you are smart enough to make the best choice for yourself, Hayes. But I also know life is very unpredictable, and when things happen that we can't control, living with regret is hard." I wanted Hayes to understand that. All of us Lawton kids had been able to say good-bye to our mother before the cancer stole her away. And we all kept in touch with our father to varying degrees, even though he drove us all nuts and stole away most of our youth because the memory of our mom dying haunted him. It wouldn't be the same emotional heartbreak to say good-bye to our father, but none of us kids could completely cut ties. "This is the last time I'll bring it up. I need to jump in the shower and head to the hospital. They're releasing Mrs. Barlow today."

Hayes picked up his dishes and glanced at me over his shoulder. "Where is she going? Her house is unlivable."

That was a good question and one of the reasons I wanted to see her before she was released. She had promised to keep me updated as to her whereabouts, but as of yesterday she still hadn't decided where she was going to go. She'd mentioned visiting her mother for a while, but she cringed when she said it. Her soon-to-be ex was badgering her to move back in with him, which was the most logical choice. He lived in a huge home in a gated community with a state-of-the-art security system. Aspen would be safe there, and it was clear David Barlow would move heaven and earth to get her back. She didn't want to go, but the man she was still reluctantly married to was wearing her down.

I headed upstairs so I could take a quick shower. I had too much on my mind and too many conflicting emotions swirling under my skin to make the most of the quiet, private time. Getting off alone in the shower was nothing new. I was too busy and my schedule was too chaotic to date with any kind of regularity. I was also an admitted commitmentphobe. After the way my marriage with Becca crashed and burned, I refused to tie myself to anyone else. I was never losing anything to another woman again, including my heart. In a town full of women looking to settle down, I tended to keep all my romantic liaisons short and sweet and with women from neighboring towns. I had a couple of regular hookups I could call when I had a free hour or two and when Hayes was at an out-of-town game. I tried to remember the last time I'd felt the press of a soft, warm, willing body against mine.

Too long was the answer, because I had to think about it for several minutes.

Grumbling under my breath and promising to rectify the situation the next time Hayes had an away game, I got dressed in my usual outfit of jeans and uniform shirt, made sure I grabbed my badge, my gun, and my hat before I headed out the door. I could make the drive to the hospital with my eyes closed now, and I could find Aspen's room on autopilot. I nodded to a few of the nurses I'd bumped into repeatedly while checking on her. When I got to Aspen's door, I paused momentarily because it was opened a crack and the sound of a loud voice was making its way into the hall. I recognized David Barlow's haughty, bossy tone right away, and I was surprised to hear Aspen reply. Her voice sounded broken and was hardly above a harsh whisper, but she wasn't letting her former husband order her around.

"I told you if you want me to come stay with you, and not in a hotel, sign the papers, David. I've been waiting for almost a year for the divorce to be final. It's time to move on. We both deserve more." I put a hand on the door and lifted my eyebrows. It seemed like the courtroom wasn't the only place Aspen played dirty. That was one hell of an ultimatum to lay at the poor man's feet. "And stop asking my mother to talk to me on your behalf. The last thing I need is conversations with her when I can barely speak. She already talks over me as it is."

"I can't believe you. All I want is what's best for you. You'll be safe at our house. I can keep an eye on you. And your mother knows you should've never left. You should listen to her." David sounded whiny and petulant.

"All I want is for you to finally sign the divorce paperwork. It's called give-and-take." She sounded frustrated beyond belief and highly annoyed. I pushed into the room, causing both of them to turn and look in my direction. I propped a shoulder up against the doorjamb and shifted my gaze between the two of them.

David was dressed in an immaculate navy suit. Aspen was wearing something I was sure came from my sister's boho-chic closet. Her stretchy pants were turquoise, her flowy top was a wild swirl of orange and pink. It was more color than I'd ever seen on the small woman, but it looked good with her dark hair and pale skin. "Just stopping by to see if you decided where you were going to post up for the next few days. Last I heard you were considering a hotel or a visit to your mother's."

She used her unbandaged hand to push back her hair, and I watched as she chewed on her lower lip. She was still bruised and battered from head to toe, but her gaze was sharp and clear.

"I'm going to a hotel." She said the words at the same time David stated, "She's coming home with me."

I saw Aspen's jaw clench, and her uninjured hand tightened into a fist. Her dark eyes narrowed. "I'm not going with you unless you do as I've asked. I'll have Sheriff Lawton take me to a hotel." She turned her head in my direction, and it was only because I was watching her so closely I could see the exhaustion and fear hidden in the midnight depths. "You can do that, right? Take me somewhere safe. That way you'll know exactly where I am and no one else will."

I dipped my chin down in agreement. "I can do that." Normally I would've made her suffer, but she wasn't in tip-top shape, and throwing her under the bus right now wasn't playing fair.

The man in the suit puffed up his chest and whirled around to confront me. I lifted an eyebrow and purposely put a hand on my hip next to where my badge was clipped.

"You can't do that."

I snorted. "Yes I can, and yes she can."

I caught Aspen's lips twiching as she fought a grin when I effectivly shut David up.

A frowning nurse popped her head around where I was

leaning. "You all need to keep it down. The elderly gentleman in the next room is complaining about the noise. Mrs. Barlow, you've been discharged. A wheelchair is on the way up so you can go. You really shouldn't be using your voice for much until you get it checked out again by your regular physician."

Aspen flushed, and David apologized profusely. I made my way farther into the room and paused next to the side of the hospital bed. Aspen looked small and delicate with all the bandages she had scattered on her limbs. She also had dark circles under her eyes, and her skin seemed so translucent and pale, I could make out the fine blue lines of her veins under the surface. She needed somewhere she could rest and recuperate without having to manipulate and bargain.

"I'll take you wherever you wanna go." Our eyes locked for a moment and she nodded gratefully. There was no explanation for the zing that shot up my spine when those dark eyes met mine.

A moment later an orderly appeared at the door with a wheelchair. It took a few moments for Aspen to maneuver her way off the bed and into the device. Her sprained ankle and burned hand were on the same side, so she was awkward and unwieldy. When David moved to help her, he was brought up short by a snarl. It was clear the woman didn't want the man's hands anywhere on her, and I needed a minute to wonder why that fact made a swirl of relief wind it's way through my chest.

I followed the silent group down the hall and opted to take the stairs instead of the elevator when they all huddled inside. There was so much tension vibrating between the former couple—it felt alive and dangerous, like an electrical current. David Barlow was a man used to getting his way, and he wasn't taking Aspen's decision to walk away from their relationship lightly. I recalled Hayes mentioning the local gossip surrounding the fire. Was it possible the busybodies were on to something but had the intent backward? Could David be behind the fire in an attempt to get Aspen back under his roof? It wasn't completely out of left field the more I watched him hound her and saw how resistant he was when it came to ending their marriage.

I met the wheelchair at the front doors. Aspen was repeatedly sighing and assuring David, "Once the sheriff determines who broke into my office and set my house on fire I'll let you know where I am. I'll be fine, David. Relax."

"This is ridiculous, Aspen. The safest place for you is at home with me." Everyone pushed into the warm Texas morning, the sun glinting brightly off of the cars in the parking lot.

"You want her at your place, she told you how to make it happen. If this is how you listen, no wonder she wants you to sign the papers so badly." I dropped the barb without a backward glance, telling Aspen to wait for a second while I pulled my SUV around to the entrance. I was running through a list of possible places to stash her for a few days—and ignoring David Barlow's shouts of outrage in my direction—when the hairs on the back of my neck suddenly stood up on end.

I paused midstep, pushing my hat back and squinted out into the sunlight.

Something was wrong. I could sense it in the air and feel the pulse of it in my bones. It was an instinct I'd honed not only as an officer of the law but also as a soldier. I would be dead ten times over if I hadn't learned early on to listen to my gut.

"Get her back inside. NOW!" I turned on the heel of my boot and lunged in the direction of where Aspen was virtually a sitting duck in the wheelchair.

I saw her eyes widen, heard David demand to know what was going on, but it was all a blur. An instant later the orderly was on the ground, following a distinctive crack. Aspen screamed, as much as she could with her ravaged throat, and her estranged husband dove for cover behind a huge potted plant. Another crack filled the air, sending more people scattering and trying to find shelter. The orderly was bleeding profusely behind the wheelchair, so there was no moving him or Aspen.

"Is someone shooting? What's going on?" The questions were coming from every direction, but all I could focus on was getting the intended target out of the line of fire.

Another shot rang out and I felt my shoulder ignite in a fire trail of pain. I grunted as I practically tackled Aspen, taking her and the wheelchair to the ground. It tipped over sideways, and we landed with a thud on the hard cement walkway at the entrance of the building. Her eyes were twice their normal size and filled with stark terror.

I made sure I covered her entire body from head to toe as I waited for another bullet to hit my back. The pain in my shoulder radiated down my arm, and I heard screams echoing from every corner of the building.

I kept my face close to Aspen's, I could feel her breathing erratically and whispered in her ear, "Someone is definitely trying to kill you."

I felt her nod against my throat where I had her head tucked protectively. "Why me?"

Everything around us suddenly went very quiet and alarmingly still. I risked a peek over my shoulder and couldn't see anything but the sun reflecting off the windshields of nearby cars. I wasn't sure how long we stayed like that, huddled together and shaking against one another. Maybe it as a minute, maybe it was ten. But eventually the burning in my stomach died down and the sense of unease faded away. I was sure the shooter was gone and lifted my head up to fully look around. The only people injured seemed to be the orderly and me.

"Sherrif! What should we do?!" More questions were fired in my direction as I hesitantly lifted myself up off of Aspen's much smaller frame.

"I'll call it in. Someone get this guy some help." I pointed to the orderly. "If anyone saw anything, I need you to stick around and give a statement. If anyone saw where the shots were fired from that would be helpful. But be on alert. And try not to touch anything that might be evidence." It was easy enough to slip into work mode once the chaos and confusion died down, but as soon as I looked at the shaken, terrified woman still huddled on the ground, there was no denying something personal was also pushing at me. I hated to see someone who was normally so strong and composed completely broken down.

"I don't know why it's you, Aspen. I'm going to figure it out though. In the meantime, I'm going to make sure they don't get another chance to hurt you. I know a place where no one will think to look for you, and you'll be completely safe." I wrapped my arms around her, holding her to my chest as her entire body quaked with tremors. I should have let her go once we were on our feet, but I didn't. For one thing I wasn't sure her legs would hold her. It was another thing entirely that I wanted to keep her close, keep her safe, and hold her until she stopped shaking.

She gave me a wide-eyed look before tucking her head under my chin and carefully placing her trembling hands on either side of my waist. I could hear police sirens wailing in the distance, so I didn't have time to reassure her, or think about why I felt her touch through the fabric of my shirt more intensely than the bullet wound in my shoulder. Instead, I told her, "Just trust me."

It was asking a lot, but she nodded after a moment. I refused to stop and examine why having her trust meant so much.

CHAPTER 7

∞

ASPEN

"This is a terrible idea. I can't stay here." I wished there was more force behind my voice, more sound, but all I could get out was a squeak of protest.

Between arguing with David, answering a million questions about the shooting, and even more from the hospital staff to determine whether my head had been damaged further, what little voice I had was shot. It had been a long, arduous morning. The shock from being shot at was still buzzing underneath my skin, but it was now secondary to the utter disbelief that the place Case believed I would be safest was under his roof.

When he told me he was placing me in protective police custody and taking me to a safe house, never in a million years would I have guessed he meant *his* house. I was wondering if maybe he was the one who hurt his head when he took me to the ground.

"What about Hayes? Someone shot at me today. You took a bullet for me this morning. You can't put your son in the line of fire. I won't allow it." All of the things I wanted to do to emphasize my point, I couldn't. There was no crossing my arms over my chest thanks to my jacked-up elbow. There was no stomping my foot in aggravation thanks to the soft splint holding my ankle in one position. There would be no yelling, since my voice could barely be heard, so all I was left with was a glare. Unfortunately, Case ignored my dirty look and continued to usher me inside the house.

His morning had been even longer than mine, and he looked as haggard as I felt. After making sure I was secured inside the hospital with an armed guard, he'd had to deal with the crime scene and the slew of reporters who showed up on the scene. Since a shooting in a high traffic and very public place like the hospital was bound to make national news, Case mentioned it was more than likely the Texas Rangers were going to get called in to help investigate. He didn't sound thrilled at the prospect, he also didn't seem too concerned by the fact he was shot. He still had a red stain and a hole in his tan uniform shirt from where the bullet, which was meant for me, skimmed his shoulder. The wound required ten stitches and now was dressed in a stark white bandage much like the one wrapped around my injured hand.

We were quite a pair.

But we'd both made it out in better shape than the orderly who was shot in front of me. The young man's injuries had required major surgery and he still wasn't out of the woods yet. I was never going to forgive myself if he died, and I could see the guilt Case was carrying around for not being a few seconds faster as well. He promised he would keep me updated on the man's condition since I was technically in isolation from this point on out. I was hoping the young man pulled through with everything I had.

"I would never put Hayes in danger. I spent years trying

to tell you and the judge that. He's going to stay with my brother out on his ranch for a few days. Crew has a tricked-out motor home he travels in when he's competing during the rodeo season, and Hayes likes to take it over when he stays with him and pretend he's a rock star. It isn't unusual for him to spend time with either of my siblings, so no one will question why he isn't here." He pushed his hat back in a gesture that was starting to become very familiar. He did it when he was about to make a serious point and wanted to make sure whoever he was talking to couldn't look away from those summer-sky blue eyes of his. "The fact that you and I don't get along is well known all throughout this town. My house is literally the last place anyone would think to look for you, and after this morning"—he arched a dark brow at me—"do you really want to risk being somewhere else? There are only two hotels in town. It won't take very long for someone to track you down if they really want to. Your best options for your safety are my guest room or hitting the road and putting some distance between you and Loveless for a while."

The second option was the one I should go with. Only, there was no way my mother would understand my showing up out of the blue in the current shape I was in. She would turn the situation into yet another opportunity to badger me into going back to David. Just like my estranged husband, she would insist over and over again, the best place for me to be was at his home.

I'd already instructed Case to ignore three calls and five text messages from her demanding to know where I was going and asking what right he had to sequester me away. He was polite enough during the first call, curious where she got his number but refusing to put me on the phone. He wasn't so nice the next time he answered, telling my pushy mother to back off and threatening her if she kept involving herself in a police investigation. It was starting to be impossible to tell who was worse, my mother or my ex. I wanted to strangle David for getting her involved and decided ignoring both of them for a few days was in my best interest. I was done with them until I had enough of a voice to argue back.

I had physical proof staying with David wasn't actually any guarantee of safety. When the bullets starting flying, David's first instinct had been to duck and hide. Not that I should blame him. The situation was terrifying, and I would never forget the image of the young orderly bleeding on the ground because of me. Case was the one who put himself between me and the onslaught of bullets. He was the man who got the injured orderly help. So, while one man claimed to love me more than anything else, and the other swore he hated me with the passion of a thousand fiery suns, it was the second man who risked his life for mine. I needed to do a better job reminding myself it was Case's job to put himself between civilians and danger. He wasn't doing any of this as a favor or out of the goodness of his heart. He was doing what he thought was best as the sheriff and as a natural-born protector. I'd always admired him, even more so now, and if things were different...if *we* were different...that stupid crush of mine would have absolutely taken flight once again. He made it really hard to resent him, and far too easy to remember all the reasons why I liked him so much when we were younger.

As for going on the run on my own...I could hardly walk from the garage where Case parked his SUV to the living room of his house without leaning against him for support. I could hop on my good foot for short distances, but if I was going anywhere that required me to move more than a few feet, I was going to need a wheelchair. I wasn't mobile enough to try and keep myself safe. Plus, I still had the mess from the fire to deal with and clients who were counting on me. As nice as the idea of running away from my entire life sounded, it wasn't possible. I'd never been one to back down from a challenge, and I wasn't about to let some unknown force start dictating my life now. I also didn't want to be alone with my thoughts—or my fear. My head was going crazy, and my heart was still trying to pound its way out of my chest. I needed to be around someone who understood how quickly and dramatically my life tilted sideways . . . Which meant I was crashing at Case's house until he figured out who had it in for me.

Sighing, I slumped against the wall closest to me. "I don't want to be an imposition. Having me here can't be ideal for you."

"Ideal? No, it's not. But keeping you alive long enough to figure out who might want you dead is. I honestly believe this is the right call to make for the immediate future. We're both adults. We can coexist without too much fuss for a few days." He waved a hand absently around the tidy entryway. "Besides, everything is on one level. It'll be easy for you to get around on those crutches when you can use them."

I nodded wearily. Maybe if my house hadn't burned down and I hadn't been shot at all in the same week I could come up with a more convincing argument as to why this idea of his was going to blow up in both our faces. Right now, it took everything I had within me to keep my eyes open and to stay upright. I put more of my weight against the wall and let my silence indicate my surrender. If Case believed he could keep me safe, and this was the best place to accomplish his goal, I believed him. He took his job seriously.

"Come on. Let's get you somewhere you can rest comfortably. The guest room is right this way." He hefted the bag his sister had packed for me up off the ground and moved to my side so he could help me hobble to the room. "If we need to rewrap your hand and clean that wound on your head, let me know. I'll help you with it."

I prayed he didn't feel the shiver that ran through my body when his strong arm wrapped around my waist. God forbid he realize I reacted so strongly to him. The man already played havoc with my emotions, and the last thing I needed was for him to see how vulnerable and soft I was when it came to him. I knew how to feud with him. I wasn't sure I was ready to learn how to play nice after all these years of animosity. He was potent. Calling a truce with Case almost certainly meant my feelings were going to go rogue and I'd end up back in love with him in no time flat.

I hopped and skipped while holding on to his broad shoulder. I noticed him wince slightly under the pressure and remembered belated I wasn't the only one who was hurt. I made sure to keep as much weight as I could off his injured shoulder but nearly toppled over when I couldn't use my sprained ankle to help balance. Sucking in a breath I whispered, "I'm sorry. I hate that you got hurt because of me. I hate all of this." The lack of control in what was happening to me was going to drive me out of my mind.

Case growled under his breath and locked his arm more fully around my waist. We were glued together from hip to shoulder, and I could feel the heat radiating from his big body. It made my head spin.

"Don't worry about it. It's part of the job description, and I'm a much bigger target than you are." The top of my head really did only just reach his shoulder. He was always larger than life, but right next to him, he seemed like a giant, and I felt like an itty-bitty scrape of nothing.

Luckily the room was only at the end of a short hallway. But I was sweaty and had my teeth gritted together painfully by the time we reached our destination. My head was starting to hurt, and my hand was throbbing painfully. All I wanted to do was lie down in the dark and have a silent pity party for myself. I'd earned a few moments to wallow.

Case tossed the bag on the end of the nicely made-up bed and muscled me into a sitting position on the side of it.

"Bathroom is through there. Kody keeps it stocked up and tries to keep Hayes and me mostly civilized. Mrs. Clooney generally helps Hayes keep the fridge full, so you won't starve. You should have everything you need. The house isn't very big, so if you need help with anything just holler and I'll hear you. I have a few calls to make and some work to follow up on, and I need to change out of this shirt. You look like hell. Try and get some rest unless you want me to find you something to eat first."

I shook my head and told him I was fine, even though I felt anything but.

I was as far from fine as I'd ever been in my life.

My house was trashed. I was going to have to replace everything I owned. And the few mementos I'd hung on to from the few actual happy memories in my life were gone. My office was destroyed. I'd worked so hard to be independent, to stake my own claim on this town, to be my own person, and someone had obliterated all those difficult steps I'd taken. I could've died today. Someone really did want me dead, and they weren't afraid to hurt other people if they got in the way. I felt like someone had dropped me in the middle of a bad action movie. I was missing the entire plotline though, and I had no idea how any of this had begun. On top of all of that, I still couldn't get David to sign the damn divorce papers, my mother wouldn't quit hounding me, and the only person I wanted to lean on was one who didn't see me as anything more than an obligation.

When the tears started, there was no stopping them.

When the sobs began to rack my body, I shook from head to toe with the force of them.

It was loud and ugly. It was wild and uncontrollable. It was overwhelming and painful.

Trying to manage that level of emotion was beyond my current capabilities, so I simply let go and broke down into nothing more than exposed feelings and raw reactions. I'd wanted a moment to fall apart. Unfortunately, I wasn't able to hold myself together quietly enough. Case reappeared and got front-row seats to my sudden hysterics. Through the veil of tears flooding my eyes, I could barely make out the look of absolute horror on his handsome face.

First, I'd invaded his private sanctuary, now I was shattering into a million delicate pieces, which he no doubt felt responsible for cleaning up and putting back together.

"I'm s-o-rr-y." I hiccuped the words out of my damaged throat. "I don't usu-ally act like th-is." I lifted my good hand to swipe at my face, but it was shaking so badly it never made it.

Somehow, I had vibrated my way off the side of the bed and was curled up on the floor. I heard Case swear from somewhere over my head, and a moment later his big frame was folded into a sitting position next to me.

"Come on, Counselor. I'm not the best with crying women. I'm at a loss as to what to do here." His hard shoulder pressed into mine, and I could feel the warmth of his thigh where it was pressed against the outside of mine. "We've know each other a long time, even if we were never very close. I've never seen you break. Not even when we were younger. You never let anything the other kids said about you bother you. And not now when you're cold as ice in court, even when things don't go your way."

He sounded slightly impressed, and my heart didn't know what to do with that new information.

His admission that he was in over his head with my outpouring of emotion was oddly endearing. I was sure he had to comfort victims of crimes and the loved ones of those who were taken while he was on the job. He couldn't be as much of a stranger to tears and hysterics as he was making out, which meant he was struggling with how to comfort *me*, not just another victim.

I sniffed loudly and went still as stone when I felt Case wrap one of his arms around my shaking shoulders. It was the first time he'd ever touched me not out of necessity. My already overtaxed system felt like it was going to short-circuit. I finally managed to wipe some of the moisture covering my face away, but I couldn't stop the shivering, or the silent sobs making my body quiver.

"Every single time I've pushed, you've pushed me right back. That doesn't happen a lot when your last name is Lawton. My father had so many people living in fear of retribution it became commonplace for most locals to simply move out of my way. Not you. You've always stood right in the center of the path. It was cute when we were teenagers. I should've checked up on you when I came home after the army. Still not sure why I didn't. But I do know, without question, that even though you have a lot on your plate right now, none of it is anything you can't handle. You are one of the strongest people I know."

His quiet assessment of my character and our shared history stunned me into silence and shocked the flood of self-pity right out of me. Not to mention the fact he called me *cute*. Even if he was talking about teenaged me, it still made my bruised heart flutter. My reply was stark and honest because all of my defenses had taken a hell of a beating the last week.

"I'm really good at hiding how I feel. I was back then, and I still am." I sniffed again and told myself not to sink into the comforting heat radiating off of his big body. I wanted to crawl into his arms and hide away from the rest of the world. "I hated what those kids called me in school. No one wants to be known as the weird girl." And no one wanted to feel alone and lost. I turned my head slightly, so I was looking at him. My words put a small frown on his face and pulled his dark eyebrows down. "No one has ever seen me break before now. I've always been broken, I'm just very good at keeping the cracks covered up. Right now, I'm not sure I can keep them from showing. I honestly don't know if I'm equiped to deal with all of this. I feel very much in over my head. I'm used to helping other people escape the danger they're in. I don't know how to handle being the one who needs protection."

We grew quiet, staring at each other wordlessly. His eyes were impossibly blue this close. I wasn't sure what I was searching for in their azure depths, but I couldn't seem to look away.

Case's arm tightened where it was slung around my neck, and he used his hold to slowly tug me closer. For a very fleeting second, I felt the brush of his lips against my forehead. If I had two working hands, I would have pinched myself to make sure the barely there caress was real and not imagined. How could such a small, insignificant gesture feel like the most important thing to ever have happened to me? Who could cry when they could no longer breathe? I let my head rest against his shoulder and took a shuddering breath. I felt completely surrounded by him, totally engulfed within his heat and his scent. It was a heady sensation, one that quickly had my head spinning in all kinds of dangerous directions.

"I know a little something about building a life on a shaky

foundation built mostly of lies and deceit. About projecting a confidence you don't feel. I spent so much time pretending to be someone I wasn't, so no one looked too closely at what was going on at home, I forgot the man I actually wanted to be." He sounded slightly forlorn about it.

"So who did you end up as? The man you were pretending to be, or the man you wanted to be?" I was still trying to figure out a way to be the woman I always intended to be, and I was curious if he felt like he'd grown past the kid trying to be perfect as a smoke screen.

"I think I ended up being half of each. There is no changing the past. At some point, we just have to learn to live with it. It's always there, always something we should learn from. I'll never lose sight of the person I had to become to survive my father, and I'll never not be the man who made a long list of drastic, desperate decisions to protect his family. I live with those choices, both the good and bad, every single day. But I've lived enough life at this point, and I know I need to set a good example for my son, that I think I managed to get a little bit of the man I wanted to be mixed in there. I couldn't be the man I am now without being the man I was back then. I'm a better man, a better father for each and every struggle I faced. And you'll be better when the dust settles and you see you're still standing."

I sighed and felt him squeeze my arm reassuringly in response. The simple touch was so much more settling and calming than any of the thousand times David told me everything would be fine after a good night's sleep. I didn't feel like I was being placated or patronized. I felt like I was being heard and sympathized with. I never would have guessed a big, tough, hypermasculine man like Case was so full of empathy and compassion. I was starting to see him in an entirely new light, and I liked what I was seeing.

"Thank you." The words were hardly more than a murmur but I felt like I screamed them from the top of my lungs.

"For what?" He sounded genuinely curious over where my gratitude was coming from.

"For listening and not telling me everything is going to be fine. For being nice to me even with all the history we have between us. You're a good man, Case Lawton. That's the kind of man you ended up as..." I let my thrashed voice trail off as he shifted where I was leaning against him.

I tried not to feel bereft as his warmth pulled away.

He climbed to his feet next to me, a scowl screwed into place on his rugged features. Without a word he reached down and helped me get awkwardly back to the side of the bed. I blinked in surprise at the sudden movement and the shift in energy between us. It was almost as if I could feel him firmly shutting the door he'd tentativly opened to a possible truce between the two of us.

"I tried to tell you I was a good guy when you took my kid away from me, and I missed most of his growing up. I've done my best to prove it over and over again, but none of my actions mattered because I was still Conrad Lawton's son, which made it far too easy for everyone to believe I would be no better as a father than he was. Even you." He plowed his fingers through his dark hair. "I have to make those calls. Let me know if you need anything."

He was out the door in a couple of long-legged strides. I thought he was going to slam the door behind him, but he left it open wide enough so that he could hear me if I did call for him. I listened as his heavy footsteps tapped across the hardwood floors, carrying him a safe distance away.

He said there was no way to forget the past, that it was always there to learn from. In our case our common history felt like a wide chasm there was no getting across. We're standing on opposite ledges with very different views on how the events between us played out. I could never tell Case things could have been so much worse if Becca had gotten her way and manged to spread those damning rumors about his time working under his father.

If Becca's accusations got out, no one would trust him to do the right thing, and the scandal that ensued would have all but guaranteed the judge took away his son for good. Plus, it would ruin his career. People would accuse him of being exactly like his father. I didn't want Case—or Hayes—to have to go through that.

I never decided if my decision was totally ethical. But I truly believed it was the best choice for Hayes—the most important person in the Lawton custody battle. He needed Case in his life. It was a choice I thought about a lot. If it ever got out, I would be in the tricky postion of having to anwser for never doing anything with the accusations Becca made. Initally, I could cover my bases with attorney-client privillage. The things Becca said about Case didn't need to go past my office door. But once she fired me, I could have done something about the claims she made. Obviously, I couldn't tell the former sheriff what Becca accused both of them of, but I should have said something to someone so they could investigate any wrongdoing. It was too late for the traumatized young woman, but there were so many other people out there in the same situation who needed to know if they asked for help they were going to get it. It was my biggest secret. One of the reasons I kept my distance from Case was because I didn't want him to ever have the chance to prove to me I made the wrong choice by keeping my mouth shut. As long as Case did his job and upheld the laws, as long as he protected *everyone*, my concious was clean.

Choking down a moan of pain, one that had nothing to do

with all my bumps and bruises and everything to do with the way my soul was starting to ache, I wiggled my way fully onto the borrowed bed and stretched out. I closed my eyes and blocked out everything spiraling out of control.

There wasn't enough Spackle in all of Texas to patch up the way I was cracking apart now.

CHAPTER 8

CASE

Fuck you and fuck that bitch lawyer." I stepped back as a cigarette butt was flicked in the direction of my boots. "Kayla woulda come back if that prissy bitch hadn't talked her into taking my kids and leaving me. Aspen Barlow didn't have any right to get involved in our personal business. What happens between a husband and a wife should stay between them."

It had been a very long week. I was still dealing with the fallout from the shooting at the hospital. My shoulder still felt like it was on fire if I moved wrong. I missed having my kid around every single day. And I was exhausted from tiptoeing around my own home all the time. I knew it was the best place for Aspen to be right now, but that didn't mean I was at all comfortable having her there, especially since she was still so weak. How close she came to death was obvious every time I had to help her do the simplest of tasks. And the emotion that welled in me when I thought of her no longer being around was confusing the hell out of me.

Needless to say, I was more short-tempered than normal and in no mood to deal with Jed Coleman's attitude.

I cocked my head to the side and regarded the man in front of me through narrowed eyes. Jed Coleman was a repeat offender. I'd arrested him for everything from driving while drunk to domestic battery. I was able to make the charges stick on the DUI, but my father had been of the same mind as Jed on the domestic battery. Dad wasn't big on keeping wife-beaters and child abusers behind bars, believing, like Jed, men who raised their hands to their families had a right to do so. Fortunately, the last time Jed went after his wife my father no longer got a say in how he deserved to be punished. Conrad no longer had his title; I did. I put Jed's violent ass in the slammer and gave an internal cheer when his wife agreed to press charges against him. When I heard Kayla Coleman hired Aspen to handle the divorce, I honestly believed she was going to finally be free of the man who made her and her kids' lives a living hell.

"So, you were pissed about Kayla hiring Aspen? Did you decide to do something about it?" I crossed my arms over my chest and gave the wiry, twitchy man a hard look.

He took out another cigarette and stuck it between his chapped lips. "I ain't seen Kayla or the kids since the judge put the restraining order in place. I had to have my brother pawn everything I owned to post bail. All my guns, my truck, my TV. Sure, I want to give that cunt lawyer a piece of my mind, but I wouldn't put it past her to have me locked back up. She's got connections and money I don't have. I wouldn't be surprised to hear she was boning the judge who handled the case. He didn't waste any time taking my kids away from me."

A waft of acrid smoke was blown in my face from the new cigarette he lit up, but I refused to react. I'd been met with pretty much the same kind of animosity from every disgruntled spouse who took up a spot on the list of possible suspects who might want to put a bullet in Aspen's head. She was not popular among the degenerates and reprobates. It was also highly unnerving to hear the less-than-favorable thoughts I'd once had about Aspen spoken out loud by people I would never want to associate myself with. A sliver of shame lodged its way under my skin, and all I wanted to do was pick it out.

"Your brother pawned all your firearms?" I knew Jethro Coleman, Jed's older brother pretty well. I'd actually run against him for the sheriff's position when my father finally agreed to walk away. Jethro was one of the old guard. A cop my dad had molded in his own vision. They guy was just as dirty as my old man, and just as prejudiced and biased. I'd gotten rid of him as soon as he gave me a viable reason to take his badge and gun. He hated me almost as much as I told myself I hated Aspen. I tried to look past Jed into the interior of the trailer he was now calling home. "I don't suppose he saved the pawn ticket for them?" It would be really hard to shoot up the hospital without a weapon.

Jed sneered at me. "You'll have to ask him."

Of course. Nothing was ever as easy as the cop shows on TV made it look. "Where were you Monday morning between ten and noon?" There was a narrow window for the shooter to get into position and take a shot. They would've had to know Aspen was getting discharged and what time she was leaving the hospital. Considering one of the nurses had revealed Aspen's condition to my sister with very little prodding, it wasn't a stretch to imagine another member of the staff passing her discharge information along if asked.

"Why? I told you, I ain't seen my whore-wife or my kids in weeks. If Kayla says otherwise she's lying." He puffed his thin chest out and blew out another cloud of smoke in my direction. "I can prove I was nowhere near her Monday or any other day of the week."

I arched an eyebrow and rocked back on my heels. He might have an alibi for the shooting, but every single derogatory word he'd used during our conversation matched the ones painted on the walls of the lady lawyer's office. Maybe I was looking at more than one perpetrator after all. "How can you prove it?"

Jed smirked at me and gave me a grin that made my skin crawl. "I got me a new girl. I was with her Monday morning. Since I ain't got a truck no more, she's been driving me around. You can ask the neighbors. They were outside when she dropped me off."

I bit back a sigh and jotted down the woman's name and contact info in the note app on my phone. I had no doubt Jed was going to take his hands to his new girlfriend as soon as she pissed him off. That was just the kind of guy he was. He'd gotten used to his older brother being able to clean up his messes for him.

"I'm gonna follow through with this, Jed. If you're lying, things aren't going to be good for you."

He snorted and flicked his still lit cigarette in my direction. I was considering writing him a ticket for littering just to make a point when his next words had me going on alert.

"Things ain't been good for anyone in this town since you forced your old man out. He understood how things work. He got it. You're still pissed you couldn't get out of this town and now you're taking it out on those of us that like the way things used to be around here."

The way things used to be meant picking and choosing who was guilty or innocent based on my father's long-held prejudices and not the actual law. I lived with it for as long as I could, because I didn't have a choice. I couldn't leave Hayes, and when I first took the job working under my old man as a deputy, I really thought I was doing the best thing for my family. I was used to looking the other way when my father did things I didn't agree with, even if they turned my stomach and made my skin feel too tight. I originally had this idea I would be able to change things from within, that I would be the one to balance out my father's blatant corruption. I underestimated how quickly my father's influence and position could poison me, and taint what little faith in justice I had left. It took almost no time at all for me to be as miserable at work as I'd been growing up under his heavy thumb. I'd started drinking and getting angry at all the choices I'd made that put me right back at the starting line of my life. Eventually, I was so caught up in my own downward spiral I forgot about trying to subvert my father's influence over Loveless. But I was smacked in the face with his crooked ways when he put the nail in the coffin of my custody case by trying to strong-arm the judge. That was the moment I said enough was enough, and I determined that I, and Loveless, deserved better than Conrad Lawton in control of the reins.

"My dad let you beat on your wife and treat your kids like garbage. Your brother helped him cover it up. They both let far too many locals slide on things like that when they shouldn't have. Holding you accountable for your shitty actions isn't me taking out my failures or faults on you, it's me enforcing the goddamn law." Which wasn't something I'd learned from my dad. "Like I said, if I find out you're lying to me about messing around with Aspen Barlow, I'll make sure you go down for it." I would love nothing more than to put the smug bastard back behind bars for a long, long time.

After calling me an asshole and spitting on the ground in my general direction, Jed stomped back into his rickety trailer, slamming the thin aluminum door behind him. The action rattled the entire trailer and made me roll my eyes. I made a note to track down Jethro Coleman and ask about the guns. That was going to be a highly uncomfortable conversation. The man rubbed me the wrong way long before I kicked him off my team.

I pulled up short as I was walking back to my SUV.

A tall man with a hat very similar to my black Stetson tugged low over his eyes was leaning casually against the front bumper. He had his arms crossed over his chest and one of his boots resting on the chrome bumper. It was a ballsy move, even for a man wearing a badge and a gun. The only reason this guy got away with it was because we'd practically grown up together and I hadn't seen the cocky son of a bitch in far too long.

"The Rangers send you up to investigate the shooting at the hospital?" I took up a position next to him at the front of my vehicle. I squinted against the sun, trying to piece together what my next move should be.

"I requested the assignment. Don't like the idea of someone shooting up my hometown. My boss was happy to hand it over. Apparently, you were pretty difficult the last time we tried to run a joint task force with your team." He shot me a look out of the corner of his eye, and I couldn't help but smirk.

"Not a fan of your boss, Gamble. His guys tried to push mine out of the investigation, and then tried to take credit for the takedown when my little brother was the one who ended up with a knife sticking out of him." Crew had a knack for finding trouble, and his last run-in with it had nearly cost him his life. "I would have much rather worked with you on that op."

The tall man next to me nodded. "I was sorry I couldn't

be there for Crew's case. Had something go bad down by the border. Couldn't get away from it. Ended up with a DEA agent in intensive care barely clinging to life. How is everyone up here doing?"

"By *everyone*, you mean Kody, don't you?" I looked at him out of the corner of my eye. "You could call her and ask her yourself, you know?"

The man stiffened next to me and exhaled heavily through his nose. "I've called her a time or two. She doesn't answer, and she never calls me back."

I grunted. "She's stubborn, but you already know that." I pushed off the SUV and put my hands on my hips. "How involved in my investigation are you going to be, Gamble?"

Hill Gamble was a damn good cop. He was also an old friend who, at one point, had been really close to being family. Hill's younger brother, Aaron, was engaged to my little sister for a far too short period of time. Kody was always a little wild and uncontrollable, but Aaron Gamble had calmed her down and given her the stability all of us Lawtons so desperately craved. When he passed away, it had been tragic and unexpected. Even though Aaron had been gone for going on five years, no one really believed Kody was over him. She was also twice as difficult and even more rebellious than she'd been before falling in love with the quiet and shy Gamble brother.

"I'm going to be as involved as I need to be. I tried to track down the primary target, but no one seems to know where she is. I assume you have something to do with that." He pushed his hat back and gave me a bland look. "Did you put her in protective custody and not bother telling your team the plan?"

I grunted again. "I put her somewhere no one will look for her, but I'll let her know you want to set something up."

"You have a lead on the shooter?" He also pushed off the SUV and crossed his arms over his broad chest. "Folks in town are scared. They don't like seeing Loveless on the national news."

I sighed. "That's because a lot of them have secrets they want to keep hidden." I squinted at him and muttered, "I don't like the target's husband. He's got too much attitude and way too much money at his disposal. She's been hounding him for a divorce, but he won't sign the papers. I had my suspicions about him until the first bullet was fired. But no way he could have faked his panicked reaction when the gun went off. Other than him there's a whole slew of people she's pissed off in court, including me. It's like trying to find a needle in a stack of needles."

"I'll dig into the rich husband. See if we can find anything he might be trying to cover up. You need me to knock on any doors? My badge is better than yours." His teeth flashed white in his tanned face, and his pale gray eyes glinted with humor.

"I've got a couple names I can pass your way. I need to run down Jed's alibi for the time of the shooting. He's a dirtbag. He might be cleared as the shooter, but he's pissed that his wife kicked him to the curb. He blames Aspen for her finally growing a backbone." I sighed. "And I have history with his older brother. The guy used to work for my dad and I canned him as soon as I could. It didn't go over well and he's always carried a grudge against me."

Hill made a sound of agreement and pushed the brim of his hat back. "Aspen's a small woman to be carrying around the entire town's ire. It's a miracle her back isn't broken." It was a pointed barb that hit home just the way he intended it to. I was very uneasy having been forced to face a lot of my own misguided perceptions of Aspen during this investigation. "Shoot me a text when I can meet with Mrs. Barlow. And let your sister know I'm in town for the foreseeable future. I don't wanna catch her off guard if our paths happen to cross. I don't want to guess which one of us that would be worse for."

We exchanged a brisk handshake, and I promised to give Kody a heads-up. I watched as Hill made his way to a nondescript sedan parked behind my SUV. I flicked a couple fingers away from the brim of my hat in a pseudo wave as he drove past. I'd asked both Kody and Hill what the deal was between them. Their relationship had been strained and practically nonexistent since Aaron's death, which made no sense. I got vague replies and a stern warning that it was none of my business when I tried to pry. Hill had treated both my younger siblings like family when we were growing up, and all of us had been close. But it was like they couldn't find any common ground to walk, now that Aaron was no longer around. I was a curious man. It wasn't in my nature to let the weirdness between one of my best friends and my sister go, but first I needed to figure out who had it in for my reluctant houseguest.

So far, living with Aspen was a test of both patience and restraint. My feelings toward her swung wildly from one extreme to the next every time I saw her. Daily I was torn between annoyance at how fully she'd invaded my life, and deep compassion for all that she was going through and over how much she had lost. Other than her breakdown the first day I brought her home, she seemed to be keeping it all together, and I felt slightly bad about it. The second she opened up, the minute she showed a hint of vulnerability, I ran. I wasn't ready to deal with the way seeing her with her shields down, and so very human and fragile, made me feel. I didn't want to be drawn to her, hated remembering how soft I felt toward her when we were young. If she wasn't so battered and broken, I would've made it a point to avoid her altogether, but that wasn't an option, so I was forced to face the fact I didn't completely loathe her the way I wanted to. It'd been nice to hold her, to forget she had thorns that had made me bleed repeatedly.

Aspen mostly stayed in the spare room and hardly made a sound. She asked to use my laptop so she could follow up with the insurance claim on her house and access her digital files from her law firm. I offered to feed her breakfast and dinner when I was around, but she waved me off and told me she could take care of herself. As far as I could tell she was living off of peanut butter and jelly sandwiches.

Reluctantly, I headed in the direction of my house after sending Hill on his way. I wanted to check on Aspen, let her know the Texas Rangers were involved in the investigation now, and set a time for her to meet with Hill. I would track down Jed's brother and his new girlfriend afterward. I also wanted to drive by my brother's place and spend some time with Hayes. Like the trouper he was, my kid took the sudden uprooting of his life pretty easily. He liked my brother's ranch. He got his own space, and he got to be around horses. I disliked not having him around, but I would die before endangering him in any way. And Hayes had proven to have an endearing soft spot for Aspen. When I explained why I needed him to leave for a few days, he'd seemed almost eager to be helping in some small way to keep the attorney safe.

I parked in the garage and walked into a house that smelled delicious. I was used to coming home and having something homemade from Mrs. Clooney, but I'd spoken with my elderly neighbor and explained I would stop by her place to check on her for the next few weeks because Hayes was gone and I would be working longer hours. So the smell couldn't be something from the elderly woman. In fact, it reminded me of my mother's home cooking. She had been an amazing chef and took pride in her ability to put on a full spread each and every night. It sucked those memories were always followed by the ones of my dad getting angry if she didn't have the table set and dinner ready by the time he got home from work.

Following my nose, I ended up in the kitchen, where Aspen was propped up against one of the long countertops. She was dressed in more of Kody's colorful clothes; this time her top was mint green, and her shorts were dark purple. She looked good in color. Not that she looked bad in her standard black, it was just nice to see her in something less somber and serious. I wanted to kick myself for noticing how she looked at all in the first place.

I moved to the stove behind her and peeked into the heavy Dutch oven she had on one of the burners. It looked like chicken and dumplings, one of my favorites. I didn't even know I had the stuff to make it in the house.

"It smells good. Was this something Mrs. Clooney left behind in the freezer?" I put the lid back and turned to look at her, figuring she heard my boots on the hardwood. When she didn't turn around or say anything, I frowned and moved forward to lightly tap her shoulder. "Aspen?"

A sudden shriek echoed through the kitchen as she spun around. Belatedly, I noticed she had earbuds in her ears and was focused on the open laptop in front of her. Her injured ankle wasn't up for the sudden movement as she whirled around to face me. I watched as she started to topple over, her good hand flailing around ineffectively in the air in front of her.

I jerked forward, hands reaching instinctively so she

wouldn't hit the floor. "Whoa, there. Sorry, I didn't mean to scare you."

Her momentum pushed her against my chest, sending one of my hands sliding across her ribs and the other across her backside to keep her upright. My intentions were good, but my starved libido registered the way her curves felt pressed up against me. For a woman with such a slight build, my hands had no problem finding a handful of soft skin.

Her nearly black eyes gazed up at me, wide with shock and a hint of fear. Her breath was warm against the base of my throat, and I could feel her fingers trembling against my biceps where she caught me for balance.

Her lips parted on a breath, and my eyes zeroed in on how soft and pink they looked. When the tip of her tongue darted out and licked across the round curve of the lower lip, I may have groaned. I know my body tightened in reaction and I was pretty sure my mouth started to water with the desire to chase after the trace of moisture she left behind. I couldn't recall ever wanting to put my mouth on anyone else's more than I wanted to breathe, but I felt like I might die if I didn't find out how she tasted, how she responded to me.

I could feel her heart pounding against my chest, and when she curled her good hand around the back of my neck, I really couldn't see her as the enemy any longer. No, now all I could see when I looked at her was an incredibly strong woman in the middle of a really unfortunate situation. She was handling everything thrown at her with grace, quiet dignity, and the bare minimum of fuss. Aspen was still the sweet, wide-eyed girl who caught my attention in high school, but now she had a backbone made of steel. When I really gave myself room to think about it, I couldn't deny any longer that attraction and admiration were at the top of the list of all the things she made me feel recently.

She made it hard to tell if I was coming or going anymore, but one thing was for sure: my cock liked the way she fit against me a whole lot. It thickened and pressed against the front of my jeans with a surprising intensity. I'd felt a lot of things in regards to the woman in my arms—but the desire, want, and need were all fairly new. I couldn't deny all of those things were suddenly flooding my system and making my head spin. She was the last woman I should have my hands on, but she was the only one who could make me lose all sense of reality.

I can't say who moved first. Time paused, the moment suspended between us on fragile, gossamer strings. If felt as if any sudden movement would send us crashing back to a place where we could never exist like this. I would never be able to pinpoint if I kissed her or if she kissed me. Not that it mattered. One second, we were staring at each other as I held her like she was the most precious thing on the planet, the next my mouth was all over hers, and I was kissing her the way you kissed someone you loved and hated at the same time. A little sweet, a little mean, and with enough passion to make us both forget we had a long, twisted road paved with mistakes and memories running between us.

CHAPTER 9

∽

ASPEN

If my other hand was working correctly, I would've used it to pinch myself. Because it was only in my secret, never-to-be-acknowledged dreams where I got the chance to kiss Case Lawton. In the dark when I was alone and lonely, I let myself wonder what it would feel like to have his often cruel, but always lush and alluring, mouth pressed against mine. I wondered if he would kiss with as much passion as he did everything else. I tried to picture the sounds he would make, and whether or not the blue of his eyes would change color when he was turned on. I envisioned the rough scrape of his stubble across the soft skin in intimate places far more often than I would ever admit to. In my head, kissing Case was a fairy tale. I romanticized it because it was something that would never happen.

My senses were not prepared for all those dreams to come crashing into reality. All I could do was cling to the tall, strong man in front of me, and hope I didn't melt into a puddle of surprise and desire at his booted feet. He was literally the only thing keeping me upright, since I was off-balance and had no shot at matching his impressive height. It was hard to keep up with the sensations overwhelming me, but I didn't want to miss a single thing. I wanted to hold on to the memory of how much better kissing Case for real was than kissing him in my fantasies.

He tasted like coffee and something sweet, which I found surprising. Nothing about Case ever came across as sweet.

His lips were soft but moved with purpose as they slid across mine. The contrast between the supple brush of his lips and the harsh scratch of his stubble sent goose bumps shooting across my skin and had my breath lodging in my lungs. There was untapped passion behind the flick of his tongue across the seal of my lips. But there was also anger present in the way his hands tightened their hold on mine, almost as if he couldn't decide if he wanted to pull me closer or shove me away. Before he could decide to do the latter, I opened my mouth and gave him the access the wet glide of his tongue requested.

It was hard to remember he didn't like me when the tip of his tongue flicked against mine. It was nearly impossible to stop myself from drowning in the flood of desire washing through my entire system. I wanted to let go and be swept away, but there was a niggling voice in the back of my mind reminding me: this moment with him was the exception, not the rule. Any minute now Case was going to realize who he was holding in his arms. He was going to come to his senses, and if I let myself get carried away, I would be lost at sea with no way to get back to shore.

I shivered when I felt the not-so-gentle bite of his teeth against my lower lip. I had to swallow a moan when he used the tip of his tongue to soothe the tiny sting he left behind. My fingers clutching at the back of his neck like a lifeline found their way into the short, dark hair at his nape. The silky strand slid easily through my grasp, and once again a bolt of shock shot through me. *Soft* wasn't a word I would associate with Case either. The man was full of surprises.

The hand he had resting on the curve of my backside moved just a fraction, getting a better hold on the rounded flesh underneath my colorful shorts and pulling me purposely closer to the unmistakable hardness that had been thickening and growing between us. Without a doubt, whatever Case was packing in his Levi's was as impressive and intimidating as the rest of him. I wantonly leaned closer to the heat and hardness.

Feeling his reaction to kissing me made me a little lightheaded and had me a whole lot of turned on. I'd always wanted to get a rise out of Case that wasn't tied to our tumultuous past with one another. I secretly longed for him to see me as something more than the weird girl from high school or the woman who came back to town only to pull apart his family.

His tongue twisted and tangled around mine as he pressed me back against the counter. One of his hands skated up my side, thumb tracing the line of ribs until it reached the soft curve of my breast. I was already struggling to breathe and to not lose my head, but when I felt the barely there sweep of his finger along the soft swell of my breast my system shortcircuited. My nipples tightened into hard, aching points, while my knees turned to water. I gasped because it felt like flames were licking along the surface of my skin. My body pulsed with a low, desperate thrum, and places I hadn't given much thought to in far too long started to quiver and flutter with anticipation. There was something about the contrast between the aggressive, demanding nature of the kiss, and the almost reverent, appreciative caress that unraveled me.

I was coming undone in his hands and had no idea how to stop it.

Luckily, I didn't have to save myself. Case's phone rang right before I attempted to climb him like a tree. He pulled away with a sudden start, setting me back on my wobbly feet very carefully. His hat had gotten knocked askew, and there was a flush on his high cheekbones under his scruff. His eyes felt like they cut right through me as we gazed at each other in tense, stunned silence.

Somewhat clumsily he swiped at his phone and put it to his ear. "Lawton." He barked the word out, shifting his gaze away from mine.

While he was distracted, I touched my tingling lips with shaking fingers and tried desperately to pull my head out of the Case-shaped clouds. I fell heavily against the counter, so thankfully I didn't end up on the floor as my knees knocked together.

"It's only been an hour, Gamble. I told you I would set up the meeting and I will." Case's eyes cut in my direction, and he frowned. "Come by my place tonight when my shift is over. You can question her then." He scowled at whatever the person on the other end of the phone said and hung up without saying good-bye.

He reached up and fixed his hat, dragging his hand over his face in a weary gesture after he was set back to rights.

"Aspen." He said my name and nothing else, but I could hear so many things inside the single word. Regret. Anger. Embarrassment. Guilt. Shame. But there was also a hint of arousal, the rough rasp of excitement hidden under all the other things. He didn't want to want me, but he did. I was going to have to take a minute and figure out what to do with that new information.

I took my hand, which was still touching my tingling

mouth, and held it out defensively in front of me. "Don't say anything. Just don't." It was a lapse in judgment that was a long time coming. This moment was a tear in our actuality, one I could still mend as long as we didn't rip it open any wider. "Who wants to talk to me? I thought you didn't want anyone to know I was staying here." I crossed my arms over my chest and tried to create as much space between us as possible.

"Since the shooting has made national news, the Texas Rangers sent up an investigator to help with the case. They always get involved in any high-profile or special investigation. The Ranger on the case wants to ask you a few questions, since you were obviously the target. Hill Gamble actually grew up here in Loveless, but I think he was already graduated when you moved here. We all hung out together when we were younger. He's a good cop, one I don't mind butting in on my turf. I told him you wouldn't mind talking to him, but I want to be there, and I still don't want you leaving this house." He shifted his weight on his feet. "That is if you're still comfortable staying here."

The flush was back on the blades of his cheekbones. He was too rugged and hard to ever be called cute, but the flush was incredibly endearing, and it was nice to see he could still be a gentleman, even toward me. He really was a good guy.

I sighed and turned back to the open laptop. "That's fine. It's all fine. I told you, let's just forget about what just happened." I'd picked up the art of ignoring the elephant in the room at a young age, so I was really good at it. I waved a hand in the direction of the stove. "Take some lunch. I was starving, and a PB and J wasn't going to cut it, so I made chicken and dumplings. Your neighbor does a good job keeping your pantry stocked."

"You made this?" I was slightly offended he sounded so surprised.

"I did." I was a pretty good cook. At David's insistence, I'd taken a class or two when he and I were dating. All good wives in the South were supposed to know how to cook. Luckily, it turned out I liked it.

"I thought you were a vegetarian." He gave me a critical look and I nearly fell over when I realized that he remembered the fact I didn't eat meat back in the day.

"Umm...I was up until I went to college. It was hard to keep up with when I was on my own, and I realized I didn't stop eating meat because of any strongly held convictions, but rather because I liked to annoy my mother. Back then she refused to pay attention to me. Now, I can't get her to leave me alone. I can't believe you didn't recognize me that day on the steps, but you remembered I was a vegetarian in high school."

He blinked at me slowly and then shrugged. "It's weird, the things that stick with you. I probably would've remembered you right away if things had been different that day. I was focused on the end of my marriage, not reconnecting with an old friend."

I lifted an eyebrow at him. "I always wondered if you considered us friends back then."

He lifted an eyebrow back. "We were something close to it. I wouldn't have tried to include you in things if we weren't. I liked spending time with you in high school." Changing the subject, he mumbled, "My mom used to make chicken and dumplings whenever my dad was being particularly ugly. She said it was comfort food and we would feel better once our bellies were full." A bitter laugh broke free from his broad chest. "Needless to say, we ate it a lot."

I gulped a little and looked over at the stove. "I'm sorry."

The last thing I wanted when I made lunch was to bring up bad memories for him in his own home.

He shook his head. "Don't be sorry. It's one of my favorite things to eat. Reminds me of my mom, which doesn't happen very often. You should get off that ankle though. It still looks pretty swollen."

When I agreed I would go lie down on the couch, he mentioned he didn't have time to eat right now because he still had work on my case to do and wanted to make time to go see Hayes. But he promised he would be sure to have some for dinner. Then he exited as silently as he'd come in. I couldn't breathe right until I was once again alone in his kitchen.

Once I heard the garage close, I groaned long and loud. I slumped forward and let my forehead thunk onto the countertop. The situation was already so convoluted and tricky between me and Case. The last thing either of us needed was this new level of awkward. I was going to do my best to ignore the fact that he kissed better than I ever imagined. I was also going to force myself to forget that I now knew he could be gentle and considerate when he wanted to be.

Knocking my head against the hard surface one more time still didn't result in my common sense making an appearance, so I set about cleaning up the kitchen and portioning out the chicken dumplings I'd made so I could freeze the leftovers. I figured I would stash the extra in the freezer so Case and Hayes could reheat it on a night when they were both busy.

I hobbled my way to the laundry room a couple of hours later to wash my borrowed bedding. If I hadn't had my earbuds back in, I probably would've heard a set of keys rattle in the front door. Case always came in and out of the door in the mudroom that led to the garage. He swore no one else would be coming and going from his house while I was there, so it never occurred to me to be on the lookout for unexpected visitors.

When I came out of the laundry room, I don't know who was more startled, me or Case's carbon copy. Father and son couldn't look any more alike if they tried, though Hayes Lawton was missing the sharp edges and hard lines his father had. He'd grown into a beautiful young man, one who was looking at my hands where they were stretched outward, warding him off as I screamed bloody murder. Hayes's eyes went huge and he became slack-jawed as he covered his ears while I shrieked.

He backed up a step, tripping over rushed words. "Uh. Sorry. I tried to call and let someone know I needed to come by and grab something for a class tomorrow. No one answered the house phone, and my dad isn't replying to my texts. Sometimes he has to patrol out of service, and he's hard to get ahold of." Slowly Hayes lifted his hands and took a step back. "I figured you were asleep or something and I could sneak in and out without anyone noticing." It was such a teenaged mind-set. Completely ignoring any possible danger he might be in.

I went slightly limp, and held out a hand and asked him to help me walk back toward the kitchen. "No one is supposed to know where I am, so I can't answer the phone. You shouldn't be here, Hayes. It's dangerous. Your dad is going to have a fit when he hears you stopped by. He was planning on coming to see you today, just so you know."

He spoke as he held my arm and matched my achingly slow pace down the hallway. "I figured it would look weird if no one saw me come and go for a few days, and I wanted to stop in and check on Mrs. Clooney. Even when I crash at Uncle Crew's place, I still stop by and see Dad. I don't like leaving him on his own. But I didn't mean to scare you. That's a dick move, considering everything you've been going through lately. I'm so sorry."

The worry in his familiar blue eyes was enough to have my heart turning over in my chest. I dropped against the edge of the same counter where his father had kissed the life out of me and cocked my head to study the young man who towered over me. I hadn't seen him up close in years, only in passing when he was in town. His resemblance to Case was startling, but so was the clear understanding in his gaze. He'd always been a bright, self-aware child. It looked as if he'd grown into a remarkable young man.

"No, I'm the one who's sorry. I always seem to be disrupting your life, and that has to feel completely unfair. I'm sure all of the Lawtons would be happy if they never had to deal with me ever again." I was allowed to feel a little sorry for myself after all, and I would regret putting this child in the middle of his parents' battles until the day I died. Things had never been fair for Hayes.

Hayes copied my head tilt and lowered his tall frame on to one of the stools at the breakfast bar. He tapped his long fingers on the counter and watched me carefully.

"It wasn't your fault back then, and it isn't your fault now." His tone was serious, and his eyes were kind, but his words gutted me.

"There were times when I was younger that I really hated you."

I lifted a hand and rubbed absently at my chest and forced myself not to look away as he poured his young heart out to me. He must have gotten his raw transparency from his father. There never had been any guessing when it came to how Case felt about me, good or bad.

"My mother didn't want me. Not when I was a baby. Not

when my dad got home from deployment. Not when they started to have problems, and not when they got divorced. One of the reasons they fought all the time was because my dad wanted her to care about me more than she did. She wasn't a good mom, but she was always really, really good at playing the victim. When she got full custody, I thought my life was over, and I blamed you. But I realized when I got older, she was the one I should be mad at. She's the one I should hold accountable. You were just doing your job, and I know how hard you pushed her to agree to let my dad have more time with me. She always gets her way. If you hadn't been there to advocate for me behind the scenes, I don't know that I would've *ever* been able to see my dad."

I blew out a long low breath and tried to get my thundering pulse under control. The fingers of my injured hand twitched as I imagined strangling Becca Lawton for the thousandth time. "You're a great kid, Hayes. I can't imagine anyone not wanting you."

When I'd first encountered Hayes Lawton, he was a quiet, serious little boy. The fact he looked so much like his father never failed to get me right in the heart. No one knew, but at the time, David and I were on our second round of in vitro, and I kept thinking how wonderful it would be to bring a kid like Hayes into the world. I wanted that more than anything, and it infuriated me no end that Becca Lawton treated her son like an afterthought. I hated that, in order to protect Case, who was an incredible father and loved his kid more than anything, I had to help keep them apart. The whole situation made my skin crawl, and when the second in vitro failed, my desire to abide by Becca Lawton's demands also withered away. I started to wonder if I was meant to be a parent if I could repeatedly send Hayes home to a woman who didn't care for him in the way he deserved. Honestly, the whole situation was one of the reasons I was reluctant to keep trying in vitro when David pressed. My emotions were all over the place. There were still days I wondered why motherhood was the only thing in my life that always seemed just out of reach.

Now that I was taking my life back into my own hands, I was going to have to take a serious look at myself and determine if pursuing being a mother through other ways was still in the cards for me. I wasn't sure it was a dream I was totally willing to walk away from.

Pulling me from my thoughts, Hayes chuckled and smacked his hand flat on the countertop. "My mom isn't capable of putting anyone else's needs before her own. It took me a long time to accept that. I think my dad feels guilty he didn't see the selfishness in her before it was too late. He's given me everything, but the one thing he can't give me is a mother who is worth a damn. So, I can see clearly you weren't behind my mom's bad intentions, it was all about Dad." Hayes shook his head. "He's too blinded by all the things he could have done differently to see clearly." A raven-colored eyebrow winged up, and a charming grin tugged at his mouth. "He had his shot to ask you for help, and he blew it."

I blinked in surprise. "He told you about that?" Our run-in on the stairs of the sheriff's office felt like it had happened in another lifetime, and a lot of things had gone so wrong between now and then.

"Yeah, he told me. He used it as a lesson to never judge a book by its cover. It doesn't matter if someone seems like they don't belong or if they don't exactly fit in. What matters is how qualified they are and if their intent is good. Sometimes he has a hard time not being the guy my grandpa tried to turn him into. If he had to do everything all over again, I think he would make a bunch of different choices." Hayes nodded, as if he knew for certain his father had regrets haunting from his past.

Unable to stop myself, I balanced the best I could on my good leg and reached across the space separating us. I covered the hand he had resting on the counter with mine and gave a squeeze. "He may have regrets." Didn't we all? "However, you are absolutely not one of them, regardless of how or when you came into his life, you've always been what he is most proud of."

Hayes lowered his chin in a brief gesture of agreement. "He's a great dad, and he's an amazing cop. But I want more than that for him, especially since I'm leaving for college soon. I worry about what he's going to have to focus on once I'm gone. I worry about him being lonely."

I swallowed past the lump in my throat and released my hold on his hand. "He'll figure it out. He always does. Your dad is one of the most resilient men I've ever met. He wouldn't want you to worry." I lifted my eyebrows in his direction. "He also wouldn't want you willingly putting yourself in a dangerous, unpredictable situation. You should grab what you need and hit the road. If something happens to you while you're with me . . ." I trailed off with a slight shake of my head. We both knew Case would cast blame on me if any harm befell his son in my presence.

Hayes snorted and rose to his feet. I had to look way, way up to keep meeting his gaze. "He needs to let go of all that resentment he carries around. It's heavy, and it weighs him down. Have him give me a call when he gets back. I'll tell him you kicked me out and let him know you were good and pissed I walked into a dicey situation. You're still trying to protect me when you get nothing out of it."

I offered a lopsided grin. He wasn't the only one I tried to protect all these years. At this point, all three of us were tangled together in a web of secrets and silence. "I doubt it will help, but I appreciate the effort."

I jolted when Hayes suddenly shot a hand out and clasped my good wrist. His gaze was heart-wrenchingly sincere, and his voice was low and steady as he solemnly told me, "I know you tried to protect me when I was little. I didn't want to live with my mom, but now that I know the kind of things she is capable of..." He frowned and narrowed his eyes. "I can't imagine what she would've done to my dad if you hadn't been there. He would have lost more than a few years with me."

I gulped and quickly looked away. He was right on the money. I wished his father could see through the subterfuge as clearly as Hayes did.

"I would make different choices along the way if I could as well. I think we all carry the burden of 'what-if' to some extent." I couldn't say I wanted to go back and never have met David or joined the Barlow law firm, but I could say I wished I'd stayed true to my original reasons for wanting to return to Loveless. "Your only job is to go out there and make your own memories and mistakes. Just remember to learn from every single experience you have." It was the same advice Case had given me only a few days ago. I was working on taking it to heart.

He chuckled and excused himself so he could grab whatever it was from his room he forgot. He sounded like a herd of hippos stampeding through the house and I was reminded that he was still a kid even though he spoke and carried himself like someone much older. I sent him on his way with one of the containers of chicken and dumplings, and he promised not to endanger himself by showing up at the house unannounced again.

By the time I was done dealing with the swinging pendulum of emotions caused by both the Lawton boys, I was exhausted and barely able to stay on my feet. I needed a nap in the worst way, and I absolutely, positively, wasn't going to dream about having Case's mouth on mine.

CHAPTER 10

∽

CASE

Jed's new girlfriend was a terrible witness. She was strung out, jittery as hell, and rambled in a completely nonsensical way. She did, however, swear up one side and down the other that Jed had been with her at the time of the shooting, and unfortunately, she had several neighbors who witnessed them arguing at her car around the time Jed insisted she drop him off. She couldn't remember where he was the day of the break-in and fire, so I kept the younger Coleman on the top of my suspects list for those infractions and went to find Jed's brother to ask about the guns.

Jethro was almost as unhelpful as the girlfriend and just as unpleasant as his brother, which was expected. I got another cigarette flicked at me and was told to piss off once again. When I told Jethro Coleman he could be charged as an accessory if he didn't cooperate, he begrudgingly produced the pawn ticket I asked for and insisted there wasn't a single weapon left in his brother's possession. Unsurprisingly, Jethro also had some choice words about Aspen and Jed's soon-to-be ex-wife. When I asked if *he* had any weapons inside his trailer, I got a door slammed in my face while he told me I could come back with a warrant. That was the thing about tangling with a former cop; Jethro knew all the tricks of the trade.

I was going to have to touch base with the county district attorney and see if I had enough circumstantial evidence to scare up a warrant for Jethro's place. Something wasn't sitting right where the brothers were concerned, and I wasn't going to be able to let it go until I figured out what it was.

I was hoping to get back to the house fairly early so I could talk to Aspen about that shockingly hot mistake of a kiss. I appreciated her waving it off and acting like it was nothing, but I still needed words between us. She had to know I wasn't the type to take advantage of anyone in a vulnerable position. I had to promise her it wouldn't happen again and let her know I'd simply lost my head in the moment because I felt protective and she felt so small in my arms. It never occurred to me that once I touched her, I wouldn't want to stop. I was honestly stunned at how good she felt when I held her. It had been a very long time since I had experienced that level of intimacy with another person. Kissing Aspen had left me shaken and stripped down to the bone in a way the quick, emotionless sex I typically indulged in never did. I wasn't numb where she was concerned, never had been. She always made me feel *something*, unlike the way I was with every other female who crossed my path after my divorce.

Sadly, my plans to visit my kid before I went home to check on Aspen and eat chicken and dumplings were shot to hell in about a second flat. I had to respond to a call about a brawl at my sister's bar, which led to two arrests. Then I got a call out for a possible intruder, which turned out to be a loose chicken setting off the neighbor's floodlights. And just as I was finally walking out of the station, a call came about a multicar pileup on the highway leading into town. That was a real nightmare and took several hours to get cleaned up. One of the drivers was DOA, and unfortunately one of the passengers died on the way to the hospital. By the time I finally dragged my ass back to my house, the last thing I wanted to do was go toe to toe with Aspen or mediate a conversation between her and Hill. All I wanted to do was take a shower, change the bandage on my shoulder—which was itchy as hell and constantly reminding me I'd taken a bullet recently—and go to bed. But that wasn't going to be an option anytime soon, since Hill was already parked in front of my house and looked like he'd been waiting there for a while.

I left the SUV parked in the driveway and waited for Hill to join me. His gaze slid over me in an assessing way, and his tone was sympathetic when he muttered, "You look like shit."

I rubbed a hand over my tired face and blinked gritty eyes. "It was a long day. Unlike you, I don't get to focus on one case at a time."

Hill clapped me on my bad shoulder, and I had to fight back a wince. "Let's go talk to Aspen so you can go to bed, old man."

I nodded. There was no way for me to contact Aspen, since she hadn't replaced the cell phone she'd lost in the fire yet, so I could only hope she was still awake and remembered Hill wanted to speak with her.

The house was quiet when we entered, but I could hear the soft murmur of the TV coming from the living room. Following the sound, I cleared my throat loudly so as not to startle the woman posted up on my couch, laptop balanced on her legs, a glass of wine in her hand, as she watched something I didn't recognize on my flat-screen. It looked like Aspen had made herself right at home and wasn't losing her mind over that kiss the way I was.

Her eyes widened when she caught sight of me, and before I could tell her I wasn't alone she muttered, "You look tired. Did you have a rough day at work?"

The only person who ever asked about my day was Hayes. I wasn't used to the way her quiet concern hit me squarely in the center of my chest. She actually cared how my day was and it warmed me all the way to my toes. I nodded at her, "Unfortunately, it isn't over yet. The Ranger I told you about is here to talk to you."

Her dark gaze immediately flashed to a point over my shoulder, the soft concern for me instantly changing to wariness as she took in the space where I knew Hill was silently waiting. He was the same height as me but looked more like a Texas version of a Disney prince with his blond hair and pale gray eyes. He also had a face that leaned toward being classically handsome. I remembered being glad when he finally graduated so I could take his place as the heartthrob of Loveless. It irritated me to no end that Aspen couldn't seem to take her eyes off the other man as he cautiously approached her with an extended hand. Hill even took his hat off, all gentlemanly and shit. My back teeth clamped together so tightly it made my jaw ache.

"Special Agent Hill Gamble, ma'am. Thank you for agreeing to speak with me on such short notice and so late in the evening. I only have a couple of questions for you, and then I'll get out of your hair." Hill was all practiced charm and studied southern graciousness. No wonder he was such a good investigator. How could anyone resist that smile and the dimple that dug into his cheek? Good-looking bastard.

"Uh, no problem. Case said you were here to help find out who shot at me outside the hospital. I just want to get back to my day-to-day routine, so whatever gets me home and out of Sheriff Lawton's hair as quickly as possible, I'm happy to help with." Aspen shut the computer she had open on her lap and leaned forward to balance her wineglass on my coffee table. I knew for a fact I didn't have wine anywhere in this house. The closest thing I owned was a bottle of expensive scotch I kept for special occasions and for the time I had really bad days on the job. I was going to have to figure out where it came from when Hill was done giving her the third degree.

Hill let Aspen's hand drop and moved farther into the room, taking a spot on the couch closer to the woman than I thought was appropriate. Crossing my arms over my chest, I propped a hip on the back of the sofa and narrowed my eyes at my old friend.

"I know you gave Case a list of people in your professional life who might be holding a grudge against you or wish to see you harmed, but how about your personal life? You're in the process of getting divorced?" He asked it as a question even though he knew the answer.

Aspen cocked her head to the side, and I saw her assessing the other man carefully. It would do Hill well to remember she was an attorney and spent a lot of her time asking the questions. She wasn't your run-of-the-mill victim.

"Yes, I'm in the process of getting divorced. It's taking a little longer than I would like, but the split from my husband has been amicable." Aspen kept her voice calm, but I watched her good hand tighten into a fist where it was resting on top of her thigh.

I snorted from behind her and received a dirty look in return as she tilted her head back to glare at me. "What? David

Barlow is fighting you tooth and nail on the divorce. That's hardly amicable."

Aspen sighed. "The separation was my idea. I'm the one who asked for a divorce. David has been reluctant to accept the change in our relationship status."

"Did you have a prenup?" Hill kept his tone calm and even, but I could hear something else underlying the false friendliness.

Aspen gave a small shake of her head. "No, no prenup, but I didn't ask him for anything. I didn't want the house or any of his retirement. I had enough money to get my own place, and I have my own retirement fund. I wanted to leave the marriage with exactly what I went in with." She reached up to fiddle nervously with her hair. "You know David was standing right next to me when the shooter starting firing, right? He very easily could have been shot."

"You think it's possible your husband was the target and not you?" The question caught both Aspen and me off guard. It never occurred to me that she wasn't the intended victim. Not after what had happened to her office and home.

Aspen shifted her gaze in my direction and sat up a little straighter. "I honestly don't know. David practices criminal law, so I suppose it would be more likely that he has violent enemies out to get him than I do."

Hill made a humming noise and flashed his disarming grin once again. "Can you tell me about the tens of thousands of dollars you and your husband spent a few years ago? That's a lot of money to not be discussed in the process of separation."

I watched as Aspen balked and went white as a sheet. She lifted a shaking hand to her throat and blinked too wide eyes at Hill. "Why are you asking me about that?"

I was confused by the utter devastation that was suddenly tainting her voice and stamped so clearly on her pale face.

Hill shrugged a shoulder. "Because money is always a motivation, and this is a lot of money we're talking about."

Aspen narrowed her eyes at the blond man. I couldn't stop myself from reaching out and putting a reassuring hand on her shoulder. She was so tense under my palm, it felt like she was made of stone.

"I had a hard time conceiving when David and I started trying to have a baby. I suffered through four miscarriages and was eventually told I would never likely be able to carry a baby to full term. David wanted to try in virto fertilization. It's incredibly expensive, and we went through several rounds. After the initial failure, I wanted to look at adoption or surrogacy, but David insisted we didn't just give up on in vitro. So, I agreed to try again. He agreed to pay. There is no way he would ask for me to reimburse him for that. I already put my body and my mental well-being on the line."

Hill nodded solemnly. "I see."

I narrowed my eyes at my old friend and moved my hand so I could gently smooth it down Aspen's long, dark hair. I was stunned by the revelation. Sure, there had been speculation around town as to why the young, successful couple didn't have kids. Most just assumed it was due to their growing business and busy schedules. A few, of course, claimed Aspen didn't want kids so she could focus on her career. They scoffed and claimed she kept that attitude from the city, even though there were plenty of young women and men in Loveless who also decided having children wasn't for them. I never gave it much thought because I was too busy fighting for my own kid, but now that I'd spent some significant time with her, there was no doubt in my mind Aspen would make a wonderful mother.

Aspen did such a good job putting on a brave face considering everything she'd been through lately, but I could tell Hill's line of questioning was poking at old wounds and rattling her to her core. I didn't like it, not one bit. It was obvious she was upset by having this information dragged out into the light, and that made me hurt for her. I shot a warning look at the other man, which he promptly ignored. The surge of protectiveness toward the tiny woman, silently leaning into my touch for comfort, was no longer as surprising. Something undefinable had shifted between us after that kiss. I didn't like the idea of her being hurt and wanted to stand between her and whatever was causing her such obvious pain.

Aspen leaned forward slightly, making my hand drop. She was practically vibrating off the couch in front of me. "Do you? Do you see how rude it is for you to bring up something so personal and painful with no warning? Do you have any clue how difficult it was for me to agree to go through such an emotionally and physically painful process for the sake of my marriage? How awful it was to push through disappointment and heartbreak time and time again?"

Hill didn't say anything after her outburst, but his pale eyes were sharp and calculating. Aspen's sincerity was obvious in every word ripped out of her.

"I'm sorry if I touched a nerve, Mrs. Barlow. I'm just trying to see all the angles. For instance, did you know it was actually your father-in-law who paid for the continued treatments? You and your husband both made a very good living, but for some reason, Mr. Barlow doesn't seem to have much of a nest egg to fall back on. Daddy Barlow is also paying for the mortgage on the big house behind the gate where your husband lives. Do you have any idea where all your husband's liquid assets are going?"

Aspen slowly shook her head, disbelief clear in every stiff line of her body. "No. I have no idea. He never said anything to me about borrowing money from his dad, and we never lived like we were having financial issues. In fact, I send money to my mother fairly regularly since she remarried, mostly to keep her off my back, and David never once asked me to stop or told me we were stretched too thin. I honestly believe he would have talked to me if we were in financial trouble." But there was a tiny waver in her voice, indicating maybe she wasn't as certain of David as she claimed to be.

Hill leaned forward, all traces of affability and charm long gone. "You sure about that? Heading for divorce was bound to bring it up. He'd have to turn his financials over to the court, regardless of you not asking for much."

"Well, I . . . honestly I'm not sure of anything at the moment. I was positive someone was shooting at me, not David, and I was confident we lived a comfortable life, until a minute ago. But maybe I'm wrong." She shifted back, and I immediately reached out so I could squeeze her shoulder. I was helpless against the urge to touch her, to let her know she wasn't alone as the rug was being ripped out from underneath her. I thought I heard her release a sigh of relief, but it was lost when Hill cleared his throat.

"It's my job to ask the unsettling questions, ma'am. Especially when we have an active shooter on the loose and no clear target." There was no apology in Hill's voice. While I understood rattling someone in order to get an honest reaction out of them was part of the job, I resented the hell out of him being so forceful with Aspen. When he was gone, I needed to look at exactly why I was fighting the urge to put my fist in his face for being so harsh with her, when I'd questioned countless victims and witnesses the same way myself.

Aspen narrowed her eyes. "I understand that. I'm not sure how I can help you though."

The disarming grin was back on his face, and he rose to

his full height. "You were more help than you realized. Once you get a new phone, I'd appreciate you getting my number from Case and giving me a call so I can contact you if anything else comes up. I appreciate your time, and I do sincerely apologize if any of my questions made you uncomfortable."

He stuck out his hand again, only this time Aspen ignored it.

"I believe the point was to make me as uncomfortable as possible, Special Agent Gamble." She sniffed slightly and reached for her discarded glass of wine. I couldn't hold back a grin at the return of her sass. It looked so much better on her than the stark sadness she wore when she spoke of her difficulties trying to have a baby.

Hill chuckled softly and plopped his Stetson back on his head. He shot me a sharp, pointed look and inclined his head in the direction of the entryway. I squeezed Aspen's shoulder once more and got to my feet so I could follow my friend out. Once we were standing on the front steps, I gave him a level look and warned softly, "If I didn't trust that you were doing your job to the best of your ability, I would lay you out right about now. Did you have to spring all of that on her with no warning?"

"I did. I wanted to see if she was going to lie about what the money went to. If she lied, then it wouldn't come as a surprise if she tried to help David Barlow hide his money troubles. She didn't lie, and I believe she was genuinely surprised when I told her who was paying for her lavish lifestyle." He took a step down and tossed his keys in the air. "Might want to let her know David Barlow hadn't exactly been faithful. It seems she didn't really know the man she was married to as well as she thought. Some of the missing money went to pay off mistresses, another big chunk of it went to pay for strippers and escorts in Austin. Doesn't totally explain why a successful lawyer with family money is broke, or why he pushed for a baby so hard, but it might help her move the divorce forward. She's way better off without him." Hill winked at me and turned to walk away but not before tossing over his shoulder, "She's been through a lot, Case. I don't think I've ever seen anyone who needs someone to lean on more than that woman sitting in your living room. Whoever gets to be the person holding her up should consider themselves lucky. Look how long she stood by that idiot husband, and how much she put herself through for him because she loved him. Imagine how good she'd be to someone who actually appreciated her. Imagine being loved like that." He flicked his fingers at the brim of his hat and left with those words hanging heavily in the air.

Not wanting to leave Aspen alone for too long after the emotional upheaval Hill had put her through, I went back into the house. I checked all the windows and doors on my way. After I did my nightly walk-through, I eventually found Aspen in the kitchen topping off her glass of wine. When she caught me looking accusingly at the bottle, she lifted a shoulder and let it fall carelessly.

"I had a couple of visitors today. Your son scared the hell out of me, and your sister stopped by with dinner and the wine. She told me to wait until I was off the painkillers to drink it, but then she winked. I'm pretty sure she's angling to be my first bad influence. I really need to get a phone so people can get ahold of me. Being cut off from the entire world isn't working for me." She was trying to sound blasé and unaffected, but I could see she was raw and on edge from the meeting with Hill.

I knew Hayes had been by the house already. When I finally got free from work I returned his missed calls and told him I wasn't going to make it out to the ranch to see him tonight. He came clean about scaring Aspen out of her skin, and mentioned they talked for a bit. I didn't pry, trusting him to tell me what I needed to know. But my sister's surprise visit was news, and not the welcome kind. Of course Kody didn't listen and steer clear of my house while Aspen was there. She never did what she was told.

Breathing out long and slow I flattened my hands on the counter separating us and simply said, "I'm sorry, Aspen."

She let out a shattered-sounding laugh. "Sorry for what exactly? That I have no clue who I married? That someone is trying to kill me? That I can't have children? That you kissed me?" Another jagged laugh was forced past her pursed lips.

I heaved a sigh so heavy it landed like a rock between us. "All of it. I'm sorry for all of it. But I saw your face when Hill brought up what the money was for. You looked devastated."

She didn't say anything for a long time, and when she did, her words caught me off guard. "Yeah, well I've pretty much made my peace with what I can and can't do when it comes to being a mother. I'm not used to sharing those struggles with anyone else, so it caught me off guard to end up in a discussion about my reproductive limitations with a stranger... and you. Sometimes I'm sad about it, I can't help but feel that way. But mostly, I know that if I ever do decide to become a mother, then I'm going to have to be the one to take the steps to make that a reality. For now, I like my life the way it is. I've put a lot of work into making it one I can be proud of. There's still so much more I want to accomplish. I feel like I'm just getting started. Most days that's enough to keep me happy and fulfilled."

I lowered my head and rubbed my hand across the back of my neck. I figured I might as well go all in with discussing tough topics tonight. There was no reason to ruin another day for her by telling her about David Barlow's infidelity later down the line. Putting it later all on the table at once seemed like the best way to get her some closure.

Glancing at her from under my lashes I muttered, "Uh, well I know the conversation with Hill was rough and unexpected, but I have something to tell you that is going to be just as unpleasant. So, brace yourself."

Her inky eyebrows winged up, and her fingers tightened on her wineglass. She gave a barely discernible nod and muttered, "Hit me with it."

I lifted my head to meet her gaze fully. "The reason David Barlow is in so much debt is because he's been paying for sex. High-end escorts. Expensive trips with mistresses. I don't know how he's kept it all hidden, but his bad habits have increased in frequency and cost exponentially over the last few years."

Aspen's fingers tightened on the stem of the wineglass so much they turned white. I was worried the delicate glass was going to break under the pressure. She lifted the wine to her lips and chugged what was left back in one swallow. Carefully setting the empty glass down on the counter she shook her head and barked out an ugly laugh.

"Part of the reason I finally moved forward with the divorce was because David started acting strange the last couple of years we were together. When I told him I was done trying to have kids I noticed a significant change in his behavior. He still treated me like a queen, but he started working later and later. He would disappear and be impossible to get ahold of. I was curious but also kind of grateful. It made leaving easier. I had my doubts about him, so I made sure I got tested for everything under the sun as soon as I moved out. At least he was apparently careful while he was making his bad choices."

I grunted and dragged my hand down my face. Someone needed to kick David Barlow in the nuts and teach him how to act right. "I'm sorry, Aspen. For everything. You deserve better all around."

She shrugged and forced her trembling lips into a faint smile. "Don't be sorry about the kiss then. It was actually one of the nicer things to happen to me in a while."

"It was a mistake. One that can't happen again." The denial was automatic and weaker than I anticipated. I shifted and winced as the stitches in my shoulder pulled. I tried to soften my too-quick statement. "I think the close quarters and stressful circumstances went to our heads."

She gave me a look that plainly wanted to call me on my bullshit, but instead of continuing the argument she nodded to where I was rubbing my stiff shoulder. "Do you want me to help you clean that and change the bandage? Turnabout is fair play after all."

I'd helped her rewrap her burned hand and clean around the staples in her head when she first left the hospital.

I wanted to refuse her help but couldn't find a logical reason other than stripping down near her didn't seem like a great idea when my self-control where she was concerned was so questionable. Instead, I reluctantly agreed. "Yeah. I could use a hand if you don't mind."

She didn't respond other than to follow me silently to the master bedroom and into the bathroom. She waited near the vanity while I ditched my Stetson and my uniform shirt. When I got back to the bathroom, she had warm water running in the sink and a fresh bandage and medical tape laid out. Her eyes caught mine in the mirror when I walked up behind her, and I watched them drop to check out my upper half.

I stayed in shape because my job demanded it. My ego

and certain parts of my anatomy—which were particularly reactive where Aspen was concerned—liked the dark heat that flared to life in her obsidian gaze as her roving eyes took in the defined lines of my abdomen.

She cleared her throat and twirled her finger in the air. "Trade me places, hero. Let's get you fixed up."

Our bodies brushed together as I slid in front of her. I didn't want my breath to catch or my dick to get hard, but that's what happened.

I couldn't take my eyes off our reflection. Her dark head barely peeked over my shoulder, and her hands looked so pale and delicate against my darker skin. I braced my hands on the edge of the vanity and leaned forward. I dropped my chin down and concentrated on keeping my breathing nice and even. I hoped like hell she couldn't feel the way she made my entire body stiffen and clench.

I hissed when she pulled the tape off the old bandage. She clicked her tongue at me, and I saw her head shake. "This is all crusty and gross. You're lucky it didn't get infected. You should have had me change it days ago."

I grunted. "Been busy. It didn't seem important."

She scoffed behind me. "Sure, it's not important. Who needs two working arms?"

I grumbled again when she wiped some kind of goo on it that caused my skin to tingle uncomfortably. Her movements were quick and efficient as she got the new bandage in place and secured it. When she was done, she patted me on my un-injured shoulder and took a step backward.

"Almost good as new." I was opening my mouth to thank her—and get her out of my personal space so I could do something completely idiotic like jerk off to memories of that kiss—when I felt the barely there brush of her fingertips skate down the column of my spine. "You have a lot of scars, Case."

I shuddered slightly and bit out, "Hazard of the job. Some are old, from football in high school. A couple are from my time in the desert." Most of them were from my old man. He had a wide leather belt with a huge-ass silver belt buckle he liked to use when he felt like I'd been particularly disobedient.

I felt her fingers trace along the waistband of my jeans and my skin rippled in response.

"You have a road map on your skin. Clearly the path you traveled has never been easy."

Her caress slipped across my hips and tickled along the edge of my abs. My stomach muscles contracted in reaction, and my cock throbbed painfully behind my zipper.

"But I'm here, mostly unscathed. I'm here for my son, and I'm here for this town. Nothing has been able to stop me from being where I was supposed to be." It'd taken me a long time to accept that Loveless was as much a part of me as I was a part of it. It no longer felt like I'd lost my chance to escape when I was younger.

I sucked in a loud breath when her fingers dipped beneath the waistband of my jeans, precariously close to the achingly hard erection there was no hiding. My hands tightened into fists in front of me, and I lifted my head so I could look at her in the mirror. Her dark eyes met mine with a mischievous gleam.

"What exactly are you doing, Counselor?"

She laughed, and the puff of air was warm against my shoulder. "I honestly have no idea, but it's the only thing that's felt right in a very long time. You said no kissing. This isn't kissing." Her thumb traced the delineated lines on my lower abdomen, and her fingernails dragged through the thin trail of dark hair that arrowed below my belly button. My cock kicked in response.

"It's a mistake. You've had a long night." The words sounded strangled and thin.

"Doesn't feel like a mistake. Didn't feel that way when you kissed me earlier either." I felt her lips touch the back of my neck, and my entire body convulsed.

"You're still married." It was the last argument I had, the last-ditch effort to put the brakes on something I didn't fully understand.

Her soft sigh made me shiver and had my eyes drifting closed all the way. A moment later her palm was gliding along swollen, rigid flesh and I couldn't put a coherent thought together.

"Doesn't feel like it."

No, no it did not. It felt like we were supposed to be exactly where we were in this moment...together.

CHAPTER 11

∞

ASPEN

I wasn't sure what came over me.

Maybe I was obsessed. Possessed. For sure I was depressed and possibly repressed.

There were a lot of things flying through my head, but they all quieted down when I had my hands all over Case's hot, hard flesh. I closed my eyes and pressed my forehead against his spine between his shoulder blades. His skin was warm, and he smelled earthy and real. He looked like a hero. He wore the battles he fought and won on his skin with pride. The scars, the marks life left all over him, didn't detract from his attractiveness at all. I liked that it was obvious by looking at him that he wasn't a man who sat on the sidelines. He was someone who acted, who had purpose, who wasn't afraid of jumping in with both feet. He was everything I wanted to be. I wanted to act first and think later. I wanted to be fearless and brave.

The first step was touching Case, even though he clearly thought it was a terrible idea. He emboldened me, and maybe, just maybe I needed to know that I could still draw a reaction out of him now that he knew to what extent I'd been rejected by my husband and just how broken I really was. I'd learned to accept my body's limitations. Not being able to bring a baby into the world was as much a part of me as being short and having black hair. For the most part I was okay with that—at least I was until someone else found out about it and made me feel like I was somehow intrinsically lacking as a woman. It was hard to miss something I'd never had until others reminded me most others had it. I was already different in a lot of obvious ways, but being different in such a personal and private way hadn't helped matters when it came to trying to find my way in the world.

But Case knew, and he had yet to push me away. He knew, and he was still hard in my hand, the tip of his cock already slick. He knew, and his breathing was still choppy and rough. He knew my biggest secret, the one I cried over, grieved, kept close to my heart, and yet his abs still contracted underneath my exploring fingers. Maybe I needed the validation that someone, well mostly this man, who I'd always been inexplicably attracted to, could want me.

One of us sucked in a sharp breath. One of us pressed closer. It was so hard to tell who was following whom. But when it became clear neither one of us was going anywhere, I tightened my hand around the pulsing erection in my hand.

I held my breath, waiting for him to stop me, waiting for him to tell me we couldn't do this. When his rough fingers locked like a vise around my wrist, my pulse kicked up in tempo, and my hand stilled. His fingers tightened like a clamp, and I felt his entire body shudder and quake under my forehead where it rested on his back. I let my lips touch his heated skin, prepared to walk away if it was what he wanted. I was never this bold, and I'd long ago gotten accustomed to handling rejection.

My eyes flew open in shock when he used the hold he had on my hand to push my hand farther into his pants and all the way down to the base of his cock.

"If you're going to touch me, then don't play around." His voice was barely more than a rasp of sound, and when I braved a look over his broad shoulder, his eyes were staring directly at me in the mirror.

My lips parted on a silent sound as I wrapped my hand entirely around his girth and started to slide it up and down. When I reached the tip, I used the pad of my thumb to collect the moisture beading up at his slit and spread it around to reduce the friction of my palm skating along his rock-hard length. My fingertips traced the heavy vein I could feel running along the base, and I heard his breath catch. His eyes were so bright I wondered if they would glow in the dark. I swore I could feel the touch of them on my face as we watched each other in the mirror.

I was too short to look over his shoulder to see what he looked like in my hands, so I had to watch myself in the mirror with wide eyes as I touched him like he belonged to me. It was a seriously sexy sight. His skin was a dark honey color next to my much paler complexion. All of him looked huge and hard against my much smaller and softer parts. Plus, with his lean hips revealed by his pushed-down jeans, carved torso, cut abs, ruggedly handsome face, and unforgettable blue eyes, he was pretty much every woman's dream of what a hot cowboy should look like. He was picture-perfect, and I was scared to blink because I felt like he might disappear if I moved wrong or said something to break the spell we were both under.

Before I could question my sanity, I tightened my hold on the straining erection in my hand and started to work him over with deliberation. I wanted to feel Case Lawton come apart in my hands. I dragged the nails of my free hand across his abs and up over his ribs, leaving lines in his skin and causing him to gasp my name in surprise. There wasn't much else I could use that hand for other than to memorize every line and dip of his body, since most of it was still wrapped in gauze. I used the tip of my tongue to trace a long line across the wide plain of his shoulders. It wasn't a kiss, so I figured I was still within the boundaries he'd set. I was used to having to stand on my tiptoes to reach the parts of my partner I wanted my mouth on. With Case, I really had to try to reach, but if anyone ever asked I would tell them it was totally hot how much bigger he was than me. I liked that I could almost completely hide behind him, that if he was inclined he could cover me from head to toe with his bulk.

He grunted when I circled the sensitive line that ran under the flared head of his cock. His arms locked, and the veins in his forearms started to bulge. His eyes dropped to half-mast, and twin flags of red started to burn on the sharp blades of his cheekbones.

"Aspen." My name was a broken sound full of warning. His hips pressed back toward me and then rocked slowly forward into my slippery grip.

I sighed against his skin and closed my eyes. I rested my cheek on his shoulder without the bandage, loving how strong and resilient he felt underneath me. I still wasn't 100 percent steady on my feet, but Case could handle both our weight with no problem.

"Let go." My voice was soft, but the order laced throughout the quiet words were loud and clear.

In this moment I knew that's what I wanted. For him to let go of the past. For him to let off the resentment and anger, so I could do the same. I desperately wanted him to let go of who he thought we were so he could see who we could be if he gave us half a chance. I didn't need to think about the crush I'd had on him when I was younger, because the way I was feeling about him now was very grown-up. I wouldn't have been able to handle him then, our differences would have gotten the best of us. But now, now the things that set us apart from one another were beautiful and would keep things interesting and exciting.

A moment later his entire body rippled and quaked under my hands. He barked out a string of dirty words that would have made me blush in a different situation. Warm liquid coated my fingers—it felt sticky and rewarding.

The only sound in the bathroom was our labored breathing. But then came the sound of water running in the sink when Case leaned forward to turn it on. I ended up plastered to his bare back as he used his tight hold on my wrist to thrust my hand under the faucet. I inhaled the last lungful of his scent and took a second to revel in the fact I could make Case Lawton lose his mind and go against his common sense if I tried hard enough. But as all evidence of his release and our closeness washed away, so did the intoxicating, powerful mood we'd been enveloped in a moment ago.

Case wiped my hand dry before grabbing my shoulders and forcibly moving me sideways so he could turn and put more than an arm's length of space between us. We stared at one another without speaking for a long time. Eventually, he sighed so heavily I was surprised the gust from the sound didn't knock me over. He lowered his chin and lifted a hand to run across the back of his neck.

"Aspen." This time when he said my name it made my heart sink into my stomach and had a painful ache kicking to life in my chest. "This has to stop. We have to stop. This isn't going anywhere, it can't. I can't. I'm trying to figure out who's trying to kill you. To do that and get you back to your life, I need to be able to think straight. I need you in the box you've been in for all these years, the one that doesn't have any kind of emotional attachment to it. I can't deal with trying to find a new box to put you in right now."

I snorted in his direction and flicked my hair over my shoulder. "Can't or won't?"

He met my eyes unflinchingly and gave me the answer I was afraid to hear. "Won't. When you're not living under my roof, when I can't smell you throughout my house, and when I can move without bumping into you every day, all the reasons we've always had for avoiding one another are still going to be there. It's hard to remember them when all I want to do is kiss you and touch you, but they haven't vanished."

It was my turn to sigh. I hobbled past him, careful not to touch him as I limped my way across his very masculine bathroom. "My reasons for avoiding you are very different from your reasons for avoiding me. You'll never understand how deeply I compromised myself for you, and for your son. You have no idea that there were times I hated myself almost as much as you seemed to hate me."

I slipped out the door on that parting shot, evading his reaching hand and ignoring his barked, "Wait. Aspen! What are you talking about?"

I didn't have the energy left to keep running around in circles after him. I was not chasing after his affection any longer. When I really thought about it, I'd been running after the barest hint of attention from this man since I was fourteen years old. And I was over feeling rejected by him. Every single time I was brave enough to get close, it felt like he purposely found a reason to shove me away. I was embarrassed and angry. I felt stupid for getting my hopes up that things might turn a corner, only to realize we were never going to be on the same page because Case didn't have the full story and I was too afraid of hearing and sharing the truth.

I swung by the kitchen for another glass of wine and by the living room to collect the abandoned computer. I knew sleep was going to be hard to come by, so I figured I might as well do some work instead of obsessing over what happened in the bathroom. I needed the distraction and could claim to be busy if for some reason Case decided he was going to demand answers about why exactly I'd stayed out of his orbit all these years.

He was standing outside of the guest bedroom door when I made my way back down the hallway. He had a determined scowl on his face and his arms were crossed over his chest. Gritting my teeth, I switched the laptop to my good hand, knowing he wouldn't grab for my injured one as I reached around him to push open the door.

"What did that mean?" He extended a hand but let it drop when he realized he would have to grab my bandaged hand in order to keep me still.

Without saying a word, I slipped around him, one of the benefits of being small, and silently shut the door behind me. It was rude to ignore him in his own home after everything he's done for me, and after he'd shown so much compassion tonight. But I literally was at the end of my rope when it came to dealing with the emotional upheaval from being around the man. I needed a break.

Before I started working I checked my e-mail and was pleased to see my insurance adjuster had sent a note asking if I could meet at my house to sign some paperwork and talk about options for rebuilding. Excited at the prospect of actually doing something productive to move my current situation forward, I agreed to find a ride to my destroyed house sometime tomorrow afternoon. I knew Case was going to throw a fit that I wanted to leave the safety of his house, but I needed the space to breathe. It was clear we both could use a break from each other, so I decided not to tell him what I was doing. Maybe it was a bit spiteful, and I was still angry from his reaction in the bathroom, but I was an adult after all, and the risks I were taking were my own. Plus, no one would have any idea where I was or where I was going. I figured I could meet a cab or an Uber a few blocks over and slip in and out of Case's neighborhood undetected. Feeling like I'd taken a little bit of control of my life back, I climbed into bed after finishing my glass of wine.

Sleep was unsurprisingly elusive. So much so that I was still wide awake when I heard Case banging around the next morning before he left for work. I did have to hold my breath and pretend to be asleep when I heard him outside my door. I held completely still when it creaked a little as it opened. Him checking on me before he left for the day was new, and my brain was too tired to try and puzzle out what it meant, or if it meant anything at all. Instead, I waited until I heard the garage close and forced myself out of bed. I cleaned up as best I could, checked a few e-mails, made myself some breakfast, and figured I would kill some time on Facebook before I had to meet the adjuster at my burned-out house.

Unsurprisingly, my Facebook messenger inbox was filled with questions about where I had gone after the shooting at the hospital. My friends who ran the coffee shop across from my office had left several messages inquiring if I was all right. My paralegal also sent several get-well-soon messages and asked repeatedly if there was anything I needed or anything she could do for me. I realized I missed the small interactions I'd had day in and day out with the people in my life. People really did care about me, which made it slightly easier to swallow Case's dismissal. As I scrolled through more messages I noticed several old acquaintances had popped in looking for information on what had happened, and I was not surprised to see that David had left a string of messages demanding that I check in with him.

I was going to have to have a serious talk with my former husband sooner rather than later, but not today. No, today I was doing things my way and making it clear I didn't need David or Case to take care of me. I could do things on my own. It suddenly felt very important to remember that.

I was getting ready to sign off and figure out how to find a ride to my house when I saw that Kody Lawton was online.

I liked Case's sassy, vibrant sister quite a bit. I loved that she gave Case an endless amount of hell and he simply took it because he adored her. I loved that she wasn't afraid of her older brother and that she refused to let her family's complicated legacy define her. I didn't like her taste in clothing, however. I was surprised she was awake this early, since she kept bar hours, but seeing an opportunity, I didn't linger.

Opening a chat window, I fired off a short, to-the-point message.

> Hey Kody. I need to run a few errands. I need a phone and some new clothes. I also need to swing by my old house. Are you free at all today? I could use a ride. I'll buy the coffee.

The little bubbles at the base of the box indicated she saw the message and was replying. We weren't exactly friends, but if anyone was going to defy a direct order from Case, it was going to be her. At least I hoped I could convince her to play chauffeur for me this morning.

> Does my brother know you want to play hooky from protective custody today?

I sighed and resisted the urge to hit my head on the keyboard.

> No. But I'm going stir-crazy living in his pocket all the time.

Chewing on my lower lip, I decided being honest with her was my best bet.

> If you can't make it, I'm calling a cab. I don't care if it sends Case through the roof. I have to get out of this house for a few hours.

I really did. It felt like my sanity relied on it.

The tiny bubbles flashed on the bottom of the box again, and I breathed a sigh of relief when she finally responded.

> I need to run home and change. Give me an hour. I'm only saying yes because I figure it's better you risk your fool neck with me rather than alone. You have two hours tops to take care of what you need to get done. If Case finds out you skipped out of protective custody, I'm throwing you under the bus so fast you won't know what hit you.

I replied with a simple thank you, relieved she didn't ask a million questions about why I was desperate to escape from Case's sanctuary.

I dressed in one of her colorful hand-me-down outfits, ecstatic at the thought of getting my hands on something to wear that was neutral and dark. The bright colors were pretty and eye-catching. I could see why Kody favored them, but they made me self-conscious. They didn't match how I felt on the inside most days.

As eager as I was to go, I was waiting for her in the garage when she opened the door. She blinked at me in surprise when I climbed into the passenger seat of her Jeep without needing any help. I still needed the crutch I tossed in the back for long distances, but I was much more mobile than I'd been the first days out of the hospital. By next week, when I had a checkup, I might be able to put my full weight on the injured ankle.

"Thank you for doing this." I was breathless as she pulled out of the driveway.

She shrugged. "Case is going to murder both of us, but I know what it's like to feel like you're suffocating inside a safe place. I assume there's a valid reason you felt like you couldn't ask him to take you around town. One aside from the fact he would have refused."

I huffed out an irritated and frustrated sound and turned to look out the window. "We're getting on each other's nerves, and it's only a matter of time before we start to go for each other's throats. It doesn't matter how big or how nice the cage is, we're still locked up together. I don't want to ask Case for permission to manage my life." And I didn't want to be the only one tripping over our dangerous attraction time and time again.

"I understand, but that doesn't change the fact this is an unnecessary risk and he's going to burst every blood vessel he has and blame me for going along with it."

"Then why agree?" I turned a curious look in her direction.

She shrugged. "Because I like winding both my brothers up and pushing them off-balance. And I think it's good for

Case to realize there are some things in the world he can't control. Plus, I like you. I wasn't expecting to, because I don't really like anyone who messes with my family, but here we are."

I felt a grin tug at my mouth. "I like you too." She was someone I would actually like to consider a friend. I didn't have many—most of my "friends" fell away with the separation—and Kody would be a fun person to have around. She didn't seem to take anything too seriously and I could use some of that levity in my life.

The conversation lapsed after that and Kody seemed content to sing along to the classic rock playing from her old radio. We stopped to get the phone first, and since it took longer than anticipated because of a line, we had to rush across town to meet my insurance adjuster. The older man was visibly annoyed to be kept waiting. His overall demeanor lacked sympathy, considering everything I owned currently looked like it belonged in a landfill. He asked me a million questions about the fire, the cause, and my plans for the home. I tried to explain there hadn't been time to evaluate any of those things and he harrumphed at me and gave me a narrow-eyed look. Next, he practically accused me of starting the fire myself for an insurance payout. I could feel Kody tensing up and bristling at his treatment from where she was leaning against the Jeep, but this entire outing was to prove I could manage my own problems without someone holding my hand.

Eventually, I told the cranky adjuster I was a lawyer and well aware of my rights and what was covered by my plan. I informed him the fire was part of an active police investigation and if he were inclined to hurry things along I would inform the sheriff. Apparently, Case's reputation preceded him because the adjuster backed off and mumbled he would be in touch after conducting a little more research. I assured him there would be no need for that because I was going to be on the phone with his boss as soon as we parted ways. I wasn't going to stand being treated like a suspect when I was the victim.

"That guy was a total jerk, but you handled him all right." Kody wheeled the Jeep out of my old neighborhood and asked me where I wanted to shop.

I told her Target was fine and muttered, "I just did all right?" I thought I dealt with him calmly and effectively.

She flashed me a toothy grin and looked at me over the edge of her retro, cat-eye sunglasses. "I woulda kicked him in the nuts. But I also would have threatened to sic my brother on him, the same way you did. Case isn't a fan of men disrespecting women. It comes from the shit way our dad always treated our mom when she was still alive."

I choked, torn between a laugh and a sound of sympathy. I was never prepared for what came out of Kody's mouth.

I also wasn't prepared for the way her solid Jeep abruptly lurched forward, sending both her and me rocking toward the dash and against our seat belts.

"What the hell was that?!" Kody's voice was thin and irritated as she whipped her sunglasses off her face and glared into the rearview mirror.

We both yelped again as the Jeep lurched forward again, the sound of tires grinding on asphalt, and the smell of burning rubber assaulting my senses.

"The SUV behind me is deliberately running into us. The driver is trying to run us off the road." And if we hadn't been in a sturdy, durable, well-made Jeep, they would have succeeded. If I were in my Audi, I would've ended up in a ditch by now. Not to mention Kody was rock solid behind the wheel. Her knuckles were white, and her mouth was set in a grim line, but she kept the Jeep moving forward and straightened out after every violent bump and the grind of metal on metal.

I wanted to ask if there was anything I could do, but I didn't want to distract her. I fished my new cell phone out of my pocket and snapped a couple of pictures of the dark blue SUV trying to push us off the road.

Kody swore long and loud after a particularly hard tap. The wheels of the Jeep screamed, and the big, heavy vehicle skipped across the lines on the highway into oncoming traffic. We both let out ear-piercing screams, but by some act of god, Kody managed to wrestle the Jeep back into the right lane of traffic. Only, the SUV didn't stop racing toward us.

I reached out a hand and squeezed Kody's thigh. Case was going to do more than burst a blood vessel if I end up getting his little sister killed. He was also going to more than hate me if anything happened to her, and this time he would be justified in feeling that way.

A roar louder than the Jeep's engine and the rush of blood between my ears suddenly thundered along the highway. Between one blink and the next, a swarm of chrome and black motorcycles was between the bumper of the SUV and the back of the Jeep. There had to be at least twenty of them, and every time the SUV tried to lurch around them, or jumped ahead of them, the agile two-wheeled beasts blocked him.

Eventually, the SUV pulled back, careening around and darting off down the road in the opposite direction.

Breathing hard, Kody pulled the Jeep off to the side of the road and gave me a wide-eyed look. "Holy shit."

Kody's Jeep was immediately surrounded by the swarm of motorcycles.

"What's going on?" I would bet good money I looked as bewildered as I felt.

Kody banged her head on the steering wheel. "The cavalry is here."

"Who?" I was completely lost, and my heart was lodged firmly in my throat.

She sighed and turned to look at me. "The Sons of Sorrow. Your not-so-friendly outlaw motorcycle club. Why am I not surprised you have no clue who they are? I sometimes do business with the guy in charge of the club. Case is going to lose his mind for real when he hears about this."

A tall man wearing mirrored sunglasses and a black baseball hat approached Kody's window. He had a bandanna with a grinning skeleton jaw on it wrapped around the lower half of his face, giving him a creepy appearance. He knocked a knuckle on Kody's window, and I noticed he had a heavy silver ring on almost every single finger. He pulled the bandanna down when Kody opened the window, and took his sunglasses off. He flashed a fierce frown at the blonde sitting next to me, and if I'd been in her seat I would've melted to the floorboards under the intensity of his dark-eyed glare.

Kody blew out a breath and quietly greeted, "Hey, Shot. Long time no see."

I lifted my eyebrows at the nickname and tried not to flinch when his dark eyes moved in my direction.

"What kind of trouble you in now?" The guy's voice was deep and missing the soft drawl most born-and-bred Texans couldn't hide.

She shook her head and hooked a finger in my direction. "Not my trouble this time. It's hers. I was just along for the ride."

He shifted his gaze between the two of us and turned to look down the long stretch of road we'd just raced for our lives on. "Saw the SUV driving erratically back down the road. Didn't seem right, so we followed along. We put a call in to your brother already. Sending some of my boys to see if they can run down the SUV." He cocked his head and leaned a little closer to the side of the Jeep, eyes raking over me where I was quivering on the passenger seat. "Hey, I think your old man represented me once in court."

I cleared my throat nervously. "We're separated." Stupid, but it was the first thing that popped into my mind.

The biker snorted. "He sucked. I ended up serving three months on a jacked-up charge. A public defender could've got me off."

I sniffed. "I'm sorry."

The biker shrugged. "Not your fault." He reached a hand inside the open window and tugged on a piece of Kody's wild hair. "Told you to holler if you got into trouble again. Next time listen before you end up as real-life bumper cars on the highway." Kody nodded mutely as the scary, leather-clad man moved away from the car. "Tell your brother to keep a closer eye on his shit. I don't have time to do his job for him."

Sirens shrieked in the distance, and all the bikers fired up their engines at once. The ground rumbled and shook as they disappeared in a cloud of dust as quickly as they appeared.

Shivering, I turned to Kody and whispered, "You have some very scary friends."

She laughed, but it quickly turned into a groan as she once again banged her head on the steering wheel. "Tell me about it." She closed her eyes and warned, "But Shot doesn't hold a candle to Case when he's pissed. No one does. So, brace yourself, because things are about to get very ugly."

CHAPTER 12

CASE

When the call came through dispatch that there was a high-speed chase happening on one of the highways running along the outskirts of town, I didn't think anything of it until the make and model of the vehicles involved came through. Kody was the only person in Loveless who drove a lime-green Jeep Wrangler. She was also reckless enough·to try and outrun a pursuer at top speed in the middle of traffic.

I was already losing my mind with worry when a second call came in from the leader of the local motorcycle club. I had a tenuous truce in place with the Sons of Sorrow, and Shot in particular. Begrudgingly, I had a lot of respect for their president, Shot Caldwell. He was a former marine, so I understood him on a soldier-to-soldier level. I never liked how chummy he was with my little sister, or how blatantly he skirted the edges of what was and wasn't legal. But I appreciated his attention to detail when he gave me a full description of the SUV trying to run Kody off the road. My heart dropped to my toes when he mentioned Kody wasn't alone in the Jeep. She had a pretty, petite, dark-haired passenger along for the wild ride.

I saw red.

I was so distracted after hearing that Aspen was in the Jeep with my sister, I didn't utter a word of protest when Shot told me he was sending a couple of his guys after the SUV. I wouldn't normally permit anyone who wasn't a member of my department getting involved in such a volatile situation, but Shot and his boys could handle themselves, and I wanted the driver of the SUV, no matter what shape he was in by the time I got my hands on him.

But my first priority was making sure my sister and my confusing, confounding nemesis were all right.

Siren screaming, I raced out of town and down the highway with little regard to the speed limit. I actually flew past a couple of the bikers as I made my way to where Kody had pulled off onto the shoulder of the road. One of my patrol cars and a deputy were already on the scene. He was obviously doing his best to keep his patience in check while talking to my little sister. She would try the patience of a saint, so I gave him credit for keeping his cool as Kody rolled her eyes and scowled at each question tossed her way.

Aspen was also leaning against the side of the brightly painted Jeep. She had a crutch under one arm, and her black hair was a wild tangle around her alarmingly pale face. She was answering the questions coming from the uniformed deputy much more calmly than Kody, but I could tell she was nervous by the way she kept fidgeting around on her good leg and the way she kept tugging on her lower lip.

Both women turned and looked in my direction when I pulled the SUV to a stop behind the Jeep. I watched as Kody stiffened, posture automatically going defensive and ready to fight. Aspen was the opposite. If it was possible for her to get even smaller, she did. She seemed to shrink in on herself.

I stalked the short distance separating me from the two women. I was so agitated I forgot my hat back at the station, so I pushed a furious hand through my hair as I glared at my younger sibling.

"What in the actual fuck, Kody?" She turned to face me, and we squared off, just like we had a million times before when she was growing up and purposely pushing every single button I had. My deputy tactfully made his escape, telling me he had enough to file a report and would use the picture Aspen took to put out a Be on the Lookout alert for the SUV.

"What were you thinking? And why is she with you?" I glared to where Aspen was hovering over Kody's shoulder. When our eyes met a fresh wave of rage swept through me. The woman literally had someone gunning for her, and she dragged my baby sister into the line of fire. "Protective custody means you don't leave the safe house, Counselor. I'm sure you know that."

Kody poked me in the center of the chest with her index finger. "Calm down, Sheriff. No one is hurt. That's the important thing to focus on."

"No. It's not." I swatted her hand away and stepped around her, so Aspen had no choice but to look at me. Angry, hurtful words shot out before I could think through the implications. Just like that day on the steps when my life came crashing down around me and she was in the center of the wreckage. "You can't stop playing games with my family, can you? It doesn't matter who gets hurt as long as you get your way. Will you be satisfied when I finally lose someone I love completely? How many different ways do you want me to suffer, Aspen?"

My voice was rising, and I could feel my temples throbbing as unchecked fury coursed through my veins. But there was something else there too. Another feeling trying to push its way to the surface. Something warmer and softer than the familiar anger. Something that scared me and made me nervous because I had no clue what I was supposed to do with it. So, like the mature, well-adjusted man I was, I clung to the familiarity of being pissed as hell at Aspen Barlow so I didn't have to admit I might, possibly, be worried sick about what might have happened to her right alongside my flesh and blood.

"Case!" Kody's voice was sharp as a knife, and her hand was back on the center of my chest pushing for all she was worth. "Stop it. I didn't have to go and pick her up. That's on me. You can't be mad at Aspen for my choice. You know better than anyone, no one makes me do anything I don't want to do."

"She shouldn't have left in the first place. It's too dangerous. Someone wants her dead." I bit out the obvious.

Kody threw her hands up in exasperation. "Yeah, we all know that. But Aspen has a life that didn't simply grind to a halt because someone has it in for her. Maybe if you could stop being hardheaded all the time, and took the time to talk to her instead of yelling at her or ignoring her, she could've asked *you* to help her instead of me. Or maybe you would've realized it on your own if your head wasn't so far up your ass."

"*She* is right here, and *she* is perfectly capable of speaking for herself." Slowly, Aspen maneuvered herself on the crutch over the uneven ground until she was facing both of us. "Kody, I really am sorry you got dragged into this mess. I knew it was a risk leaving the house and I had no right to ask you to put yourself in danger like I did. Case is right. I was selfish. I shouldn't have involved you."

Aspen narrowed her eyes in my direction as the shockingly white pallor of her face gave way to a scarlet flush. "As for not leaving the house, we never discussed that. No one is supposed to know where I am staying, and I stuck to that. We never talked about the fact I would practically be under lock and key until you have someone in custody." She gave me a pointed look, and I bristled automatically. I didn't like the implication that if I were better at my job, we wouldn't be having this conversation at all because whoever was out to get her would be behind bars. "I have things to take care of, a life to manage. I can't do that cut off from the entire world. I'm not going to be punished any more because someone out there wants to hurt me. I'm not hiding forever. I didn't do anything wrong."

Kody piped up before I could respond to Aspen's defiant rant. "I'm glad you called me, Aspen. Case taught me defensive driving before I even had my license. If you'd been with someone else, in a taxi, or in an Uber, today might have ended very differently. Not to mention Shot only got involved because he recognized my Jeep." Kody sniffed and lifted her eyebrows in my direction. "Instead of huffing and puffing, and trying to blow the house down, why don't you look at the upside of the situation for once."

I growled and pointed a finger at my little sister. "That's another bone I have to pick with you. Why are you and Shot Caldwell still buddy-buddy? I thought I told you to steer clear of him and the SoS. You don't know what they get up to, and if things ever go sideways, the last thing we need is a Lawton tied to an outlaw motorcycle club."

"You don't get to tell me who my friends are, Case. You don't get to tell me where I can go, or what I can do, either. You're my brother, not my keeper. How many times do I have to remind you of that fact? Be happy Shot has a soft spot for me. That SUV wasn't backing off and had already shoved us into oncoming traffic once. Shot ended the situation with no fatalities, and he called you to tell you what was going down. Sounds like he was a Good Samaritan if you ask me." Kody tilted her chin back and flipped her hair over her shoulder. She was dug in, ready to argue her position until she was blue in the face or until I gave in. We'd always been this way.

I sighed and lifted my hands to my hair and tugged. Frustration pounded at me from all directions. There was no making Kody reevaluate her choices when she was certain she was in the right. So I shifted my attention to Aspen. At least she had the sense to seem contrite over the near heart attack they'd given me.

"If you wanted to leave the house I would have sent a deputy over so you would have had protection while taking care of what you needed to do today. I would have sent someone whose job is to put themselves in the line of fire. My sister likes to meddle where she shouldn't, and lord knows she enjoys pissing me off, so I'm not surprised she jumped at the chance to run you around town. But she shouldn't end up smeared all over the asphalt because you suddenly got cabin fever." My tone was cold, and I knew the pointed barbs hit their mark when Aspen flinched hard. "You're playing with lives and hearts that don't belong to you. I know you're used to doing that at your job, but this is different. You had a choice this time, and you made the wrong one."

Kody snapped my name once again, but I didn't look her way. Aspen blinked her wide, doe eyes at me and slowly nodded. "You're right. I did make the wrong choice, I do that a lot where you're concerned. I won't do it again."

I grunted my response, buried my confusion and inclined my head toward my SUV. "Get in the car, and I'll take you back. I'm going to assign someone to stay with you when I can't be there. That way if you need to leave for some reason you can do it safely."

Before I was done speaking she was shaking her head violently back and forth. "Oh no. I'm not going back to that house. I'm done."

I turned to blink stupidly in her direction. "Done? How can you be done when we still have no idea who's after you?"

Aspen shook her head again, dark hair catching in the wind and blowing wildly around her face. "I'm done with *you*, Sheriff." She shifted her gaze toward Kody and almost whispered, her voice was so low and quiet, "I need my new phone out of your Jeep. I'm calling for a ride and catching the first flight I can get out of town."

Kody jumped from foot to foot, clearly unsure of what she should do. Eventually, those big, dark eyes of Aspen's must've won her over because my sister suddenly bolted for the opposite side of the car, leaving Aspen and me facing off on the side of the road.

I should be relieved. Getting her out of town was actually a really good idea, but something heavy and unwieldy settled in my gut at the thought of her being out there on her own with an unknown threat breathing down her neck. If she left my county, she would no longer be my problem, and everything inside of my chest tightened up at the thought. I liked knowing where she was and that she was tucked away, somewhere safe and sound.

I liked going home and having someone besides my son there. Someone who asked about my day and watched me with soft eyes and a perfectly pouty mouth. Someone who seemed genuinely glad to see I made it home from patrol in one piece and sometimes understood the bad days were so bad there was no getting past them. Someone who forced me to slow down and appreciate the good days because it felt like there were fewer and fewer of them.

"Aspen..." I took a step in her direction, and she practically scrambled backward. Her crutch she was using for balance slipped on the gravel, sending her off-center, and I reached out to catch her. I swore under my breath when she immediately fought my hold and tried to break free.

"Let me go, Case. I'm sick and tired of you finding fault with everything I do. Was I stupid today? Yes. But you have no idea, no clue how hard I worked, how diligently I fought for those lives and hearts that weren't mine. I hate that you lost so much time with your son, but you could have lost even more than that. No one is exempt from making the wrong choice. That includes you, Sheriff." She used her bandaged hand to pull her wayward hair out of her face as she glared at me. "The difference is, I can accept responsibility for my screwups. Can you?"

I scoffed at her and tilted my chin down so I could match her, dirty look for dirty look. "Of course I can."

She snorted. "Really? Because you've been blaming me for everything that's gone wrong in your life for the last decade. I had nothing to do with you knocking up Becca in high school. I wasn't the one who kept you from leaving Loveless. I never suggested you go work for your father, knowing how corrupt he was. I had nothing to do with your marriage falling apart, and it was never my idea to take custody away from you, and I wasn't the one who threatened the judge. The only thing I did was try and save the very last good thing you had in your life at the time... your reputation. If it weren't for me, this entire town would believe you were no better than your father." Her voice was steadily rising, and her cheeks were getting redder and redder. I'd never seen her in a full-on temper before, and I had to admit she was still beautiful even when she was mad. Her anger made her seem bigger than she actually was, and I fought flinching away from the heat in her eyes and acid in her words.

"Do you know Becca claimed you admitted to helping your father with covering up a case when you were a deputy? She told me you had a direct hand in letting an abusive husband go. He later kidnapped and attacked his wife. She swears you got drunk and admitted to her you knew the guy was dangerous, that you saw your father hide evidence that would have kept the husband behind bars, but your father let him go, and you didn't do anything about it. She told me you knew all along your father took money from the man to cover it up and keep what he did to his wife quiet. The only reason she never came forward with the accusation during your divorce and custody hearings is because *I* talked her out of it each and every time. I'm the one who convinced her she needed actual evidence for the claims to matter. I'm the one who reminded her if you lost your job, if you went to jail, you couldn't pay the outrageous amount of money she was asking for every single month. Everyone in this town had been dying to see you fall from grace. I saved you from that, and I saved *Hayes* from that, because I never believed it was true. Even after you threatened me. Even after you treated me like I was a leper. I always believed the best of you, Case. You kept your job, your repuation, and most importantly, you kept the time you did get with your son. All because of me."

I couldn't fight it any longer. I fell back one step and then another. I couldn't breathe. And I couldn't tear my eyes away from the woman standing in front of me. It was like the sun suddenly peeked out from behind a thick covering of clouds, and I was finally seeing her without the shadows and murkiness from the past.

"Why didn't you ever talk to me about what happened back then?" I whispered and watched as Kody cautiously came around the back fender of her car.

Aspen gave me an are-you-kidding-me look and snorted so loudly a flock of birds in a nearby field took flight.

"How was I supposed to talk to you, Case? You hated me. I tried to help you once that day on the stairs, and you shut me down after insulting me. You made it clear you wouldn't believe anything I had to say. Then I didn't talk to you because your ex-wife was still my client and I was legally obligated to keep my mouth shut. And even when she wasn't my client, you *still* hated me, yet I didn't do anything with the accusations, even though it's my job to uphold the law. I couldn't convince myself the boy I was so very attached to and cared so much about in high school became a man who was so blatantly corrupt. And it has eaten at me all these years. Made me question who and what I am." She must've caught sight of Kody coming around the car and held out her injured hand for the phone. "But I'm done being a martyr. I'm done being your convenient excuse for everything that doesn't go the way you want it."

I was stunned stupid and silent. I had no clue. All these years she was sitting on a secret so huge, so damning. All for me and Hayes...

It wasn't true, of course. Well, my role in the events the night the young woman reported her husband wasn't true. Yes, I believed my father accepted a bribe from the deacon to make the pictures of his wife's injuries and her medical reports disappear. And yes, I was aware that he was fully responsible for sending the abused woman on her way and letting the husband go, but I had nothing to do with any of it. I took the woman to the hospital. I urged her to press charges and told her she needed to get a lawyer and go above my father's head if he wouldn't listen. I worked for weeks to prove my father tampered with the evidence, but he was so good at covering his tracks it was like beating my head against a brick wall. I diligently checked up on her, and when she was taken by her ex, I was the one who coordinated with the FBI and local officals to find her as quickly as possible. I'd even gotten a chance to make amends when she returned to Loveless several years later looking for closure. An apology didn't seem like enough after all she'd been through, but I was glad I got to say "I'm sorry."

I did vaguely recall getting hammered one night back then and telling Becca that seeing that young woman black and blue, with broken bones and a broken soul, was finally my breaking point. My father was really good at being a bad guy, and I was tired of him getting away with it.

I forced myself to take a breath, and before my sister could pass the phone off, I intercepted it. Kody let it go without much of a fight, so I figured she knew this conversation I was having with Aspen was far from over and for once was cutting me some slack and not intervening. I slipped the thin device in my back pocket and took a step in Aspen's direction. She swore at me and bumped against the side of the Jeep as she tried to evade me.

"Aspen...we need to talk about this, about what happened back then. It's not true. I would have never helped my father hide evidence. But, either way, no one asked you to throw yourself on the funeral pyre." Which made the fact that she had even more impressive and poignant.

"No more talking. I'm leaving." There was finality in her tone I didn't care for at all. She turned and started to limp away, but the crutch hampered her mobility, and the uneven ground slowed her down.

Without giving much thought to my next actions, I reached

out and caught hold of her crutch, pulling her in my direction. When she started to twist sideways, cursing my name the entire time, I locked an arm around her waist, catching her small frame easily against mine and lifting her wiggling, squirming body into my arms with ease. I started toward my SUV like I was carrying her over the threshold. I could hear Kody giggling from somewhere behind me, but I refused to stop my forward momentum. If I paused, I would have to consider just how inappropriately I was manhandling a civilian in broad daylight. I was always so careful to do things by the book, but right now no words were going to tell me how I should deal with Aspen Barlow once and for all.

"What are you doing?" Her voice was sharp, but she stopped trying to escape the closer we got to my vehicle. I made sure to wince and play up the fact my busted up shoulder wasn't exactly up to sweeping a woman off her feet at the moment. Anything to get her where I wanted her. Anything to get rid of the foreign feeling at the center of my chest when I thought about her disappearing from Loveless when there was so damn much to settle between the two of us.

I shook my head, wishing I had my hat to hide under. I hated feeling exposed, and she was the last person I needed picking through all my confused and conflicting emotions.

"Taking you back to the house. Keeping you safe. Figuring out how you got under my skin so easily. Listening to what you have to say about the past, and actually hearing it for once." I looked down at her and arched an eyebrow. "Take your pick."

It took some juggling to get her into the front seat without banging any of her hurt bits and pieces. She let me strap her into the passenger seat, dark eyes watching me like a hawk every step of the way.

I braced an arm on the roof and leaned down. Our faces

were so close our noses almost touched. "I'm far from perfect, Aspen. I know I screwed up back then. I still screw up. I'm going to screw up in the future. Back then I was in the middle of losing everything, my father was a nightmare I couldn't get out from under, and all I wanted was to go back to the beginning and start all over. I'm not surprised Becca took something out of context and blew it out of porportion. I am shocked you sat on something you thought was so damning and critical all these years. I couldn't see much beyond my own miserable circumstances for so long. But I see it all so clearly now. I see *you* now."

I heard her gulp, but her impossibly long, soot-colored lashes fell, covering her reaction to my words.

"What do you see?"

I pushed off the car, satisfied she wasn't going to run, or limp, away as soon as I walked away. "I'm not entirely sure. But I know I can't look away." I cleared my throat. "Talk to me, and after everything is on the table, if you still want to catch a plane I'll take you to the airport."

It took a minute, but she eventually nodded in silent agreement. Satisfaction spiraled inside my chest, and I found myself biting back a grin as I rounded the SUV to the driver's side. Maybe my kid was right, and I had to move forward for my view to finally change. I'd been staring at my past for so long it had all started to blur together in one big void of regret. But I could say for certain when I got a good look at the future I was facing, there was a small, dark-haired woman standing directly in the center of it.

CHAPTER 13

∞

ASPEN

The ride to Case's house was one seriously quiet and intense affair.

It also took a lot longer than it should have because Case insisted on following Kody home, and then driving the most roundabout way back to his house possible to make sure we weren't being followed. The precaution seemed excessive until I remembered being tossed around like a ragdoll in Kody's Jeep as the SUV slammed into us over and over again. I wasn't sure when my life turned into a knockoff of a James Patterson novel, but I was at my limit with how much I could take.

Other than asking how the person who tried to run us off the road would know where to find me and Kody, Case hardly spoke. Even when I told him I had gone by my house and met with an insurance adjuster—meaning it was more than likely whoever wanted my head on a plater was watching my house and waiting for me to put in an appearance—he did nothing more than offer up a low grunt for a response. In hindsight, had I been thinking clearly and not acting out of panic and unchecked emotion, I would've realized the only two places someone would be expecting me to make an appearance were my office and my house. They were the two main locations I should've avoided while I was in hiding. I was supposed to be smarter than that. But something about the man sitting next to me sent my common sense on vacation. I'd never really been able to think clearly around Case, and now that there was a new level of intimacy added to our dynamic, I felt like I could barely function at all.

Case Lawton was hell on a girl's heart and on her judgment. Both of mine were taking a beating lately.

When we finally pulled into the garage, I allowed him to help me into his house. I hurt pretty much all over, and I was due for a major adrenaline crash. I didn't argue when he guided me in the direction of the guest bedroom. Sure there were better places to finish hashing out differing views of the past, but lying down so I could elevate my abused ankle sounded absolutely awesome. I wasn't sure how much fight I had left either. Foolishly, I thought my being on the bed would automatically create some distance between me and Case. After last night, I was certain he was going to make it a point to keep a respectable distance between us, so there was no getting the wrong idea or getting close enough to touch.

He surprised me when he pried his boots off and climbed up onto the bed and stretched out alongside of me. He laced his fingers together behind his head and looked up at the ceiling, as if he had all the time in the world and no clue that he was sending my system into overdrive.

"Why?" I felt the deep rumble of his voice all the way down to my bones. "Why couldn't you tell me? Why did it have to be you who acted as the scapegoat all these years? Why risk your career and your convictions for me?

It can't simply be because you had a little crush on me in high school."

I turned my head slightly so I could look at his chiseled profile. His jaw was locked, and a muscle in his cheek fluttered occasionally, letting me know he was clenching his teeth. I didn't have an answer that would make him any less rigid or tense.

I used my free fingers to toy with the bandage on my burned hand. The skin underneath was beginning to get itchy, so I hoped it was a sign it was starting to heal.

"It had to be me because if *anyone* else represented her, they would have let her pull every dirty trick in the book, and you would have lost any right to see your son. Becca was prepared to ruthlessly ruin you. And after you started working for your father, it's like people in this town wanted to see you fail. I knew her story would sound believable because of who your father is. So I did what needed to be done because I wanted what was best for your son. At the end of the day, keeping children safe—keeping *Hayes* safe—is the most important part of my job. And Hayes needed you around—not potentially locked up, unable to fight for custody down the line." I heard his teeth grind together and winced. "I was on your side. Still am. And it wasn't as simple as a crush. You were the only person who ever reached out to me, made me feel welcome. You have no idea how powerful that was to a girl who always felt all alone. You meant the world to me back then."

And he had grown to mean an awful lot to me now. I always seemed to want more than he was capable of giving. "Aside from losing Hayes, what's always been your biggest fear in life?" The question was quiet because I knew the answer, even though I didn't know him as well as I wanted to. I was pretty sure everyone who spent any significant time in Loveless, Texas, knew the answer.

Case tilted his chin and looked down at me. Shadows of something powerful and profound moved across his eyes. They looked like angry storm clouds rolling in to ruin an otherwise beautiful day. I hated the way the blue in his eyes dimmed when he was reminded of the man who he never wanted to define him. The man he spent a lifetime trying his best to defy.

"My biggest fear has always been being like my father. I've always been terrified of being someone my family is scared of. I never wanted to be a man people feared rather than respected. I've worked my ass off to undo all the damage Dad's done to this town, to my siblings, to our name." He released his hands and dragged a wide palm over his face. "If my father hadn't threatened that judge, things would've been different. It's as much his fault as it is Becca's I lost so much time with my kid when he was growing up."

It was the first time he openly admitted I wasn't the cause of the separation. Progress, but he really had no idea how tricky and manipulative his ex-wife could be.

"No. If the judge even hinted that he was going to relent and give you any leeway, Becca would've found a way to sabotage the ruling. She was determined to win and to punish you by any means necessary. She would have forced me to bring up the cover-up and the accusations against you. She would have cheated and conned everyone in that courtroom. She knew how much you worried people believed you were like Conrad, and she knew people would believe the worst. Even if she didn't have proof you were involved in the tampering of evidence, she would've put it out there just to trash your reputation. You would've never been able to run for sheriff. And that judge would have given you no chance to appeal the original custody ruling. I don't think you know how deeply she resented you. You ruined all her plans, Case."

He shifted so that he was also stretched out on his side. The new position brought his handsome face really close to mine. The ends of our noses almost touched, and I could count all his long, dark eyelashes. They were really pretty on such a rugged, masculine face.

"Yeah, well she ruined my plans long before I ruined hers, so we should've been even. The only reason I stayed in this town and anywhere near my father was because of Becca and Hayes. I gave up my future for her and tried to give her the life she wanted, even though I knew good and well she got pregnant on purpose. She was always worried once I left for college I would meet someone else, someone better. I really did try and make her happy, until she made it clear nothing I ever did was going to be good enough."

Without thinking about it, I lifted my bandaged hand and used the tips of my fingers to touch the fierce frown painted on his lips. His mouth was another feature that was unexpectedly soft and pretty when he wasn't using it to scold or scowl.

"She did whatever she had to so you wouldn't leave. But you ended up leaving anyway." I felt like I was pointing out the obvious, but Case looked stunned.

"I didn't leave. I got deployed. That's a huge difference." His breath was warm against the tips of my fingers, and it felt like I could almost touch the frustration in his words.

"Not to someone as selfish and spoiled as your ex. The baby was a means to an end and all of a sudden she's stuck raising Hayes alone while the entire town bemoans their golden boy joining the army instead of the NFL. She loved being the center of attention, but not when it painted her in a bad light. She couldn't wait to turn all of that negativity and disapproval back on you, but she had to bide her time. No one was going to hate a hero, but they had no problem being disgusted by another dirty cop following Conrad Lawton's lead."

His eyes narrowed, and it felt like the space between us did as well. I wasn't aware I'd been leaning closer and closer the longer we talked, but our knees were touching, and my chest was almost flattened against his.

"I was never a dirty cop. My father never had that much influence over me. I've always gone out of my way to do the right thing. I never wanted to let that woman's husband go. I was going to bring him back in as soon as I found a doctor not scared of my father to confirm the initial examination results. I just needed some time to undo the damage my dad did, but I never got to because the girl took off. I promised her I would protect her, but she didn't believe me, because my dad destroyed her trust. I never blamed her for running, but I also never got an opportunity to make things right." Suddenly he lifted the hand not holding his head and slide his fingers through the hair at my temple. It was a light caress, but it sent goose bumps racing across my entire body. "Aside from Hayes, me *not* taking after my father is the one thing in life I know I can take pride in. I did everything I could after she left to prove my dad was the one behind the missing evidence, including getting internal affairs involved. No one was ever able to prove anything. The man has always been a better criminal than cop."

I sighed, leaned into the gentle stroking and let my eyes fall closed. It felt really good, soothing even. Not that my pounding heart and tightening nipples could tell the difference between a touch meant to comfort and one meant to arouse. I was torn between settling into the soft care and moving closer as desire started to thrum low and hard in my belly.

"You're a good man, Case. I stand by that, which is ultimately why it was me standing between you and her all these years, and why I never said anything. I don't regret it, even though it meant you were bound to hate me. I would do it all over again if I had to."

"Maybe this is too little, too late, but I'm sorry. Sorry I was a clueless kid in high school. Sorry you had to deal with Becca and her games. Sorry you had to carry that secret around for so long. Sorry I had any part in you questioning whether or not you were doing the right thing. You really are one of the strongest people I've ever met. I like respecting you a whole lot more than hating you, Aspen. Thank you for doing what you did...for me and for Hayes." He was very quiet for a long time, but his fingers never stopped moving through my hair. When he spoke his lips almost moved against mine. "Not so sure you would be saying I'm a good man if you knew all the bad thoughts going through my head at the moment. You've always made me feel too much, Aspen, but I never thought you would be the woman I was willing to do just about anything to get into bed. But here we are."

My eyes flew open, and a small gasp escaped when I felt the tip of his tongue dart out to trace the small dip in my upper lip. "What exactly are you willing do to, Case?" I had to hear him say it before we moved any further.

The wet slide of his tongue moved to my lower lip, and I inhaled sharply as his knee suddenly pressed its way between my legs. My nipples hardened into aching points against the unyielding wall of his chest, and the fingers resting against his cheek started to quiver.

"I'm going to let go. Of the past. Of the blame. Of the mistakes I made. I've needed a new perspective for a long time. Wish I could've found it on my own, but sometimes you need a shove in the right direction. I'm going to thank you for everything you sacrificed for me in a way neither one of us will be able to forget."

I wanted to tell him no one needed to push me toward him, I'd been leaning that way since I was a lovestruck teenager, but I lost the ability to speak when his denim-clad thigh slid along mine, only stopping when it was pressed against the apex of my thighs. My entire body tightened and pressed closer to his. I felt him harden against the lower part of my stomach, and I could see the rapid flutter of his pulse at the base of his neck as we got as close as we could.

This time there was no question he was the one who initiated the kiss. He was the one moving things forward. He was the one taking us away from where we'd always been, to someplace entirely new.

His lips were insistent against mine. His tongue demanded immediate entry to my mouth. I yielded and practically melted against him when his tongue twisted and danced skillfully around mine. The hand he had to play with my hair moved to the side of my face. His thumb traced the line of my cheekbone, and he used his index finger to carefully outline the outside of my ear. Holy hell, how did he know how sensitive and responsive my damn ears were? I felt like I was going to come right out of my skin when he repeated the gesture as he simultaneously used the edge of his teeth on my lower lip.

My legs shifted anxiously against his, all my soft places going warm and wet when I felt his body respond to mine. I could feel the weight of his cock pressing against his jeans as our hips collided and rubbed deliciously together. Case was no longer keeping his desire in check, and when let off the leash it was a big, consuming thing.

He used his weight to roll me over on my back. He planted one beefy forearm next to my head and sent his other on an exploration of my body. I wrapped my good arm around the back of his neck to keep his mouth on mine as I wantonly lifted my hips into the solid ridge filling out the front of his jeans. I already knew he was impressive. But I wanted to feel the fullness in someplace other than my hands. There was a steady ache throbbing between my legs that was too persistent to ignore.

Case managed to get my shorts open and my shirt halfway off without breaking the kiss. I had to let him go so he could strip the brightly colored fabric all the way off. My bra followed quickly after. Before I could feel shy or freak out over the fact I was half naked in bed with the guy I'd pined over for most of my life, his mouth closed over one of my nipples, and all coherent thought fled. The heat from his mouth and the drag of his teeth over the tender peak made my eyes roll back in my head. The intimate contact also had my fumbling fingers wrestling clumsily with the buttons on his shirt. It took triple the time it normally would've to expose his broad, thickly muscled chest, but when we were skin to skin, the struggle was totally worth it.

I hooked my good leg around his lean hips and rocked against him, searching for the kind of friction that would make my head spin and bring about some kind of a relief to the pulse thudding in all my most sensitive places.

I shifted restlessly when he moved his attention to the neglected nipple on the other breast. I wanted to get closer but also push him back so I could watch what he was doing. I wanted the image of Case Lawton's mouth all over my body burned into my brain for eternity.

I shoved a hand down the length of his torso, my destination clear. I wanted his heavy silver belt buckle and the stiff denim out of the way. I wanted to feel his velvety soft shaft, slippery with pleasure sliding between my legs. I wanted his rock-hard abs pressing me into the bed as he took me over the edge. I wanted to hold on to flexing muscle as he rocked into me over and over again.

I yelped in surprise when Case's strong fingers wrapped around my wrist the minute they ventured below the little indent of his belly button. My eyes locked on his and my tongue darted out to taste my kiss-swollen lips.

Case groaned, the sound full of frustration and regret. He dropped his forehead down, so it touched mine. "Aspen..." My name was a guttural sound that would have completely been a turn-on if it wasn't for the apology I could see floating to the surface of his ocean-colored eyes.

"I want you, but not like this."

I felt my mouth drop open, and I stiffened underneath his much bigger body. "Not like what?" Needy? Desperate? Out of control? I was only those things with him. He should be trying to take advantage of the effect he had on me, not hitting the brakes.

"Still married to Barlow." He sounded honestly pained, but it didn't change the fact he promised to lead me somewhere beautiful and instead left me hanging high and dry.

"I haven't been intimate with David in over a year, and no one after him either. You know how hard I've been pushing for him to sign the divorce papers. This is you finding something else to hold against me that I have no control over, Case." I pushed at his massive shoulders and tried to wiggle out from under him. Once again I was done with the emotional whiplash that came with caring about Case Lawton.

He caught my flailing hands in one of his and pinned them above my head. "You're wrong. This is me trying to do the right thing. I haven't had a woman in my house or in my bed in years, Aspen. Nothing wrong with wanting to do right by the one I've got there now, the only one who's mattered in a very long time. I'm not going to fuck another man's wife, but I will wait for her." My heart hammered against my ribs, and my pussy clenched in response to his smirk and raised an eyebrow that accompanied his next sultry promise. "And I'll keep her happy, and make sure she's taken care of while she handles getting rid of her excess baggage." It sounded like a promise and a threat all wrapped up in one.

Before I could ask for specifics, his mouth was back on mine, stealing away any protest I may have made as his hand disappeared under my panties.

His mouth devoured mine as thick fingers parted wet folds and slid unerringly into the welcome heat of my body. The initial stretch and invasion made my back bow off the bed and had my body clamping down against the intimate pressure. My head tossed side to side, ripping my mouth free from his punishing kiss. Case took advantage of the jerky moment and send his lips skipping down the side of my neck. Each nibble, every caress made my body soft and pliant under his touch. His fingers dipped deeper inside of me, finally feeling that void I'd felt since our lives intersected and twined together.

I gasped his name and dug my heel into the base of his spine when his thumb circled the overly sensitive nub of my clit. The sensation was like being electrified and had every nerve in my body lit up and alive.

Case kissed his way across my collarbone, and down the valley between my breasts. His fingers never stopped moving in and out of my now drenched center, making obscene sounds that matched the low moans and rough murmurs filling the room.

"Lift up."

I obeyed the rough command without a second thought. I barely had my hips arched off the mattress when impatient hands pulled my remaining clothes down my legs. My breath caught when he paused and took a moment to make sure my bad ankle didn't get jostled around as he arranged me where he wanted me.

I ended up with my legs hooked over his shoulders where he knelt by the side of the bed. I wanted to be embarrassed at how up close and personal he was getting with all my private places, but it was hard to feel anything but want and need when I felt the bristly brush of his cheeks against the inside of my thighs. His lips blazed a burning trail to all the intimate areas his fingers had thoroughly mapped out moments ago. I felt him drag the tip of his nose along the crease of my thigh and locked my fingers in his hair when I felt the first swipe of his tongue through my wet, willing flesh.

My legs shook next to his head, and I heard him chuckle in satisfaction right before his lips closed around me and he sucked with enough force to scatter what was left of my mind in a million directions. I might have screamed. I may have pulled his hair hard enough to get a grumble of complaint out of him. I knew I thrashed under the tender assault because nothing ever felt as good as Case's mouth on me at the same time he pushed back inside of me with his talented, dexterous fingers. It was sensory overload. The way everything felt and sounded. The way he looked so confident and right between my legs. The scent of sex and something earthy and manly that I would always associate with the man taking me apart.

Case used the edge of his teeth to trap and then torture the tiny, aching little bundle of excited nerves he was lavishing attention on. At the same time, he twisted his wrist, driving his fingers deeper and hitting that spot I'd almost forgot existed.

I saw white. A burst of light exploded behind my eyelids.

"Case!" His name was wrenched out of me with a hoarse cry. "Don't stop." If this was his way of apologizing, maybe I didn't mind arguing with him.

It'd been a very long time since anyone had played my

body so perfectly, and I'd never been with anyone who seemed to instinctively know exactly when and where to touch in order to make me forget who I was. My fingers tingled, and my toes twitched. I felt my body clench around his fingers, and a rush of warmth spread slowly with each thrust and wiggle. The orgasm wasn't a slow spark that took a minute to ignite. No. It was an explosion that wrecked me and left me limp and shaking in Case's very capable hands.

"I think you made me actually see stars." I couldn't remember any other man who made me feel drunk off of sex and loopy in the aftermath. Case was intoxicating. It didn't take much to imagine getting quickly addicted to his particular brand of distraction.

I felt a wet kiss on the inside of my leg. "That's just the start. You and me, we'll be worth the wait. Trust me." He sounded so confident I had no choice but to believe him.

CHAPTER 14

∞

CASE

$\mathbf{T}$he next night, after a frustrating day of dealing with dead ends and no new prospects on Aspen's case, a call came through that Shot and his boys had tracked down the SUV. However, Aspen was on her knees in front of me, and my cock happily nudging against the back of her throat when my phone rang, so I missed the call. The fact the car was abandoned and the driver gone was almost enough to zap the delirious haze of satisfaction she left me in. According to the biker, a second set of tire tracks near the vehicle indicated the driver ditched the car and already had a getaway driver waiting for them. I'd visited the Coleman brothers once again, but I had nothing to leverage against them, and they predictably alibied each other for the time of the car chase. Jethro seeming particularly smug about everything and was really rubbing in the fact I couldn't touch either of them without evidence no matter how strong my suspicions were.

Shot sounded as frustrated as I felt at having the best lead so far go nowhere. I was tired of the bad guys always being one step ahead and the threat on Aspen's life continually growing. Now that I could openly admit to myself I had feelings for her beside resentment and anger, I wanted to put her under lock and key and make sure nothing ever touched her again.

Frustration, and literally having nowhere else to turn, was the only reason I got up early the next morning and took the long, desolate drive out to my father's property.

The winding dirt road made me feel like I was traveling back in time. I remembered being so isolated out here, so far away from anyone who could help. It had felt like no one cared what living under Conrad Lawton's cruel regime was like. The place and property had never been pretty or well maintained, but after my mother died it really went to shit. Dad didn't care. This was his tiny, vicious kingdom and he never wanted anyone close enough to see past the carefully curated mask he wore for the people of Loveless. Sure, it was well known the patriarch of the Lawton clan was a tough taskmaster, a strict father, and an unbending disciplinary. All things that made him appealing as a no-nonsense lawman. What no one could see, since we were hidden away here on the outskirts of town, was the violence, the punishments, and the emotional torture. It was all done in the name of making sure we toed the line and didn't disrupt the sweet gig Conrad had lording over the small Texas town.

My father should never have been voted into his position as sheriff, and it shouldn't have taken as long as it did to vote him out. Really, until I decided to play hardball with him and threatened to pull all the family skeletons out of the closet, he had no competition. No one was brave enough to take him on. Small towns feared change, and this one feared my father for far too long. I wanted to ask him for help almost as much as I wanted to do my own dental work with a pair of rusty pliers, but I needed someone with his particular connections. It wasn't only the regular citizens who were daunted by Conrad Lawton, but the criminals also walked the other way when they saw him coming. My father had his finger on the pulse of every bad deed done in this county. He made more taking bribes from the bad guys than he ever did as a civil servant, and still made his living hustling and helping criminals break the law. It aggravated me to no end I could never catch him in the act.

I parked in front of the old farmhouse. It had been in my father's family for years. My dad learned his unforgiving ways at the hands of a master, and the lessons learned in the Lawton home were passed down from generation to generation. Luckily, we'd had my mother to finally break the cycle. Her love, her kindness, were enough for me and my siblings to see a better way. When my mother was still alive, she tried her best to make the place feel homey and bright, but all that remained of those efforts were the long-dead rosebushes and faded yellow paint.

I pulled to a stop in front of the house and sat in the car, staring at the front door for a long time. It'd been years since I'd willingly walked through that door. It was never a good idea to try and negotiate with my father on his home turf. It was never a good idea to try and reason with him at all.

The curtains ruffled in the front window, and I heard a dog bark. Well, now he knew I was here, and if I didn't go to him, he would come to me. I steadied myself and slipped out of the car and stomped up the front steps. The old wood creaked under my boots, and the front door swung open before I could knock. My father propped himself on a shoulder on the entryway. His green eyes were always cool and assessing, and it never failed to unnerve me that we looked so much alike minus the eye color. Age had thickened him around the middle some, but he was still a large man, and I would never forget how heavy his fists were.

"What are you doing out this way, boy? One of the damn neighbors complain about the dogs?" He narrowed his eyes and stroked his thumb along the side of his mouth. The move couldn't be viewed as anything other than maniacal and menacing. "I'll take care of it if they did...*Sheriff.*" Never had the title been spoken with more scorn.

"No. Not here about the dogs. Came to ask you about some trouble going around town. I'm sure you've heard someone took some shots outside the hospital. You have any idea who might be up to taking such a stupid risk?"

He stared at me silently for a long moment, and when he finally spoke, I felt like the little kid who was never fast enough to get away from him. "Was it really a risk? You don't have anybody locked up, do you? Don't have a clue who's doing what under your watch. I'll never understand why anyone thought you could do my job better than me."

I inhaled sharply and counted back from ten. Letting him antagonize me was exactly what he wanted. He always tried to drag me down to his level.

"Women were tired of you not listening to them, so were the all the folks who just happen to be from somewhere else originally. You were supposed to protect and serve *everyone*, not just the people you decided were worthy." It was a fact. I won the vote when I ran against him because all of the people he screwed over during his tenure finally decided to take a stand. I was lucky they realized it was my life's mission to undo all the damage my old man had done. I hooked my thumbs on either side of my belt buckle and asked again. "So I'll ask again, you hear anything I should know about, old man? Don't think I won't drag you down to the station if you decide to give me shit. We both know I'll do it."

My father rolled his eyes at me and crossed his ankles like he didn't have a care in the world. "How's your sister? I heard she ran into some trouble on the highway and needed those bikers to rescue her. Where were you when someone was trying to run her off the road? You're letting an outlaw biker gang do your job for you now?"

I gritted my teeth and told myself he wanted me to hit him. But I knew I'd find myself neck deep in police brutality charges before I could blink.

"The bikers were in the right place at the right time." And I would be forever grateful. The last person I wanted to owe a favor was Shot, but it was too late for that. "And I was working. Like you so helpfully pointed out already, I still don't have a suspect."

"Doesn't it bother you that your baby sister is keeping company with a bunch of bikers? Do you know what she gets up to in that bar of hers? How do you look the other way, Mr. Straight and Narrow?" He was picking at every weak point I had. It was the world's worst kept secret that Kody liked to run numbers out of the bar. Nothing serious, just a line on college and pro football during the season. She skirted the edge of being a full-on bookie by not handling the money directly. That's why she knew Shot and the boys as well as she did. They handled all the dirty work so I didn't have to toss my baby sister in the slammer.

I sighed and tossed my head back so I was looking up at the sky. I had to put a hand on my hat to keep from losing it to gravity. Why did I think coming out here was going to get me anywhere? When had my father ever been helpful or given something without demanding more in return?

"If she breaks the law, I'll handle it just like I would if she was anyone else. So far, we haven't had to cross that bridge. She's an adult, one who fully understands actions have consequences. You're the only Lawton left in town who thinks he's above the law." I kicked at the dusty ground and sighed again. "Sorry to bother you, old man. Not sure why I thought you might have the common decency to throw me a bone." One of the dogs howled, and I could see why the neighbors might have an issue. I was sure they wouldn't dare complain though. Not when those mutts belonged to Conrad.

"It was a good shot, right? Would've hit the target dead center if you hadn't dived in front of her?" The question caught me off guard, so I nodded mutely. "Town's got a few skilled hunters and a couple decorated veterans. Only a handful of people aside from you could've made that shot. Most of them not against taking money and looking the other way." He scoffed at me and pushed off the door. "If you didn't have the intended victim in your bed, you might've figured that out for yourself, boy." How he always knew what was going on behind everyone's closed door would always remain a mystery to me.

I narrowed my eyes and ran through a short list in my head. I narrowed my eyes at him and cocked my head to the side. "Your name could go at the top of that list." He was one hell of a shot and had no morals to speak of.

"Put my name on any list you want, Case. I'll be dead and in the ground by the time you prove anything. Since you can't seem to do your job as the sheriff, do your job as a big brother and keep your sister out of trouble."

He put a hand on the door and was about to disappear back inside when I asked, "Why has Kody always been the only one you treat halfway human?"

He cast me a blank look over his shoulder as he pulled the screen door shut. But then I heard him quietly say, "She looks just like your mother," before disappearing back into the dreary house.

Swearing under my breath, I stomped back to my SUV. I called the station and ordered twenty-four-seven surveillance on the Coleman brothers. I wanted them brought in if they so much as jaywalked. Jed knew how to handle a weapon, but Jethro enlisted around the same time I did. I knew from the years I'd worked alongside him at the station that he had zero morals, and it wasn't hard to imagine the man taking money in exchange for a life, steadily moving him up the ladder of who was behind all of this. Jed needed Aspen out of the way to win his upcoming divorce battle. And Jethro was the type of big brother to go above and beyond for his family.

Luckily, Jed wasn't the brightest crayon in the box. It only took us a day of tailing him to catch him blatantly violating the restraining order his estranged wife had in place. My deputies arrested him as he was following the harassed woman into the grocery store. He screamed obscenities at her and threw a punch at one of my cops. I was more than happy to slap him with additional charges when we hauled him into the station. I let him sit and stew, not surprised at all when he demanded a lawyer as soon as he sat down in the interrogation room.

I was, however, caught off guard when David Barlow showed up, looking harried and harassed, claiming Jed was his client. I should've looked for a connection between the two men before now, but it never occurred to me Jed could afford someone like Barlow to represent him. My dad was right. I was too close to the victim to see anything beyond keeping her safe. That fact grated on my last nerve.

I ushered the well-dressed man into the interrogation room as pieces of the puzzle started to fall into place. I told them both it would be a minute and called Hill so I could run my theory by him. Since I was personally involved with Aspen, it was going to make interacting with her jerk of a husband a conflict of interest. Hill agreed to come into the station and take the lead on questioning.

The Texas Ranger walked through my station house like he owned the place. He gave me a nod and looked pointedly at the door to the room where Barlow and Coleman were talking in hushed tones. "We didn't find any large withdrawals from Barlow or his father's account that would indicate he paid either of the Colemans to hurt Aspen."

I nodded. "I don't think they asked for money. Jed is looking at fifteen to twenty years behind bars for assaulting his wife and kids, not to mention the time attached to the new charges he racked up today violating the restraining order. I think Barlow agreed to represent him in court in exchange for the brothers going after Aspen."

Hill rubbed his chin. "To what end? What's Barlow gain if Aspen is out of the way? He's not the beneficiary on any of her accounts or her life insurance policy. The marriage is over for all intents and purposes so he can fuck whoever he wants, guilt-free. What's the motive?"

I rolled my eyes. "Go in there and find out."

Hill nodded again and silently slipped through the door. The man was an intimidating bastard when he was in investigator mode. I settled at a desk with a computer monitor showing the live video feed from the interrogation room. I watched as both Barlow and Jed stiffened and sat up straighter when they caught sight of the Ranger badge on Hill's belt.

"Gentleman."

"My client wants to lodge a complaint against the Loveless Sheriff Department and Case Lawton. They've been following him, harassing him, and impeding his ability to conduct his day-to-day business. As of now, my client has not been charged with any crime relating to his wife, so this treatment is biased and uncalled for." Barlow was good, smooth even.

But I could see a thin line of sweat dotting his upper lip, and he couldn't quite meet Hill's gaze.

"Your client disobeyed a protective order placed by a judge. He also took a swing at a cop. Charges are pending and steadily growing. Your client is also the prime suspect in the ongoing harassment and multiple attempts on your wife's life, Counselor."

Barlow balked and sputtered. "Excuse me?"

Hill sprawled back in the chair and reached out so he could tap his fingers on the table in front of him, appearing completely unbothered and at ease while both men across from him were squirming.

"I personally ran your financials, Mr. Barlow. I know you can't afford to take on pro bono cases at the moment, so why exactly are you representing Mr. Coleman?" I grinned. Hill went right for the throat and Barlow wasn't ready for it.

"You ran *my* financials? Why?" He reached up and tugged on his tie.

"Because you refuse to grant your wife a divorce and the husband is always a suspect when there is an attempt on the wife's life."

Barlow cleared his throat and looked at Jed out of the corner of his eye. "It isn't what you think."

Jed tried to jump to his feet, but his hands were handcuffed to the table in front of him. He attempted to kick the lawyer but couldn't reach, as Barlow jumped to his feet and scrambled away.

"Shut your mouth, you rich bastard. Don't say another goddamn word." Jed was breathing hard, eyes narrowed to slits as he swore at his attorney.

"I'd like to remind you, Mr. Barlow, that while the sheriff has enough to hold Jed, his brother is still in the wind, and more than likely not going to take kindly to his baby brother being locked up. It might be a good idea to cooperate, or I have a feeling you're going to find yourself experiencing the same threats your wife has been dealing with as of late."

"Shut up! You're fired, Barlow. I want a new lawyer!" Jed continued to lose his mind as Barlow sweated and shook under Hill's unwavering gaze.

Eventually, the man in the suit sighed and shook his head. "You don't understand. Without Aspen, my father stops paying for my house, my car, and he won't keep me on at the family firm. He's barely tolerated me since she left. I promised I would salvage my marriage, that I would bring Aspen back to the firm. I didn't have any choice."

Jed howled like a wild animal and pulled at his cuffs so violently the entire table shook. Hill continued to watch the outburst dispassionately as the suspect threatened to kill his lawyer repeatedly.

Barlow winced and dragged a hand down his face. "I spent all my money. Wasted it. I like to gamble. I like expensive women and cocaine. The bad habits started in college and got worse when I came back home and was under my father's microscope. Marrying Aspen saved my ass, and she always sees the best in everyone. My father loves her, and she's a better attorney than either of us. She brings in a ton of revenue for the firm. He agreed to bankroll our life together as long as she kept my ring on her finger." He let out a bitter-sounding laugh and dug his palms into his eyes. "I tried to knock her up so she couldn't leave, but it didn't work. I was running out of options. When she took on Mrs. Coleman's case, I saw an opening. Jed needed representation, and I needed my wife back. All I wanted was for Jed to scare Aspen into coming back home. She wasn't supposed to get hurt. No one was supposed to get shot at, and her house definitely wasn't supposed to get burned down. And Jethro wasn't supposed to be involved at all."

"No way! I didn't shoot at her, and I didn't set no fire. I trashed her office and yeah, after you told me she was going to her house, I may have followed her and tried to run her off the road, but I didn't try to kill that snotty bitch. Even if she does deserve a bullet between the eyes." Jed huffed and gave Barlow a hard look. "You're a dead man. You were supposed to get me out of jail, not get me more time."

Barlow gulped and looked at Hill with wide, pleading eyes. "This all got so out of hand. I swear, Aspen was never supposed to get hurt."

Hill lifted both his eyebrows up, and I wanted to reach through the video feed and wrap my hands around Barlow's throat.

"How did you know she was going to be at her house to meet with the adjuster? She's been in protective custody since the shooting." Hill kept his voice totally calm and cool, which is why I sent him in. I would have been breathing fire in that room.

David Barlow flushed and tugged at the hem of his jacket. He cleared his throat and looked everywhere but at the man interrogating him. "She never changed any of her e-mail passwords from when we were married. I've been checking her personal account, trying to figure out where she was so I could talk to her. I saw the e-mail exchange between her and the adjuster. She really wasn't supposed to be injured in any way, just scared."

"It takes a special kind of son of a bitch to try and scare his woman home. And she did get hurt, so that's on you." Hill flattened his hands on the table in front of him and pushed up and out of his seat. "Looks like you're going to need some legal help of your own, Counselor. I'm going to talk to the sheriff and see how he wants to proceed."

Barlow practically wilted in front of Hill. "Get me out of this room. He's not going to calm down, and I don't feel safe."

"I think you're safer in here than you are out on the streets with his brother." Hill tapped on the table and left with the parting shot, "Sign the divorce papers, Counselor. Don't you think that's the least you can do for the woman after setting all this in motion?" He exited the room, and I heard him come up behind me after a few minutes.

On the monitor, Jed was doing his best to get at Barlow while Barlow himself looked like he was on the verge of tears.

"I'm leaving them in there for a little while longer. Maybe Barlow will admit to putting a hit out on Aspen."

Hill cleared his throat. "You really think he tried to kill her? It seems to me like she's more valuable to him if she's alive."

I exhaled and took my Stetson off so I could push my hands through my hair. "I don't know, but someone tried to put a bullet between her eyes, and I can't see Jed or Jethro Coleman doing it without reason. Barlow's the only person who has a reason."

Hill made a noise and cocked his head to the side as Jed continued to howl like a wild animal. "She strikes me as a smart woman. How did she not know Barlow was acting at the end of their marriage?"

I snorted and looked over my shoulder at him. "Coming from a man who's never been married, that statement doesn't surprise me. You'd be shocked what you miss, the things you overlook when you're trying to hold your relationship together."

"With Barlow in custody and Jed Coleman on the hook, do you think you need to keep Aspen under protective custody? You don't think the older brother will still risk going after her, do you?" Hill leaned against the wall and watched me carefully.

Did I think she was still in danger? I wasn't sure. I didn't trust Jethro, and honestly, I wasn't ready for her to go. Leaning forward in the chair, I tapped a finger on the screen right over David Barlow's incredibly pale face. "I need that idiot to sign the papers, then I'm going to run everything by Aspen and see what she thinks. If she wants to leave, I'll put a unit on her until I can bring Jethro in." If she wants to go... well I would have to let her, but not before I secured a promise that she would be back.

CHAPTER 15

∞

ASPEN

David is the one who set everything that's happened to you in motion." Anger was evident in every word Case practically spit out, but he was trying to soften the blow. His eyes watched me carefully for any sign I was about to have a meltdown at the shocking revelation.

I sat in stunned silence at Case's dining table as he covered my shaking hands with one of his and told me that David had hired Jed Coleman in order to scare me back home. "Jed's behind bars, David is too, for the time being, but I have no doubt he'll bond out before the end of the night. Jethro Coleman is the one we have to worry about. It looks like he stepped in when his little brother couldn't quite get the job done, and he is dangerous. I don't think you'll be totally safe until he's locked up."

I was shocked by the burn of tears in my eyes. David and I were long past the point of there being a way to salvage our relationship, but it still hurt to know he'd been so reckless, so careless with my safety. Because of him I was effectivly homeless and the new life I'd started to rebuild was in ashes. I pulled my hands free of Case's comforting grip and put one to my chest. I thought Case hated me in the past, but it felt nothing like this. David attacking me, dismantling everything I'd worked for and built so he could have his own way. That felt like true hatred.

"I can't believe this." My voice was harsh and unsteady. I didn't even sound like myself. "Who does something like that to someone they claim to love?"

Case made a low, rough noise in his throat and reached out to grasp the back of my head. He tugged me forward and dropped his forehead down so it touched mine. I blinked against the tears, but a few of them fell anyway.

"Someone who is stupid and desperate. He had no idea once Jethro got invovled he wouldn't be able to control the damage. He unleased a monster with no idea what would happen. I honestly believe he just intended to scare you enough to send you running back into his arms, but he ended up with more than he bargined for." I appreciated Case trying to make the situation seem less awful, but someone shot at me. A stranger and Case both took a bullet meant for me beause of David's selfishness. There was no excuse for his dangerous, thoughtless actions.

I felt Case's thumb swipe across my cheek and took a deep breath to get my rampaging emotions under control. "If he doesn't sign the divorce papers after this, I'm moving forward without him. I can't have his last name anymore. I don't want to be tied to him in any way." Part of the feeling of betrayal came from knowing he used one of my client's husbands to implement his plan. David knew how hard I worked to protect the people who came to me for help, how scared and nervous most of them were. He literally used that fear against me.

Case's forehead bumped mine as he nodded slightly. "He'll sign."

I reached out and grabbed the front of Case's shirt in both my fists and fought to pull myself together. "So what happens now?"

Case misunderstood me and went on to explain that David was probablly going to flip on the Colemans and take a plea deal. He wouldn't be in jail for long. I'd already figured most of that out on my own. Being married to a criminal attorney for years gave me a basic understanding of how the criminal justice system worked. I wanted to know what happened, now that Jed was locked up, and how big a threat Jethro Coleman really was. I wanted to know if it was time to move on. Did Case really need to keep me under lock and key anymore? Did he want me to go, or would he ask me to stay? All those questions churned painfully in my heart and under my skin while I processed that David was no longer the man I married.

I pulled back so my head was no longer resting against Case's and whispered, "With David's plan shot to hell and his brother behind bars, is Jethro really that big of a threat? He has to know he's not getting anything, now that David and Jed have been caught. Maybe it's time for me to go so you can bring Hayes home. I'm sure you guys have been missing each other. You should get your life and your home back." I struggled to get the words out, but this man had gone above and beyond for me. The least I could do was give him his space back, even though I secretly hoped he wanted me to stay. I felt like I'd been wanting Case Lawton to claim me as his own for most of my life.

Case shifted his hold on me so that one of his hands could cup my cheek. His thumb traced a random pattern along my cheekbone, and I wanted to melt into a puddle at his feet. When he was sweet, it unraveled me.

"I am ready for Hayes to come home. Graduation is right around the corner and then he's moving away for school. I want as much time as I can get with him before then, but I also want you safe. I'd feel better if I could keep an eye on you until we have a lock on Jethro. He's unpredictable and very dangerous. He shot up an entire hospital just to scare you. You're safer here than you are anywhere else. I'm not going to let him get anywhere near you. He'll have to go through me first." He was watching me so carefully I really had to fight to hold back an automatic flinch at his words.

I appreciated that he wanted to keep me safe and that he wanted to keep watching out for me, but I didn't want to be a victim he felt compelled to protect. I wanted to be the woman he couldn't bear to see walk out the front door because he needed me and wanted me so much.

I let go of his shirt and sat back in the chair, spine going straight and shoulders stiffening subconciously. I cleared my throat and nervously fiddled with the ends of my hair. It was an anxious habit I thought I had left behind in law school, but this conversation had anxiety racing through my blood and was making me twitchy. It was on the tip of my tounge to ask him if he wanted me to stay because he *wanted* me, but I was scared of his anwser. What if he really only wanted me under the same roof so he could keep me safe? He seemed to see that as part of his job.

"Case, that's sweet, but really, what are you going to tell Hayes about me still being here? Am I going to go back to sleeping in the guest room? I don't know that I'm comfortable staying here with both of you when I'm not exactly sure what you and I are doing together. Are we friends with benefits? Something more than that? He's going to have questions." The same ones I was currently having to be honest.

"Hayes is almost eighteen. I think he can handle seeing his father with someone and not be traumatized. He's been on my case to date more and get out of the house. He'll probaly be thrilled I found someone to put up with me. If you leave, all I'm going to do is worry about you, Aspen."

I sighed and watched as he finally took note of my stiff body language. His dark eyebrows quirked in question, but he made no move to reach for me. "I appreciate that. But I think it's time I get back to my life. I'm not going to leave you, but I am going to leave your house. I think we need to figure out if we can make this thing between us work when we aren't in each other's pockets." I needed to know if he would still feel the same way about me when it wasn't convenient.

His eyebrows dipped low over his brillant blue eyes and a dark scowl thundered across his face. "I don't think you should go, but I won't stop you if that's what you think is best right now. I know you worked hard to get your independence back when you left David, and I'm not going to stand in the way of that. I'm not going to leave you unprotected though. You'll have to get used to having one of my guys following you around at all times until I can catch Jethro."

It was a good anwser. But not exactly the one I wanted to hear. I loved that he wasn't going to try and clip my wings and order me to stay for my own good, but it would've been nice if he'd pushed a little harder, fought a little more to get me to stay. All I needed to hear was that he wanted to keep me close because he couldn't stand the idea of us being apart, since it took us so long to finally end up together.

Biting back another sigh I leaned forward slightly so I could touch my lips to the tip of his nose. "Thank you for being so concerned about me. I promise to be careful until you find Jethro, and I'll be back to see you soon. I don't have it in me to walk away from you, Case."

He sighed and I tasted his exhaled frustration against my lips. "Good, because I'm having a hard time convincing myself doing the right thing means letting you go. As for explaining our relationship to Hayes and anyone else who asks, we're together. It's you and me, trying to figure this out, taking our time, because we both want to make sure we get it right this go-around. You're special. I'll tell anyone who asks me that."

Again, when he was sweet it was my undoing. When he said things like that it made me feel like I wouldn't be waiting in vain to hear him actually ask me to stay with him. I could wait until he told me his home, and his heart, were empty without me being around every single day.

I was leaning forward so I could give him a real kiss and tell him he was special to me too when my new phone vibrated on the kitchen table. Shifting to the side my eyes widened in surprise when I saw a text message from David's number on the screen.

"Who is it? You just went white as a ghost." Case's voice dropped to a growl and he reached for my phone, but I snatched it up before he could read the message.

"David. He must be out of jail." I felt my jaw drop when I read the short message.

I'll sign the papers. Just tell me when and where.

I clasped the phone to my chest and blinked at Case's like an owl. When I found my voice I told him, "He says he's going to sign the papers. Oh my God. I never thought this day would come. It's finally over." I couldn't help the feeling of relief that suddenly swamped me. The man who had lied to me, deceived me, tricked me, set out to hurt me, was almost out of my life for good. I couldn't wait to say my final good-bye. Once those papers were signed I could focus on Case and where we went next from here.

Before Case could say anything, I moved forward so I was practically in his lap. I kissed him with all the elation and frustation I felt bubbling under the surface. Although Case was still stuck on us not having sex until I was divorced, I was getting addicted to everything else we were doing. And not knowing when I was going to get another chance to spend the night snuggled in his bed, I met that intense blue stare with one of my own and told him, "Let's celebrate."

His wicked grin told me he was all in with that plan.

The next morning Case chuckled and shooed me out the door in front of him, smacking me on the butt on the way. I could feel his reluctance the entire time he drove me to Kody's bar, where David and I had agreed to meet. It took a miracle and all of my lawyerly persuasion skills to get Case to agree to let me have this meeting with David on my own. I needed to say good-bye to my marriage and the man I no longer loved alone. I didn't need Case to get the wrong impression if I cried or yelled. There were no regrets in leaving, but it was still hard to give up on something that had been such a huge part of my life for so long.

Case gave me one last punishing kiss before I climbed out of his pickup truck and headed to the bar. David was easy to spot as soon as I entered. His suit and tie stuck out like a sore thumb in the rustic, western interior.

I took a seat across from him and pushed the pen sitting next to the stack of papers in front of him across the table with more force than necessary. David's hand was shaking when he reached out to grab it. He was a disheveled mess. His hair was standing up at odd angles all over his head, his glasses were smudged and sitting crooked on his face, his suit was wrinkled, and he was both pale and unshaven. I hardly recognized him. Not surprising, since the man sitting across from me was now a stranger. There was no sign of the man I had married, because the David Barlow I thought I knew didn't exist.

"Sign them." I didn't offer a greeting of any kind or show any concern about his haggard state. I tapped my fingers on the table in front of me impatiently. I'd wanted to meet somewhere neutral and public. He had wanted to meet somewhere secluded and private. Looking at him, I could understand why. He was humiliated. He was also going to be disowned if the rumors going around town were accurate. Daddy Barlow had finally had enough of covering for his baby boy, and now David had officially lost everything. "I'm going to push the divorce through with or without your signature, David. Sign the paperwork, and we're done. Keep holding things up, and I'll make sure every single detail is made public. I will hang all of your dirty laundry out to dry."

"Aspen..."

His voice was shaky, and his nervous gaze darted all around the mostly empty bar.

Kody was leaning behind the bar top, pretending to do inventory while watching me and my soon-to-be ex with an eagle eye. Crew Lawton was also doing a piss-poor job of pretending to eat lunch instead of playing bodyguard while I had this one last showdown with David.

Case fought me tooth and nail on being present for this showdown. He didn't want me anywhere near David. I should've known the protective sheriff was going to send in reinforcements. Crew refused to look away from David, making my former husband squirm uncomfortably. I would be uneasy under that icy blue stare as well. Crew's resemblance to his older brother was uncanny. He also had the same commanding presence, which was impossible to ignore.

"Don't 'Aspen' me, David. You bribed my client's violent, abusive husband to come after me. You knew what he was capable of. You pretended to not know anything when my office was trashed, when you were the one behind it. You put my life, and Kody's life, at risk by blackmailing an unpredictable lunatic to run me off the road. How careless and selfish can you be? Not to mention all the risks you took yourself. Drugs, prostitutes, escorts. Do you have any idea how risky your actions have been? You're so lucky no one died. There is nothing else to say. I don't want anything to do with you, and I don't want your last name any longer. I don't know who David Barlow is anymore. He's not the man I married and he's not the man I fought so hard to have a family with." I was so close to being back to Aspen Keating, to being free of him and all the expectations that came with the last name Barlow. I slapped the table with my palm, making the table shake. "Sign them!"

David jumped and let out a tiny squeak that had our audience chuckling. He blushed a bright red and eventually scrawled his name across the places on the stack of papers marked with an *X*. When he lowered the pen and pushed the stack back in my direction, his lower lip was trembling. I swore if he started crying after everything he'd put me through I was going to jump across the table and claw his stupid eyes out. I was the one who got to choke back tears and be sad about the end of things. Not him. He had orchestrated this entire mess.

"When we first met I really thought I could do better, that I could be the Barlow my father always wanted me to be. You made me want to be a better man. I told myself I could be worthy of you, that we could have the perfect family." He pulled his glasses off and rubbed the bridge of his nose. "I know people always said you married up, but I always knew

I was the one punching above my weight class. You were always too good for me, Aspen."

Collecting the papers and sliding out of the booth I glared down at him. "I'm still too good for you. I'll see you in court, David." I fully intended to testify against Jed Coleman. Unsurprisingly, David had indeed made a deal to also testify against him, as well as his brother, which meant, as expected, he would never serve a minute in jail. Both Case and Hill believed the older Coleman was behind both the shooting and the fire. His motive was still in question, but Case seemed to believe Jethro wanted me out of the way so Jed's wife wouldn't have an advocate and they could coerce her into dropping the charges against her abusive husband. Case believed the Colemans thought I was the only thing standing in the way of things going back to the way they'd always been, and Jethro was just doing his brotherly duty by getting me out of the way.

I wasn't so sure I agreed with that assessment. The state was going to press charges for assault and battery againt Jed regardless of whether Kayla Coleman testified against her husband or not. That was inevitable when the law got involved in domestic cases, and I'm not sure my being her lawyer was enough incentive to kill me. But, lacking any other reasonable explanation, everyone warned that Jethro Coleman was still a threat, so I still needed to be extra cautious.

Cowboy boots clipped on the worn wood floor and I looked up into familiar blue eyes as Crew approached the table. He nodded at the papers and I flashed him a thumbs-up. I cleared my throat and tossed my hair over my shoulder. "Good to go."

He winked, his eyes twinkling playfully. He was probably the most easygoing of the Lawton siblings, but I would never make the mistake of underestimating any of them.

Charm could be deadly, and Crew had more than his fair share of it.

"That'll make big brother happy." He narrowed those intense eyes in the direction where David was still cowering in the booth. "If anything happened to my sister because of your dumbass, whatever the Colemans might have planned for you would be a picnic compared to me and Case."

David audibly gulped and shrank back as far in the corner as the space would allow. I didn't blame him. I wouldn't want to be the object of any of the Lawtons' ire either. A pissed-off cowboy was one thing. A pissed-off cowboy with the last name Lawton was another.

After leaving David with his head down, sitting alone and dejected at the table, I followed Crew toward the front doors. He tilted his head toward the bar, where Kody was actually serving customers now. I didn't want to interupt her to tell her good-bye so I simply waved and silently followed her brother. "She gave me a key to her place and told me to drop you off. Are you sure there isn't anything you need to get from Case's before we roll?" My Audi was still at the body shop. Since it wasn't parked in the garage during the fire, it had escaped the damage that destroyed the house, but the exterior had taken a beating and all the tires needed to be replaced.

I still couldn't believe Kody offered her place up for me to crash until I found a rental. I'd brought a lot of chaos into the Lawtons' collective lives. I wondered if they would ever stop surprising me.

"No. I've got what I need." And I didn't want to completely remove myself from Case's home. I felt like if I left a little bit of myself behind, I wasn't really leaving for good.

"Let's head out then." He turned and called good-bye to his sister, who shouted good-bye to us both without turning around from the tap behind the bar where she was pouring a beer.

I clutched the paperwork to my chest like it was the most precious thing in the world—because it kind of was. I'd been waiting for so long for that signature. It felt like I finally had a chance to start over, to get things right.

Crew wrapped a hand around my elbow and helped me walk slowly toward the door. I had a splint on my ankle and no longer needed the crutch if I moved slowly and carefully. We'd only taken a few steps when the door swung open, and the last Lawton stepped through it.

Crew laughed full and loud next to me, fingers giving my arm a reassuring squeeze. "Wondered how long it was going to take him to show."

Case stalked in my direction, eyes locked on the papers in my hand. He pushed the brim of his hat back and growled, "He sign them?"

Slightly stunned I nodded. "He did."

"So you aren't married to him anymore?" The questions were short and sharp.

I cocked my head in confusion. "Well, a judge has to sign off on it, and the paperwork needs to be filed with the court, but no, not married anymore..."

It was on the tip of my tongue to ask him why he wasn't at work in the middle of the day, but a moment later he bent and sealed his mouth over mine in front of his family, my ex-husband, and the customers lining the bar. He might as well have branded his name across my forehead, it was such a public display of claim. I was getting very good at not knocking his hat off his head when he kissed me, but this time when it fell to the ground neither of us cared.

When Case broke away to breathe, I blinked at him like an owl. He rubbed his thumb across my swollen, damp lower lip and growled, "Mine." He dropped another biting kiss on my slack mouth, and a second later I felt the edge of his shoulder dig into my stomach as he swooped me up in a firefighter's carry over his shoulder. I scrambled to hold on to the papers against his broad back as he turned and headed for the door. I lifted my head in time to see Kody laughing behind the bar and Crew shaking his head. David looked like he wanted to say something from his seat but stayed silent with one warning look from the younger Lawton brother.

I should've been outraged, after all, I wasn't property to be hauled around. But it was kind of remarkable to have Case openly declaring our never-ending war had ended, and we were now on the same side, fighting the same battle. No one could question that Case Lawton literally swept me off my feet.

"You could have asked me to come with you, you know? I would have gone willingly." I was pretty much ready to follow him wherever he wanted to lead. "People are going to talk." It wasn't every day the sheriff carried someone out of his sister's bar over his shoulder with the intent of taking them to bed rather than to jail.

Case dropped a wide palm on my ass, and I felt his shoulders shake underneath me as he laughed. "If it were possible to die from an overdose of foreplay, we'd both be in the ground. The papers are signed. The house is empty until my kid comes home tomorrow. It feels like the stars aligned, and I'm not one to let an opportunity slip by." He used the hand on my backside to give it a little love tap before he set me down on my feet next to his huge, black pickup truck. He looked so good in his lightweight, gray Henley and a pair of faded jeans.

Case took my face between his large hands and placed the sweetest kiss imaginable on the tip of my nose. "Will you come home with me, Aspen? Please?"

Like there was any question. "Of course I will." I grinned up at him and gave a little shrug. "Though I'm not sure I can wait that long. I've never been so sexually frustrated in my life."

I got another kiss. This one quick and hard on the lips as he opened the door to the truck and helped me climb inside. The thing was lifted so high, I would've needed a damn step stool to get inside of it if Case hadn't been there to give me a boost. I guess everything really was bigger in Texas.

Snickering at the thought, I turned when Case climbed up into the cab next to me. He took his hat off and tossed it on the dash. He used a hand to push his dark hair back, and I was overwhelmed with the urge to sink my teeth into his razor-sharp jawline. Throwing next to his hat the paperwork that signaled I was free to do what, and whomever, I wanted, I slid closer and dragged my nose along the outside of his ear and gave in to the urge to nip at the curve of his jawbone.

"This is like all my high school fantasies coming true. Making out with a hot cowboy in the front seat of his truck." I ran my fingers down the strong column of his neck and rubbed my thumb over his Adam's apple. "Teenaged me would be dying right now. Adult me is impatient as hell."

Case swore and shifted in the seat, making the leather creak. He turned his head slightly so our mouths could align. Eye to eye, his gaze was serious, and his voice was sure when he replied, "If I could be here with anyone in the world, I would still choose you. You might've spent a lot of time alone when we were kids, but I've been on my own since my marriage ended. Maybe we just needed the timing to be right so we could finally be alone together. But there is no reason for either of us to ever be lonely again."

We stared at each other for a moment, a lot unspoken in the heated look we shared. Eventually, we'd have to put words to everything we were feeling, but not right now.

Quirking my eyebrow, I let my hand fall to his lap, where the softly worn denim lovingly clung to his muscular thighs and the heavy weight pressing between them. He sucked in a breath as I palmed his growing erection through the fabric. His eyes narrowed as he reached out to wrap a hand around the back of my neck so he could pull me closer. I went willingly and whispered against his mouth, "I lied. I don't think I can go home with you. I'm not going to make it. I want you, want you inside of me, so bad I can taste it." Having him in my mouth and hands was no longer enough. I wanted him inside of me, filling me up, claiming me.

Case gave a little growl and set about devouring my mouth in a kiss that was going to leave my lips bruised and swollen. I grabbed ahold of his shoulder and maneuvered myself so I was straddling his lap. One nice thing about being on the small side was that I fit in the space between him and the steering wheel with plenty of room to move. I wrapped my arms around his neck and kissed him back with just as much ferocity.

Teeth clashed. Tongues tangled. Breathing became a nuisance as hands started to find their way under clothes. The windows started to fog up, but I couldn't care less, because Case's hands were on the back of my thighs, moving under the fabric of the loose, black shorts I'd put on today. I sucked on the tip of his tongue and shoved my hands through his soft hair. When we eventually broke free so we didn't suffocate, we were both panting and flushed. His dark eyebrows arched almost to his hairline as I untangled a hand so I could wrestle with his ever-present mammoth-size belt buckle.

"We're gonna get arrested for indecent exposure." He said it jokingly, but the humor in his tone fled when I finally had his pants open and a hand wrapped around his straining cock.

The flared head was already filled with color and the heavy vein running underneath was plump under my fingertips.

"Doesn't matter. I'm pretty close with the sheriff." I kissed the side of his neck, using my teeth to nibble my way down to his collarbone. I had nuzzled my way past soft cotton to get at skin, but I liked it. It was like going on a treasure hunt for all the places on his big body that I knew would make him lose his mind. "I also know a good lawyer."

"Aspen..." I liked the way he said my name, but I needed him distracted beyond the point of saying anything.

I tightened my hand around his thickening flesh. I wasn't one who threw caution to the wind on a regular basis, well I hadn't been. But maybe that was all part of figuring out who I was supposed to be, now that I was no longer living my life through a filter of what everyone else thought.

I wiggled off his lap until I stretched out on my belly along the long bench seat. Thank goodness he had his personal vehicle. This never would've worked in his SUV. Plus the likelihood of me convincing him to fuck me before we got to his house would have dropped dramatically in a city-issued car.

Before he could gather his wits to protest, I swiped my tongue across the wide head of his cock. The slightly bitter taste of pre-cum hit my tastebuds as I pulled the swollen head of his erection into my mouth. I felt Case's body arch up from the seat. One of his hands landed on the back of my head as I bobbed down, the other went to the small of my back, sliding down my spine and into the waistband of my shorts. I felt his fingers on the curve of my ass and heard him gasp my name in an entirely different tone when I sucked hard enough to hollow my cheeks out. I used my hand to squeeze the base of his erection. Urging him without words to lift up so I could get more of him in my mouth and my hands between his legs.

If he was going to argue about propriety and decency, the words died a pretty quick death when his jeans ended up around his knees, and his balls ended up in my hands. He was warm everywhere, and I could feel tension making all of his muscles vibrate. I appreciated the restraint, but I needed him to let loose. I needed him to feel as out of control and reckless as I felt. Maybe it wasn't fair. I'd wanted him for a lot longer than he'd wanted me, but anticipation was killing me. I had to know if we would be as good together as I'd always imagined.

When I used my teeth, just slightly, he swore, and his fingers dug painfully into the curve of my ass. A moment later I felt them glide through the valley between my cheeks, a feather caress that didn't stop until it reached the wetness gathering between my legs.

I gasped around the rigid length in my mouth. I moved too fast in surprise when I felt his fingers start to slowly, softly part my wet folds so he could stroke the hungry entrance to my body. A throb of pleasure made my inner muscles clench, and I wanted to know what it would feel like to have all those fluttering, quivering places he was touching moving against his heavy, hard shaft.

I continued to work Case over with my mouth until he growled my name and started tugging on my hair in warning. He was almost down my throat, I was practically humping his fingers, my nipples were so hard they hurt, and we were both finally so far gone we could have been in the middle of a church service on Sunday, and there would be no stopping what was coming next.

I pulled my mouth off of his straining erection with a wet pop. I scrambled to shove my shorts and underwear down my legs as he stripped my plain, black T-shirt over my head. I gasped when he lifted me up like I weighed nothing and put me back in his lap, only this time when I lowered myself down, it was so I could take his entire, throbbing, heated length inside of me.

The initial contact forced my eyes closed and had him swearing up a storm. They popped back open when I felt his lips land on my cheek, and his hands on my waist pulling me closer. I dropped my forehead to his shoulder, realizing he was still mostly clothed while I was exposed. That shouldn't have been a turn-on, but it was. Seemed like the new me liked a little bit of risk. Which was a good thing, since every inch of Case that was pushing its way inside of me was as raw and as naked as the want shining out of his blue eyes

"Is this okay?" The rough question growled after the fact was almost endearing. It was kind of a pat to my ego to know he wanted me so much that I scrambled all his normal responsible instincts.

"I'm clean," he continued. "I told you, I've been alone a long time, and we just had our yearly physical for the department a few months ago. I'm Mr. Clean."

I let out a surprised giggle.

We hadn't talked about what was going to happen when we moved to the next phase of our budding relationship. It seemed like with everything else we did, it was all or nothing.

We either loved or hated.

We were either in or out.

There was no middle ground.

"It's more than okay. I told you already that I got a clean bill of health when I left David last year. I feel like I've been waiting a lifetime to have you inside me. I love that having all of you, that I can feel everything."

Right now he was all the way inside of me and I was feeling extremely loved. We shared a tender kiss, and I whimpered a little when he used his hold on my waist to lift me up and guide me back down. It didn't take long to find a rhythm that worked, given the confines of the front seat and the impatience that had been hounding us.

I rocked against him frantically, hands sliding under his shirt to rest on his chest, which was now slippery with sweat. One of his hands palmed my breast and I moaned into his mouth when he used his thumb to rub my nipple into an aching point under the silky fabric of my bra. He felt huge inside of me, and every single time I lowered myself down, so he was fully seated, I stopped breathing for a second because I felt completely consumed by him. There was no room for the past when Case was taking up every available centimeter of the room inside of me.

"Give me your hand." He grumbled the order into the side of my neck where I could feel his teeth leaving a mark. I unlocked shaking fingers from his hair and put my hand in his.

Watching me without blinking, he dragged my palm over my skin. Guiding over my chest, down across my belly, until it finally reached the place between my legs where we were joined. I opened my mouth in mute surprise when he put his fingers over mine and slowly started to manipulate my clit. I felt how wet I was, could feel the heat coming from our connection. It was such an erotic sensation to feel his hardness moving through all my softness.

I threw my head back and moaned his name. He shifted so he could use his teeth on my still-covered nipple. My clit was tight and so sensitive under our combined touch. All of it was too much at once, and I shattered

I yelped a shocked sound as my body locked down on Case's. I felt my release rush around his still thrusting cock, but the drag and pull of competition he wrung from my body must've triggered his own, because a heartbeat later he stiffened underneath me and a new wave of warm, wet pleasure flowed between us. Case dropped his forehead to the center of my chest and moaned.

His fingers were still locked with mine between my legs, and every touch sent lights exploding behind my eyelids. I rested my cheek on the top of his bent head and struggled to catch my breath. I pushed my fingers through the short hair at the base of his skull and muttered, "Totally worth going to jail for."

It was also totally worth waiting for. Case was right.

CHAPTER 16

CASE

My body was tired, happily worn out and sore in all the right places, but my mind was wide awake and running at a thousand miles a minute.

After the unexpected interlude in the parking lot behind my sister's bar, I took Aspen home and barely made it through the front door before I was all over her again. It was a rush to make up for lost time, and luckily she seemed just as desperate for the contact as I was. We took a short break to refuel before moving to my bedroom. After a shower that ended up doing more to get us dirty than clean, we fell into bed exhausted and blissed out. Aspen fell asleep almost instantly, her face serene and pretty as her eyes fluttered in time to whatever she was dreaming. Her parted lips were cherry red and swollen from too many kisses, and the elegant line of her neck was marred with tiny bruises left behind from my teeth. She looked thoroughly debauched and perfectly edible. I wanted to be greeted with the same sight every time I opened my eyes.

Reaching out a finger, I gently pushed a stray piece of ebony hair away from her face. The ends caught on her lip and brushed over the tip of her nose, making it twitch and causing one of her dark eyes to pry open. She watched me sleepily as I used my index finger to trace the high arch of her midnight-colored eyebrow.

"I was jealous of you when we were younger." The admission felt like a dirty secret I'd been holding on to for a very long time.

Aspen's other eye popped open, and she shifted so one of her hands was settled on the center of my chest.

"How is that possible? I was a mess back then. I spent so much time trying to be the opposite of everything my mother wanted me to be, I could barely figure out who I really was. And I had no friends. You were the only one who made an effort to be nice to me."

I shook my head a little and pulled my fingertip down the delicate line of her nose. "I knew who you were, even if you didn't. You were the girl who dressed how you wanted. The one who believed in something tangible and real, when everyone else was only concerend with status and being popular. You were the only person in our entire school who knew what it was like to live somewhere other than Texas, so your worldview was bigger and more interesting than anyone else's. From the minute I was born everyone in Loveless knew my name. By the time I took my first steps everyone already had an idea who I was supposed to be. Other than you, I didn't meet a stranger until I joined the military. My world was so small, and yours seemed so big. Even coming home after deployment, I was jealous. I hadn't seen you in years but I heard all about you coming home and getting married. How you were this ugly ducklig turned swan...not that you were ever ugly...but you get the point I'm trying to make." I sighed and looked at her out of the corner of my eye. "I had to come back here. I didn't have a choice. You decided to come back. When you could have gone anywhere, lived a bigger life somewhere else. I was envious of your options. I think that may have been part of the reason it was so easy to hold on to a grudge for so long. All the things I'd wanted in my life that I lost my shot at, I felt like you had and tossed away."

She hummed a little sound that could have been one of sympathy or distress. I rubbed my thumb along the pillowy curve of her lower lip and let myself drown in the darkness of her eyes.

"I didn't want to stand out in a bad way when we moved here. In Chicago I was one of many, and no one needed another friend like me to fill the void. When I got here, no one knew what to make of me, so I was always left on the outside looking in. I felt like I was always searching for the place where I belonged. The first time you asked me if I wanted to come to a football game was the first time I'd ever been included. It made me feel special. You made me feel like I mattered, like I had a place here." The long, tapered fingers resting on my chest tapped a rhythm matching my heartbeat. "I came back, not because I found a place I could fit in, but because I found a place I wanted to help make better for other kids like me...and like you." Her eyes shifted to black velvet. "No one should have to live up to the kind of corrupt legacy you did. There should be an even playing field, so all of us can just be who we are and be accepted for the things that set us apart. I came back to fight for the underdogs."

I gave her a lopsided grin and curled my fingers around the side of her neck so I could tug her close enough to kiss. "My ego was hoping you were going to say you came back because of me." I was only kind of kidding.

A soft puff of laughter hit my lips, and I felt the impact of it right in the center of my chest. I was soft for this woman. Somehow, when I wasn't looking, she'd reached inside of me and locked her hands around my heart.

"Maybe there was a very small part of me that wanted to come back and see if you ever found your way out from under the cloud of being Conrad Lawton's son. You know I always had a crush on you in high school. I thought you were so impressive, and maybe there was a touch of hero worship at play, but then you went to work for your father." She sighed, and the edge of her nails dug painfully into my skin. "I was disappointed. But not in the same way the rest of the town was. I thought you deserved more."

I made a noise low in my throat and pulled her even closer. I skimmed a palm down her silky thigh, lifting it until it was resting along the outside of mine. The new position had my newly awakened cock brushing lightly against her soft, tender opening. I wasn't a kid anymore, but my body missed the memo and started to respond to her welcome heat again. Her foot rubbed against the back of my calf as she shifted closer.

"I had an agenda." The admission was rough. Keeping track of the conversation grew more difficult when she kissed my collarbone and dragged her hand down my chest toward my stomach. My abs contracted under the caress and my cock thickened and lengthened even more. The tip nudged against her velvety entrance, toying with tender skin and playfully bumping against the tight bud of her clit. Aspen gasped, and I dropped a kiss on her head. "I wanted to make Loveless a better, more equal place as well. I had a lot of idealistic dreams, but then everything in my personal life turned into a nightmare, and I was busy trying to save myself. I forgot I promised to save everyone else."

I felt her fingertip dip into my belly button and then dive lower, tracing the line of hair that narrowed down to my now eager and very ready cock. I sucked in a breath when she fisted the wide base and squeezed. The pressure had my eyes threatening to roll back in my head. I liked the way she handled me—fearless and unafraid. There was never any question she wanted me as much as I wanted her.

Her tongue flicked at the pulse hammering at the base of my throat, and her forehead brushed against the side of my neck when she nodded. "And look at you now. You are making it better. You pushed your dad out. You took over as sheriff, and you actually did something for this town. Even if it took a little longer than you planned. I wanted to do that but got caught up in perpetuating the image of a perfect marriage. When I was finally accepted, even though it was only for show, it felt so good, I also forgot I was supposed to be working toward doing good. I feel like we both found the path we need to get on in order to be get us to who we were always meant to be. And it's kind of an awesome bonus we get to walk the last few steps together."

She hitched her leg higher on my waist and pressed even closer. My breath caught when she used the hold she had on my cock to guide the head of my erection through the satiny, wet slit between her legs. Every time the flared head of my cock bumped against her clit, her eyes widened and her breathing quicked. It was a delicious tease, soft and mellow, since we were both sexed-out and languid from a day spent devouring one another.

I let my hand trace along her ribs, climbing until I could palm her breast. I hummed in satisfaction when I felt her nipple dig happily into the center of my palm. She was such a perfect handful—like she was made just for me.

Her arms wrapped around my side and shifted just enough

to lodge the first few inches of my cock inside of her. Her inner walls fluttered around me, like an internal kiss. I nudged her head back so I could reach her mouth, lips barely touching as my tongue moved on her lips. The kiss turned from a leisurely, slow seduction of her mouth to something far more aggressive when I used my weight to roll her onto her back so I could settle more fully against her. I mimicked the rhythm I started following between her legs in her mouth. In and out at an unhurried pace, drawing the sensation from overstimulated senses slowly and deliberately. Her legs wrapped around my waist, ankles digging into my ass as I started to thrust. I loved the way her body enveloped mine with zero hesitation. It was the sweetest feeling on earth.

Her fingers drifted through my hair. Her eyes slid closed, and we moved together like we'd been doing this dance in the dark for ages. It never even occurred to me that there should be any kind of barrier between us. My entire relationship with Aspen was about knocking down walls and finally allowing myself to be naked, without any mask or facade to hide behind. She was the only person who saw me for who I really was. I wanted her to have all of me, and I wanted to be able to have all of her, whatever may come.

I braced one arm above her head, hand fisting in her long hair as we rocked together, the pace increasing along with our breathing and heartbeats. I rolled her nipple between my fingers making her arch up into me. I grunted in surprise when her fingernails scored a line of fire down either side of my spine. I was going to have marks on my skin tomorrow, and I couldn't wait to see them. I kept our mouths sealed together, tasting her moans over and over again as we slowly, leisurely climbed toward the crest of pleasure.

I felt my orgasm start to coil and wind tight around the base of my spine. My hips kicked in reaction, moving more intently, pounding harder to chase after the all-consuming feeling leaving no part of my body untouched. I released my hold on Aspen's pert breast and moved my hand to the curve of her ass, tilting her hips higher, aiming for that spot inside of her that would break her apart. My rhythm faltered as my orgasm broke me apart. My forehead fell to rest against hers, causing our noses to brush together as her body unraveled much more languidly and lazily around mine.

Her sigh was a whisper of sound against my mouth as I wrapped my arms around her and flipped us, so she was sprawled across my chest. We smelled like sex and each other, the darkness of the evening wrapping us up in a private, cozy veil. I wasn't ready to let her go.

Aspen nuzzled her nose in the hollow of my neck, keeping her face hidden as our bodies slowly slipped apart. She hissed a satisfied sound and tightened her arms around me. All of her responses and reactions were so honest and real. It was so refreshing to be with someone I could trust.

I sighed and held her close. "Being with you means so much to me." Because it was so unpredictable what the future held. She almost took a bullet, and I never knew what kind of dangerous situation could go south on me on any given day.

She kissed my shoulder again, and I could tell she was getting sleepy.

As I held her, I thought about how she had changed me since the very beginning. I was drawn to her because she was so very different from everything I'd ever known. She was new and exciting, smarter than anyone I'd ever met. Now, I was pulled in by her strength, her resilance, her loyalty. She was always special, and I found myself trying to improve because she deserved someone as special as she was.

I was good at my job, gave my all to it every single day. I really considered it a calling, which was why I'd always had so many issues with how my father ran his office. But I'd always been emotionally removed from my duty and the badge. It took having someone I cared deeply about being smack dab in the center of one of my cases to make me realize what I did was always going to be so much more than an occupation. I was starting to see how being personally invested in the lives and well-being of the people I protected might make me a better sheriff and a better man. Regardless if so many of those people wanted to see me fail. Having Aspen believe in me, knowing she held on to that secret all those years, was a game changer. Her faith in me lit a fire inside of me that had been snuffed out a long time ago.

Pulling her close, I heard her whimper something incoherent in her sleep. Kissing the top of her head I told the darkness, "I'm going to ask you to stay." I was. There was no time for fear or doubts—hers or mine. I didn't need to be apart to figure out this was real. I wanted to start our lives together as soon as possible.

I just had to be as brave as she was.

CHAPTER 17

∞

ASPEN

You're going to be careful today. Jethro Coleman is still out there, and we still don't know what his agenda is." Case's tone was deadly serious, and the expression on his face was stern and unforgiving. He had his hand braced above my head on the wall behind me and was looming over me in such a way that was equally sexy and threatening.

I had to lift up on my tiptoes so I could pat his bristly cheek with my palm. "I'm just going to the office for a few hours." A cleaning crew had tackled most of the damage, and the front window had finally been replaced. It was time to get back in business. I had people relying on me for a paycheck, and others relying on me to help them out of a bad situation. I couldn't ignore what I was meant to be doing any longer. Not even for Case. "You have one of your deputies patrolling Main Street, and I'll make sure to keep the doors locked, and the blinds closed the whole time I'm there. You're dropping me off and picking me up later on tonight. It'll be fine."

"Unless it's not." His annoyed growl was actually adorable.

I lifted up so I could press a kiss against his frown. "I can't live my life afraid of my own shadow." Not if we were going to figure out how to make a relationship work. There would always be an element of danger in our lives, considering his job and, on occasion, mine. It was better we faced the ramifications of those dangers head on rather than pretend like they weren't always going to be there. "I'll be careful and take the necessary precautions. Don't worry about me, instead focus on the fact you get Hayes back home tonight." Case asked me to come and have dinner with the both of them tonight, but I'd declined much to his annoyance. I gently reminded Case that his son hadn't been home in over a week and probably wasn't ready to share Case's attention just yet. Though I greatly appreciated his desire to include me. It warmed me all the way down to my soul, the same way it had when we were younger.

Case dipped his chin down and deepened the playful kiss I placed on his mouth. It was a nice way to face the day, even if I could feel his anger—and a hint of fear—in the possessive way his mouth moved over mine. When he pulled back, he said, "Gonna worry about you and not just because it's my job, but because you matter to me. I can't stand the thought of anything else bad happening to you."

God, how long had I been waiting to hear that? It felt like forever. I threw my arms around his neck and planted another, wet, noisy kiss on his fiercely frowning mouth. "And I'm going to worry about you, but we can't let fear change who we are, or what we're meant to do." His bravery and his fearlessness were just a few of the reasons I'd always looked up to him.

Case narrowed his eyes at me but grunted a reluctant agreement and let me pull him out the front door. I patted his cheek and followed him out to his SUV. The ride to my office was a fairly somber affair. Case was tense, and I was distracted, but I could barely contain my excitement when I saw the outside of my office building looking like it had before the damage. It was almost like a sign I finally had a little slice of my life back under my control.

Case caught the hand not clutching my new briefcase and gave it a squeeze. I could see it stamped all over his face he wanted to walk me inside the building and stay with me until the sun went down, but to his credit, he simply dropped a tiny kiss on the back of my hand and grumbled, "Have a good first day back."

If I hadn't been halfway in love with him already, the sweet sentiment from such a hard man would have shoved me over the tipping point. I flashed him a wink and hopped out of the SUV with more confidence than I actually felt. Being on the street in the middle of the day, even in a small town, knowing there was potentially someone out there who wanted to hurt me, was unsettling. I rushed to the front door, fumbling with my keys in the new lock. Once I was inside, I made sure the door was secure and waved to Case as he drove away, knowing he wasn't going anywhere until he was sure I was locked inside.

The entire office smelled like industrial air freshener with an underlying hint of pine, but none of the red paint or ugly slurs were left on the carpet or walls. Every surface gleamed, making the place look brand-new. I wasn't ready for my secretary and paralegal to come back full-time just yet. I needed to get my ongoing cases in order and my schedule up-to-date before I jumped back into the deep end with both feet. I'd lost a couple of clients due to my sudden disappearance, and I couldn't blame them for finding new representation. But I didn't want my caseload to thin out any more than it had. The last thing I wanted was to appear unreliable. Not after working so hard to rebuild my reputation after leaving the protection of the Barlows' established firm.

I had no idea how many hours passed as I plowed through file after file. My eyes crossed as I changed meeting dates and filed for changes in court hearings. It was all monotonous and tedious work, but I found the rhythm calming and reassuring. It was lovely to be back in my element and walking on familiar ground.

My stomach rumbled a couple hours later, and I realized most of the day had slipped by. Standing, I lifted my arms over my head and stretched. My spine popped all the way down, and the base of my neck ached. I lifted a hand to rub at the tight spot, nearly jumping out of my skin when there was a sudden pounding on the glass door at the front of my office space. Glancing at my phone, I didn't see any missed calls, so I knew it wasn't Case checking up on me, and it wasn't my staff being overly eager. Cautiously I crept to the window next to my desk and used a finger to part the wooden slats of the blinds so I could peek outside, expecting to see either the husband or wife who ran the coffee shop across the street checking up on me. My jaw nearly hit the floor when I caught a glimpse of the familiar figure using her fist to bang noisily on my door.

"Holy hell." I breathed out the shocked exclamation and hurried around my desk. I rushed out into the reception area so I could pull the door open before my mother broke it down.

Yes, my *mother*.

I jerked the heavy door open with one hand and reached out to catch my mother's flailing arm with the other. I pulled her into my office and shut the door with a bang behind her.

"Mom. What on earth are you doing back in Loveless?" She hadn't stepped foot in this town since she and my father left right after I moved away for college. Dad went from representing a Texas fracking company to being lead counsel for a Florida *Fortune* 500 CEO who ripped off his employees' retirement funds. It really was no wonder the man had suffered a massive heart attack in his fifties. The stress of ruining the environment and lives had caught up with him.

My mom wasn't dressed for Texas weather. She had on too many layers, all of them dark and heavy. Her hair was already rebelling against the dry weather, and her normally flawless makeup was starting to melt and run. Her bag was designer and landed with a thud on the floor when she stomped into the room. She still looked more like she should be shopping on Fifth Avenue than standing in my office on Main Street. Sourly I wondered how much of her obviously expensive outfit I'd paid for.

"My daughter's home burned to the ground. Someone took a shot at her when she was leaving the hospital. One of her client's husbands tried to run her off the road, and on top of all of that, you're a divorcee. You've been impossible to talk to lately and totally unreasonable. I can't believe you refused to loan me money the last time we spoke. Where else would I be, Aspen? I had to come see for myself what was going on with you." She wrinkled her nose at me and lifted her hand to block the smell. "It smells awful in here."

"The office was vandalized." I sighed and lifted my hands to my head, so I could tug on my hair. "Wait..." I narrowed my eyes at her. "How did you know the divorce was finally a done deal?" I cocked my head to the side. "And how did you know I was here in the office?" The only person who knew I was going back to work today was Case.

My mother sniffed again and narrowed her eyes at me. "David called me and told me you strong-armed him into signing the paperwork finally. He was quite distraught. He also told me you've seemed to have moved on. Really, Aspen? Going from a Barlow to a Lawton? What on earth would possess you to downgrade like that?" She looked around the reception area with disdain. "Aren't you going to offer me a cup of coffee or something? Have you forgotten all your manners already?" She huffed out an annoyed breath that made me grit my teeth.

I bristled and turned my back on the woman who birthed me but did very little to raise me. She'd always treated me as more of a nuisance than as a child unless she needed money. I busied myself at the new Keurig so I didn't say something I'd regret.

"I can't believe David had the nerve to call you." What a worm.

"I'm glad someone did. It's not like you've bothered to keep me updated on your disaster of a life as of late." The judgment in her tone was thick enough to cut with a knife.

Sighing I turned and handed her the coffee. "I didn't realize you were interested in what was going on in my life. Every time we talk it's all about what you need, and you telling me what you think I'm doing wrong. I tried to explain for the last year that David and I were done, but you refused to believe it." Or support me. I gritted my teeth in frustration. "I'm better off without David in my life, and Case is a wonderful man. He's gone above and beyond for me. He literally took a bullet for me. I don't know where things are going with us, but I'm happier with him than I ever was with David." And that was even with all the chaos controlling my life at the moment. "You should've let me know you were coming. I'm sort of homeless at the moment. I'm not sure how long you plan on staying, but I don't have the proper accommodations to put you up right now."

"I'm not staying for long." She made a face as she sipped the coffee I handed her. I couldn't tell if the distaste was over the drink or the thought of staying in Loveless any longer than necessary. "I'm only here to check on things." I arched an eyebrow and reflexively crossed my arms over my chest. I wondered if by "things" she meant me... her child. "And I didn't let you know I was coming, because you would have tried to talk me out of it." After making another face, she motioned for me to come and take the cup of obviously inferior brew away from her.

"Things have been up in the air since the shooting and after the fire. I've barely had time to breathe. It's not that I don't want to see you, there's just a lot going on right now, and the timing isn't the best. If you wanted to visit, we could've found a better time." I wasn't sure how she made all the terrible things I'd endured lately about her, but here we were. "I honestly didn't know you were worried. You never said anything to me about being concerned how I was doing." Motherly concern was not in her wheelhouse, but she'd made it clear she was horrified by my marriage ending.

My mother sighed heavily and dramatically. "Really, Aspen, have you given any thought to what happens next? You're not exactly young anymore, and you have... limitations. Have you completely given up on the idea of having a family of your own? Doesn't that make you feel like a failure?" My mother lifted her eyebrows, and I felt the implications all the way down to my bones.

I fought back a wince and forced myself to keep my voice calm. "No, Mom. I am not a failure in any way. There are so many different ways to build a family."

I was wondering if she really visited just so she could make me feel like garbage? What a waste, but not entirely unsurprising. She always went the extra mile to let me know I was a disappointment. My fingers flexed around the warm mug in my hand. The urge to toss it in her face was strong, but I refrained. "Let me finish up what I was working on and then we'll figure out where you're staying, and we can discuss why you're really here." She wanted money, as always. But I was done being her personal ATM machine. She was never going to be the mother I wanted, and it was time I stopped trying to buy her love and approval. My stomach growled again. "Maybe we can get something to eat. I'm starving." Turning, I faltered midstep and asked again, "Mom? You never said how you knew I was at my office. I've been keeping a pretty low profile with everything going on. I haven't been out and about much."

"Just a good guess. Your house is gone, where else would you be during the middle of the day?" She gave me a pointed look, which I found completely unnerving. Her appearance already had me off-center and out of sorts, but something about this visit felt off.

"Did David tell you about my client's husband trying to run me off the road?" I paused midstep and turned to look at her.

My mother shrugged, not meeting my gaze as she moved toward her abandoned bag. "He must've. How else would I know about it?"

"That's weird. He was the one who made a deal with the man who tried to run me down. David's a criminal attorney." A bad one, but still he knew the law and how it worked. "Why would he be discussing the attack with you? He shouldn't be admitting to anything."

My mother blinked at me slowly and a lead brick settled

in my stomach. I lifted a hand to my mouth, trying to cover a gasp as a horrible realization blindsided me. "Did you tell him the only way to get me back was to try and scare me? Was this all your idea?"

"Aspen..."

I held a hand out in front of me. "No. Tell me you didn't do this. You didn't try and manipulate me into getting back with David because you were worried about money." A dry, brittle laugh escaped. "He doesn't have any. Did you know that? When we realized we weren't going to have a baby the traditional way, he decided it was okay to spend it all on hookers and drugs. Not to mention what he lost gambling. He's broke. In the end, he was a terrible husband."

My mother shook her head and pulled her purse to her chest. "I know he had no money. I'm not stupid."

"Then what's going on, Mom? Why are you really here? What do you want?" I backed up a step, watching her warily. A shiver was sliding up and down my spine. I wished I hadn't left my cell phone on my desk in the other room. I wanted to call Case. It was never comfortable being alone in a room with my mother, but this was the first time I felt unsafe.

She sighed again, eyes cold as winter as she assessed me. "You know things have been difficult for me financially since your father passed away."

I jolted a little at the admission. "Because you married an idiot and you let him handle your finances. You shouldn't have let your new husband blow through everything Dad left you." I was done playing nice. "What do your money troubles have to do with me? I send you money whenever you ask." And it wasn't pocket change.

She shook her head slightly, mouth pulled tight. "Yes, but now I need more than you would ever be willing to give. And you turned me down last time I asked." She cleared her throat. "There's a loan shark involved now. Playing the stock market wasn't enough anymore. He kept risking more and more, believing there was a way to break even. If we don't find the money, my husband is going to end up dead, and then they'll come after me."

I opened my mouth and closed it repeatedly, sure I resembled a fish. The shock was making me stupid. "So you encouraged David to hire someone to scare me back to him, knowing he didn't have the money to give you even if it worked? Why?"

She didn't say anything, so I went to push past her toward the front door. "I'm going to find Case." I was already angry David had gotten away with mostly a slap on the wrist. Even though she was my mother, I was going to let Case deal with her. I felt like the top of my head was going to explode I was so angry. I couldn't believe I'd given this woman everything she'd asked for all these years, for her to manipulate and hurt me this way.

She caught my arm as I went to move by her, but I shook her loose. "Let go of me. I don't want to hear anything you have to say. You can explain yourself to the sheriff." And knowing Case, it wasn't going to be a pretty scene.

My mother's next words froze me in my tracks. "I needed everyone to focus on David and his connection to Jed, so no one would question why Jethro Coleman was trying to kill you." She said it so matter-of-factly she might have been describing the weather outside.

How did she even know that? I sucked in a breath and whispered, "Why is Jethro trying to kill me?" It was the million-dollar question, and I never would have suspected my mother was the one with the answer to it.

Her next words made me bitterly regret not walking out the door when I had the chance. Curiosity really did kill the cat, or rather the attorney in this instance. I should've run when I had the chance.

"Because I hired him to. I need the money from your life insurance policy. It will save my husband's life and provide just enough for us to start over somewhere. Jethro was taking too long though. I told him to forget about it. I decided to finish the job instead."

I was shoved roughly against the wall behind me. Surpised by the violence and my mother's strength, I watched with unnaturally wide eyes as my mother pulled a wicked-looking handgun out of her designer bag and pointed it right at the center of my chest. I put a shaking hand to my thundering heart and gaped at the woman who'd brought me into the world. The one who apparently wanted to take me out of it as well. "I'd say I'm sorry things have to end this way, but I think we both know it would be disingenuous."

I shook my head. "How do you think you're going to get away with this? Case will be here any minute. There is no way someone didn't see you out on the street. This is a small town. Everyone is in everybody else's business. You can't just shoot me and walk away." Not to mention she would be killing her only child. How could she live with herself? What kind of monster did I come from? She was a thousand times worse than Conrad Lawton.

"Oh, I plan on people knowing I'm here. I came to check on my daughter, knowing her life has been in danger. What a tragic turn of events when I found her deceased." She exhaled a long, low breath, and I swore the temperature in the room dropped several degrees.

"This is insane." My voice cracked, and I felt bile rise in the back of my throat. I kept shifting my gaze between the stoic, unemotional woman in front of me and the weapon in her hand.

"You did make my plan slightly more difficult when you got involved with the sheriff. I wasn't expecting that. He never liked you much." She hummed a sound of annoyance and moved a step closer to me. "I was planning on paying Coleman to make it look like a suicide after David signed the divorce papers. Single, no prospects, defective. There was going to be an epic suicide note, but then you went and cozied up to a Lawton." She shook her head. "You've never made things easy, Aspen. Such a difficult, obnoxious child."

"Case is coming." He had to be. I refused to believe any differently.

"No. He's not. Jethro isn't very bright, but he is a good soldier. He follows orders. He understands strategy and the endgame. He's been watching and waiting. It doesn't hurt that he hates Case Lawton with a passion. Once you had the office cleaned he knew it would only be a matter of time before you came back to work. He also knew there was only one way—one other person more imporant than you—to make sure the sheriff has his entire attention and resources on someone else."

She waved the gun in the air. "Do you really think I just happened upon you at the right time and the right place? Naive girl. You've always had such a bleeding heart. You didn't get that from me."

My heart lodged in my throat at her words. "You wouldn't."

She arched her perfectly groomed eyebrows at me. "Do you know how much your insurance policy is for? There isn't anything I wouldn't do to get that money."

I gulped and fisted my hand on my chest. "If Coleman went after Hayes, Case is going to burn this town to the ground going after him. There won't be anywhere he can hide, so whatever money you promised him is worthless. Case will end him, even if nothing happens to his son."

The gun waved again, and the smile that crossed my mother's face was so calculating and evil it made my skin crawl.

"That's what I'm counting on. I never intended to give that redneck a dime."

There was no holding the bile back after that. I gaged and made a mess all over my nice clean office.

CHAPTER 18

∞

CASE

Dad, something's wrong."

The call made my heart drop and had my blood running ice-cold. It was the middle of a school day, and there was no reason Hayes should be calling me. He was supposed to be safe and sound in his AP English class.

"What's going on, kiddo?" I tried to keep my voice calm, but I was already moving out of my office and headed toward my SUV. A couple of deputies called out greetings, and a young cop who operated the front desk during the day shift asked where I was going. I waved them all off, steps quickening as I hit the front door.

"I'm not really sure. Mom's been blowing up my phone. She's called twenty-three times and sent me around fifty text messages. She's been annoying lately, but not like this." Hayes sounded confused and worried. His voice was also hollow and echoing, making me think he had snuck away to the bathroom to call me, since phones were forbidden during classes.

"What do the messages say?" Becca could be erratic, and she was unquestionably manipulative. No one was off-limits when it came to her brand of emotional warfare. But she'd never interfered with our son's education. She was dying to say her kid played football for one of the top colleges in the nation, and she was looking forward to the possibility of Hayes going pro so she could bask in the secondhand celebrity. I instantly agreed something was very, very wrong.

"She didn't leave a voice mail, but the texts are weird. They start out asking me to come over to her house right away. When I didn't respond, she switched to saying she was coming to the school and that I needed to meet her out front. She says it's an emergency. You don't think that jerk boyfriend of hers did something to her do you?" He sounded antsy. I knew my kid. Even though his mother drove him up a wall, he would throw all caution to the wind if he thought she needed his help. "I tried to call her back, but now she won't pick up."

I slammed the door to the SUV and cranked the engine to life. "Don't leave the school, Hayes. Go to the principal's office and stay there until I call you back. I'm on my way there right now."

He huffed an irritated breath that let me know he didn't appreciate me treating him like he was still a little boy. "What about Mom? I checked the find-my-phone app, and it shows her phone at my school. I don't understand what's going on."

"Do not step outside of that school, Hayes. I'm serious. I'm going to send someone to your mom's place right now to see what's going on. Just because her phone is at your school doesn't mean she is, you got me?" The warning was clear in my voice. If he disobeyed me, we were going to have a huge problem.

"Fine. But you better call me back and tell me what's going on." He disconnected the call, and I knew if I didn't get answers soon he was going to blindly walk into danger to find them on his own.

I called Hill, because I needed help and he was the one person with a badge I trusted implicitly. I started barking orders before he even said hello.

"I need you to go to my ex-wife's house. Something is going on with my son, and I have a bad feeling about it. I'm on my way to his high school right now." Thank God Hayes was smart enough to call me when things seemed hinky. "Jethro Coleman is still unaccounted for, and if he somehow gets his hands on my kid..." I trailed off. I would hand over just about anything in the entire world to ensure Hayes's safety.

Hill grunted, and I could hear the sound of traffic and wind rushing, indicating Hill was driving. "What about Aspen? This could just be a big distraction." Our minds worked the same way, which meant I didn't have to explain every little fear I had about the current situation in detail.

"I have a patrol unit on Main Street. She's at her office today, and I haven't received any reports of anything suspicious. My next call out is checking in on her."

Hill made a sound of agreement. "Just pulled up at your ex's place. Nothing looks out of the ordinary from the outside."

I breathed a little easier at that news. I pulled into the front of the high school with a screech of tires. The campus was mostly empty aside from a stray teenager scurrying between classes. "So far the school looks clear as well. I'm going to run in and check on Hayes and let the principal know there may be a situation."

"Well...shit." Hill's voice went low in my ear. "There is definitely a situation. No one is answering the door, but I can see in the front window. I don't see Becca, but there's an unconscious male on the living room floor. And there's blood. Lots of blood. I'm going in based on probable cause."

I swore under my breath and slammed the heel of my hand against the steering wheel. "He went after Becca for her phone."

"Coleman?" I heard a heavy thud and assumed Hill was trying to shoulder the door to Becca's house open. I sent up a silent prayer the woman was unharmed. I couldn't imagine how Hayes would react to learning Becca got hurt in order to lure him out of the school and into the middle of a game of cat and mouse.

"Who else could it be? He's been at the center of all of this. Keep me updated. I need to check on Aspen and make sure Hayes doesn't leave the building." Hill muttered an absent agreement, and the phone went dead. I reached for the radio attached to the dash, jolting just as it crackled to life.

Bending over to respond to the call very well may have saved my life. The deputy I had on patrol watching Aspen radioed in to inform me everything appeared normal. He did mention a well-dressed woman stopping by the office and assumed she was one of Aspen's clients. He went on to say Aspen let the woman into the building without hesitation, which was weird. I knew she wasn't ready to open her doors for regular business hours yet. I was getting ready to send the deputy into the building to double-check that everything was okay when the passenger window on my SUV shattered into a million pieces.

I swore long and loud as another bullet blasted the back window. My ears were ringing as I clutched the radio in my hand, scrambling across the front seat, keeping my head low as the stuffing from the driver's seat suddenly exploded outward as yet another bullet lodged in the leather. My ears were ringing from the noise, and I couldn't decide if I should be looking out over the parking lot for the shooter, or toward the school to make sure no one came out the front doors.

Breathing hard, I gasped the code for active shooter into the radio. I got the passenger door open and tumbled out, landing hard on my hands and knees. The impact was jarring, sending my teeth clicking together. I saw my phone light up where it fell on the floorboard. It was covered in glass, but I could see my son's name on the screen. It was my worse nightmare come to life, an active shooter in the one place where he was supposed to be safe, and it was my fault. I'd let these dominos fall. I couldn't begin to imagine how terrified my kid must be. Hopefully he'd gone to the principal's office like I told him to. I was sending up a silent prayer the school official would do whatever it took to keep Hayes from doing something stupid.

I heard a bullet ping off the frame of the SUV too close to the top of my head for comfort. I reached up reflexively, realizing I had lost my hat somewhere in the dive out the door. I pulled my service weapon out of the holster, hand sweaty and finger itchy. I wasn't looking for a shootout or a firefight. This wasn't a war zone. This wasn't the desert. This was a sleepy small town where people, and especially children, should be safe. It was my job to prevent something like this from happening. I couldn't believe how spectacularly I had failed. Taking a deep breath, I practically crawled my way toward the front tire of the SUV, crouching down behind the engine block because it was the safest place to take cover from the incoming rounds. I had no clue how far away backup was, or how much ammunition Jethro Coleman had. I did know my SUV was getting shot all to hell.

I saw the mic from my radio dangling out the passenger door and was tempted to reach for it, but as soon as I shifted, a bullet dug into the asphalt right where the top of my boot had been. Coleman was a good shot. If I gave him a target, he was going to hit it. I wiped the back of my hand across my sweaty forehead and looked up at the school. Luckily the administration seemed to have put everyone on lockdown. No one was coming or going from the building, meaning I only had to worry about myself. There would be no staying hidden and trying to survive by keeping my head down if an innocent victim ended up in the crossfire.

Finally, I heard sirens competing with gunshots. They still sounded really far away, and I wasn't sure if the shooter was moving closer, or how much longer I could hunker down and do nothing while a madman terrorized the high school. Tightening my hand on my weapon I slowly, painstakingly, leaned around the front end of the car to see if I could get a bead on where Coleman was positioned.

I gasped when the headlight exploded right next to my face. Glass and plastic embedded in my cheek and the coppery scent of blood filled my nose. My eyes burned, and my head screamed in pain as my skull collided with the fender of the car as I jerked back behind the vehicle. Putting a shaking hand to my face, I wasn't surprised when it came back stained scarlet and sticky with blood. I could feel the sear of pain all through my jaw and down the side of my neck. I had to blink both sweat and blood out of my eyes as my vision swam. For the first time in a long time, I was scared down to my bones. I wasn't used to being in a situation I couldn't control. I wasn't sure how to operate when there were literally no viable options for success.

Panting, I turned blurry eyes toward the front of the school when I noticed motion at the front doors.

"No!" I wasn't sure if I said the word out loud or if I silently screamed it, but I was moving before I could think the action all the way through.

I heard the gun go off again, but it was nearly drowned out by something louder, almost meaner. There was no time to turn my head and evaluate the situation, all I cared about was getting to the teenaged girl with wild-colored hair before a bullet did. Even with the distance separating us, I could see her eyes were huge and blind with fear. Her skin was nearly white, and tears were running down her face as she blasted through the heavy metal doorway. A blond woman who was slightly younger than me appeared in the doorway behind the teenager. She was screaming and frantically motioning for the girl to get back inside, but the teenager was operating on a level of fear and adrenaline that didn't understand logic.

When she caught sight of me running in her direction, she took one look at the gun in my hand and started to backpedal. I heard her scream, another gunshot, and then suddenly everything went deadly silent.

For a second I wondered if I'd taken a bullet somewhere fatal. But I could still feel the way my cheek was burning, and I could feel sweat trickling down my spine. The teenager fell to her knees in front of me and wrapped her arms over her head. I stopped running when I was directly in front of her but still a few feet away. The teacher in the doorway was watching with wide eyes, and I motioned her to get back inside.

I was still waiting to feel the burn of a bullet, but the sirens were closer now, and the gunshots had gone silent. Looking over my shoulder and squinting into the sun I tried to locate where the shooter had been positioned. I caught the reflection of the light off what I could only assume was a gun scope on the rooftop of the gymnasium. I also noticed that every available officer in the county was now surrounding the school and exiting their vehicles with weapons drawn. The entire event felt like it'd lasted for hours, but in reality, it had only been minutes.

I looked back at the crying, hysterical girl in front of me. Clumsily I put my gun back in the holster and took a step back. "Hey. It's all right. You need to go back in the school so all the students can be accounted for. We'll need to contact all your parents. I'm Sheriff Lawton. I'm not going to hurt you."

The teenager started crying harder and was shaking so badly I wondered if she'd gone into shock. Taking note of the bright burst of color in her hair, I wondered if she was the new student Hayes had told me about. Breathing out a long breath I nodded as several of my deputies surrounded me. Everyone was asking questions and demanding answers, but I held up my hand and continued to focus on the girl.

"I'm Hayes's dad. I promise I'm not going to hurt you." I tried to keep my own voice from shaking.

Finally, wide eyes looked up in my direction. She looked like a ghost with her too white skin and too dark eyes. She reminded me so much of Aspen when she was younger, I felt it like a punch in the chest.

"Hayes is nice." Her words were slurred and choppy. She sounded almost drunk, possibly delirious, and again I worried about her going into shock. I crouched down and held out a hand, which she looked at in horror.

I grimaced when I realized my fingers were covered in blood from my face. I retracted it and tried for a reassuring smile instead. "He's a good kid. I need to go check on him. Why don't you come inside with one of these nice deputies or me?" One of the female officers I had on staff took a hesitant step forward and nodded when the girl didn't flinch away.

It took a minute for her to get to her feet, and when she took her first step back toward the school, she stumbled. The female officer caught her before she went down and gave her a sympathetic pat on the back. They were talking in quiet tones, and the teenager looked less like she was going to pass out, now that she had someone to lean on.

"Case, you there?" I looked around at the sound of my name, frowning when I realized it was coming from one of the radios on a nearby officer's shoulder. I motioned for him to come closer so I could respond to Hill.

"I'm here. Where are you?" He was supposed to be making sure my ex-wife wasn't dead.

"I'm on the roof with your shooter." Hill's tone was dry, as if his location should've been obvious. "Becca was fine. Found her locked in the basement of the house. Coleman pistol-whipped the boyfriend, so he's in a world of hurt, but they'll both live to tell the tale. Becca was already playing the sympathy card when the paramedics showed."

I pulled my shirt out of my jeans so I could wipe at my face. "The shooter Coleman?"

The radio crackled again. "The shooter *was* Coleman."

I frowned. "*Was*?"

"Yep. Looks like someone took a shot at your shooter. Nailed him right between the eyes too." Hill sounded slightly impressed.

"Wasn't me. He had me pinned down like a sitting duck." I was still furious over the fact.

"Naw. This wasn't one of us. This is a kill shot. Professional, done with a high-powered rifle from a long distance." Again there was a note of awe in the Texas Ranger's voice. "He's got a go bag up here with him. It looks like he was planning to take his shot at you and run." With our small police force and limited resources, he might have gotten a good jump on getting away if someone hadn't gotten to him first.

"Fuck me." I remember the roar drowning out the sound of gunshots right before I'd started to run toward the girl. It could've been the rumble of motorcycle tailpipes. Groaning I ordered, "Hill, call Aspen for me. My phone's in the car, which is now a crime scene. I need to make sure Hayes knows both Becca and I are all right, then I need to check on Aspen. My patrol officer said she had a client show up, but she didn't mention anything to me about having an appointment." It was still a strong possibility this was all a distraction. Every single cop in Loveless was now posted up somewhere around the high school. If someone wanted to get at my girl, now was the time to do it. I would deal with the possibility of the Sons of Sorrow taking out Coleman later.

I thanked the deputy for letting me use his radio and strode purposely toward the school. I needed to see my kid. Needed to let him see me because I was sure he was worried sick. When I got to the principal's office, it was chaos. Teachers were screaming, the phones were ringing off the hook, and several of my officers were trying to keep the peace. In the midst of it all, I could hear my son screaming at the top of his lungs to be let out of the office. He was pounding on the door so hard the wood was shaking in the frame. The principal apologized for keeping him locked in the room but told me it was his only option when Hayes had tried several times to leave the school. The first time was when the first shots went off. The second time, he tried to go after the girl who'd slipped past everyone and ran directly into danger. All I could do was thank the staff for keeping my kid safe. At the end of the day that was all that mattered to me.

When the door to the office was opened, my six-foot-three, 180 pounds of solid-muscle son fell into my arms like a five-year-old. He took one look at the blood on my face and started to sob into my chest. I shut the door so he could have his moment, assuring him I was fine and that his mother was okay. It took a solid minute for him to catch his breath and compose himself.

When those eyes, which were the same as mine, finally cleared, I knocked my forehead against his while squeezing the back of his neck and warned, "You know better than to try and leave a secure location when there's an unknown threat." We talked about it all the time. I was proud of his bravery, but he was also in so much damn trouble.

"Sheriff."

I looked up as the door opened and the same female officer who brought Hayes's little friend back into the school stuck her head in the room. "Special Agent Gamble said to tell you Mrs. Barlow isn't answering either her cell phone or the office phone."

I swore under my breath and nodded. "Thanks."

That wasn't good. Not good at all.

CHAPTER 19

∞

ASPEN

$\mathbf{M}$y mother made a disgusted face and looked down her nose at me.

For a brief second, I swore every single important moment in my life flashed before my eyes. I saw everything I wanted a chance to redo, and all the right steps I'd taken to finally get the job, guy, and life I wanted. It was a good life, one I wanted to make better, to do more with. One I wasn't giving up without a fight. There was no way I was going to let this woman, who never gave me anything, take everything from me. I was done being nothing more than a means to an end to her.

I clearly remembered the phone call in which she'd harassed me for over an hour about changing the beneficiary on all my accounts over to her after I told her I was leaving David. At the time I was almost foolish enough to believe she was supporting my decision to walk away from my marriage in some small way. Little did I know she was putting deadly, dangerous wheels into motion. I felt like I should've known better.

I watched, horrified, as her finger twitched on the trigger. The cup of coffee in my hand jolted, sloshing hot liquid on my still healing fingers. I hissed at the burn, but my mother didn't notice. She was too busy trying to figure out why the weapon in her hand didn't fire. It appeared that Jethro Coleman had provided her with a gun but hadn't bothered to explain how to use it. She'd never embraced being a Texan when she lived here. If she had, she might've known the first thing she should've done when she pulled the weapon was check to make sure the safety was off.

When my fingers tingled in irritation I looked down at the coffee she had passed off. With all her attention on getting the gun to work, there was a limited window of opportunity for me to get out of the building before she figured out the safety. Even if she had no clue how to shoot, at such close range, the likelihood of her missing some vital part of my anatomy was slim.

Catching my breath, I pushed off the wall and moved closer to where my mother was hovering in the middle of the room. Her head jerked up, and the gun snapped back in my direction. I had no clue if she had figured out how to take the safety off, and I wasn't going to wait around and find out.

With a flick of my wrist, I sent the mug and hot liquid flying in my mother's direction. My aching fingers were proof that the coffee was still hot enough to scald. My aim must've been on the money because I heard my mother shriek as I shouldered past her and barreled my way to the glass front door. Luckily I'd been so distracted by her sudden appearance I hadn't locked it after letting her inside. The impact when my shoulder hit the glass as I stumbled into it jarred my teeth together. My hands shook violently as I pushed the heavy door open, and I was lucky I stayed on my feet because my knees felt like they were made out of water and my ankle still wasn't 100 percent.

The warm air from outside rushed by, and so did a platoon of police cars. The sound of multiple sirens screaming was deafening as the entire sheriff's department raced down Main Street. The sound was loud enough that not one of the cars stopped when the glass door shattered behind me as I bolted for the sidewalk. Instinctively I lifted my arms and covered my head, ducking down, eyes searching for someone to realize what was going on. The gunshot was muffled by the sound of sirens, but I heard it because it was uncomfortably close. It seemed Mom had figured out the safety.

"Aspen!" My name was a shrill sound that made my skin crawl.

The woman really had gone off the deep end if she thought I was going to stand still and make myself an easy target while letting her put a bullet in me. I'd survived her hired gunman for weeks, and he actually knew what he was doing. There was no way in hell I was going to give up now. Not when I had a future with Case in front of me. And not with the possibilty of building the family I'd always wanted with him and Hayes on the horizion. My lunatic of a mother wasn't snatching any of the beautiful possibilites I now had away from me.

I waved my arms wildly around my head and screamed for help at the top of my lungs, but none of the patrol cars stopped. Vaguely, I thought I heard a loud, repeated popping sound coming from the direction of the high school, but there was no time to stop and figure out what was going on elsewhere in town. I had my hands full with what was happening here and now.

I jumped and tripped over my own feet as the newly

replaced window to my office exploded seconds after I ran past it. Mom didn't follow me outside when I ran, but she was still taking shots as I ran frantically past the big windows that covered the building and faced the street. I wasn't sure where the bullet ended up, but a car alarm on the street started wailing loudly. I couldn't imagine my mother was crazed enough to try and shoot me down in cold blood in the middle of Main Street, but then again I never would've guessed she hated me enough to hire someone to kill me either. I just needed to get out of her line of sight and call for help.

I hobbled into an uneven run, planning on darting into the first open storefront I came across. But before I could duck for cover, a familiar lime-green Jeep rounded the corner and came flying down the street. Kody was driving twice the speed limit, a cloud of dust kicking up around her tires as she raced in the same direction all the patrol cars had gone. Luckily she caught sight of me trying to desperately flag her down. The Jeep came to a screeching halt in the middle of the road, and Kody stuck her head out of the window as I jogged toward the vehicle.

"What's going on?" Kody ran her eyes over my disheveled form and frowned. I was panting and quivering like a leaf when I collapsed into the passenger seat of the Jeep.

"My mother is trying to kill me for insurance money. She's the one who hired Jethro Coleman to take me out, but she got impatient and decided to do the job herself."

"Oh my God! Coleman just shot up the front of the high school. I was going to make sure Hayes and Case are okay. Every cop in town is on their way to the school. Case has to be out of his mind with worry. He's going to blow a gasket when he hears about your mom on top of this." Kody turned her head just as another bullet exited the office window. It was a good thing my mother had no aim. The bullet went wide, harmlessly hitting the asphalt a few feet in front of the Jeep.

Kody swore and turned so she could search for something on the floorboards of the back of the Jeep. "I thought my old man was a piece of work, but I think you win when it comes to having the worst parent in the history of parents."

I really did. This situation was unbelievable.

"Kody!" I gasped when she straightened, holding a scary-looking shotgun clasped in her hand. "What are you doing?" She couldn't possibly be getting ready to turn downtown Loveless into the O.K. Corral...could she?

She kicked open the door to the Jeep and climbed down to the street. She barely glanced over her shoulder at me when she cocked the shotgun with an intimidating click and lifted it in her hands. I yelled and jumped a foot in the air when she fired the gun, blasting out the rest of the window to my office.

"Didn't learn much from my daddy other than how to be mean and how to shoot back when someone takes a shot at me. I'm not letting anyone else get the upper hand again. I was pissed when we got run off the road. I'm beyond angry my brother got shot because of that lunatic woman in there." She kept a tight hold on the shotgun and took a few steps toward the office building.

"Kody!" I scrambled across the front of the Jeep, practically falling on my ass when I launched myself out of the abandoned driver's side of the vehicle. I caught her shoulder as she lifted the gun once again when there was movement by the destroyed window. I would be heartbroken if anything happened to her because she was trying to protect me. Those Lawtons, their hearts were too big. They were always trying to stand between me and all the bad things following me around. I wasn't sure what I'd done in this lifetime to deserve that kind of loyalty, but I knew I would never take it for granted.

Kody was breathing hard, and she was also shaking. I didn't think her vibrations were from fear like mine were, they felt like angry waves rolling outward. We watched as a small handgun came flying out through the empty window frame. It landed on the sidewalk a few feet away with a thud. My mother didn't make an appearance but her haughty, "Don't shoot. I give up," drifted out toward us.

"Do you think she has another weapon on her?" Kody cautiously dropped the barrel of the shotgun.

I shook my head. "I don't think so. She didn't even know how to use that one. Her plan spiraled out of control, and she was desperate to salvage it. She was going to try and pin my murder on Coleman. She was going to double-cross him."

Kody snorted. "Stupid. He didn't hesitate to shoot up a hospital and a school. How did she think she was going to elude him when he realized he wasn't getting paid?"

I shook my head. "She called him a redneck. She always hated this town and the people in it. She thinks she's better than everyone, that she deserves more. I doubt she considered Coleman coming after her, because she was counting on Case getting to him first. She was going to conveniently find my dead body in my office, and take the money from my life insurance policy."

Kody rolled her eyes. She opened her mouth to respond, but her response was swallowed up by the arrival of several police cars. I almost collapsed when I noticed Case climbing out of one of them. His eyes were wild. His hair was standing up all over the place. He had streaks of blood on his cheek and on his hands. He looked slightly more than worse for the wear, but he was still a sight for sore eyes. I barely registered Kody stiffening next to me, her gaze locked on the tall man exiting the other side of the car as Case rushed toward both of us.

When Case's arms wrapped around me, the world that was spinning wildly out of control finally righted itself. I could feel his heart racing and the fine tremble quaking through his big body. I wrapped my arms around his waist and buried my face in the center of his chest after whispering, "My mother just tried to kill me."

I wasn't sure if he heard me or not because Kody's voice was loud and sharp as she yelled, "What are you doing here, Gamble? How long have you been in town? Case, did you know he was here?" Each question was shrill and rose in volume as she spat out one after the other. "Don't even think about touching my shotgun, Hill. It was self-defense. That crazy woman in Aspen's office fired blindly out into the street. I was well within my rights to fire back." Kody was always excitable and dramatic, but this was the first time I'd heard her sound nearly hysterical.

"Is Hayes all right? What happened at the school?" I clutched handfuls of Case's shirt in my hands, not sure I was going to be able to let go of him.

"Hayes is fine. Coleman is not." His voice was a deep rumble at the top of my head. I felt his lips lightly touch my hair. "Is your mother still inside the office? I need to take her into custody."

I nodded, forehead bumping against his sternum. "She hired Coleman. She manipulated David as a smoke screen. All for money." I couldn't keep the hurt and disgust out of my voice.

Case gave me a tight squeeze, and I felt another kiss on the top of my head. "They call it the root of all evil for a reason."

I sighed and forced myself to let go of the death grip I

had on him. I blinked up at him, lifting a hand so I could lightly brush my fingertips over his cheek. "I can't believe it's finally over."

Case grinned at me, blue eyes crinkling at the sides, teeth flashing in his handsome face. "Yeah, but we're just getting started."

I'd never looked forward to anything more.

CHAPTER 20

∞

CASE

It took hours and hours to answer all the questions and fill out all the reports surrounding the events of both shootouts. That was a lot of bullets flying in my normally sleepy town, so the media had descended in droves. They just complicated matters even more. By the time I managed to leave the office I was running on fumes.

Luckily I'd been able to send Hayes home with Aspen after he saw for himself his mom was okay, and after Aspen had given a very detailed statement as to what went down with her mother. I couldn't leave, but Aspen jumped in to take care of Hayes. I was glad my son had Aspen to lean on while I was tied up with red tape and never-ending interviews. Neither one of them needed to be alone right now, and they were both strong enough to lean on each other and not collapse.

My ex was good and shaken up over the break-in. I hoped that maybe she'd finally gotten the wake-up call she so desperately needed that life was too short to take advantage of the people who mattered most. She'd actually sounded terrified when she asked about Hayes, and she started crying when I informed her that he was unharmed. For the first time since we were teenagers, her tears seemed real.

Aspen's mother refused to say anything, simply asking for a lawyer and stonewalling anyone who tried to question her. I was going to put the woman away for as long as I could. I wanted her to rot behind bars.

Watching my son help Aspen into his truck so he could take her home solidified the need to keep her under my roof. She belonged with us. She was ours to take care of and to love. She filled up all the empty spaces I hadn't realized were there until she broke through all the barriers that I had put in place to protect my heart after my divorce. I needed to move on asking her to stay with us. Asking was a lot less scary than the thought of losing her for good.

However, tackling my love life had to take a backseat to getting my town back to a secure safe place. Every Coleman in a hundred-mile radius had shown up demanding answers I didn't have about Jethro's involvement in the school shooting. Shot Caldwell was also sitting in an interrogation room, cool as a cucumber while Hill questioned him about his whereabouts for the day. The president of the motorcycle club was a decorated sniper back in his marine days. It was common knowledge the man was deadly when he wanted to be. He was also way too smart to implicate himself in a murder, no matter how justified the kill might be. Skill and smarts were how the Sons of Sorrow had thrived in Texas since they'd moved their chapter here. Shot seemed completely unbothered by the interrogation, which annoyed Hill to no end.

The Texas Ranger had been on edge since the showdown on Main Street with my little sister. Hill was one of the most reserved, logical, and stoic men I'd ever met. However, it took fewer than five minutes in Kody's company for him to turn into a grumpy, snarling, short-tempered beast. My sister seemed to thrive on pushing the man's buttons, and surprisingly Hill let her. It was an interesting dynamic, but being all riled up didn't get Hill anywhere with the biker. In fact, Shot's attorney, some woman from Austin, in a two-thousand-dollar suit had him released within a few hours of us picking him up for questioning. Hill was annoyed, which might have had more to do with the fit my sister threw when she heard we were bringing the biker in for questioning.

It was obvious she was closer to Shot Caldwell than any of us thought, and that knowledge turned Hill into a brooding, sullen asshole. I, on the other hand, had a hard time being pissed off that the man was walking free. Eventually, if there was proof Shot was the one who took out Coleman and saved my ass, then I would do my duty and arrest him. But, as long as there was zero evidence tying the man, and his club, to the shooting, I was just going to count my lucky stars I was getting to go home to my kid and my lady when everything was said and done.

Hayes was asleep on the couch when I finally dragged myself in my front door. He had the news muted on the TV. His high school was the lead story, and the rest of the town was featured as people reacted to the events of the last few days. His mouth was open, and a gentle snore escaped every now and then. His cell phone was clutched in his hand, and it looked like Aspen had covered him with a blanket at some point. He looked exhausted. Even in sleep, there were dark circles under his eyes and deep lines indented in his forehead. He was too young to have so many worries chasing him in his sleep, but I couldn't protect him from the horrors of the world forever. He was going to be out there on his own soon, and all I could do was hope I'd given him the tools to make good choices not only for himself but for others as well. I lightly brushed the lines, trying to soothe them away without waking him up. He muttered something nonsensical under his breath and curled on his side toward the back of the couch. I tucked the blanket up around his shoulders and dropped a kiss on the top of his head. He was too damn big to carry to bed the way I had when he was little.

I hauled myself toward my bedroom, excited to strip and do a face-plant onto my bed. The only thing better than getting twelve hours of sleep would be finding Aspen waiting for me between the covers. Only, my bed was empty. It would've been a crushing disappointment if I hadn't heard the shower running in the master bathroom. Not only was she still here, waiting for me, but she was also wet and naked. I couldn't think of a better present to come home to after the nightmare of the last few days.

I left my clothes in a pile on the floor and headed toward the lure of the woman standing under the steamy water. The entire bathroom smelled like something citrusy and sweet. Aspen was humming something I didn't recognize, her dark hair a slick, heavy veil covering her back and sliding over her creamy shoulders. Her typically pale skin was a rosy pink from the heat of the water. She was such a lovely sight. She literally stole my breath away and made me realize how much I had to lose if I couldn't work up the courage to ask her to—and get her to agree to stay.

She glanced over her shoulder when I pulled the glass open and slipped into the small space behind her. I inhaled her fragrant scent and reached for her soft skin. Her tiny frame immediately curved into mine, the line of her bare back fitting effortlessly against my chest. I smoothed my palm over her shoulder, brushing her heavy, wet hair to the side so I could kiss along the side of her neck.

"How you holding up?" She was tough, but today was enough to make anyone break.

"Right now, I'm kind of numb to it all. It doesn't feel real. I'm sure it'll all hit me like a ton of bricks, but right now I just want to forget about everything." She leaned her head against my shoulder. "Aren't you tired?" Her voice was husky and went right to my dick.

I pressed my hardening cock against the soft swell of her ass and hummed in appreciation when she rocked back against me. "Never too tired for you."

She muttered in approval and tilted her head to the side, giving me better access to the curve of her jaw. I nuzzled my nose in the hollow beneath her ear and was rewarded with a shiver. I rested my palm on her lower stomach and pulled her back tighter into the cradle of my hips. My erection lodged happily against her backside, throbbing in time to my heartbeat. She placed one of her hands over mine and leaned her head back on my shoulder. I wanted to come home to this—to her—every day. But it occurred to me in a blinding flash of insight, I'd never really *asked* her what she wanted, or what she expected of me.

"Aspen." I tightened my hold on her waist and pressed my forehead against her temple. "I know I told you that you could stay here until you figure out what you're doing with your house, but I never told you that I *want* you to stay here. I want you to stay with me, I want you to be here when I come home from a rough day, like today. I want to be there when you come home and need someone to lean on. I want you to take care of Hayes, and let him take care of you. I want him to see me happy. And you're the only one who makes me feel that way. I just want you, Aspen. More than I can remember wanting anything in my life. Will you please stay?" It was fast, but the reality was we'd spent a lifetime feeling a lot of different ways about one another.

When she turned her head slightly to look at me, I lifted an eyebrow and smirked at her. "If I'm honest, I'm going to tell you that I love you regardless of your answer. I love you, no matter what you decide to do."

Her fingers tightened on mine over her stomach, and her free arm lifted so she could curl it around my neck, stretching out her lithe form along the front of my body. "I want you, Case Lawton. I've always dreamed of loving you. I just never thought you would consider loving me back."

I sighed and let my hand drag down the soft plain of her tummy. Her skin quivered under my fingertips, and her breath hitched in her throat. "No need to dream. Not when the reality of you and me together is this good. Don't go, Aspen. Stay with me."

I slid my hand between her legs and grinned in satisfaction when her legs immediately shifted to allow me better access. She was so slick and sweet down there. I loved how instantly responsive she always was to my every touch.

"I'll stay." Her voice was barely above a whisper. "But I still have to figure my life out, so if I need to go for a little while, you have to trust that I'll be back."

Trust and love were the two hardest things for me to give to anyone, but if it meant I could keep her, I would hand both of them over. I could be brave enough to trust her to do right by me, especially considering she'd been doing it all along without me knowing it.

"I guess my job will be making sure you always want to come back. I think I'm up to the challenge." And if she weren't convinced today, I would work harder the next day, and the next, until she was certain her place was right in the center of my life, smack dab in the middle of my crazy family.

She leaned forward, head touching the tiles as my fingers brushed across her clit. Her arms lifted to brace herself as she circled her hips and rubbed enticingly against my erection pressing instantly along the curve of her ass. It was easy to lose myself in the sensations of softness and warmth surrounding me. Being with her felt like it was meant to be—safe and exciting at the same time. She embodied all the things I'd been searching for in my life. She was a place to call home, a port in the storm. But she was also an adventure, a journey into the unknown that was so much bigger than the narrow world I'd allowed myself to live in for so long.

Considering our ridiculous height difference, there was no way I was getting low enough to slide inside of her from this position. So I contented myself with gliding up and down along the sweet valley between her rounded cheeks while I used my fingers to drive her out of her mind. Her body contracted around mine, and the sounds coming out of her mouth had lust coiling tightly in my gut. It didn't take much for me to realize how much we could have lost today if things had shifted even slightly to the left of perfect.

Aspen must have felt the same way, because she suddenly wrenched away and turned to face me. She locked her arms around my neck, tilted her head back for a kiss, and practically jumped into my arms when I grabbed the back of her thighs and lifted her up so I could press her back against the slippery tiles. My tongue unerringly found hers at the same time my cock slipped into her welcoming heat. I bottomed out almost instantly, letting me know how ready she was, how much she wanted me. It was nice to know she always matched me need for need. She made a strangled noise low in her throat as we effortlessly moved together, bodies syncing with perfect rhythm.

I kept one hand curled lightly around the swell of her

backside, and lifted the other to her flushed breast. The raspberry-colored nipple was peeking out from the curtain of long, dark hair clinging to her chest. I used the slippery strands to torment the little point until she was gasping against my mouth. Her eyes were heavy-lidded and unfocused as she slid up the slick wall and dropped back down on my hard length.

This woman was at the center of all my best and worst moments in life. She'd been driving me in one way or another without either of us realizing we were headed to the same destination. It was so much better now that we both knew where we were supposed to end up. Together. With my name on her lips when she came apart in my hands, and hers was tattooed across my heart as it exploded with pleasure and a sense of rightness that couldn't be matched by anything else in the whole wide world.

The water was cold by the time we stumbled out of the shower and into my bed. I watched Aspen as she ran a towel over her hair before climbing under the covers with me. She stared back with a fond smile playing around her kiss-swollen lips. "Hayes was very worried about his friend that ran out of the school. I thought I was going to have to sit on him to keep him in the house. He was also worried about you and Becca. He's very much your son. Concerned with everyone aside from himself. He didn't want to eat, and he wouldn't take his eyes off the news. Exhaustion won out, but it was one hell of a fight."

I pulled her across the king-size bed until she was completely surrounded by my much larger body. I rested my cheek on the top of her head, her hair cool against the bandage she'd helped me put on my lacerated cheek. "See, we need you. The Lawtons are good at looking out for everyone else, but we aren't so good at taking care of ourselves." I heard her murmur an agreement, and let my eyes drift closed, the weight of the day finally pulling me down. "Comes from trying to protect everyone from my dad for so long. We got used to taking the blows while making sure they never landed on anyone else who was innocent." I yawned so loud and wide my jaw popped. Staying awake was no longer an option. I was surrendering to the darkness whether I wanted to or not.

Vaguely I sensed Aspen huddle in closer and felt the touch of her lips on the center of my chest where my heart was finally resting easy.

"As long as I'm able to, I promise I will do whatever I can to help other families who are battling their own Conrad Lawtons. I will make sure the next Case, Crew, and Kody get every opportunity that was taken from you." I felt the warm air of her sigh against my skin and pulled her closer so I could hold her through the night before the pull of sleep got too strong. I'd have to wait until tomorrow to tell her that she may have had a hand in breaking my heart in the past, but she'd been the one to single-handedly repair it. It was whole now because of her, and I was going to use it for great things. Loving her the way she deserved being at the top of that long list.

EPILOGUE

∞

ASPEN

Hayes's Graduation Party

I rested my head on Case's shoulder and watched as the pretty teenaged girl with the brightly colored hair laughed at whatever Hayes was whispering in her ear. The girl was skittish as a newborn colt. But she lit up like the sun around Case's handsome son. When Case asked Hayes what he wanted to do to celebrate his graduation, it didn't come as a surprise when Hayes told us all he wanted was a backyard barbecue with the family and a few friends. This intriguing girl was the first person on his invite list. They'd been inseparable since the shooting.

"Are you sure they're 'just friends'?" I could see a heartbreak waiting to happen from a million miles away. Hayes watched the girl like a hawk when he thought she wasn't looking, and she stared at him with her heart in her eyes whenever his attention was elsewhere. Since my house was still in a state of constant repair and renovation, I'd had front-row seats to the teenage drama unfolding for months now. It was a hot topic of conversation when I went and had tea with Mrs. Clooney every Sunday when the Lawton boys did their football thing. I loved Case's elderly neighbor and adored how she'd quickly accepted me into the fold. She was a thousand times nicer than my mother ever had been, and she was a good shoulder to cry on as my mom's case prepared to move forward to trial. I was going to have to testify against her, and some days I couldn't believe this was what our fractured relationship had come to.

Case shrugged, nearly dislodging my head. I glared up at him and got a kiss on the forehead in response. I grabbed the beer out of his hand and took a drink, deciding I wasn't going to give it back as a passive-aggressive punishment.

"I don't think they're old enough to know what they are. She's got another year of high school left, and Hayes is moving halfway across the country in four weeks. They're trying to make sure they don't hurt one another. I think they're smart to keep things light." That was such a guy way of seeing things, and anything that kept him from becoming a grandfather before Hayes was done with college was a win in his book.

I rolled my eyes and handed him back his drink when he gave me puppy dog eyes. Innocent was not a look Case Lawton could pull off, but I gave him credit for trying.

"I think they're going to end up hurting regardless." Hayes was a Lawton through and through. His heart was too big and too vulnerable, and his natural instinct was to protect and defend. It was such an easy target for someone who was obviously in need of an endless well of love and affection. "She looks at him the way I used to look at you when we were teenagers."

"You still look at me that way." Case bent down and

brushed his nose along the rise of my cheek, before placing a gentle kiss on my temple. "If it's meant to be, they'll figure it out, just like we did."

I got a squeeze before he let me go and moved toward the grill. The man was an okay cook, but he was a genius on the grill. I was building an outdoor kitchen off the back of my house for that reason alone. I figured it would be a key selling point when I tried to convince him to move in with me once all the work was done. I'd subtly been asking for his input on the renovations since they started, but the man was a good investigator, so I think he caught on to my plans when I insisted he help me pick out new hardwood floors. I was pretty sure I'd found "the one" when he didn't even blink an eye at the outrageously expensive, slightly garish vintage-style wallpaper I picked out for the living room and dining room. Even if Case didn't totally understand my obsession with bringing new life to old, forgotten things, he appreciated it was important to me. Once everything was done the place would be brand-new. I thought it would be a nice place for both of us to start over. Once we landed somewhere permanently, I knew Case wanted to talk about the future. He was about as subtle as a train wreck when he tried to feel me out about the future. The man once swore he was never getting married again, but he was the one dropping hints left and right that he very well might put a ring on my finger in the future.

I didn't need a ring to know we were going to make it. I didn't need be Hayes's official stepmom or to have Case's last name to know we were forever. We were a family no matter what, but if he ever asked, I was going to say yes. I knew it was still hard for him to put himself out there, and there was no one else I would ever promise my forever to besides him.

Leaving Case stationed behind the grill, I wandered over to where a stunning blond woman was lingering off to the side by herself. Inheriting Della Deveaux along with the rest of the Lawtons had been one of my favorite things to happen in the last few months. The cosmetic company CEO was also a former big-city transplant who'd found her home in Loveless with Crew. She was quiet, but when she spoke it was with a hint a French accent and pure refinement. We got along famously as soon as we met, recognizing a kindred spirit in each other from the get-go. I was ecstatic about the pear-shaped diamond that could be seen from space on her left hand. Crew proposed not long after life settled down after the shooting. Della was going to officially become a Lawton in the near future, which meant I got to keep her.

"Ahhh...young love. It's so beautiful." She sighed as she also watched the teenagers lost in their own world. She cocked her elegant head to the side as Hayes lifted a hand to tenderly move a piece of dyed, highlighter-green yellow hair away from the girl's face. "He was willing to run into a firefight for her. Those Lawton men are something special."

"The Lawton women too." Kody's tone was full of gentle admonishment when she popped up out of the blue to hand me a beer and give Della a playful glare. "In fact, I think we're even better because we somehow manage to survive loving the Lawton men."

Della hummed a soft agreement as I tossed my head back and laughed. I did that a lot lately. There was joy and laughter in my life now, so many moments that were so bright and happy they almost felt too big for my heart to hold. Somehow, it kept expanding, kept widening to take it all in. I was embracing all of it—family, friends, and forever with open arms. I'd finally found the place where there was no question I fit in and belonged. And there wasn't a single day that went by where I was ever lonely.

Kody tilted the bottle in her hand in the direction where Becca Lawton was standing with her surprisingly age-appropriate date. "I'm still getting used to not hating her guts."

The couple was talking quietly with their heads bent together, not mingling much, but every so often Hayes would wander over to his mother and check in. Becca seemed genuinely interested in whatever her son had to say, and she had to turn to wipe away tears more than once. It seemed like the shooting had finally opened her eyes. Case was only cordial, but the rest of the family made it a point to go out of their way to make the woman feel welcome. Everyone was trying really hard to mend fences for Hayes. Becca even apologized for how awful she was in high school, and for putting me in the middle of her and Case's war. She seemed to have found some genuine regret for her past behavior, so I stayed polite, even if I didn't trust her as far as I could throw her.

When Hayes asked if he could invite his mom to the barbecue Case's knee-jerk reaction was to refuse. He wasn't as magnanimous as his son, but when I pointed out if he hadn't forgiven me, and let go of his grudge where I was concerned, we wouldn't have what we did together, he relented. Forgiveness was hard, but he was working on finding his way there. As long as his ex put forth an effort to be present and accountable in their kid's life, he was willing to let her be included in family functions. He was in no way ready to forgive her for taking Hayes from him in the past, or for wielding false accusations against him to manipulate me into helping her get her way. No apology or newfound appreciation for all she might have lost was going to get back that stolen time. But Case and the rest of the Lawtons made the effort to include her, which seemed to be enough for all involved, and it made Hayes happy.

Kody snorted. "Still can't believe Case let her come and wouldn't let me invite Shot."

I shook my head and narrowed my eyes at the rebellious blonde. "Your brother puts up with a lot, but he will never accept your bestie being the leader of the local motorcycle club. Even *you* have to realize that's asking too much."

Della nodded in agreement. "Crew isn't a fan either."

Kody shrugged and took a chug of her beer. "My brothers don't get to pick my friends." Her eyes narrowed, and her shoulders straightened as she bit out, "Especially when their taste in friends leaves a lot to be desired. Who invited him?"

Every head in the backyard turned to watch as Hill Gamble strode purposely across the grass. The tall, blond Texas Ranger had stayed in Loveless until my mother was formally charged. He'd left quickly after, off on another case somewhere down by the border. I could see by the surprise stamped on Case's face he hadn't been expecting his friend to show. Hill stopped to kiss Mrs. Clooney's cheek and to shake Hayes's hand. He slipped an envelope into the teenager's grasp and said something that made Hayes blush brightly enough to be seen all the way across the yard.

Hill tipped his pale gray cowboy hat down in greeting, but the grim expression on his handsome face didn't change even after welcomes and the offer of a cold beer.

"Sorry, but I'm not here on a social call. Case, can I talk to you privately for a minute?"

Case's eyes met mine, and I immediately hurried over to his side. "We can go inside. Everyone is in the yard, so we'll have some space."

Hill nodded solemnly and must've caught Kody's angry gaze because his step faltered slightly. His tone was brisk when he told Case, "You might want to ask Crew and Kody to join us."

I rushed over to Mrs. Clooney and asked the elderly woman to keep an eye on things while we were inside. Mostly I wanted her to keep Hayes occupied so he didn't question why his entire family wasn't outside.

The older woman patted my hand, the motion sending her sky-high teased hair bobbing in every direction. "I've been watching out for that boy since he moved in next door. I'll make sure nothing happens to his special day." She winked at me. "I'll make sure he doesn't sneak off with that little girl with clown hair as well. Boy's in deep with that one. Never seen him focus on one girl before."

I wanted to laugh but I was too worried about Hill's sudden appearance and the grim look on his face. I kissed her wrinkled cheek in thanks and rushed toward the house.

A couple of minutes later, all the Lawton siblings, as well as myself and Della, were gathered in the kitchen of Case's house. Hill seemed nervous and he wouldn't meet anyone's eyes, not even after Kody stomped her foot on the ground and demanded, "Out with it, Gamble. What's with the sudden appearance and the cloak-and-dagger act?"

Hill sighed and whipped his hat off his head. It was the first time I could remember seeing the man flustered. He shoved a hand through his hair and lifted his head so he could meet the curious eyes trained on him.

"Yesterday I was called in when a body showed up in a junkyard outside of Austin."

Case crossed his arms over his chest and tilted his head to the side. "Why'd they call in the Rangers? Austin Homicide should've been able to handle a basic call."

Hill looked down at his boots and curled his hands into fists at his sides. "They called me in to assist because the deceased was a former law enforcement officer, and because I have a personal history with him and knowledge about his career."

Of course, Case was the first one to put it together. I gasped in surprise when he suddenly slumped next to me, my arms darting out to catch him, even though there was no way I could keep us both upright. Luckily, Crew had lightning quick reflexes and grabbed Case's other arm before he hit the ground.

"No. Hill, no. It can't be." Case's voice cracked, and I watched as his brother and sister both instinctively moved in front of him, trying to protect him from the harsh truth Hill Gamble was about to lay at the Lawtons' feet.

"I'm sorry, but the deceased was identified as Conrad Lawton. I'm so sorry to be the one to tell you this. Your father was murdered."

I wrapped my arms around Case's waist and pressed myself against his back. I could feel him shaking, could feel a storm of emotion building inside of him. Out of the corner of my eye, I watched as Della grabbed onto Crew in a similar way. They were strong, capable men, but learning that both the man and the monster they'd always feared was gone was enough to turn them both into lost little boys.

Kody was the one who reacted the most intensely. She didn't cry. She didn't shake. She didn't fall apart or take a moment to reflect. No, she launched herself at Hill, eyes wild and fists raised. She called the man every name in the book. She cursed him to hell. She clocked him on the cheek and went for a punch to the gut before he caught her in his arms, locking her down and refusing to let her move as she struggled to get free. She was breathing fire as she asked him, "How many times are you going to tell me someone in my life is dead, Gamble? How many times are you going to stand there and look so cold, so removed, while you rip my heart out?"

The big, blond man sighed and for a brief second something painful and raw flashed in his moody, gray gaze. "Hopefully this will be the last time, Kody."

Kody wrenched herself out of his hold and poked her index finger in the center of his broad chest. "It will be... because I never want to see you again."

She stormed out of the kitchen with an angry stomp. The rest of us watched her go as Hill muttered, "I really am sorry, but I figured the news was better coming from me. I'll have to take a backseat, since I knew Conrad and there can't be a conflict of interest, but I am involved in the investigation now."

Della let go of Crew after pressing a quick kiss to the back of his neck. "I'm going to check on Kody." The elegant woman slipped silently out of the room, and I could practically feel the tension rise as Case and Crew faced off with the Texas Ranger.

"You'll keep me in the loop." Case issued it as an order, not a request.

Hill nodded grimly. "As much as I can." He dragged his hands down his face and suddenly looked exhausted. "You think she'll be okay?" There was no question as to whom he was asking about.

Case and Crew nodded simultaneously. "She will be. We'll take care of her." And they would, because the Lawtons stuck together no matter what.

"Good. That's good." Hill's tone lowered, and anyone looking at him could see he was the one who wanted to make sure stubborn, wild Kody Lawton was all right. Good thing for him neither one of her bothers were paying attention, each lost in their own twisted and complicated mixture of grief and relief at hearing that their father was no longer a threat.

But I was watching, and I could see every ounce of unrequited love this man had for Kody shining like flakes of silver in the stormy gray of his eyes.

Interesting.

It wasn't until much later when the party was over and Hayes left to go hang out with his friends that Case finally allowed himself to react fully to the news of his father's death. Collectively, all the remaining Lawtons decided it was best to break the news to Hayes about his grandfather on a day that wasn't all about celebrating his accomplishments. It was supposed to be a happy day, one full of family and friends. In true Conrad Lawton fashion, he's managed to rain on everyone's parade. The man had an uncanny knack for bringing nothing but pain and sorrow into his children's lives.

When I walked into our bedroom, Case was sitting on the floor, back to the bed, much the same way I'd done the first day he brought me home from the hospital. His head was in his hands, and there was an open bottle of Crown Royal on the floor next to him. Silently I lowered myself next to him and quietly reached out so I could stroke the back of his neck. I kissed his temple and brushed my nose across his damp cheek. His wide shoulders shook slightly when I wrapped my arm around them.

"I shouldn't be upset or surprised. He was a mean, nasty bastard. He treated my mom terribly, and he never did anything without a hidden agenda." He reached for the bottle of whiskey and rubbed the rolled-up sleeve of his plaid shirt across his eyes. "But murdered...Don't know what to do with that. Makes it worse, makes it hurt more."

I kissed his temple again and squeezed him harder. "You feel however you're feeling. There isn't a right or wrong way to process this kind of news. Tonight we're going to focus on you, and whatever you need. Tomorrow we can focus on the rest of the family. We'll get through this. All of us will because we have each other to lean on. We're family."

I finally understood just how powerful and unstoppable having a real, loving family could be. Nothing was going to take us down as long as we had each other.

AUTHOR'S NOTE

Hi guys!

There is nothing as exciting as starting a new series and bringing a whole new set of characters into your lives.

I just wanted to drop a few notes here so if you're a new reader, or a longtime one, so that all the connections in Loveless to my other series are clear! I'm very tricky like that. I've been leaving crumbs to Loveless for *years*!

First, there's Case. If our handsome sheriff seems familiar it's because he appears in *Salvaged*, in my Saints of Denver series. He plays an integral role in the characters in that book getting some much-needed closure. He also makes a brief appearance in my Getaway series. We find out just how irresistible he can be in *Runaround*.

Hayes also plays a part in my stand-alone novel *Recovered*. Affton, the girl who got away from him, actually has a whole book. If you love angsty New Adult I strongly suggest you pick *Recovered* up.

Now for the trail that goes the furthest back. The Sons of Sorrow first are introduced in my internationally bestselling Marked Men series. Rome Archer has a run-in with the Denver Chapter in his book, and honestly, people have been asking me for a book about the bikers for *six years*! Finally, I found a place to make that work. Also, the major outlaw MC based out of Colorado is named the Sons of Silence, so I kind of wanted to keep something similar with the club name. Fun side note: my dad dated the president of the club's daughter in high school for like five minutes. If you ever wanted to know exactly how badass my old man is...lol.

Are you enjoying the Lawtons?

Keep reading for a preview of the next book in the Loveless, Texas series, coming in early 2020.

PROLOGUE

∞

HILL

My little brother had always been my best friend.

It was common knowledge around our tiny hometown of Loveless, that where one Gamble brother went, the other followed.

Our home life wasn't the best. Our parents had a complicated, volatile marriage. They loved each other deeply, passionately, almost obsessively . . . they hated each other the same way. At times it felt like Aaron and I were nothing more than props in some dynamic, overly dramatic soap opera our parents were living out. So, my baby brother and I learned early that it was better to be anywhere other than home. I never minded him following me around. I liked being his hero. I enjoyed being the one who taught him the basics, like how to play catch, and how to fish. I also indulged him by passing along my little tips and tricks when it came to getting girls. Although I tended to stick with sports and any extracurricular which might help me get into a good college, girls were always Aaron's favorite distraction from what was happening at home.

It helped that Aaron was a good-looking kid. Tall, lanky and filled with teenage angst that made him broody and unpredictable. He cruised around Loveless on a battered old dirt bike I helped him fix up and had just enough disdain for authority to place him squarely in the "bad-boy" category. Teenage girls found him irresistible, adults found him to be uncontrollable. He was a quiet kid, often lost in his own thoughts, but he never had a problem opening up to me. I didn't think there was a single secret between the two of us.

I was wrong. Very wrong.

I had no idea Aaron was cutting himself. Leaving scars on his body to hide the ones that refused to heal on his heart.

I would have never guessed his wild mood swings were anything more than puberty and testosterone taking their toll.

I didn't have a clue my younger brother was silently suffering, internally agonized every single day. His mind was telling him lies...and his mind would turn out to be his worst enemy.

Unfortunately, I also never in a million years would ever have predicted that Aaron and I would fall in love with the same girl. Or that she would be the reason our relationship ended up falling apart.

Kody Lawton became the center of Aaron's entire world in the blink of an eye. The Lawton kids and Aaron and I were all friends growing up, but as soon as Aaron met Kody, they became thick as thieves, almost inseparable, and forever up to no good. Kody was a troublemaker, a fearless rebel, a sassy, smart-mouthed brat who my brother thought the sun rose and set upon. But it wasn't until Kody's mother passed away right as Kody was about to enter high school that my brother realized his feelings for her went deeper than friendship.

I'd graduated by then, but before I left asked her brother, Case, to keep an eye on Aaron. I knew the death of their mother hit all of the Lawton kids hard, but Kody was devastated and Aaron, even though he was emotionally fragile at best, was the one she leaned on the heaviest. Almost overnight they went from best friends to something so much more. For Aaron, there was no other girl beside Kody Lawton, and for Kody, Aaron was always going to be the first boy she ever loved. I was too far away—too engrossed in finally finding some freedom and getting to live life on my own terms—to recognize the warning signs. But I did know the way Aaron loved Kody Lawton wasn't unlike the way my parents loved and hated one another. There was zero balance, and little else mattered in my brother's life than the girl who had stolen his heart. They were living together before she was old enough to vote and got engaged the day before Kody graduated high school. To the casual observer it appeared to be young love working out, but on the inside, things were a mess. Aaron needed help, but he was too young and too scared to admit it to anyone . . . even Kody.

She was the one who called me in the middle of the night, crying because she found Aaron huddled in a ball on the bathroom floor slashing his skin with a razor blade. Kody was the one who texted me in a panic when Aaron was so listless and drained he wouldn't leave bed for days and days at a time. She begged me to come. Pleaded with me to fix my brother, but I panicked. I didn't know how to fix him, didn't have the tools required to convince Aaron he needed help. I tried to comfort him, but still I kept my distance. Deep down, I was jealous. Even with all the turmoil and upheaval Aaron brought into her life, Kody adored him. She loved him like it was the only thing keeping him alive, and maybe it was. There was no telling how deep and twisted the depression that lived inside my brother had taken root. When I did go home to check on him, it felt like I was visiting a stranger.

I was no longer his hero. In fact, I had somehow morphed into his number one enemy. Aaron acted as if he hated me for leaving, for living my own life. It made me wonder if he knew how hard I worked to be a good brother while also hiding my ever growing attraction to his one true love.

I didn't want to like the grown-up Kody Lawton. I didn't want to find her beautiful and vivacious. I didn't want to be charmed by her sharp tongue and no-holds-barred attitude... but I was. On my first visit back home, it suddenly hit me that Kody was no longer a little girl, but a young woman. One who was strong, savvy, and endlessly patient with my baby brother. I'd spent my entire life taking care of everyone else, and I couldn't deny I was envious of the kindness and compassion she was always showing Aaron. It was an inconvenient crush, especially because I couldn't distance myself from her emotionally since we were both tied together by our growing concern for Aaron. Talking to her about how much she loved my little brother and how worried she was about him often left me hurting—for her and for Aaron—but I suffered through. What other option did I have?

Knowing my feelings for Kody could never go anywhere, I focused on my life away from Loveless. I graduated college, joined the Texas Border Patrol, and eventually worked my way up the ranks of law enforcement until I had the opportunity to apply to be a Texas Ranger. I dated here and there. Told myself I couldn't settle down because my career came first, because I didn't have enough to offer just yet. The truth was, my whole heart was never invested in finding love. It was stuck back home, hung up on my little brother's soon to be wife. I distanced myself more and more from Aaron and Kody, not knowing that Aaron's issues were escalating. I stopped taking Kody's calls, but I never stopped caring about my brother. I called him directly, urged him to get help, and begged him to see someone about his emotional unpredictability. I tried to connect with him. I even tried to get my parents involved, but as usual, they were more concerned about themselves than either of their children. No matter what I said, or how hard I tried, Aaron brushed off my concern and assured me he would be fine. And I selfishly believed him. It was easier for me that way.

But he wasn't fine. Far from it.

A couple of days before Aaron and Kody's wedding, I received a call from Case Lawton, who was working as a deputy for the Loveless sheriff's office. Someone who lived next to Aaron and Kody called in a disturbance complaint. When Case got to the house, Aaron was nowhere to be found, the small home they rented was trashed, and Kody was sporting a fat lip and a sprained wrist. Case was pissed at the state his sister was in, and even more pissed my brother was missing and unable to answer for his actions. I was tangled up in an extremely complicated sex trafficking case at the border, so I hadn't planned on making it home for the wedding as it was. Not that Aaron bothered to invite me. The distance between us felt insurmountable anymore.

Nevertheless I knew there was no way Aaron would hurt Kody if he was in his right mind, so I called in someone to take over my case and went back to Loveless for the first time in years.

I found Kody before I found Aaron.

Seeing her tearstained, pale, horrified face did something to me. All the feelings and emotions I'd learned to deny did their best to burst free. I couldn't resist pulling her into my arms, and couldn't stop myself from touching my lips to her forehead and apologizing for not taking better care of my brother...and her. It was the first time in my life I recalled feeling like an absolute failure. It was also the first time Kody touched me, making it a memory seared in my mind forever.

I would also never forget the look of absolute betrayal and utter devastation on Aaron's face when he suddenly appeared. I let go of Kody like her skin suddenly sprouted thorns and stepped toward my brother.

"It takes *her* getting hurt for you to give a shit, Hill? What about me? I hurt all the time and you pretend like I don't exist." He was gaunt, eyes wild, and far too pale. He was shaking uncontrollably and his arms were covered in thin, white scars. He looked like an alien. He no longer looked like the sullen kid who followed me around, but a man with too many demons to count.

Kody pushed me out of the way and reached for him, pleading, "Aaron, we have to talk about this. You have to let me help you. I love you, but we can't go on like this."

My brother lunged for his pretty, blonde fiancée. His hands were curled into claws and I swore if I hadn't gotten between the two of them, he was going to wrap those shaking hands around Kody's neck.

I put a hand on the center of Aaron's too thin chest and pushed him back. I didn't expect for him to land on his ass, or for him to immediately leap to his feet and bolt for his motorcycle. He'd long since upgraded from the dirt bike to a sporty foreign design that was faster than lightning. He disappeared before I could get my scattered thoughts together. Kody's hand locked on my arm as she yanked me around to face her.

"You have to find him, Hill. If something happens to him…" She trailed off, head shaking sadly from side to side. "I'll never forgive myself."

I nodded absently. I wasn't going to let anything happen to my little brother and it was high time I forced him to get the help he so obviously needed. I was a pro at pushing my feelings aside and would continue to push them aside so that Aaron and Kody could have the happy-ever-after they'd always dreamed of. Well, as long as Case didn't murder my brother for roughing Kody up before I got my hands on him.

I made Kody text me a list of places Aaron might go, and asked Case to help me track down anyone he might be close to. But it was almost as if Aaron disappeared into thin air. Kody called every fifteen minutes asking for updates, even though she was turning Loveless upside down trying to find him as well. Eventually, the last place to look was my parents' house. I couldn't fathom why Aaron would go to the one place he'd spent so much time trying to escape, but sure enough, his bike was parked out front when I arrived.

It took my mother forever to answer the door and she blinked at me like she didn't recognize me.

"Hill? What are you doing here? I thought you were skipping the wedding." She narrowed her eyes at me. "Aaron was devastated when you told him you weren't coming."

I highly doubted Aaron had shared anything so personal with her, but the well-aimed barb did sting.

"Is he here?" I maneuvered around her before she could answer me.

"Yes, he is. He showed up a few hours ago. He said he was spending the night here while Kody was at her bachelorette party." She reached for my arm, but I was already running up the stairs, headed toward the small bedroom Aaron and I shared growing up.

I smelled it before I hit the door.

The coppery, metallic scent of blood. There had to be a lot of it for the smell to be as strong as it was. Freaking out, I kicked the door open and rushed into the room, my heart immediately sinking into my stomach.

Aaron was slumped on the floor, head bent, sitting in a pool of blood. There was an empty bottle of pills on the floor near his legs, and a bloodstained razor blade abandoned on his lap. I had no idea how long he'd been there, but it was long enough for his pallor to turn a faint gray and for his breath to be incredibly shallow and ragged.

Shouting Aaron's name, I fumbling with my phone to call 9-1-1.

I pulled a pillow off the bed, wrenching the case off so I could wrap it around Aaron's wrist. I did the same on the other side, barking orders into the phone.

The commotion brought my parents into the room. My mother immediately burst into hysterics, while my father stood stoically.

Refusing to take my focus off my brother, I growled, "Neither one of you bothered to check on him. He showed up out of the blue, looking like a zombie, and you left him alone. How can you be so thoughtless? So careless." It was a pointless statement. Neither one had ever had the first clue what to do with either of us. Aaron and I had always been bit players in their theatrics.

My heart skipped a beat when Aaron's eyelids suddenly fluttered. He looked at me through hazy eyes and tried to say my name. Everything inside of me froze and then burst into panicked flames a moment later when he stopped breathing.

Time ceased to exist.

I had no idea how long I sat on the floor of my childhood room after the paramedics left. I stayed there covered in my brother's blood, crying over everything I'd lost, and agonizing over all the mistakes I'd made.

Eventually I pulled myself together enough to tell my parents I never wanted to see them again, and dragged myself to Aaron and Kody's so I could tell her what happened.

Only, I didn't get a chance to get a word out. Kody took one look at the dried blood on my hands and staining my clothes, and collapsed into a boneless heap of grief at my feet. I wanted to comfort her, to tell her we could face this together. No one loved Aaron the way we did. No one understood him the way we did.

Twenty-two years old was way too young to die.

However, as soon as she was able to speak through the tears and violent shakes, she smacked me in the face and told me, "This is all your fault. All he ever wanted was to make you proud. He did everything he could for your time and attention. Why weren't you here when he needed you the most?" Her voice was almost as cold as mine had been when I spoke to my parents as she told me flatly, "I never want to see you again, Hill Gamble. I hate you."

I watched her heart break right in front of my eyes. I could also see that she believed I'd let Aaron down. And I didn't disagree with her.

After the funeral, I silently promised both of us I would stay out of her life and move on with my own, but it was hard. I'd known her since we were kids, I was still close to her brothers...and I still cared about her more than I should. But I did keep our contact to a minimum. It was easier for both of us and eventually, things between us got less hostile. As time went on we matured, learned a little more about ourselves, and a whole lot about bipolar disorder and depression. I buried myself in work and became even more of a chronic bachelor, and Kody, she committed to being even more of a pain in the ass than she already was. She didn't bother to rein her wildness and everyone in Loveless sort of gave her wide berth. We would never be friends, but we would always be almost-family. I was content with the unspoken truce because even if she only acknowledged me when she *had* to, at least she stopped pretending like I didn't exist.

It was my unfortunate luck that fate was determined to have love, death, and Kody Lawton pulling my strings for an eternity. I never wanted to tell her she lost someone else. Never planned on being the guy who continually trampled all over her heart...but here I was, so many years later, getting ready to explain to all the Lawton kids that their father had been murdered. And that I was the one responsible for finding his killer.

ACKNOWLEDGMENTS

As always, I owe the biggest thanks to all my readers. If you're new, or if you're here after twenty-some books, you will never know how much I appreciate you picking up *this* book. I know how many choices there are out there, and how limited free time to read can be. So your sharing your time, and your money, with me, it means everything to me. I think you are some of the bravest readers out there, sticking with me. I know you never really know what you're going to get when you pick up one of my titles, but I hope the surprise and adventure have proven worth the risk time and time again.

Also, here is where I shamelessly ask you to leave a review of this book somewhere, anywhere! Since it's the start of a new series with a new publisher, your review makes such a *huge* impact. Save an author's life... leave a review.

I also want to thank every blogger, reviewer, book pimper, book pusher who's out there spreading the word. It's always nice to be part of a group who typically spends their time talking about the books they love. It's so beautiful, and I know it's often a thankless job. So here I am, shouting *thank you* from the rooftops.

Thanks to my kick-ass team, Stacey, KP, Melissa, and my new addition, Lexi. It's always a little intimidating working with a new editor on a new project, but Lexi made this a breeze. Good thing she doesn't mind my penchant for writing real jerks with hearts of gold. It's always fun to work with someone who pushes you to do better. There's a long, boring business story about how this series ended up in Lexi's hands, but let's just say, I'm glad she didn't let a bunch of unruly skater boys scare her off.

My awesome BETA team didn't get to tackle this book before it went into editing, but still, they are rad and I missed them a lot during this book... lol.

I need to thank BTS and the Stray Kids, who I listened to nonstop during the twenty days I wrote this book. Thank god for K-pop. It's fun, upbeat, and the perfect soundtrack to jam out to when you're under a killer deadline. Plus, the dancing. OMG... show up for the dancing alone.

Huge, mega, gigantic shout-out to my girl Rebecca Yarros. I have no idea how I conned her into writing a book with me for promo for *this* book, but I did and I love her endlessly for getting on board with my crazy plan. She's an amazing writer, a great friend, and the world's best neighbor. I'm so glad she likes me.

Last but not least, I'm sorry, Mike!

I know I was a jerk while I was working on this book but you tolerated my violent mood swings and crap attitude for a month with great aplomb. Thanks for still sticking around! You da best.

If you want to keep up with me these are all the places you can find me on the web. I strongly suggest joining my reader group on Facebook and following me on Bookbub. Those are the best places for updates!

Bookbub: bookbub.com/authors/jay-crownover

Website: jaycrownover.com
My store: shop.spreadshirt.com/100036557
FB page: facebook.com/AuthorJayCrownover
Twitter: twitter.com/jaycrownover
Instagram: instagram.com/jay.crownover
Pinterest: pinterest.com/jaycrownover
Spotify and Snapchat: Jay Crownover
I strongly suggest joining my reader group on FB. I hang out in there a lot and you get pretty much unlimited access to me:

facebook.com/groups/crownoverscrowd

ABOUT THE AUTHOR

Jay Crownover is the international and multiple *New York Times* and *USA Today* best-selling author of the Marked Men Series, the Saints of Denver Series, the Point Series, Breaking Point Series, and the Getaway Series. Her books have been translated into many different languages all around the world. She is a tattooed, crazy-haired Colorado native who lives at the base of the Rockies with her awesome dogs. This is where she can frequently be found enjoying a cold beer and Taco Tuesdays. Jay is a self-declared music snob and outspoken book lover who is always looking for her next adventure, between the pages and on the road.

Learn more:
  www.jaycrownover.com
  Twitter @JayCrownover
  Facebook.com/AuthorJayCrownover

For a bonus story from another author you may love, please turn the page to read

It's All About That Cowboy by Carly Bloom.

CHAPTER ONE

Jessica Acosta sat alone at Big Verde's single stoplight, fingers gripping the steering wheel of the bright red Porsche, feeling conspicuous as hell. Her sensible crossover SUV was in the shop for scheduled maintenance, so yesterday she, her eleven-year-old sister, Hope, and her boss, Carmen, had driven all the way from Houston in Carmen's tiny red attention whore of a car. *As if Carmen, with her bright blue hair and multiple piercings and tattoos, needed it.*

It had been cramped but fun. They'd jammed to *all* the girl jams, talked *all* the girl talk, and squealed *all* the girl squeals when they'd hit the 130 toll road outside of Seguin with its eighty-five-miles-per-hour speed limit.

Hope had loved it. Like Carmen, she was an adrenaline junkie. Jessica was more of a white-knuckled party pooper. But somebody had to be the grown-up of the trio, and it was usually her.

They'd checked into the Big Verde Motor Inn last night, only to check right back out. Carmen hadn't liked the way the room smelled. Or the way it looked. She said the duvets had probably never been washed. She looked at a speck of something and insisted it was a bedbug.

Jessica hadn't been able to detect the smell—or bedbugs—and she knew Carmen's criticisms were only meant to land them in the nearby Village Château, a fancy hotel with a really great restaurant Carmen was dying to try.

Since Hope had asthma, allergies, and was getting over a cold, Jessica couldn't risk the chance that Carmen's delicate nose really had detected mold. So, now they had a suite at the Village Château, where Hope and Carmen were probably living it up in luxury this very moment.

It was just as well. It would be easier for Carmen to entertain Hope there while Jessica was at the funeral.

Jessica looked up and down Main Street. Big Verde was her hometown, but she might as well be a stranger here. She and her mom had left the morning after high school graduation, and she'd never been back.

Until now.

She was here for Mavis Long's funeral and what she assumed to be a reading of her will. The lawyer hadn't called it that, but what else could it be? *If you could be at my office on Monday at 9:00, we have some items to discuss at the request of Miss Mavis.*

It was no surprise to Jessica that Hope would be mentioned in the will. Mavis had promised, and she kept her promises. But if word of it got out—and it would—the folks in Big Verde would be extremely surprised. Perplexed. Titillated. Other words that indicated excitement over gossip fodder.

Whispers.
Scandal.
Drama.
Welcome Home!

Jessica shuddered and drummed her fingers on the steering wheel.

Her goal had been to get in and out of the funeral like a ninja, not to roll in like a drag queen firing a glitter bomb. Not that drag queens necessarily drove red Porsches, but both would draw about the same amount of attention in downtown Big Verde, Texas.

She slunk down in her seat. *Change, light. Change.*

The town hadn't even *had* a stoplight when she'd grown up here. And since nobody had driven through the intersection during the approximately eleventy-billion hours she'd been sitting at it, Big Verde *still* shouldn't have one.

It had to be broken. And if it was, everybody in town knew it, and they were probably watching through their storefront windows to see how long it would take the stranger—*her!*—to figure it out.

She tapped the gas pedal in frustration, which resulted in inadvertent engine-revving. A sideways glance at the boutique called Cathy's Closet confirmed she had drawn some attention. A face peeked through the green shoe polish letters on the window—FE FI FO FUM...*KEEP THOSE BADGERS ON THE RUN!*—to stare at her.

It was Friday, and the Big Verde Giants would apparently be battling the Smithtown Badgers at the football field later tonight. The band would play, the cheerleaders would cheer, and unless they'd hired a new coach since Jessica's cheerleading days, the Giants would lose.

Cathy's Closet was new. Cute clothes in the window. It had been a hardware store back in the day. A woman who was probably Cathy came out to sweep the pristine sidewalk and covertly stare at Jessica.

Jessica squinted back from behind her big sunglasses. *Was that Cathy Schneider?* Holy cow! It was! Cathy had hardly changed at all. Not only was she still rocking her seventh-grade hairdo, but she wore enough accessory items to sink a ship. Thankfully, Jessica's dark sunglasses shielded her eyes from the glare of Cathy's bangle bracelets.

Jessica nearly waved. She and Cathy had been friends once. But Cathy didn't seem to recognize her now, and anyway, Jessica wasn't here for reunions. She was here to pay her respects to Mavis Long quickly, quietly, and without fanfare.

In a bright red Porsche.

Jessica swallowed a lump the size of Texas. Cathy wasn't going to be the only person from her past she'd see this weekend. In a town the size of Big Verde, literally everyone was someone from her past, but it was Casey Long who had her concerned. She'd prepared a little speech—*Hey, Casey. How have you been? Remember how you took my virginity and tossed me aside like yesterday's garbage?*—but hoped she wouldn't have to use it. Who knew? Maybe Casey wasn't even in Big Verde anymore. Maybe he'd hit it big in the rodeo world, just like he'd always dreamed, and was halfway across the country trying not to fall off a bull.

She imagined him being tossed across an arena by an angry black bull with flaring nostrils and cartoon smoke coming out of its ears. And then she realized she'd accidentally revved the Porsche's engine again. *Getting ready to charge.*

She sighed. Even if Casey didn't live in Big Verde anymore, he'd come home for his great-aunt's funeral. He was a Long, so there would be no getting out of it.

This was ridiculous. How long could a woman sit at an intersection? There was nothing coming as far as the eye could see, so when Cathy turned her back, Jessica eased into the intersection, and then hurried across. The tires squealed just a little, because she wasn't used to so much power.

And that's when she heard the siren.

Her body broke out in a sweat. Her skin felt like it was being poked by a million needles. A rush of adrenaline and pure, white hot panic overtook her.

Breathe. At worst, it's a traffic ticket. Just breathe.

* * *

Dammit. Dammit. Dammit.

Casey was going to be late for his great-aunt's funeral. Some dumbass in a red Porsche had run the light just as he'd turned onto Main Street.

He'd have been happy to ignore it—pretend he hadn't seen it—except he couldn't because (a) You couldn't pretend not to see a red Porsche in Big Verde, and (b) There was an audience. He had no choice but to pull the guy over and provide some much-needed excitement for Big Verde's downtown business district.

Cathy Schneider held up a...*broom?* as he drove by, and Danny Moreno, the pharmacist at the Rite Aid, waved and smiled in approval when Casey turned the cruiser's lights on.

The idiot pulled over in front of the Pump 'n' Go, so at least Casey wouldn't have to chase him. Four old ranchers, who'd probably been talking shit at the coffee bar, came out to the sidewalk, ready to watch the show.

Casey pulled up behind the Porsche. Big Verde was a small town of locals, but the pretty Texas Hill Country views and green, clear waters of the Rio Verde attracted tourists and city folks looking for country homes. Most of them were nice families who pumped much-needed revenue into the town during the summer. But a few of them were assholes.

He squinted at the Porsche and ran the plates.

It was registered to Carmen Foraccio. The name sounded vaguely familiar, but he couldn't place it. He got out of his cruiser and waved at the sidewalk gawkers before adopting his most menacing scowl.

"Go get 'em, tiger!" one of the ranchers yelled.

Casey couldn't let a grin ruin the scowl he'd perfected, so he ignored the fan club. He'd give the lady a warning and be done with it.

The car's window was rolled halfway down, but he couldn't see inside. At six feet four inches tall, he towered over the car, which seemed like a damn toy next to him. The top of it barely passed his belt buckle. "Good morning," he said, in the general direction of the window beneath him. "You just blew through a red light."

"I'm sorry, officer. I think that light must be broken."

It wasn't broken. But it did tend to have a mind of its own. Casey had sneaked through it a few times himself, although never while on duty.

"License and proof of insurance, please," Casey responded. He didn't have time to stand here socializing.

"Okay, hold on a sec."

Casey sighed and tapped his foot.

The voice, like the name, sounded familiar. It stirred up a feeling of nostalgia, which was weird, because when he tried to locate Carmen Foraccio in his memory banks, he came up blank.

He backed up a bit and peeked through the window. And what he saw was a very nice, round ass in a tight black skirt as the woman dug around in the glove compartment. The skirt crawled up her thighs as she struggled, and Casey straightened quickly, feeling as if he'd sneaked a peek on purpose, which he absolutely had not.

"I'm trying to find the insurance card," the woman said with a muffled voice.

Casey shifted from foot to foot as he experienced... *Irritation? Excitement?*

He'd definitely heard that voice before.

"Still looking!" she called.

Casey looked at his watch. "Ma'am, that's fine. Just your license please. I'll look up the insurance."

"Um, okay. Hold on..."

He glanced in the window again. Got an eyeful of curvy thigh as Ms. Foraccio switched course to dig behind the passenger seat.

"It's in my purse."

Casey stared up at the blue sky. Whistled. Tried not to look back into the car or at the sidewalk Pump 'n' Go gawkers who were by now hoping to witness a pat down.

"Oh..." the woman said with a shaky voice that made Casey wonder what was coming next.

"My..."

He glanced back inside the car to see the woman frantically patting herself down and squirming in the seat.

"God."

She looked up at him. Big movie star glasses concealed nearly the entire upper half of her heart-shaped face. Below the glasses were pouty lips, pink and shiny from something that probably tasted like bubble gum, not that he was thinking about what her lips tasted like.

A part of him was definitely thinking about what her lips tasted like. And another part of him, for some stupid reason, felt like it already knew.

"Is there a problem, ma'am?"

He hoped his voice sounded firmer than he felt, because for some damn reason his legs were shaky.

"I think I left my purse at the hotel."

Casey stood up straight and pinched the bridge of his nose.

"Ms. Foraccio, I'm afraid I'm going to need you to step out of the vehicle."

He sighed and cracked his knuckles.

Shit.

CHAPTER TWO

Jessica couldn't believe she'd left her purse at the hotel. The car was registered to Carmen, so this should be interesting.

She lowered the window the rest of the way. She couldn't see his badge. Just his waist, which was bedazzled by a huge silver belt buckle. HILL COUNTRY-COUNTY RODEO CHAMP.

Not surprising in Big Verde. And she didn't doubt his cop status, since in addition to the belt buckle, he also had a nightstick and a holstered gun.

"Please step out of the vehicle," the officer repeated.

"Am I going to be arrested?"

"Not if you do what I ask and exit the vehicle. Unless you're wanted for murder or have a shit ton of parking tickets."

Jesus. Would this guy back up or bend down? She really didn't want to continue talking to the belt buckle. She was nervous, and that made her want to do things like lean out the window, put her lips right up to that ridiculous chunk of rodeo metal, and yell, "I'll take a burger and fries! And supersize it!"

She swallowed those words right down and instead said, "I need to make a phone call." Dang! Her phone was in her purse.

"We're not at the part where you get to make a phone call yet," the smart-ass said. "Now I need you to get out of the car, nice and slow."

The man took a couple of steps back and bent down to peer in the window. It was a relief to put some distance between her and the belt buckle.

Aviator cop glasses rested on a long Roman nose, over lips drawn into a tight, straight line. And below those lips, which were full and promising despite being pursed like they'd just sucked on a lemon, was a very familiar chin. With a cleft.

Jessica gripped the steering wheel as her body went into fight-or-flight mode.

Fight: *Hey, Casey. How have you been? Remember how you took my virginity and tossed me aside like yesterday's garbage?*

Or

Flight: *This Porsche could outrun a cop, right?*

Also: *Casey was a cop? What the hell?*

Without thinking—because thoughts were impossible once your lizard brain took over—she revved the engine.

"Ma'am—"

That voice! It was lower than she remembered, but it was definitely the voice of Casey Long.

What was he doing in law enforcement? She never would have seen that coming. In high school, Casey had been the town's rebel teen, and they'd been such a dumb cliché— Good Girl falls for Bad Boy—before Casey had gotten what he'd wanted and then forgotten her.

She'd never forgotten him though. And even in her terrified rage, something softened inside her. Dang it. That was what made him dangerous.

The engine raced again. She must have depressed the pedal without realizing it.

"Don't even think about it," he said.

She was totally thinking about it.

"Ma'am, I'm late for a funeral. And I hate funerals almost as much as I hate weddings. I do, however, love a good car chase. So, you can damn well bet I'll catch you. And then I'll spend the rest of the morning doing the paperwork associated with your arrest, which will get me out of having to go to the funeral. If I'm lucky, I can drag it out and escape the reception as well." He cracked his knuckles. "Your call."

Jessica bit her bottom lip so she wouldn't fuss at him for wanting to miss his own aunt's funeral. Heartless. The bastard was still completely heartless.

His jaw jutted out stubbornly. She knew a pair of icy blue eyes glared at her from behind the shades. Eyes you could fall into. Eyes that were so hypnotic they could make you do just about anything.

She turned off the ignition. Unbuckled her seat belt.

"Nice and slow now," Casey said, hand hovering near his gun.

She opened the door and stepped out, shrinking beneath the scrutiny of the growing crowd at the Pump 'n' Go.

"Remove your sunglasses, please."

The sound of his voice sent vibrations through her body; vibrations that were not entirely unpleasant. Some things might have changed, like Casey being a freaking cop, but the effect of his voice on her body hadn't. She suspected her pupils were dilated.

She pursed her lips in annoyance, and glanced at the nightstick and holstered gun on his belt. Slowly, she took off her sunglasses and looked up. Way up, because Casey had added a couple of inches to his height since the last time she'd seen him. He was at least a foot taller than she was.

His stubborn jaw went slack with recognition.

She gave a little wave. "Hi, Casey."

So much for the prepared speech.

Casey yanked his aviators off, and she had to blink *once, twice, three times* at those baby blues.

"Jess? Jessica Acosta?"

She sighed. At least he remembered her name.

"The one and only. Sorry I'm not the fabulous Carmen Follacio—"

"Pardon?"

Jesus! She'd said *Follacio*, which sounded dang close to *fellatio*.

"I'm not Carmen *Foraccio*," Jessica tried again. "She's loaned me her car."

Casey, still looking stunned, ran a hand through his dark wavy hair. His face indicated he was drawing a blank. Was it possible he hadn't heard of Carmen Foraccio, famous celebrity chef and star of the Food Channel's hit show *Funky Fusions*?

But that hair. He still wore it longer than he should. It curled past his collar and showed no signs of thinning. It took everything Jessica had to keep her hands to herself. As usual, she ran her mouth as a distraction. "Are you really a cop, or did you steal that car?"

"Darlin', I'm the sheriff of Verde County. If one of us is driving a stolen car, my bet is on you."

Did he really just call her *darlin'*?

She crossed her arms over her chest, but then Casey grinned at her, and she felt it all the way to her angrily tapping toes. She couldn't tell if he was grinning in a teasing way, or in an *I can't wait to put you in handcuffs* way.

Both options made her tingle all over, so maybe she shouldn't be thinking about handcuffs. But there they were. Hanging on Casey's belt.

The grin finally reached his eyes, as if he found the idea of himself as a sheriff every bit as amusing as she did, and it set a herd of butterflies loose in her stomach.

Casey Long had been the town's teenaged hooligan. Only he hadn't ridden a motorcycle. He'd ridden bulls. And if the gigantic rodeo belt buckle was any indication, he still did.

Casey started writing in his little book. He ripped out a page and handed it to her. "This is for the stoplight."

He ripped out another. "And this is for having no proof of insurance."

And another. "And this is for not having a driver's license on you."

She looked at the three pieces of paper. Warnings. He'd given her warnings.

"Thank you, Casey. Seriously, I'm just trying—"

"Jess," he said, cutting her off. "Why are you back?"

Suddenly, the fuller face and lower voice and broader shoulders disappeared, and she was looking into the emotional blue eyes of eighteen-year-old Casey Long. It made eighteen-year-old Jess pop to the surface of her consciousness like a cork.

And eighteen-year-old Jess had not been very smart.

* * *

What the hell was Jessica Acosta doing back in Big Verde? God. His hands were shaking.

Unacceptable.

She looked 100 percent the same. And that meant 100 percent hot. But lots of women were hot. They didn't do to him whatever the hell it was that Jess was doing to him. He wanted to laugh. He wanted to vomit. He wanted to handcuff her and throw her in the back of his cruiser and never let her out of his sight, because the last time he'd let her out of his sight, she'd run off and he'd never seen her again.

Until now.

He struggled to maintain control over his facial features. But it was hard. He'd fantasized about this encounter for years, and it typically played out in one of two scenarios.

Scenario One: He reads her the riot act. *You think you can just waltz out of somebody's life without so much as a good-bye and then just show up out of the blue like nothing happened?* Then they attack each other and have sex.

Scenario Two: He falls to the ground in a heap and cries like a baby because he's so damn glad to see her again. Then they attack each other and have sex.

She stood there with her arms crossed, her toes tapping, and her eyes flitting back and forth from him to her car, no doubt ready to jump right in and leave him standing in her dust. Maybe he should have thought of a third scenario involving a car chase.

He cleared his throat. "Coming home for a visit?"

"Funeral," she stammered.

There was only one funeral in Big Verde today. "Aunt Mavis's?"

Jess nodded.

Why on earth would she be going to Aunt Mavis's funeral? Of all the reasons to come home, why would it be for that? A million questions were piling up in his throat. He swallowed, so they wouldn't fly out of his mouth, but they got stuck halfway down.

"Jess..."

Why did you leave? Where did you go? Didn't you know it would crush me?

She'd left the day after high school graduation. They'd shared their hopes and dreams for the future—he'd wanted to be a professional bull rider and Jess wanted to open a restaurant—and promised to be together forever, just the night before.

Forever hadn't even lasted twenty-four hours. She and her mom had skipped town without a trace.

Jess stared at the ground. Offered no explanation.

Casey found his voice. "Well, we're both going to be late if we don't get a move on. We might have to use the lights."

"What? Wait, no—"

"Let's go, Ms. Acosta." A horrible thought smacked him in the face. "It is still Ms. Acosta, isn't it?"

"Yes, but—"

"Let's go then."

She wasn't married. He tried not to feel giddy about it and failed.

Jessica got back in her car, and Casey jogged to his cruiser. Then he pulled out onto the road and passed Jess, turned on the lights, and waited for her to follow.

He didn't know why he'd turned the damn lights on. The funeral home was two blocks up. But Jessica Acosta was back in town, and that made him feel excited and happy and uncomfortable all at the same time. The occasion seemed to call for lights and sirens.

CHAPTER THREE

Jessica's stomach clenched at the sight of so many cars lining the street. Small-town funerals were big deals, and everyone in Big Verde would be at this one. People often sat around looking for who *hadn't* come instead of who had.

For a town matriarch like Mavis Long, the place would be packed. In fact, people had gathered on the lawn, where chairs were set up and speakers were mounted on tripods. The little chapel was probably out of seating already.

Jessica drove slowly past all the pickups, SUVs, and cars, trying to ignore the flashing lights in front of her.

What had possessed Casey to turn on the dang lights? Was he out of his mind?

A few folks were still getting out of their vehicles, chatting with each other and attempting to tame unruly cowlicks on little boys. Most were in their Sunday best. This meant western leisure suits for the older men, and clean jeans with shirts tucked in for the younger men and boys. Most ladies and girls wore conservative dresses. *Very* conservative dresses.

Jessica's sweaty palms stuck to the steering wheel as she looked for a place to park. She wiped them, one at a time, on her black skirt. Her *short* black skirt. When she'd picked it out, she hadn't been thinking about Big Verde's fashion trends or how appropriate it might be for a small-town funeral.

There was literally no place to park. Good grief. She was not going to drag out this freak show by circling the block.

Two piercing blasts from a siren cut through the air, causing her to jump and bite her lip, which she'd apparently been chewing in nervous angst. What had she done wrong now?

Casey had pulled into a spot farther up the block. He got out and started waving his arms. *At her.*

Everyone watched as she slowly drove toward Casey, who was now making motions one might use when guiding a jet liner to a terminal or signaling marine mammals to do tricks. Was he afraid there might be one lone holdout who wasn't already looking at her? What was next? People gathered in the splash zone to watch her park?

Sweat dripped down her back as Casey proceeded to direct her, inch by inch, into the parking space directly behind him.

Once parked, she sat back with a sigh. She just needed a moment to—

The door magically opened and a big hand extended inside.

So much for taking a moment.

"The funeral's about to start," Casey said.

She took his hand. It was warm. Strong. Both foreign and familiar. How many times had she held it at the movies or while walking down the halls of Big Verde High? She blushed, remembering how Casey's fingers had roamed her body like curious explorers of unknown lands.

He'd been the first to trace her lips with his thumb. The

first to brush her nipples with his fingers. The first to cup her ass while pulling her close...

"You okay, Jess?"

She swallowed. Collected herself. And stood up on shaky legs.

He offered his arm, which would seem dramatic in Houston, but in Big Verde it just meant he was a gentleman.

Casey Long. A gentleman.

They started down the sidewalk. People smiled politely, but most were older, and she didn't see any recognition in their faces. Just interest.

Maybe she'd survive this day after all.

* * *

Casey nodded at everybody who said *Howdy, Sheriff,* as he and Jessica headed for the door. It would be nice if they'd stop their gawking. Jessica would stop traffic in any town, but in Big Verde, she was damn near paralyzing.

She was nervous. The little things she did with her hair, the fluffing and tossing. She'd been doing it since high school. It was still cute as hell.

"I'm really sorry about your great-aunt, Casey," she said.

Lots of people had said that to him over the past few days. Some of them had meant it casually. Some had meant it deeply. Some hadn't meant it at all. What he heard in Jess's voice was heart-wrenching sincerity. As if she were not only sorry, but also somehow deeply saddened.

Mavis had been well known in the small town. But as far as he knew—and he knew damn near everything—Jessica hadn't kept up with anyone in Big Verde. How did she even know Mavis had died?

He cleared his throat. "So where are you living now?"

"Houston," she said.

She didn't follow it up with what she did or who she lived with or how long she'd been there. Just *Houston.*

Why had she driven all the way here for the funeral? Other folks in Big Verde had died since Jess had left. Folks she'd probably known better. There'd been no trips home for their funerals. There had to be more to this story.

"Aunt Mavis's death is a terrible loss for our family," he said. "But it wasn't exactly unexpected."

Jessica stopped walking and looked at him. "She wasn't even sick. It was totally unexpected."

How would she know if his great-aunt had been sick?

"Well, she was ninety years old, Jess. That's what I meant by it not being unexpected. Nobody lives forever."

Jessica shook her head, as if his response disappointed her, and started walking again.

"Howdy, Sheriff!" Casey looked up to see Matt Hurley loping cheerfully their way. "Beautiful day!"

The only thing about Matt that said "undertaker" was his dark suit. Other than that, he was all smiles and grins.

"Hey, pretty lady. I don't think I've seen you around here before."

And inappropriate comments.

Matt had started going bald in junior high, but the process had stunted somewhere around eleventh grade, leaving him with a few stragglers he grew out and combed across his forehead. The back of his head was left completely unattended, probably because Matt couldn't see it in the mirror and therefore assumed it didn't exist.

He didn't let his appearance dampen his enthusiasm for the ladies, though.

Jessica removed her sunglasses. "Hi, Matt."

Matt's skinny face suddenly became animated. His Adam's

apple bobbed as he searched for words. What he finally came up with—loudly and right outside the building where Casey's aunt lay in a coffin—was, "Goddam, girl! Look at you! Jess is back in town!"

Jess seemed to melt, as if willing herself to disappear.

Matt threw the door open. The small chapel was filled to capacity, and Jessica shrank back against Casey. His entire body lit up like someone had poked him with a cattle prod. He wanted to wrap his arms around her, pull her even closer, but he couldn't. He needed to get control of himself. This wasn't the same girl who'd left him twelve years before. She was a grown woman, and he hardly knew her.

He couldn't quite accept the truth of that.

She was probably nervous, and Matt wasn't doing anything to help matters, so Casey put his hand at the small of her back. He hoped it would reassure her that she was among friends.

Miss Mills, the organist for the First Baptist Church, sat at the front of the chapel playing "How Great Thou Art" on the funeral home's electric keyboard. The fact that she did this at a Methodist funeral said something about the importance and station of Aunt Mavis in the community.

Matt hollered, "Look everybody! It's Big Verde High's homecoming queen of the class of..." He looked at Casey. "What year was it, Casey? Let's see, you were two years ahead of me—"

Miss Mills stopped playing.

Everyone looked at them.

"Matt, I think I'll have a seat up there with my family. I was running a little late due to increased criminal activity in the town." He winked at Jess.

Miss Mills picked up where she left off, and slowly everybody went back to looking mournful. They were accustomed to Matt's outbursts.

Matt, as if suddenly remembering where they were, made a rousing attempt at appearing solemn.

"The Hurley family is honored to be here for you during your time of need. Please accept our sincere condolences."

"Why thank you—"

Matt turned back to Jess. "Where did you get that kick-ass car?"

Casey patted Matt on the back, a little harder than necessary, because that's what it typically took to shut him up, and then led Jessica by her elbow to the pews set off to the side of the casket where the family was seated.

Jessica trembled. Was she really that nervous? His own knees were a bit shaky, but it was because being around Jess again rocked him to his core.

"Casey, no. I'm not family. I'll sit somewhere else."

"There is nowhere else," he said. "And you came all this way. Everyone will be pleased to see you."

That might be a stretch. They would be surprised, though. Because Jess being here for Aunt Mavis's funeral made absolutely zero sense. To lessen the tension, he decided to do the polite thing and inquire about her mother.

"How's your mama? Doing okay, I hope."

Jessica stiffened even more. "She passed away two years ago. Heart attack."

Jesus. He had shit timing. "I'm very sorry to hear it."

And he was too. Even though Jessica's mom had hated his guts. In all fairness, most girls' moms had hated his guts.

Gerome Kowalski, owner of the infamous Rancho Canada Verde and a man Casey had known his entire life, came forward with his hand extended. He'd be delivering the eulogy. "Casey, Mavis will be very much missed by this community."

"Thank you, Gerome. This is such a nice turnout for her. In fact, Jessica came all the way—"

Jessica was headed to the coffin. And she appeared to be sniffing and weeping.

"Is that little Jessica Acosta?" Gerome asked.

"Yes, sir. She's come back for Aunt Mavis's funeral."

Gerome nodded. "That's right nice of her. I'd expect as much."

So, there *was* a reason Jessica was back. But what was it?

There were currents that flowed beneath Main Street in every small town, and the secrets they carried were hidden from most.

Gerome was one of the few who always knew. And like Aunt Mavis, he kept those secrets to himself.

It was infuriating.

CHAPTER FOUR

God. She felt like such an idiot. She hadn't intended to bawl her eyes out at Mavis's funeral. But dang it, Gerome Kowalski knew Mavis. He got Mavis. And the eulogy had captured her perfectly. Hard and unyielding. Demanding and critical. Almost impossible to please. And yet, also kind and loyal. Generous and sympathetic. Even fun.

Jessica smiled. Hope could make Mavis act silly. A person hadn't lived until they'd seen Mavis jump out from behind a chair in a power pantsuit, wielding a light-up laser gun.

And she could be fierce. Like when she'd stood between an angry landlord and Jessica's mom, who'd already paid the rent, no matter what the landlord said.

Their little family had mattered to Mavis Long, and she had mattered to them.

Dang it. The tears started up again.

The service was over, and people were lining up to pay their respects to the family, so Jessica went to the back of the alcove to wait it out. She'd leave as soon as she thought she could get away without having to talk to anybody.

Mavis's only son, Senator Wade Long, who'd once been

the sheriff of Verde County, stood on the front row accepting condolences. Jessica shivered and ran her hands up and down her arms. She'd known he would be here, but she was nothing to him. He wouldn't recognize her, and even if he did, what could he do?

Wade Long was the reason she and her mom had been forced to leave Big Verde. Her mom had been pregnant with Wade's baby. *Pregnant with Hope.*

Back then, Wade had his sites on the Texas Legislature, and although he and his wife were well on their way to divorce, he couldn't have his constituents knowing he'd fathered a child with an undocumented immigrant.

To this day, as far as Jessica knew, nobody had ever found out. Well, almost nobody. Mavis Long had discovered the secret.

Jessica sniffed and willed a new tide of tears away. She'd never forget opening the door of their sparse little apartment in Houston to see Mavis Long standing there, hair perfectly coifed, demanding to see her only grandchild. She'd only wanted to know if Hope's financial needs were being met. She hadn't intended to have a relationship with her...*to be a grandma.*

But one look at chubby little two-year-old Hope had melted Mavis's resolve. She'd lost a bit of her stiff-spined composure at the sight of Hope's sweet almond-shaped eyes, and she'd lost 100 percent of her heart.

Jessica hadn't known her hardworking mom was undocumented. Not until Wade Long had threatened to have her deported if she ever told a soul. He ordered her to leave Big Verde and never come back.

Nothing had ever been the same again. Ever since that day, Jessica had lived her life with the fear that her world could dissolve at any minute. And she'd never dared to dream of coming home to Big Verde. Not if there was even the slightest chance that Wade would make good on his threat and her mom would be deported.

But now her mom was dead. And Mavis was too. Wade Long couldn't do anything to her family. But Jessica's hands wouldn't stop trembling.

A short blond woman came zigzagging through the crowd. She was heading Jessica's way, face lit up by a smile.

"Jessica! Hi!"

It was Maggie Mackey. Jessica had always liked her. She'd been a tomboy who didn't care what people thought. Jessica had cared what *everybody* thought, so she had admired Maggie's attitude.

There was a ring on her finger. Who had she married?

Dang it. She was already falling into the small-town pattern of wondering about other people's business.

"What are you doing here?" Maggie had always gotten straight to the point. No polite chitchat for her. "How long are you staying?"

"Not long. I'm just here for Mavis's funeral."

Maggie cocked an eyebrow but didn't question her further. "I hope you're coming to the reception. It's at the Methodist Church Fellowship Hall. Everyone would love to see you."

"Oh, I don't know—"

Leaving Big Verde had been traumatic. It had taken years to get over it. Why rekindle old relationships? She was heading back to Houston—where nobody knew or cared about your business—on Monday. Houston had never been much of a home, but the anonymity it allowed was good for keeping secrets.

"Well?" Maggie asked, hands on hips. "Are you coming or not?"

"Of course, she's coming," Casey said.

Where had he come from? And why wasn't he up at the line with the rest of the family? Casey was acting as if he was afraid to let her out of his sight. Strange behavior for a man who'd never once tried to find her after she'd left Big Verde.

"Look who's hovering about," Maggie said with a grin.

Was Casey *blushing*? Her own cheeks felt a bit warm. Holy crap, was *she* blushing? She thought she'd prepared for the inevitable reunion with Casey. She'd spent the last four days fortifying her emotional shields, but all it took to decimate them was a smile and a slight blush from Sheriff Long.

Heck, her shields had disintegrated as soon as she'd heard his voice when he pulled her over.

"There's a little too much schmoozing going on over there with my uncle," Casey said, nodding at the Good Senator. Jessica could barely contain a shiver of disgust, and Casey's slight sneer indicated he didn't exactly have warm, fuzzy feelings for the man either.

"He's not your uncle," Maggie said.

Casey shrugged. "He's older than me. He's a relative. He's not my grandfather. That makes him an uncle."

"He's your great-aunt's son," Maggie argued. "And that makes him your second cousin once removed. Or maybe it's your first cousin twice removed..." She furrowed her brow. "You know what? Why don't you just refer to him as your uncle."

Or they could all just refer to him as the anti-Christ and be done with it.

Casey put his hand at the small of Jessica's back and gave a gentle nudge. It sent thrills up and down her spine, but as they exited the funeral home, she still had every intention of heading down the sidewalk to her car.

So why was she crossing the street toward the Methodist Church Fellowship Hall?

Ten minutes later she sat at a folding table, picking at macaroni salad and trying to look small so nobody would talk to her. She kept an eye on Casey while he worked the room. It was so weird to see him patting backs, shaking hands, asking about cattle and crops. She'd seen Wade Long do the very same thing. But unlike Wade, Casey seemed genuinely interested in the folks he talked to.

He was keeping an eye on her too. As if he was afraid to look away for too long. Why? He'd seduced her. And then tossed her aside. *Just like a Long,* her mom had said.

Jessica hadn't wanted to believe that Casey was like that. But then he'd ignored her letters. Never tried to find her. She thought she'd worked through it and didn't care anymore.

She was wrong though. She cared.

Casey finished chatting with an older gentleman and then came and sat down beside her. "Sorry," he said. "It's an election year."

Jessica nodded. The last year she'd spent in Big Verde had been an election year too, and Wade Long had been in full politician mode. Unlike previous elections, he'd had a challenger. He'd left no hand unshaken and no funeral unattended. There hadn't been any room for even a hint of a scandal, much less a pregnant undocumented immigrant.

Casey poked at a blob of what looked like Jell-O with fruit and nuts in it. It jiggled obscenely. "I prefer the funerals on your side of town," he said. "Food's better."

Jessica stiffened. "What do you mean *on my side of town*?"

Casey put a paper napkin in his lap and glanced at her, shooting a spark of electricity right through her body with those blue eyes. "The Catholic side."

Okay. Well, it was true that Jessica had grown up in the neighborhood adjacent to the Catholic church. And that most of the people in that neighborhood were Catholic.

Casey curled his lip at the Jell-O on his plate. "As far as funeral foods go, the Catholics win hands down."

Jessica looked at the blob of mayonnaise and macaroni dangling on her fork. He had a point. A funeral in her neighborhood had meant barbacoa tacos, trays of enchiladas, Spanish rice, and big, steaming pots of beans made by the Catholic Daughters.

"With the Lutherans and the Baptists, you might get some sausage and whatnot," Casey continued. "But Methodists are going to torture you to death with tiny little sandwiches filled with vegetables and things they call salads that are mostly Jell-O. Also, they put marshmallows where they don't belong, and they have a weird thing for mayonnaise."

Jessica grinned. She and Casey had always gotten a kick out of observing and commenting on the habits of Big Verde's social circles. It was so easy to fall into those habits. "And what's with that punch?" she asked. "Why is Methodist punch always green?"

"This is fancy punch," Casey said. "It's got sherbet in it."

He brought the tiny crystal cup up to his lips, holding up his pinky as he did so, and took a dainty sip. And then he suddenly jerked forward, spilling the rest all over his tie.

A little boy had grabbed his arm. "Casey!"

Casey remained completely calm. "Hey, there, Dalton."

A woman was right behind the child, apologizing. "I'm so sorry. Dalton, get down."

Jessica smiled at Dalton, and when he smiled back, she realized she was looking into a little face that shone just as bright as Hope's. Like Hope, the child had Down syndrome.

"I hate this tie," Casey said. "He did me a favor."

Then he picked Dalton up and set him on his lap. "Marissa, do you remember Jessica?"

"Marissa Mayes?" Jessica asked. "Oh my goodness! Hi!"

"Of course I remember!" Marissa squealed. "I recognized you as soon as you walked into the chapel. And I'm Marissa Reed now. I married Bobby."

Bobby Reed had been the high school quarterback, and Marissa had been a cheerleader with Jessica. It warmed her heart to know they'd gotten married and were still together. "How is Bobby?"

"He's doing great. Wait until he hears you're back in town!"

Jessica wasn't going to be around long enough to socialize, but she didn't bother saying so. It would be nice, though, to catch up with old friends.

"Is Dalton yours?"

"Sure is," Marissa said proudly.

"He's a handsome young man," Jessica said, and Marissa beamed even more.

"What brings you to Big V?" Marissa asked. "Surely not Miss Mavis's funeral?"

Casey looked at Jessica intently, as if that was the burning question of the day.

"I'm here for the funeral," Jessica said simply, knowing that her answer only added to the confusion.

As she looked at Marissa's curious face, ten million different stories suddenly crashed into her brain—fun stories—and surprisingly, she wanted to rehash them all. *Remember that time we toilet-papered Coach Reiner's house? Remember when I helped you sneak into Bobby's bedroom window but we picked the wrong one and you ended up staring at his mom in her nightgown?*

"JD!" Marissa shouted, earning glares from a nearby table of elderlies. "JD, come see who's here!"

Marissa's older brother, JD Mayes, strolled through the crowd with his plate of jiggly food. And even though they were indoors, he wore his signature white Stetson. Some things never changed.

JD's eyes widened at the sight of her. "Jess!"

He rushed over and gave her a warm hug.

Hubba-hubba. The cowboy still had it. He'd taken Jessica for many spins around the dance floor back in the day. They'd even held hands once in the movie theater. But that was as far as it had gone, because Jessica had only had eyes for one cowboy: Casey Long.

* * *

It felt like a high school reunion, watching JD, Marissa, and Jessica talk about old times. Casey couldn't help but grin. Jessica had been a good student—class valedictorian—and a cheerleader. Casey had been more of a troublemaker. Only two things had mattered to him: Jess and bull riding. Other than that, it had been all speeding tickets, underage drinking, disrespect for authority (he still had that issue if the authority hadn't earned it), and a chip on his shoulder the size of Texas. His crooked uncle had taken care of the speeding tickets and the underage drinking—all fixed with a wave of the magic Long wand. But the only thing that could get him to say *yes, sir* or *no, ma'am* to assholes was the threat of not being able to rodeo.

Jess had seen something in him that no one else had. She'd gotten him to pay more attention to his grades, even though he hadn't planned on going to college. He'd wanted to make her proud; to be the kind of boy she wouldn't be ashamed of. She'd been an angel, and as he listened to her chat with Dalton about his toy tractors, he figured she probably still was.

"Hey, Earth to Casey," JD said, giving him an elbow.

He'd been daydreaming. "Sorry. What was that?"

"I just told Jess about the charity rodeo tomorrow. She says she can't make it, but I think all she needs is a little encouragement. Dalton, here, is doing his part..."

Dalton put his hands together like he was praying, and with his tongue poking out from where his two front teeth should be, he said, "*Pwease.*"

Jess laughed, and it flowed through Casey's chest like a bubbling brook.

Anything that would keep Jess in Big Verde longer was a good thing. He was dying to question her, to find out why she and her mom had left Big Verde in such haste. Had her mother hated him that much? "Yeah, you should come to the rodeo, Jess. JD and I are competing in the team roping—"

"Wait," Jess interrupted. "On the same team?"

JD laughed. "Yeah, we're the current Tri-County champs, believe it, or not."

"I don't believe it," Jess said.

Casey was pretty sure that the last time Jess had seen him and JD together, JD had had him in a headlock while Mr. Preston, the principal, had been shouting at them to break it up.

"We kick ass," Casey said. JD gave him a fist bump, and then Dalton insisted on fist bumping everyone within his immediate reach while muttering *kick ass.*

"Thanks so much," Marissa said with an eye roll.

JD gave a small salute with a wink.

"You don't ride bulls anymore?" Jessica asked.

Casey flinched. Painful subject. "I suffered an injury a while back."

Exactly twelve years ago when I got on a bull not caring whether I lived or died because the girl I loved left without saying a word.

"Damn near died," JD said.

Jessica's eyes widened, and she reached out with her hand to...touch his face? He wouldn't know, because she yanked it back just as quickly. His skin yearned for the feel of her fingertips, and he fought the urge to lean toward her.

"But you're okay, now, right?"

His brain struggled to make out what she'd said. JD lifted the brim of his hat and raised an eyebrow in question. *Are you going to answer her?*

Casey cleared his throat. "Yeah. My back kinks up occasionally. I just don't care to be thrown and rolled by a fifteen-hundred-pound asshole bull again. Broke a few bones."

Seven, to be exact.

"Asshole bull!" Dalton shouted with glee.

"Dalton, that's football talk. We don't say *asshole* unless there's a game's on," Marissa chided.

"Hey, Dalton, why don't you tell Jess about Hope House? Maybe she'll want to come to the rodeo if you do."

Jessica's head snapped up, eyes wide as saucers. "Hope House? What's that?"

Why did Jess look so curious? Or was it sad? Or maybe it was happy. Her mercurial eyes seemed to display every single emotion on the spectrum.

"Hope House is fun," Dalton said.

"It's a place where special kids and adults get to hang out," Casey said. "They do all sorts of stuff. They train for the Special Olympics, and we even teach a few of them how to rodeo."

"Dalton is a mutton buster," Marissa said, referring to the children's rodeo activity of clinging to the back of a running sheep like your life depended on it.

"Who started Hope House?" Jess asked.

"Aunt Mavis," Casey said. "It's one of the reasons so many folks have turned out to honor her. She was a great woman. Gruff on the outside, maybe, but a heart of gold."

CHAPTER FIVE

The lobby of the Village Château was cool and calm. The heavy dark furniture Jessica remembered from the last time she'd been here—the graduation party thrown for Casey by the Longs—was gone. Now it was muted neutral tones and local Hill Country art.

She took the stairs to the second floor where their suite was. With the exception of the grand ballroom, which still sported thick, brocade carpeting, sparkling chandeliers, and a gigantic, ornate fireplace, the general air of the establishment was way less formal. It was really nice. Comfortable. And the aromas wafting up from the Château's restaurant were divine. Her stomach growled. Gelatin salads could carry a girl only so far.

She walked down the hall to room 204 and started to insert her key. But the door jerked open before she had a chance.

"I got my head under the water," Hope squealed. Then she threw her arms around Jessica.

"Good for you! See? I told you it was no big deal."

With Hope attached, Jessica entered the room to find Carmen lying on the bed, blue hair still wet, looking utterly exhausted. "Oh, it was a big deal, all right," Carmen said.

"And I went down the slide!" Hope said. "I went all the way under."

Hope had an irrational fear of getting her face wet. Ride a roller coaster? No problem. Trampoline? You bet. Blow bubbles in the water? Not so much. So, this was big news.

"Maybe I should let Carmen take you swimming more often."

Carmen lifted her head. "Maybe Carmen wouldn't survive that."

Ha! Carmen could look as pitiful as she wanted, but she and Hope were thick as thieves. They both loved to cook. They both loved to eat. And they neither one cared what anybody thought.

"Hey," Jessica said, sitting on the bed. "Thanks. You know there aren't many people I trust to watch Hope. In fact, I think there might just be, you know, the *one* people."

Carmen grinned slightly and narrowed her eyes. "Yeah. You owe me."

There was no way to get a smooshy *you're welcome* out of Carmen. Her real-life persona was pretty much the same as her television one. In your face. Loud. Colorful. And though she minced garlic at vision-blurring speed, she did not mince words.

Hope faked a sigh and rolled her eyes. "Carmen's tired and cranky."

"I'm not the only one," Carmen replied. "Why don't you go watch some more television and relax?"

"You're trying to get rid of me," Hope said.

Jessica laughed. Woe to the person who underestimated Hope because of her Down syndrome.

"You're right. I am. Your sister and I need to talk."

"But you've *been* talking," Hope whined.

"Retreat to the dungeon," Carmen ordered. "We'll get dinner in an hour."

Hope clapped her hands and smacked her lips. "Yum. Can we eat in the room?"

"You bet."

Hope happily went into the other room and closed the door.

"You were gone longer than expected," Carmen said.

"I went to the reception after the funeral."

Carmen sat up. "You did?"

"Yeah. It was kind of fun."

"That's what they say about funerals. Fun times."

"It's just that I saw some old friends. It was nice."

"That's a little more normal."

Normal. What was that supposed to feel like? She hadn't felt "normal" since learning her mom was undocumented. It had turned her world upside down. There'd been no stability or security after that. Of course, there'd *never* been any, but she hadn't known it. After learning the truth, she'd lived in fear of a traffic ticket or auto accident. Of literally anything and everything that could end up separating their family. And that included sharing their secret with anyone. So, they hadn't.

Except for Mavis.

Now that her mom was dead, there was no longer anything to fear. But living without a noose around your neck was hard to get used to. The noose felt...*loosened*. Not gone. That was why she hadn't been able to leave Hope back in Houston, even though Carmen could have taken just as good care of her there.

If at all possible, Hope went where Jessica went.

"I saw Casey," she whispered.

Carmen's eyes widened. She smirked, like a blue-haired elf. "Did you talk to him?"

"Yes. Quite a bit, actually. He's the sheriff now."

"You're kidding!"

"No, he really is. He pulled me over for running a red light. Did you know you don't have proof of insurance in your car?"

Carmen rolled her eyes. "How long has it been since you've been laid?"

"Carmen!"

"Well?"

Jessica went to the window. The lagoon-shaped pool, complete with slide and waterfall, brought back the memory of Casey's graduation party. It had been a luau theme, and the pool hadn't been so fancy. Just a plain rectangular lap pool. But to Jessica, a kid who'd grown up swimming in the Rio Verde, it had seemed magical and romantic. There had been floating candles and little paper boats, and then afterward, she and Casey had . . .

It had been too long since she'd been laid.

Carmen joined her at the window. "So that's where the magic happened, huh? By the pool?"

"Well, not right by the pool," Jessica said. She pointed to the right, where a fire pit blazed. "There used to be a thick clump of palm trees. Casey had laid out a blanket." The blush crept in. "We had a bottle of champagne he'd lifted from the Château's restaurant."

She'd never tasted champagne before. The bubbles had made her sneeze.

"That's so romantic." Carmen sighed. Then she grinned. "But was the sex awful? The first time is usually nothing to write home about."

A couple sat down on the lounge in front of the fire pit and snuggled.

"No, it was actually nice. I mean, I didn't have a mind-blowing orgasm. Or any orgasm. I doubt I even knew what one was. But Casey was sweet and took his time . . ."

Her voice faded as the memory took over. Casey had more than taken his time. He'd explored her body with intense curiosity and a blush-rendering thoroughness. All of the things that had been only hinted at during make-out sessions on the couch or in the back row of the movie theater had come to fruition.

Later, as they'd lain in the shadows of the palms in the moonlight, he'd confessed it had been his first time. And that he loved her.

Jess, you're my first. And I want you to be my last. Promise we'll be together forever.

She'd promised.

She turned away from the window. It was time to let it go. She'd paid her respects to Mavis. She'd seen a few friends, and it had been pleasant. Now she just had to lie low at the Château—harder than if they'd stayed at the Big Verde Motor Inn—and visit the lawyer on Monday.

"Are you going to see him again?" Carmen asked.

"I don't think so. I went into the ladies' room, and when I came out, people said he'd taken off. Something about cattle being loose on the highway."

"Lame," Carmen said.

"Well, not really," Jessica said, feeling suddenly defensive. "That's actually a dangerous situation."

Carmen snorted. "If you say so."

Jessica had been bitterly disappointed by Casey's hasty departure. There was so much she'd wanted to ask him, but what would be the point? It was probably best to hide out the rest of the weekend.

As if reading her mind, Carmen said, "So are we allowed to leave the premises of the hotel this weekend? Or are we trapped here while you hide from Sheriff Long?"

"Which Sheriff Long would you be referring to?" Jessica

asked. "The Sheriff Long who pulled me over this morning? Or the former Sheriff Long who happens to be Hope's daddy? Because I'm hiding from them both."

"Sheriff Long is my daddy?"

Carmen gasped. Jessica's throat closed up. They both turned to face Hope, who stood in the doorway. How long had she been there?

* * *

Casey sat on a fancy chair that was too small for his large frame and stared into his beer. He was dazed. The clinking plates, laughter, and conversations around him were muted, as if he wore earmuffs.

One funeral reception should have been enough. But now he had to suffer through a private family gathering at the Village Château. Mavis would have hated all the fuss.

Someone poked him in the arm. "You all right, pardner?"

JD gazed at him with concern.

"I'm just sad about Aunt Mavis," Casey said, but really, he was completely distracted with thoughts of Jessica. He'd had to leave the fellowship hall without even saying good-bye, much less getting any answers.

"Liar," JD said.

"Pardon?"

"It's not Mavis you're missing."

"Why are you even here? This is a private gathering for family only," Casey said. "And I *am* sad about Mavis."

"I know you are. But that's not why you're moping around. And I think we're related in some way or other."

He was *not* moping. Although seeing as how he was crammed into this chair in a corner, staring out the window with a warm beer in one hand and a plate of untouched food in the other, he could see how a fella might think he was.

Dammit. It had been twelve years. He should be over this teenage shit by now. But seeing Jess had brought on a rush of emotions he couldn't quite sort out. They'd talked about getting married, for Christ's sake. She'd just needed to get her mama to come around. Then they were going to live happily ever after. Stupid teenage stuff.

But it had seemed real.

He took a sip of beer but had trouble getting it to go down.

"Unless there are two red Porsches in Big Verde, she's right here at the Village Château," JD said.

Casey's heart sped up. "Are you sure? I figured she'd gone back to Houston right after the funeral."

"I didn't hear her say she was going to do that," JD said. "I heard you ask her if she was sticking around long, and she said she wasn't. That's pretty vague. Maybe she's heading back tomorrow."

Casey's heart started pounding again. Like nearly out of his chest.

"I think I'll head to the bar for a drink," he said.

You could see the lobby of the hotel from the restaurant's bar. She'd have to come down eventually, even if it was tomorrow morning...

"There's an open bar right here," JD said with a grin, nodding at the bartender doling out booze in the corner of the room. "But you go do whatever it is you've got to do."

CHAPTER SIX

Jessica sat at the bar, sipping a margarita and trying to catch a buzz. After settling Hope down, she'd asked Carmen what the hell she was supposed to do now. And Carmen had said, "Get drunk."

Normally, she'd have blown that off and set herself about fixing everything. But these were not normal times.

So here she sat.

It had been a huge mistake to bring Hope to Big Verde. Carmen was right. Nobody was coming to take anybody away. She should have let her stay with Carmen in Houston. But the last thing her mom had said was *Take care of Hope*.

Her mom. She'd die all over again if she knew Jessica had blabbed about Wade Long being Hope's father right in front of Hope! Maybe Hope would forget about it.

She caught the bartender's eye and raised her empty glass. He nodded and began measuring ingredients into the blender.

Hope wouldn't forget about it.

She'd been so excited and confused by what she'd heard that she couldn't even eat her dinner. And Hope *lived* for food.

Carmen had gone on and on about how good it was—which meant it was *really* good—while Hope had asked a million questions.

Carmen: This fried brie is to die for!
Hope: But where is my daddy?
Jessica: He's not really your dad—
Carmen: Did you taste the sauerbraten?
Hope: Will he buy me a doll?

Jessica had felt too sick to eat. How could she explain to an eleven-year-old that her "daddy" had used his power and privilege to coerce a woman into a sexual relationship? And that when the relationship resulted in a pregnancy, he'd threatened to have her deported.

Her mom had sworn her to secrecy. And Jessica had understood the importance of cooperation. It didn't need to be spelled out for her. If Wade Long alerted the authorities, her pregnant mom would have been forced to leave the country.

While sobbing, she'd written a letter to Casey.

Dear Casey,

Something horrible has happened and my mom and I have to move to Houston. I will write you when I get there, so you can come find me. I'm having to sneak this in the mail. THIS IS TOP SECRET. Do not tell a soul!

I love you. We'll be together again soon.

Jessica

She'd put a stamp on it and dropped it in a box in a strip mall when they'd stopped for fast food.

Two weeks later, she'd dropped another letter in the mail. Begging him to call. *Hang up if my mom answers! I love you, Casey. Come find me.*

Three more letters. *Come find me! Casey, why aren't you answering?*

He never did. Her mom said all Long men were horrible.

They took what they wanted and discarded you. Jessica hadn't believed it at first.

With time though...

She sighed, worrying about Hope. How could she explain this? Hope's tendency to fixate on things meant she repeated herself endlessly. And this was one thing nobody wanted to hear. Carmen had taken her swimming again in the hopes of distracting her. *She'll forget all about it after some ice cream and a swim.*

Only she wouldn't. And Jessica knew it.

The bartender set her second margarita in front of her. She decided to go for the guzzle. She sucked up about a third of the frosty beverage through the straw, and then grimaced and grabbed her head because (a) brain freeze and (b) Casey had just walked into the bar.

What the hell was he doing here? She grabbed her glass— she wasn't abandoning her margarita—and slunk off the barstool. But she couldn't escape with him standing in the doorway. A large potted tree caught her eye. Maybe she'd hide behind that until Casey moved and she could make a run for it.

Their eyes met. She probably looked like a deer caught in the headlights.

The tension Casey had carried in his shoulders since he'd first walked into the bar seemed to seep away. And then he smiled.

It made her gasp. Seeing a smile spread across Casey Long's otherwise stern and stoic face was like seeing a vibrant flower in the middle of the desert (and thinking it had bloomed just for you). It warmed every single inch of her body except for the fingers wrapped around the frozen margarita. Actually, they felt warm too. And she became even warmer—and a bit tingly—as Casey made a beeline for her.

Why hadn't she put on any lipstick? She looked down at her feet. Flip-flops! Although she'd have looked silly wearing anything else with her cutoff shorts and Hello Kitty T-shirt. What had she been thinking when she came down here like this? Her mother would have been mortified.

It's important to look our best. People judge.

Boy, did they ever. Especially in small towns.

"Tell me you weren't about to dodge behind a potted plant," Casey said with a grin.

* * *

Shit, she was cute. Would she deny that she'd been making a run for the plant? Or would she own it?

"There goes my life as a super-secret agent," she said with a shrug.

She owned it.

"You don't have to hide from me, you know," he said. It hurt that she wanted to, but he understood. It was awkward. So much time had passed...

Yet, as he looked into her big brown eyes, it hardly felt like it. Hair in a ponytail, shorts, and a T-shirt; he recognized this girl. Hell, if she put on a cheerleading outfit and went out onto the field tonight, nobody would even question it.

He swallowed. Thinking about Jess in a cheerleading outfit was making it difficult to form words into a sentence, and he had enough difficulty with that as it was.

"I wasn't hiding *from you,* per se. I just figured all the locals would be at the football game tonight and it would be safe to come down dressed like..." She looked down at her gorgeous tanned legs. "This."

She held out a foot and a flip-flop with ribbons tied all over it dangled from her toes.

"That's high fashion for Big Verde. And tonight's an away game. Folks don't necessarily want to drive all the way to Smithville to cheer the Giants on to their eighty-seventh straight loss."

"Fair weather fans," Jessica said.

She'd cheered her little heart out for those Giants once, all while stealing sideways glances at Casey while he stood along the fence with his ragtag group of rodeo pals. He remembered trying to act cool when his friends wanted to leave, pretending to care about the pathetic football game when all he really cared about was seeing Jessica do one of her famous split jumps.

Those legs. Could she still do the splits?

"I lost interest in football when a certain cheerleader moved away," he said. "But I'm here tonight for a family celebration of Aunt Mavis. It's in the hospitality suite."

"Oh, I'm sorry! Don't you need to be getting back?"

"She would have hated the fuss," he said.

Jessica nodded in agreement.

Casey was missing something. He just knew it. But he didn't have a clue as to what. "Want to go for a walk?" he blurted.

He was desperate to not let her out of his sight. When he thought she'd left earlier, damn it, he was eighteen again. Eighteen and heartbroken. Ready to put out an *APB* to track her ass down.

She wouldn't stay forever. But right now, he could barely think beyond the current moment. And in the current moment, he needed to touch her. A strand of hair had conveniently escaped her ponytail, and he gently tucked it behind her ear.

Jessica licked her bottom lip and trailed her eyes down the front of his dress shirt. She looked very much as if she was imagining what might be underneath it, and the odds of her finding out were increasing, since he suddenly felt warm. Every damn inch of him might as well be on fire, just from the heat of her eyes.

He tried not to look as if he might be doing the same to her, but it was hard. He'd already noted all the things about her that were familiar, but he was dying to discover the ways in which she'd changed. And not just physically (although she did still look cute enough for a cheerleading outfit). The way her eyes continued to roam his body indicated the years had given her confidence. And he liked the way it looked on her.

"Well?" he asked, raising an eyebrow and holding out his hand. "How about that walk? You can keep your drink; we won't leave the property."

Jessica nodded, as if she'd made her decision. Then she took the straw between her lips, and while never taking her eyes off his, she sucked down the rest of her margarita.

"Hold on there. You're going to get a—"

She winced and shut her eyes. "Brain freeze," she said. "I know."

With a satisfied sigh, she set her empty glass on a nearby table, and took his hand. When her fingers touched his, every hair on his body stood up, as if lightning were about to strike him dead.

CHAPTER SEVEN

W as she really holding Casey Long's hand?

She wanted to pinch herself to see if she was dreaming. Or slap herself in order to wake up. Or maybe just slap herself because holy cow they were heading out the French doors toward the pool, where Hope and Carmen were swimming.

Dang!

"Pardon?"

She'd said it out loud.

Casey looked at her quizzically.

Jessica could see Hope paddling around under the waterfall. She turned, forcing Casey to look away from the pool. Luckily, they were in the shadow of the corner of the building, where Hope and Carmen probably wouldn't spot them.

Being spotted would be disastrous. Not only would Carmen embarrass Jessica by making hubba-hubba eyes and giving thumbs-ups and God only knows what else, but there was a good chance Hope would accost him with *Hi! Are you my daddy?*

And wouldn't that be a kicker?

Plus, she just didn't want anybody in Big Verde, not

even Casey, knowing about Hope. There was no real threat from Wade anymore, but fear was strong glue for making habits stick.

She steered Casey toward the fire pit. They could sit on one of the outdoor couches with their backs to the pool. In the moonlight, they'd just look like any two people.

"I just meant *wow*. I hardly recognize the Château."

"It's changed quite a bit since you and I—" Casey paused. Cleared his throat. "Since the last time we were here."

The last time they were here they'd made love. Made plans. Promised to be together forever.

"They've got a fancy German chef now," Casey continued. "Rumor has it, he's trying to buy the restaurant from the hotel."

"Frederick Mueller," Jessica said.

Casey raised an eyebrow. "Somebody's been keeping up with the news in Big Verde."

"You realize I work for Carmen Foraccio, right?"

Casey gave her a blank look.

"You've never heard of Carmen?"

"The name sounds a bit familiar. Is she famous?"

"Do you watch the Food Channel?"

"Is that like a TV show?"

"Oh my God. Um, well, it's a network that features shows about food. And Carmen's show is at the top. She's a celebrity chef. Have you heard of La Casa Bleu? Or *Funky Fusions*?"

"JD and I ate at La Casa Bleu when we were roping in Vegas. Italian food."

"Well, it's Italian and French. It's a fusion place. There's one in Houston too. It's the original location."

"Oh really? Do you eat there often?"

"I manage it," Jessica said proudly.

"Wow, Jess. That's pretty amazing." A huge smile lit up Casey's face.

"What are you so happy about?"

"It's just that, well, you said that's what you wanted to do, right? Run a fancy restaurant like the Village Château? And look at you. You're doing it. And a famous one, at that."

As a kid, Jessica had been practically obsessed with the Village Château restaurant. It represented high society to her—Big Verde style—and she'd longed to be the kind of person who ate there regularly.

"They had pretty good spaghetti," Casey added with a wink.

"You got *spaghetti*?"

"The most expensive spaghetti I've ever eaten in my life. Although I think it had a special French sauce on it, so maybe that was why. Is Carmen the chef?"

"She used to be. And she still oversees the menu and all the recipes. Everything is made according to her specifications. But she doesn't spend much time in the kitchen anymore. Her show takes up most of her time."

"*Funky Fusions*," Casey said. "I think I've seen it. She goes around eating all kinds of crazy shit, right?"

Jessica laughed. "That's the show."

They arrived at the fire pit. From here, they could still hear occasional giggles and shrieks from Hope, but they were muffled by breezes and distance.

Jessica sat and patted the seat next to her, hoping Casey would hurry up and join her. The lighting was dim—ground sconces and the glow of the fire—but she didn't trust that someone couldn't make them out if they looked really hard. And Carmen was nosy.

"Somebody's having fun over there," Casey said with a grin, looking over his shoulder at the pool.

Jessica grabbed his hand and yanked. "Sit."

It wasn't very effective, as far as yanks went. Casey was over six feet of solid muscle, and he glanced down at her like she was a tiny kitten yanking his chain.

"Hold your horses," he said, and then he sat down next to her and stretched out his long legs, crossing his ankles and revealing some really nice cowboy boots. His slacks were gray, and there was no gun or badge on his belt. His shirt was white, and Jessica watched as his fingers nimbly loosened his tie.

She swallowed as those same fingers then trailed down his shirt to settle on his thigh, which was hard and muscular and straining the fabric of his slacks. When she succeeded in wrenching her eyes away from that lovely vision and directing them back to Casey's face, she was met by a very sexy smirk.

Followed by a wink.

"That margarita getting to you?"

Maybe just a little. The brain freeze had melted into a warm glow.

"How did you end up in law enforcement?"

"Surprised?"

"Understatement."

Casey laughed. "Well, believe it, or not, I got in some trouble after the bull riding didn't work out. Nothing awful. Just fighting and drinking. I think I was embarrassing the family."

She'd worried that Casey might fall back into his wild ways after she'd left. And it seems he had.

"And?"

Casey stared at the fire, appearing relaxed. "Aunt Mavis made me volunteer my time to help some truly troubled youth. Kids with real problems, way bigger than mine. And

I discovered I was pretty good at it. So, I decided to get a degree in criminal justice."

A warm swell of pride spread throughout her chest. "I knew you could do it, Casey," she whispered.

He looked up, the reflection of the flames dancing in his blue eyes. "It was hard," he said. "Without you."

Then why didn't he come after her? Why did he ignore her letters?

The words were on the tip of her tongue. *Just ask him.*

She took a deep breath, but Casey started talking again. "I was a cop in San Antonio for a couple of years. I didn't much care for city life, so I came home. Decided to run for sheriff."

"Family tradition," Jessica said, hoping the bitterness didn't show in her voice.

"I know what Wade did, Jess."

Jessica's head snapped up. Her pulse pounded in her head. "You do?"

"He's a crook. Hell, he fixed *my* record. He threw his weight around. God only knows what all shit he was... *is*...wrapped up in. Aunt Mavis was ashamed of him. She actually told me so once."

So, he didn't know. Not specifically.

He uncrossed his legs and turned to face her. They were suddenly mighty close. She could smell his aftershave. His eyes locked on hers, and she clenched the cushion of the seat to keep from falling right into those baby blues.

Casey didn't blink. "I'm not like Wade. This is my county. My town. My people. And I take care of them."

If she'd thought Casey Long the bad boy had turned her on, it was only because she'd never met Casey Long the good guy. She wanted to grab that stern face and kiss it senseless.

"Do you remember what happened here?" she blurted.

Casey furrowed his brow, as if she'd said something offensive. "How could I ever forget it, Jess?" Then his expression softened, and he gently touched her cheek with his thumb. "It was my first time."

The touch of his thumb on her cheek sent shivers all the way to her toes. "Oh, you're sticking to that story?" she asked, feeling a little breathless.

Casey smiled. "I am totally sticking to that story. Because it's the truth. And I'm pretty sure you know it, based on my performance. I don't think I made it to the eight-second buzzer."

Jessica laughed at the bull riding reference. But sincerity shone in Casey's eyes. She'd been his first. And if he hadn't been lying about that, was he telling the truth about everything else? Had he truly been in love with her?

His eyes had darkened, and he leaned in even closer. She stared at his lips and brushed his chin with her fingers.

"I'm better now," he said. "I can go well past eight seconds."

"Had lots of practice?" Jessica asked with an embarrassingly shaky voice.

"I wouldn't say lots. But I know where all the important spots are." The lips she couldn't take her eyes off of curled up in an adorable smirk. "And I know just what to do to them."

She believed him. He was practically doing it with his eyes. And all of her important spots were responding appropriately. She squeezed her thighs together as Casey's eyes settled on her lips.

Was it the margarita making her feel this way? No. There wasn't enough alcohol in it to lead to wherever this was going. The only thing leading her now was her heart.

And her important spots. Which were pretty much on fire.

The look in Casey's eyes promised he could put out fires, no problem.

As if on cue, the fire in the pit suddenly went out, making Jessica gasp.

"Must be ten o'clock," Casey said. "That means the pool is closed."

Oh dear. Jessica looked back at the pool. Carmen and Hope were both out, wrapping themselves in towels. There was nobody else around.

"The lights and pit are on a timer," Casey added. "That's why the fire went out."

"Not out entirely," she muttered. Then she put her hand to her mouth, because she hadn't meant to say it out loud.

Casey gently pulled her hand away. "Let's see what we can do about that," he said, bringing his lips to hers.

CHAPTER EIGHT

Her lips. God, even better than he remembered. In some ways, he was reliving the past—this was Jess, *his Jess*—but he was also navigating new territory. New delicious territory.

This was grown-up Jess. And grown-up Jess knew how to kiss.

She pressed her breasts into his chest, and he ran his hand down her back, mapping all the womanly curves and planes of her body. When he got to her hip, she twisted to give him better access, and he slipped his hand beneath to cup her nice, round ass.

She responded with a moan that nearly made him come undone.

He was impossibly hard. What he had going on couldn't be referred to as *wood*. It was more like granite. And speaking of *undone,* she had his tie off. He didn't even know when that had happened. Her fingers traveled the trail of his shirt's buttons.

She sighed against his lips. "We're in public."

Did she mean *We're in public so we need to stop* or *We're in public and I'm seriously turned on?*

She pulled away and gazed at him. There was just a sliver of a moon, but it lit up her eyes.

"We're probably doing a little more than we should out here. Somebody might see us," she said.

They hadn't done nearly enough.

Casey glanced around. "It's pretty dark out. They'd have to walk right up on us."

Jess licked her plump lips, already swollen from kissing. Her chest rose and fell quickly, but she wasn't quite breathless. And Casey wanted her breathless.

"But someone might do that," Jess said. "Walk right up on us."

Casey shifted nervously. He *was* the sheriff. Having sex in a public place probably wasn't the smartest idea he'd ever had. Jessica definitely brought out something wild in him, but his days of living on the wild side were over.

"Let's go to your room," he suggested. "That seems like a better plan."

Jessica had his shirt unbuttoned and was staring at his chest. It was probably a bit broader and more muscled than when he was a skinny kid in high school, and it definitely had more hair.

"Jess, did you hear me? Your room?"

She looked back to his eyes with a sheepish little grin on her face. He couldn't know for sure in the dim lighting, but he suspected she was blushing. She sighed deeply. "Actually, that won't work. I'm not traveling alone."

Ah. He should have guessed that with the Porsche. "Carmen?"

"Yes," Jess said. Casey followed her gaze to the second floor of the hotel, where a balcony light was on. The other rooms were dark. While the restaurant did a booming business with travelers and locals alike, the hotel didn't see much activity during the off-season.

He wasn't going to let this opportunity get away. But they couldn't keep making out by the fire pit. It had been a blissfully long time since a Long Family scandal, and Casey would like to continue that streak.

His place was up in the hills, only about fifteen minutes away, but he suspected if Jess had time to think about things, she'd cool off. Hell, if *he* had time to think about things...

Nah. He wasn't going to cool off. If anything, he was heating up even more.

He scanned the area. There was a patch of cedar trees, but they wouldn't provide enough cover. And besides, he and Jess weren't going to bang on the ground like animals.

He glanced at Jess. She was biting her bottom lip and eyeing his chest and looking every bit as if she was all in for banging on the ground like animals.

A loud humming sound started up as the pool pump kicked in. The pump and other equipment were concealed behind a wooden fence surrounded by shrubbery. You had to go through a little gate to get in there; Casey knew this because he'd once been called out to investigate a violent racoon. Such was life as a small-town county sheriff.

The enclosed area was roomy enough to hold a chaise lounge, of which there were plenty by the pool.

Jess saw where he was looking.

"What's behind the fence?"

"Pool equipment."

"We couldn't—"

Oh yes, they could. Casey jumped up and walked to the pool. He picked out a sturdy chaise lounge, hoisted it up, and carried it past the fire pit to the gate that led inside the small fenced-in area.

Jessica hurried over. "What do you think we're going to do on that?"

"I don't know. Maybe we'll lounge? Look at the stars? Make out like fiends?"

"What if somebody is watching us right now?"

There wasn't a soul around. "Even if someone were looking from one of the windows, they couldn't possibly see anything other than shadows, and besides, we're about to be hidden by this nifty fence."

"You sound pretty sure about that."

He extended a hand. "Come on, Jess. Let's do something wild."

* * *

Casey Long stood in the shadows with his shirt open, looking dangerous as hell and holding out a hand. How many times had Jessica dreamed of feeling his touch again? She couldn't shake the feeling that she was dreaming.

Nothing could come of a hookup with Casey. Jessica would be back at her crazy life in Houston on Monday, and she and Casey would probably never talk to each other again. But for now...

"Okay," she blurted.

It had been a long time since she'd done anything that could be considered even remotely wild or risky.

Casey gently pulled her in and closed the gate behind them. She went straight into his arms and pressed against him. God, she loved the feel of him. So tall—he'd always been tall—but now he was also *big*. She rose on her toes and kissed him, eliciting a sexy groan that was louder than the hum of the pool equipment.

"Shit, Jess," he said against her lips. "You taste so good."

He abandoned her lips and went down her jaw to her neck, licking the sensitive skin behind her ear. "I want to taste all of you," he whispered. "Every inch."

Jessica's breath hitched. Was he talking about what she thought he was? The one time they'd been together had been sweet, but they'd both been inexperienced. She hadn't even *known* about that particular activity, much less experienced it.

Casey's hands roamed beneath her T-shirt as he kissed her neck. Her knees were so weak they probably wouldn't hold her up much longer.

As if sensing her imminent collapse, Casey steered her toward the chaise lounge. "Sit," he ordered, with a low and raspy voice.

Jessica followed instructions, and Casey pressed the back of the chair all the way down. Then he stood over her, running his hands through his hair and gazing down as if she were a feast and he couldn't decide where to start.

"You've filled out a little," she said, staring at his chest.

"So have you," he replied, staring at hers.

His eyes shone with lust, which Jessica greatly appreciated. But she'd done a little more than fill out. She was thirty and although she was in good shape, her body reflected the years. She didn't have saggy old-lady boobs, but they weren't exactly perky anymore, either. She wanted to tell Casey he'd missed her best years, but her best years had been spent working, going to school, and taking care of her mom and Hope.

Everybody had missed her best years, including her.

Casey took his shirt off, dropping it to the ground. Ho. Lee. Cow.

The man looked like a Greek god. Broad, chiseled chest with *way* more hair than she remembered. Hard, sculpted abs. Her fingers itched to explore.

"Your turn," he said, sitting on the chaise next to her. The chair creaked and sank into the grass.

Insecurity crept in. "I don't know that I want to take anything all the way off. We might need to make a run for it."

"I'll accept that for now," he said, running his hand beneath her shirt, up her belly, and between her breasts, and dragging her T-shirt with it. "But next time, everything is coming off."

Next time? Was he really thinking there would be a—

Her thought was interrupted by Casey lifting her bra up over her breasts, not even bothering to unclasp it. He let out a shuddering sigh as he stared. "God, woman. You're gorgeous."

Before Jessica could say a word, Casey bent over and covered a nipple with his warm mouth.

That was it. She was gone. Run for it? Ha! If anyone walked up on them now, Jessica wouldn't even know it.

Casey's hand trailed up her leg to the inside of her thigh. *When had she opened her legs?* Probably as soon as she'd felt his lips on her breast. She panted embarrassingly as his fingers traced ticklish patterns on her skin.

The jean cutoffs were pretty short. Shorter than a woman Jessica's age should wear them, but right now they were coming in handy, as Casey had no trouble slipping his fingers inside the denim. He brushed her panties, and she moaned and arched her back. The combination of what his fingers were doing and what his lips were doing was almost too much.

Casey lifted his head and watched her while still working magic with his fingers. "Can I—"

He was talking to her. She'd seen his mouth move, but it was so freaking hard to hold her focus. "Can you what?" she gasped.

"Can I..."

"Hm?"

"Jess, I want inside you."

"Yes," she whispered. "Please."

His finger slipped inside. Followed quickly by another. And then his mouth was on hers, forceful, but not crushing, and he was exploring—with tongue and fingers—slowly and intentionally, as if he had all the time in the world.

Jessica thought she might lose her mind. She wasn't in the mood for a Sunday drive. She was excited. Starved. Impatient. And he was torturing her. It was delicious torture, but still torture.

She ran her hands down Casey's back and gripped his very firm butt in an encouraging way. He responded and ground against her, harder and faster, as if he'd picked up on her sense of urgency. One of his legs was over hers, the other one was—*where was the other one?* Probably on the ground. The chaise simply wasn't big enough for the both of them.

Casey kissed her neck. Sucked on it. When was the last time Jessica had petted and made out with someone? She reached between them and felt the hard length of him. He whimpered into her neck and rubbed himself frantically against her as the chaise lounge squeaked and squawked.

They were both hot and sweaty and panting like animals, and this was... *fun.*

She hadn't felt this excited, crazy, and *free* since the last time she'd made out with Casey Long.

Casey stopped moving and slowly pulled his hand away. The only sound was the humming of the pool pump and their haggard breathing.

"What's wrong?" she asked.

"I told you I wanted to taste you. All of you."

She watched as he brought his fingers to his mouth, licked them, and then closed his eyes as if he'd just tasted heaven.

Oh boy. That was hot. And she knew what was coming next. Or at least she hoped she did. She unbuttoned her shorts and slid down the zipper. Then she raised her hips, and Casey pulled off the shorts, along with her panties, in one fell swoop. No time for modesty now. Jessica's hormones were in the pilot's seat, and they were going full throttle.

Without even a hint of hesitancy, Casey hoisted her legs up and over the armrests of the chaise. "Still pretty flexible, I see," he said with a grin.

Jessica gasped as the cool night air kissed her sensitive flesh, and then Casey kissed it too.

Goose bumps. Tingling. *Humming.*

Was it the pool pump? Or was it her?

"Oh, Casey..."

It was definitely her.

Casey moaned in answer and continued what he was doing. Plus a few other things with his fingers. Like pinching her nipples.

"So good," he mumbled against her. The vibration of his voice almost did her in. "So." He licked her lightly. "Damn." He licked her again. "Good." He thrust his tongue inside her, and that was all it took.

Fireworks exploded behind Jessica's eyes as her body spasmed. Her toes curled. Her fingers tingled. She'd thought women who described their orgasms in that way were exaggerating. But it turned out, she'd been having inferior orgasms.

Casey held her in a gentle suction until she couldn't take it anymore. She gently pushed his face away, and he rose above her, gazing into her eyes.

"Was that okay?"

She nearly laughed. "Better than okay. You've learned some new tricks."

"Would you like to see some more?"

"What else have you got up your sleeve?"

Casey rose to his knees and unbuckled his belt. "Actually, it's in my pants."

CHAPTER NINE

Casey couldn't believe this was happening. What had started off as him heading to his great-aunt's funeral had ended with him crouched behind a fence and shrubbery having sex with the literal woman of his dreams. One who happened to be an ex-cheerleader. And judging by the position her legs were currently in, she could still do the splits.

He was doing several things he could be arrested for, including destruction of property, because there wasn't any way the chaise lounge would survive the night.

It was by far the best day he'd had in a long time. Possibly in forever.

"Do you have a condom?" Jessica asked.

Shit. The question had the effect of a dart piercing a balloon. He patted his pockets even though he knew he didn't have one. "I don't think—"

Jessica snapped her legs shut.

"Jesus. Hold on. Don't do anything hasty."

He looked around helplessly, dick out like a flagpole, as if a condom would materialize out of thin air.

"Do you have one, or not?" Jess asked.

"Nope."

"Oh no! Are you serious?"

"I didn't think to grab one on my way to my great-aunt's funeral."

Jess sat up. Pulled her bra back down over her delicious, bouncy breasts. She was shutting down the party, and Casey didn't blame her one bit. How could he? But he was still mighty frustrated and damn near ready to explode.

His hands shook as he leaned over and snagged her shorts with the panties inside and tossed them to her.

"Thanks," she said, standing up and slipping them on. "I'm sorry—"

"Don't apologize, Jess. I'm glad you had the where-withal to think about protection. I was, well, you know. Out of my ever-loving mind." And he still was. It was pretty obvious too, since he was standing there with his dick out, although it had definitely lost some of its enthusiasm. He started to zip up.

"Don't do that," Jess said, licking her lips. "There are other ways to have fun."

Casey raised an eyebrow and stopped zipping.

Jessica sat on the chaise, and its legs gave out. She grunted as she bounced on her butt.

Casey snorted. And then Jess started to giggle. It rolled through him and tickled his ribs as he fought off the urge to join in.

"Come here," she said, rising to her knees and still smiling.

"Jess, you don't have to do this," Casey said. "I'm fine. I've had a great time. Really."

Getting her off had been way more than a great time. He really didn't need to do anything more.

Jessica smirked at his hardening dick, which begged to disagree. She crooked a finger. "You're giving yourself away."

Casey took a step toward her—the lady had given him an order and he wasn't about to disappoint her—but over the humming of the pump and the pounding of his pulse in his head, he thought he heard footsteps.

Dammit. He put a finger to his lips while shoving his dick in his pants.

Sure enough, someone was coming. Casey looked over his shoulder to see Tyler Murphy peering over the top of the fence.

"Hey, Sheriff Long, is everything okay?"

Tyler was a busboy for the restaurant. He was also Casey's neighbor's kid. "Yeah, Tyler. Everything's fine."

He glanced back at Jess. She was wild-eyed and putting herself back together while trying to back into the shadows.

"Be careful, Jess—"

Too late. Jessica stepped back and tripped on the broken chaise lounge. Casey lunged and caught her, and when their eyes met, she started to giggle again.

Casey got an idea.

"This young lady has had a bit too much to drink. I heard her wandering around back here." He looked intently at Jess. "Feeling better now, ma'am?"

Jessica crossed her arms and faked a hiccup. "Yes, Sheriff," she slurred. "Much better."

None of that explained why Casey wasn't wearing a shirt, and Tyler didn't look 100 percent convinced. But what the hell was the kid doing back here anyway? Casey sniffed in the boy's direction and picked up the faint, skunky odor of marijuana. "Did you come out here to check on the pump?" he asked. "Because that's a weird chore for a busboy."

Even in the dark, Casey could see the whites of Tyler's eyes as he caught on to the position he was in. The kid probably came out here regularly to toke up. If Casey felt like looking, he was pretty sure he'd be able to find telltale signs of previous activity. He wouldn't be surprised if there were stems and papers scattered about.

Tyler seemed to come to the same conclusion. "Uh, I was just out here collecting cups and shit—uh, sorry—from around the pool and I thought I heard—"

Casey raised an eyebrow, crossed his arms over his bare chest.

"Thought I heard this lady being sick or something."

Jessica fake-hiccupped again, and Casey nearly busted out laughing. Everybody understood each other then.

He nodded at Tyler. "I've got it under control."

"Yes, sir," Tyler said with a smirk. "It sure looks like it."

"Get on back to work," Casey said.

Tyler saluted, turned, and loped back off in the direction of the hotel.

Casey picked up his shirt and slipped it on. Jess still had her hand over her mouth, but it wasn't containing her giggles very well.

"Get some control over yourself, woman," Casey said with a wink. "Or I'll throw you in the drunk tank."

"We don't have to call it quits, you know," she said. "We can go somewhere else."

"Nah. I think we should quit while we're ahead. I had a really good time." He looked at her little T-shirt, her shorts with the top button still undone, and her mussed-up hair. "A *really* good time."

"So, let's keep going. Swing by the Rite Aid and pick up a pack of condoms, head to your place, and get busy." She wiggled her hips.

God. It sounded so easy. And he loved how eager she was. But it was late, and there were other things to consider. "As much as I'd love to, I can't just waltz into the

Rite Aid with you to buy condoms. For one thing, I'm the sheriff."

"Sheriffs don't have sex?"

"They do it discreetly."

"Oh, is that what we were doing?" One corner of her mouth curled up. "Being discreet here in the shrubs behind the pool pump?"

Damn. That crooked little grin. He'd love to wipe it off her face with a kiss.

"And the Rite Aid is closed anyway," he added. "They roll up the sidewalks around here pretty early."

He picked up the broken chaise. "I'm going to toss this in the Dumpster behind the restaurant," he said. "And then I'm going to help a poor drunk lady get back into the hotel safely."

Jess pouted.

Those lips. He wanted to drop the chaise and tackle her to the ground. But he couldn't. For one thing, no condom. For another, he had an early day tomorrow.

"Are you going to come watch me and JD rope at the rodeo? It's for a good cause, and I'm really hoping you'll stick around awhile."

Jessica twisted a strand of hair around her finger, a habit that took him straight back to high school. But then she looked at him and smiled.

"I'll think about it."

"You think about it real hard."

"Will you be wearing chaps?"

"I'd get laughed out of the arena."

Jess looked bitterly disappointed. "That's too bad. I like chaps."

"I'll wear chaps," he blurted. "If it means you'll come."

He swallowed.

"To the rodeo," he added. "Not just, you know, come."

They both busted out laughing, again. Silly, uncontrollable, insane laughter. They stopped when they literally couldn't breathe anymore.

"I really, really like chaps," Jess said.

She licked her lips. *Licked her damn lips like she was thinking about him in a pair of chaps and nothing else.*

"And I'll also have a handy dandy rope, if that turns you on."

She squeezed her thighs together, realized she'd done it, and unclenched them with a sly little grin that said she knew he'd noticed.

"What time does the Rite Aid open tomorrow?"

"Now, darlin, tomorrow is Sunday. It's closed. You can't buy condoms on the Lord's Day. It's bad enough that you're even thinking about it."

"Oh, I'm thinking about it, Casey Long. We might have to drive to the nearest town to hit up a Walmart."

"That could be arranged," Casey said. "After the rodeo."

Jessica bit her lip, and Casey got up right close. "I might have to tie you up so you don't leave again."

The blush that lit up Jess's cheeks said she wasn't entirely opposed to the idea. Casey was going to be in for a long, sleepless night.

* * *

Jessica lathered up in the shower. The smile on her face was starting to make her cheeks sore, but she couldn't get rid of it, no matter how hard she tried. Not that she was trying very hard.

Hard. Holy cow, Casey had been hard. She felt awful that she hadn't been able to return any favors and do something about it. But they'd been caught!

Her smile got even wider.

She'd been like a teen again. A dumb, horny, risk-taking teen.

She hadn't risked anything in twelve years. Not for her own happiness, and not for love.

Love. She did *not* love Casey. But dang it, she definitely had a major crush going on. It felt just like old times.

Yep. She was definitely a kid again. Although a kid would have insisted this crush was something more. Because it felt like her world was going to end on Monday when she had to go back to Houston. And because the thought of not seeing Casey again hurt just as much this time as it had the last.

Only this time, she wasn't going to leave with any secrets. Wade Long couldn't hurt her. People could talk if they wanted, but she was taking Hope to the rodeo tomorrow. It had been wonderful to see old friends today. It would be even better to see them tomorrow.

* * *

Casey sat at the bar. He'd wandered around the pool after dropping Jess off in the lobby—she'd refused to let him walk her to the room—picking up the cups and napkins and trash that Tyler had missed.

The bar was empty and they were closing up shop, but Casey was a Long *and* the sheriff. He could stay as long as he wanted. He wouldn't do that though. He didn't believe in tossing his weight around with the family name. He'd just shoot the shit with the bartender until the kid was done drying glasses.

"Hey, Zeke, who does the purchasing for the pool furniture and whatnot around here? I accidentally broke a chaise lounge and I'd like to replace it."

Zeke picked up a glass from the washer and began drying it off. "Stella will know what to do about the chaise. Although she'll just tell you to forget about it."

Stella was the general manager, and Zeke was probably right. It would be best for Casey to just replace it himself.

Casey sucked down the last of his beer and pulled out his wallet.

"On the house, Sheriff. You know that," Zeke said.

"Bullshit," Casey said, slapping some cash on the counter. "I'd better get home. Early day tomorrow for the rodeo."

"You and JD roping?"

"Yeah. We don't stand a chance, though. I heard a lot of the Rancho Canada Verde cowboys are entering."

Zeke laughed. "You're going to your asses kicked."

"I know. But it's for Hope House. I'm happy to have my ass kicked for little Dalton Reed and his friends." He stood up and stuffed his wallet back in his pocket.

"Hold on, Sheriff," Zeke said, digging beneath the counter. "You know that lady you were with earlier? The one who was here at the bar?"

Casey crossed his arms. "Jessica Acosta. What about her?"

Zeke held up a slim leather wallet. "She left this when she followed you out the door."

Wow. Good thing Zeke found it. Although in Big Verde, most people would turn it in. It was just one of the things he loved about the people of his town. "Thanks, Zeke—"

Zeke's face broke out in a grin. "I guess she forgot all about it while y'all were busting the chaise by the pool pump."

"Damn Tyler Murphy," Casey muttered.

Zeke laughed and handed over the wallet. "She's in room 204."

Casey's pulse sped up. He'd get to see Jessica again, even if only for a few minutes. "Thanks."

He left the bar and climbed the ornate staircase in the lobby. When he got to room 204, he stopped and took a deep breath. He was still riding the high that came from messing around, and he had a partial boner to prove it. But what was making him sweat was something much deeper. It had been so satisfying to tell Jess about his life, how he'd pulled himself together and gone to college, become a cop, and then finally been elected sheriff. It was as if he'd worked all this time just to be able to someday look her in the eye and tell her he'd done it. He'd become the man she'd always known he could be.

I knew you could do it, Casey.

Of everything they'd said and done tonight, those words had been the sweetest. He was a better man because of Jessica Acosta. No doubt about it. He'd been a hellion who gave his family fits. Drove his teachers insane. Irritated the hell out of the fine folks in town who saw him as an entitled, spoiled brat.

But Jessica had seen something else in him. He'd thought she was crazy. Believed she just had a good girl crush on a bad boy. But at some point, he'd decided to become the guy she thought he was. Even after she left, or maybe *because* she'd left, he kept trying. And he'd done it.

He squared his shoulders. Made sure his shirt was tucked in. And then he knocked.

The door opened. And it wasn't Jess who answered. Or her friend, Carmen.

It was a little girl. "Hi!" she said.

"Hi yourself. Is your, uh…" He tried looking over her shoulder into the room, but she'd only opened the door about six inches.

"Who are you?" the child asked.

He wanted to ask her the same question. "I'm Casey."

That seemed to be all she needed to hear. She opened the door wide, and Casey peered in, but still didn't see Jessica.

The little girl put her hands on her hips. "I'm Hope."

Casey finally got a good look at her. She was probably ten or eleven years old and cute as a button. And she had the same infectious grin as Dalton Reed. She had Down syndrome.

Casey smiled back.

"My grandma used to live here," Hope said.

Casey rubbed his chin. Was she somehow local? Did he have the wrong room?

He looked at the number on the door. It was 204. That was the room Zeke had sent him to. And besides, if this little cutie was local, he'd know it.

"My, my, my," a sultry voice said.

Finally. An adult. Casey looked up to see a gorgeous woman with big blue eyes and hair to match staring over Hope's head. He realized he'd seen her on television at least once or twice. "You must be Carmen," he said.

"Mm-hm," Carmen said, looking him up and down with a little smirk that suggested he might need to have a talk with Miss Acosta about kissing and telling.

He hoped she hadn't left off the part where he'd made her toes curl.

"And you must be Sheriff Long," Carmen said.

"You're Sheriff Long?" Hope asked.

"Uh-oh," Carmen muttered. "Listen, Hope, he's not—"

"Sheriff Long is my daddy!"

What the hell? Casey took a step back. The room began to spin a little.

My grandma used to live here.

Shit.

"Uh, hold on a minute, cowboy," Carmen said. Then she shouted, "Jessica!"

Hope ran into the hall and wrapped her arms around Casey. Jess came to the door with her hair wrapped in a towel, her eyes wide, and her mouth hanging open.

"Hope, come here," she said, unwrapping the child from his legs.

"No, no! Let me go!" Hope wailed. "He's my daddy!"

All the color had drained from Jess's face as she held on to Hope. A man across the hall poked his head out the door. "Is everything okay?"

"It's fine," Jessica said.

The man looked to Casey, but Casey couldn't talk.

Nothing was fine.

Hope's little face was streaked with tears. This was his child? And he hadn't even known about her?

"Jess," he said. His voice didn't sound right. He felt like he was choking. "How could you?"

He turned and stumbled down the hall, ran down the stairs, and didn't stop running until he got to his truck. People shouted his name, asked if he was all right.

But he barely heard them.

He had to get somewhere to sort this all out. Somewhere private. A place where his own damn child wouldn't see him freak out.

CHAPTER TEN

Jessica scanned the arena from the stands. The rodeo had officially begun over an hour ago. They'd gotten there early, in the hopes that Casey would too. But nobody had seen him. They'd already sat through the opening ceremony, the mutton bustin'—Dalton had placed third—and the women's barrel racing event. The youth calf scramble was next, and then it was team roping.

That was Casey's event.

Jessica twisted the hem of her T-shirt into a knot. Surely, Casey wouldn't have gone and done something stupid? What if he'd drunk himself into a stupor? He'd been terribly upset, and Jessica had wanted to run after him. But he was an adult, and Hope was not.

Hope had needed her more.

And Casey shouldn't have run away.

Even so, her heart ached for him.

She spotted JD's white hat and stood up. "Stay here," she said to Carmen and Hope.

She worked her way down the bleachers, stopping every two seconds to say hi to someone because that's how it was in Big Verde. She finally made her way to where JD stood by the fence, phone to his ear. Their eyes met and he shook his head.

"Still not answering?" she asked.

JD shoved his phone back in his pocket. "You want to tell me what got him so upset that he just took off the night before the rodeo?"

Jessica scowled at him. "That's what you're worried about? The rodeo?"

"Well, I'm sure as hell not worried he's been kidnapped. He's pissed or something is all."

He yanked on his white Stetson with a pointed look that said, *At you.*

"We didn't fight," she said. "It was a misunderstanding, and he took off before I could explain everything to him."

"I don't need to know the details. But, Jess, that man has never stopped pining for you. He's lonely, but he functions. Sometimes he even manages to be happy. You can't just come barging back into town and mess with people's lives."

Is that what she'd done? She closed her eyes at the memory of the look on his face when Hope had blurted out that he was her father.

She swallowed down a bit of bile, but then she said, "He's never stopped pining for me? Really?"

JD looked at the arena where the calf scramble had started. The crowd was cheering and going nuts for the kids participating, and Hope was probably having a blast. "Really," he said. "So be careful with him."

Obviously, she had to tell Casey that Hope wasn't his. But she wasn't sure what would come after that. It wasn't like she could make a life with a man who—

She gasped, earning a quizzical look from JD beneath the brim of his hat. *When had she started thinking about making a life with Casey?*

Exactly twelve years ago. And she'd never stopped.

She was lonely, but she functioned. Sometimes she even managed to be happy. But she'd never stopped pining for Casey Long.

Yes, they'd been kids. But there were plenty of old happy couples who'd started off as high school sweethearts. Maybe not many. But sometimes when you know, you just know.

"Team roping is next," JD said through a clenched jaw. "That asshole better show up."

Slowly, and with her eyes on the entrance gate, Jessica made her way back to Carmen and Hope.

"Still not here?" Carmen asked.

Jessica shook her head.

"My fault?" Hope asked.

She didn't fully grasp what had happened. And even though they'd talked and talked and talked last night, Jessica wasn't positive that Hope understood Casey wasn't her dad.

"None of this is your fault."

Hope smiled. "Can I ride a sheep?"

Jessica sat down. "No, you're too big."

"Can I ride a horse?"

That could probably be arranged.

* * *

Casey pulled through the gate of the fairgrounds. He sure hoped he hadn't missed his and JD's event. JD would never forgive him.

Well, he would, but it would be a miserable two weeks waiting for him to get around to it.

He parked his pickup next to JD's and looked at his face in the rearview mirror. He hadn't shaved and there were bags beneath his eyes. Staying up all night will do that.

A daughter. He had a daughter.

It all made sense now. The Acostas had left because Jess had been pregnant. Eighteen years old with her whole life ahead of her, and he'd knocked her up. No wonder she'd called it *game over* last night when he hadn't had a condom. She'd had her life ruined once already.

He remembered the child's sweet, perfect face.

Not ruined. But definitely altered. Things had not gone the way Jessica and her mom had painstakingly planned.

Hope. It was a beautiful name.

There was an abandoned stone chapel on Harper's Hill. It was technically private property; part of the twelve-thousand-acre Rancho Canada Verde owned by the Kowalski family. But Gerome Kowalski didn't mind that Casey went there from time to time, and that's where he'd spent the night, trying to wrap his mind around this new reality.

At first, he'd been angry. Angry at Jess for keeping his own child a secret from him. But then he'd tried to put himself in her shoes. She'd been a teenager, and her mom had been in control. Had she really had a choice?

What would he have done at eighteen? He liked to think he'd have stepped up to the plate. But the truth was, he didn't know. Not for sure. This was why adults told teens they needed to be old enough to handle the consequences of sex. As a grown man, Casey knew this. He'd had that particular talk with more than one kid. But at eighteen...

None of that mattered now. Jessica had come home, and she'd probably been trying to work up the nerve to tell him about Hope. She must have felt terrified, not knowing how he'd react.

And he'd reacted horribly.

But Hope had been so happy and thrilled to meet him.

He'd seen nothing but joy in her face, and although he couldn't see himself, he had a pretty good idea of what he'd looked like. And she didn't need to see that.

He'd collected himself at the stone chapel. Regained his composure. And he was ready to face Hope with a smile and open arms. He was her daddy, goddammit. And if the way his heart ached at the thought of Jess ever escaping his sight again was any indication, he still loved her mama.

Yesterday he'd been Big Verde's most available sheriff. Today, he had a family.

They'd make this work. *If* Jess could even stand the sight of him after last night.

He grabbed his hat off the seat and stuck it on his head just as his door was yanked open. JD grabbed him by the arm. "Jesus Christ, Casey! I don't know where you've been or why you haven't answered your phone, but we're on in a few minutes. I got us pushed back as far as I could. Get your ass out of the truck."

JD gave a hard yank and Casey stumbled out of the truck, slamming the door behind him.

"Why the hell are you wearing *chaps?*" JD asked.

"What's wrong with chaps?"

"You look like an idiot."

The two of them started walking.

"Are we saddled up?" Casey asked.

"Of course, we're saddled up. And I warmed up Genevieve for you, but you need to get on that pony and ride around a bit. If we've even got time for that."

Casey glanced at the stands when they walked through the gate. He didn't see Jessica, and that worried him. But surely she hadn't gone back to Houston. Not after everything that had happened. Unless, she was so disgusted by his behavior that she never wanted to see him again.

"Get your mind off of that woman," JD said. "I know you think team roping is a breeze compared to bull riding, but you can still get hurt."

JD was right. Casey had to get his head on straight.

Fifteen minutes later he and Genevieve were in the box, looking at JD sitting atop Brazen on the other side of the chute. There was a young steer in the chute between them, raring to go. Casey's adrenaline was pumping. This was practically the best part.

He and JD had been partners for six years and friends and/ or foes for damn near a lifetime. He wasn't exactly sure what it was he did with his eyes to say *ready*, but JD saw it and gave a small, tight nod of his head.

The gates opened, and they were off.

JD was the header, and Casey rode heeler. They thundered across the arena with JD in the lead. He was on fire. He tossed the rope and it flew through the air, hooking the steer's horns. Now it was Casey's turn, as heeler, to go for the legs. The arena seemed to shrink as he honed in on the steer, rope held high in the air, and then it was gone. Flying.

The steer kicked up, and the rope ensnared its legs with perfect timing. Effortlessly, Casey got the rope around the saddle horn in a perfect dally before he looked up. The arena came back into focus and there was Jessica, hanging on the fence, with Hope next to her.

They waved, grinned, and shouted just as the rope went taut, jerking the horse. Distracted, Casey wasn't ready, and in what seemed like slow motion, he fell off the horse.

Fell. Off. The. Damn. Horse.

He landed with a thud and saw stars. Got the breath knocked out of him too.

JD rode up next to him. Concern shone in his eyes, but only for a brief second. Then he started laughing. "I told you to get your mind off that woman. Are you sure you used to ride bulls?"

"Ha-ha," Casey wheezed. "Very funny."

It didn't feel funny though. A sharp pain nearly gutted him when he inhaled. And when he went to stand up, he discovered he couldn't. *Goddammit.*

JD jumped down from his horse, concern back in his eyes. "Hey, bud. You okay?"

No. He was not okay. But he would be. "It's just my back."

Soon he was surrounded by people saying things like *Don't move* and *How many fingers am I holding up?* Someone also mentioned *ambulance.*

An EMT who looked maybe twelve years old called for a long backboard and a neck brace.

Jesus. He just needed a few minutes to come out of this spasm...

Suddenly Jessica was there. She dropped to her knees next to him and leaned over. "Casey, are you okay?"

Her dark hair brushed his cheek. She smelled like sunshine and sounded like an angel and her eyes were wide with fright.

"I'm fine," he said, although for some reason, he was having trouble getting air in his lungs. "Where's my daughter?"

Jessica put a finger to his lips. "Shh..."

"Where is—"

"Casey, Hope's not your daughter. Everything is fine."

Everything was fine?

Everything was definitely *not* fine. Because that meant—

He couldn't finish the thought. "Jess, if she's not my child, then whose is she?"

Before he could get an answer, someone stuck a stupid oxygen mask over his face.

CHAPTER ELEVEN

Jess watched the ambulance leave. She hadn't been able to answer Casey's question, because the EMTs needed her out of the way. But Casey's reaction to her thoughtless response, which she'd meant to be reassuring, answered any questions she'd had about him.

When informed that he wasn't the daddy of an eleven-year-old girl with Down syndrome whom he'd never met before, the emotion that had shown on his face was disappointment. Maybe even grief.

Casey Long was a special kind of man.

JD had heard everything but was busy acting like he hadn't. "He'll be fine," he said.

"How do you know that? He could have a broken back or a punctured lung or a concussion or—"

"He's embarrassed is all. And he should be. The idiot fell off his damn horse."

Carmen and Hope joined them as the dust settled and everybody started going back about their business. "Is he okay?" Hope asked.

JD took off his hat and held out his hand. "Howdy. I'm JD. And don't you worry your pretty little head. He'll be just fine. Sheriff Long probably needs some horseback riding lessons."

Oh no! Jessica held her breath. He'd said *Sheriff Long.*

She looked at Hope, praying she wasn't about to blurt out something that would no doubt end up on the front page of the *Big Verde News* the next day, but what she saw was a blushing eleven-year-old. *Blushing!*

"I'm Hope," she said, taking JD's hand.

Well, JD *was* very handsome. The two of them shook hands and simultaneously charmed the heck out of each other while Carmen touched up her lipstick.

"You know," JD said, "we have a place here in Big Verde called Hope House. Since it practically has your name on it, I think you should stop by and check it out before you leave. My sister teaches cooking classes there, and she has a little boy named Dalton."

"Cooking!" Hope said, clapping her hands.

"She loves to cook," Carmen said. "In fact, she's one of the best chefs at La Casa Bleu."

That wasn't quite true. Hope loved to be in the kitchen, but in a place like La Casa Bleu, the pace was frantic. She could never be in there during the chaotic dinner rush. However, she loved repetitive tasks and was a stickler for details. The pastry chef adored her, and nobody could *put a cherry on top* like Hope.

"I knew it!" JD said. "You're Carmen Foraccio, aren't you?"

"Guilty as charged," Carmen said. "And I assume you went to school with Jessica?"

"High school heartthrob," Jessica said.

Carmen fluttered her eyelashes. "No doubt."

"Man, I love your show," JD sputtered, taking off his hat as a sign of respect. "Gosh, I watch it all the time."

It was weird to think of JD watching cooking shows, and even weirder to see him acting starstruck. Although, if the blush on Carmen's cheeks was any indication, she was equally dazzled.

"Should we go to the hospital?" Jessica asked. Because *hello! Casey was hurt!*

"It would really embarrass him," JD said. "So, sure, let's go."

Jessica hated to drag Hope away from the rodeo. She'd been having so much fun up until the time Casey fell off his horse. "Carmen, do you guys want to stay here? I'm sure I can catch a ride with JD."

Two cowboys walked up. The pockets on their shirts said RANCHO CANADA VERDE. These were real working cowboys, as Rancho Canada Verde was one of the few cattle ranches in Texas that still managed cattle on horseback. Its cowboys had been sweeping the rodeo without even trying.

"JD, we feel honored to have been here to witness Casey riding a horse for the very first time," one of them said.

Both cowboys laughed and then followed it up with a high five. They looked nearly identical. They had to be twins.

"Shut up, guys. He just had some kind of—"

"Spasm? Conniption fit?" the other cowboy said, with a smirk that bordered on full-out grin.

"Ladies," JD said, "these irreverent jerks are Beau and Bryce Montgomery."

Both cowboys removed their hats. "Ah," one of them said, gazing at the three of them with his blue eyes.

"We get it now," said the other.

"Pardon?" JD asked.

"It was a woman."

"Yep."

One brother looked at the other. "The question is…"

"Which woman?"

Jessica's cheeks grew warm, no matter how hard she willed them not to. Beau or Bryce—she had no idea which one—winked at her. "Bingo."

* * *

Casey looked at Dr. Martin. "Happy now?"

The X-rays had shown nothing was broken. Casey's back was in a damn spasm and his ribs were bruised, but that was it. And he'd been carried out of the arena on a stretcher while every cowboy within a ten-mile radius had laughed his ass off.

They'd never have laughed over a serious injury. During his bull riding days, Casey had seen guys get their necks broken. He'd seen ropers lose their thumbs. He'd seen a man tossed into the air by a bull who seemed to think he was a rag doll.

But he'd never seen a man just fall off his horse for no good reason.

Except there *had* been a reason. He'd seen his whole damn world watching him from the fence and the realization had momentarily tilted the universe.

"I'm happy that you're not mortally wounded," Dr. Martin said. "Unless you're planning to die of embarrassment, that is."

Casey gave him the side-eye. Partly because he deserved it, but mostly because he couldn't turn his head.

"You'll need to take it easy for the next few days. I'll give you some muscle relaxants—"

Casey waved his hand dismissively, but the movement made him wince.

"And you should stick to the bed or recliner."

Like that was gonna happen.

"And avoid reading. You might have a slight concussion."

"Thanks, doc."

Casey got down from the exam table gingerly. He'd been through this before and knew what to do. Warm compresses. Cold compresses. He'd try to avoid the muscle relaxants, since they made him wonky and he needed his mind clear.

There was much thinking to be done.

Last night he'd been in a downright state of shock and panic when Hope had called him daddy. She'd seemed pretty damn sure about it, after all. But he believed Jess when she said he wasn't the child's father.

Then who was?

Wondering made his jaw and head hurt even more than his back. Jessica had been gone for almost twelve years. If she hadn't been pregnant when she and her mom had stolen out of Big Verde in the middle of the night without leaving so much as a note, then she'd become pregnant very shortly thereafter.

But somehow, he knew it was the reason they'd left. Jess had been pregnant. In high school. But it didn't make sense, unless she'd slept with someone besides him. And while he knew folks made mistakes, particularly young folks, he just didn't buy it. Not Jessica. She'd been levelheaded and practical, even at eighteen. The most foolish thing she'd ever done was *him,* and nothing in her behavior during their time together had indicated she was anything other than head over heels in love with him.

And he'd felt the same.

Jessica had come back to Big Verde for a reason, and he thought he'd figured out what it was. But he'd been way off.

He walked down the hospital's short hallway and out the back door where the ambulance had deposited him earlier. The bright sunlight hurt his head, and Doc might be right about that slight concussion. He reached in his pocket for his keys and looked around for his truck.

Shit.

The truck was at the arena. How the holy hell was he supposed to get home?

A silver Lexus pulled up.

Jesus Christ, not now.

The tinted window rolled down slowly, and there sat Annabelle Vasquez. She wasn't the only woman in Big Verde who regularly pursued him, but she was no doubt the most aggressive. And she was wearing a goddamn candy striper uniform.

Blue Jays. That's what the hospital volunteer ladies called themselves.

Now would be a good time to make a dash for his truck, only he couldn't dash if his life depended on it, and there was no truck.

"I heard about your little accident," Anna said with a smirk. Her eyes roamed the full length of his body. "You didn't hurt anything on your way down, did you?"

Why did everything she say sound so dirty?

"No, ma'am. It wasn't until I hit the dirt that everything started to hurt."

"Hm. Well, I'm early for my shift. Do you need a ride home?"

"That's mighty nice of you to offer but—" He looked around. It wasn't like he had many options.

Anna raised an eyebrow, then leaned over and opened the door.

And Casey got an eyeful. He could see clear down to her belly button in that getup. Surely the old ladies like Mrs. Dunbar and Miss Mills didn't wear the same outfit?

"Is that the official hospital volunteer uniform?"

"It's the same general idea," Anna said, "I had mine altered a bit."

Casey got in the car, feeling like this was the beginning of a very bad slasher film where you just knew it wasn't going to end well. Or, as Anna reached across him to help grab the seat belt, "accidentally" touching his arm, shoulder, thigh, chest, and *lap,* the beginning of a low-budget porno.

"Okay, Sheriff," she purred. "Get ready to ride."

He gulped and stared out the window.

As they pulled out of the parking lot she added, "Nice chaps."

* * *

Jessica followed a winding road to the top of Lookout Hill and stopped in front of a private lane. The number on the fence post matched the address JD had given her.

They'd gone by the hospital only to discover that Casey had been released nearly as soon as he got there. The doctor had told them he had some bruised ribs and was perfectly fine—HIPAA laws apparently hadn't reached Big Verde—but Jessica wanted to see for herself.

She peered down the lane at the white rock house. For some reason, her hands were sweaty. Casey was going to have some questions, and she wasn't sure she was up to answering them. Hope was a Long, but Jessica had never intended on anyone knowing. Mavis had loved her only grandchild, but she had never suggested bringing Hope home to Big Verde.

Maybe Mavis was ashamed. Just like Jessica had been ashamed over her mom's citizenship status. Jessica had felt like she'd done something wrong, even though she hadn't.

It didn't make sense, but shame and embarrassment weren't necessarily reasonable emotions.

But Mavis had started Hope House.

Surely that meant something.

Jessica bit her lip and slowly turned the steering wheel to start down the lane. She wasn't sure how much she wanted to tell Casey, but she needed to see him. To know he really was okay. When he'd fallen, her heart had nearly stopped. She hadn't been that terrified since the hospital had called to say her mom had had a heart attack. It was that same horrible, helpless feeling. The *I might really lose someone* feeling.

Movement caught her eye. Someone was getting out of a silver car on the driveway. And even from a distance, Jessica could see that it was Annabelle Vasquez, who hadn't changed a bit. What the heck was she doing at Casey's house?

Annabelle and Jessica had been cohead cheerleaders. Jessica had been chosen first, and then Anna had thrown such a fit that her parents had gone to the school board. Next thing Jessica knew, she was sharing the highly coveted position with Big Verde's version of Nellie Oleson.

Not that she was still mad about such a trivial thing. Much.

Anna wore a super tight blue-striped pinafore. Was she actually in a *costume?* She carried a doughnut box in one hand and a Rite Aid bag in the other.

Maybe there were condoms in that bag, and she and Casey were about to play "nurse and patient."

Casey had definitely picked up some skills in the sex department. Maybe Annabelle was a practice buddy. What did Jessica really know about Casey's life here in Big Verde?

She must have been thinking too hard, because Anna suddenly turned around and looked at her. Jessica slunk down in the seat, which was stupid, and Anna stared through squinted eyes. Then she smiled.

Dang it!

But she didn't wave at Jessica or indicate she should come on up. She just turned on her heel, flipped her hair, and then sashayed her way to the front door, where she went inside without knocking.

Jessica put the car in reverse and backed down the lane to the road.

Casey had a life. And she'd done nothing but make it more difficult since the moment she'd got here. First, she'd made him late for his great-aunt's funeral. Then they nearly got caught behind the pool pump, which would have been embarrassing for her but could have been career-ending for Casey. And finally, he'd been thoroughly traumatized by Hope calling him Daddy, before finally being sweetly disappointed to learn that he wasn't.

And there was the falling-off-the-horse thing. She couldn't forget about that.

Casey seemed to be doing really well in Big Verde. He was happy, content, successful...and maybe he had a thing going with Anna. Who was she to waltz in and ruin it?

Tomorrow, after the reading of the will at the lawyer's office, she and Hope and Carmen would go back to Houston. Casey would remain in Big Verde. They were meant to be high school sweethearts and nothing more.

Maybe you really couldn't go home again.

CHAPTER TWELVE

Casey drifted to the surface of consciousness and then promptly sank back into the warm, fluffy depths of dream-land. He'd been prancing around the arena on his horse while a nice set of pom-poms pressed into his back...

Pom-poms.

Jessica!

His eyes flew open. He kicked off the covers and gri-maced, remembering his back.

Gingerly, he shifted his hips. Not too bad. He tried rolling over on his side, and that went okay too. He swung his legs over the side of the bed and sat up, keeping his back straight.

Hot damn. The muscle relaxant Anna had forced down his throat had done the trick. But just how long had he been out?

The lighting in the room indicated it was early evening. Only the hue didn't look quite right. Surely he hadn't slept all night.

He looked at the clock on the nightstand: 8:30 a.m.

Shit! He absolutely had slept all night.

He'd wanted to get to the Village Château at the crack of dawn. Had Jessica already left? No matter. If she had, he'd call into the office and tell them he wasn't coming in. He was driving to Houston. He'd storm into that fancy spaghetti place she worked at and, well, he didn't know what would come after that. But he wasn't sitting around here wondering why the love of his life walked out. He'd done that once. He wasn't going to do it again.

He stood up, grabbed a clean shirt, looked at his dirty jeans—he'd slept in them to avoid having Anna take his pants off—and decided to just brush them off. Bending over to step into a clean pair might be pushing his luck. He was stiff as hell.

Ten minutes later he headed for the door. He looked out the window and saw his truck parked in the driveway. JD must have driven it over.

With relief, Casey reached for the doorknob. There was a sticky note staring him in the face, just below the peephole.

Gabriel Castro called. Said for you to be at his office at 9:00. Very important. He says he has something of yours. Don't be late. XOXOXO Anna

Casey sighed in frustration. It's like the entire world was conspiring to keep him and Jessica apart. He yanked the door open and walked to his truck. What the hell did Gabriel want? He was a lawyer, so nothing good.

There was barely enough time to make it to Gabriel's office, but Casey wanted to swing by the Château first. The damn lawyer could wait.

His mood improved as he drove down the hill toward town. It was a gorgeous day, and he had a good feeling. He and Jessica had both felt the connection; he just knew it. She wouldn't leave Big Verde for Houston without at least saying good-bye, especially since he'd fallen off his horse yesterday.

His face heated up over that.

But what could he say? That was the effect she had on him.

She'd looked pretty worried.

Casey grinned. A little.

The Château was just on the outskirts of town. He looked around as he pulled into the parking lot. There was no red Porsche. His heart sank. Well, it was more like it took a dive straight to the pit of his stomach.

He swung around the back of the hotel, drove around to the side.

No Porsche.

He pulled into a spot and parked. Then he just sat there.

The weekend seemed like a dream. In the course of forty-eight hours, he'd rediscovered and fanned an old flame, thought he was a father, learned he wasn't, decided he was in love and then...

Well, hell.

She'd left him without so much as a good-bye.

Again.

* * *

Jessica sat nervously in Gabriel Castro's office, flanked by Carmen and Hope. As hard as she tried, she didn't recognize the name. There was a large Castro family in Big Verde, but she didn't remember a Gabriel.

"I just can't place him," she said out loud, chewing her lip.

Carmen snorted. "Would you stop? It's so funny to watch you go all *small town* on me. I'm absolutely positive there were people in Big Verde who floated under your radar."

"But there weren't," Jessica said. "You don't understand Big Verde."

"I understand it has cowboys. Real ones. Like those twins. So, it's all good in my book."

The Montgomery twins had come by the Château last

night, and Carmen had joined them for a couple of drinks before they'd dragged her to Tony's, a local honky-tonk. It was Carmen's first time in a honky-tonk, and she'd had all kinds of fun. The kind of fun that involved twin cowboys.

The bar food at Tony's was surprisingly good," Carmen said. "Nothing fancy, but really good. Tony gave me his mom's recipe for buttermilk-battered mushrooms. Did you know she still works in the kitchen? She's ninety-one!"

Jessica tried not to be irritated by Carmen's enthusiasm for All Things Big Verde. She'd been a great help this weekend, looking after Hope and providing emotional support. She was entitled to a little fun.

"I wonder how much money Mavis left Hope," Carmen said in a loud stage whisper.

"How much what?" Hope asked.

"Nothing," Jessica and Carmen answered together. Because there was no point in explaining wills and inheritances to an eleven-year-old.

Hope was Mavis's only grandchild, and Jessica knew she'd be taken care of. If Jessica ever became ill, or too old to care for Hope... Well, it was an overwhelming relief to know Hope would have a nest egg.

She looked at her watch. Lawyers. Why did they always keep you waiting?

The door opened and a tall, handsome man in a crisp gray suit walked in.

"Good morning, ladies," he said. His smile radiated a warmth that lit up his eyes. He had a full head of thick, luscious hair, sparkling white teeth, and dimples that took the edge off of his nearly overwhelming sex appeal. "I'm Gabriel Castro."

He went straight for Hope. "I presume you are Ms. Hope Acosta?"

Hope grinned.

He looked at Carmen next. "Ms. Foraccio, I'm a huge fan. It is a pleasure to meet you. I hope you're enjoying your time in Big Verde."

Carmen pumped his hand with enthusiasm. "I'm enjoying it very much."

Finally, he turned his brown eyes on Jessica. "And you must be Jessica, the most enthusiastic cheerleader the Big Verde Giants have ever had. At least that's what I hear."

"I'm sorry. I know you're a Castro, but I just can't place you—"

Gabriel laughed. "No relation. I married into the Big Verde community. I'm originally from Austin."

That explained it. "Oh? Who did you—"

The door opened and Jessica turned. *Casey!*

He looked just as surprised to see her.

"I thought you'd left," he said.

Jessica stood, and Casey crossed the room in three quick steps. The next thing Jessica knew, she was in his arms. The world shrank to just the two of them, Casey's heart beating frantically beneath her cheek while her own pulse pounded in her head. Hope giggled. Carmen sighed. Gabriel cleared his throat.

It was quite possibly a full minute before Casey loosened his grip and took a small step back.

"I wasn't going to leave without saying good-bye," she said. "I came by your house yesterday, but you were busy."

"Busy? I was probably asleep," he said. "Anna made me take a muscle relaxant. It knocked me out."

"Yeah, I saw her."

Casey laughed. "Really? How did that go? Did y'all try to out high-kick each other?"

Jessica couldn't help it. The idea of that made her snort.

Whatever there was between Casey and Anna—if there was anything at all—it was obviously not romantic. And every cell in her body breathed a sigh of relief. Even though she was leaving for Houston today, and Casey was staying here.

"We didn't speak," Jessica said. "I saw her and I just, you know, left. I didn't want to disturb you."

"You could never disturb me."

They sat down, and Casey leaned over with a slight wince. His breath tickled her ear as he whispered, "Never with Anna. You know me better than that, Jess."

Anna had been her rival. And Casey was loyal beyond a fault.

She shivered from the feel of his breath against her ear.

Gabriel sat in his chair. "I hear you took a tumble yesterday, Sheriff Long."

Casey rolled his eyes. "I'll never live it down."

Hope sat up straight in her seat. "Sheriff Long is my daddy!"

Oh God. They were back to that.

* * *

Casey broke out in a light sweat. Why did Hope keep saying he was her daddy? It was jarring, to say the least. He looked at Jessica, and she merely rolled her eyes. She was irritated, but not surprised, so Casey relaxed.

A little.

"I know Sheriff Long is your daddy," Gabriel said to Hope.

What?

Now Jess's face went white.

"Uh, Jess..."

"And we're here because your Grandma Mavis asked us to come together," Gabriel said.

"Her grandma?" Casey blurted. Then he looked at Jess.

"Yes, Casey. That's what I tried to tell you at the arena—"

"Her *grandma*?" Casey repeated. "You're saying Aunt Mavis is her grandma—"

Aunt Mavis had one son. And it was his ass-wipe cousin or uncle or whatever he was, Wade.

The room felt like it flipped sideways as things clicked into place. Casey jumped to his feet in a blinding fit of white rage. That goddamn *asshole*. He started to shake. He needed to punch something, but instead he pulled Jess to her feet, and through clenched teeth, he said, "He...*touched you?* How? When?"

The room went totally still. She'd been eighteen. *Eighteen!* He wrapped his arms around her. No wonder they'd left town that way. Her mom had to protect her.

"Casey, not me."

Jessica was saying something. He let go and stared into her eyes. Her sweet, sweet eyes. Swallowed down another lump.

"My mom," she said. "Hope is my sister."

Gabriel came around his desk. "Have a seat, Casey. I'm so sorry. I misspoke."

"I'm her sister," Hope said, smiling proudly.

Casey sat down. He had no choice, since his knees had basically given out.

Jessica sat too, and her small hand took hold of his.

He tried to wrap his mind around what he'd just learned. Wade had been having an affair—or something—with Jessica's mom. He'd gotten her pregnant. And she had taken Jessica and left Big Verde without telling a soul where they were going.

"Did you not read the letters, Casey?"

Jessica's face. He focused on that. Why were her eyes tearing up?

"What letters?"

"I suspect these are the letters right here," Gabriel said, holding up five envelopes, all covered in hand-drawn hearts and stamped and addressed to Casey Long.

All were still sealed.

"Where did you get those?" Jessica asked.

"From Mavis," Gabriel said. He handed them to Casey.

Eighteen-year-old Jessica's swirly-girlie handwriting stared up at him. Casey took a deep breath, and with shaking fingers, he popped a kissy-lips seal that would have made him laugh on any other occasion.

"Is it okay for me to read these?" he suddenly asked Jessica.

"Yes, of course," Jessica said. But then she looked at the envelopes with their hearts and flowers and kissy-lips and added, "But maybe not this very minute."

Casey wanted to rip into them as if they contained the secret to immortality or the cure for cancer, but Jessica's cheeks were pink and getting pinker. So, he casually tucked them into his shirt pocket and gave them a gentle pat.

"I don't understand," Jessica said. "How did Mavis end up with those letters?"

Casey explored his memories from twelve years ago, the summer of his graduation. Everything was a blur of pain and panic, because Jessica had disappeared, but he remembered that his parents had gone to Europe. It was supposed to have been a graduation trip for Casey, but he'd been too crushed and depressed to go. He'd stayed home, and Aunt Mavis had come by every day to check on him and other things.

Like the mail.

Gabriel pulled another envelope out of his desk. "I suspect this will explain everything."

There was another letter?

"I had assumed we were here for a reading of Mavis's will," Jess said. And then she quickly added, "Because of Hope."

Gabriel laughed softly. "That only happens in the movies. I mean, I have your copy of the will right here. And I'm happy to go over it with you, if you need me to. Mavis left Hope very well cared for. But you were both called here today because Mavis wanted you and Casey in the same room while I read you this."

Gabriel cleared his throat dramatically. "Dear Jessica and Casey, this is an apology for a terrible thing I have done..."

* * *

Five minutes later, everyone sat quietly, digesting what they'd just heard. Jessica anxiously bit her lip and tried to remain in her seat. Because what she wanted to do was jump up and down and stomp her feet, and that wasn't appropriate at all.

Mavis had intercepted the letters. She'd known about Wade's misdeed and had been afraid Jessica would tell Casey, and then he'd tell someone, and they'd tell someone...

Honestly, Mavis might have been right. They'd been teenagers, and there had been too much at stake. Way more than simply the Long family's reputation.

Casey sighed and leaned forward to rest his elbows on his knees, shaking his head. "I just don't know how my family could have done yours any more wrong."

"In her confession, Mavis asked for our forgiveness. I loved her way too much not to give it to her," Jessica said.

Casey looked at her as if she had two heads. "You really did love her, didn't you?"

"I really did."

And Mavis wasn't the only person she'd loved in Big Verde. What she'd felt for Casey had not been a teenage crush. And what she felt for him now was even stronger. From the moment he'd walked in the room and enveloped her in his arms, she'd felt safe. And for her, that was a strong and rare emotion.

She'd been adrift for twelve years, and Casey was an anchor. She couldn't stand the thought of leaving him again, but she couldn't conceive of a way around it.

"Man," Carmen said. "You folks certainly know how to dish out the drama in this town."

Upon hearing the word *drama*, Hope put a hand to her forehead, as if she were about to swoon. Carmen had taught her to do that whenever someone was being overly dramatic. It made Gabriel laugh and relieved at least some of the tension in the room. And when Hope's stomach chose that moment to growl loudly, that relieved the rest.

"Somebody's hungry," Jessica said. "Should we head to Corner Café for a late breakfast?" She wanted to spend as much time as possible with Casey before heading back to Houston.

A little spark of panic fluttered in her chest. She clutched his hand tightly, and it went away.

"Can we make it brunch?" Carmen asked. "I have a bit of business with Mr. Castro here."

Jessica looked at Gabriel. Was Carmen kidding?

"She's my ten o'clock appointment," he said.

What possible business could Carmen need to conduct in Big Verde that involved a lawyer? Whatever it was, Jessica recognized her friend's stubborn impish grin. There was no point in asking. She wouldn't get it out of her. Not right now anyway.

Jessica looked out the front window of the Corner Café. A girl who looked about sixteen was busy scrubbing off green shoe polish that spelled out BEAT THE BADGERS!

"Well," she asked Casey. "Did they?"

"Did who what?"

"Did the Big Verde Giants beat the Badgers on Friday?"

Sally Larson, owner of the diner, refilled their coffee cups. "You're kidding, right?" she asked, not even bothering to pretend she wasn't listening to their conversation. "Darlin', the last time the Big Verde Giants beat the Badgers was 1979."

"Oh. Well, there's always next year."

"That's the cheerleader spirit," Sally said, pretending to wipe crumbs off the table. She'd been hovering around their booth like a bee bothering a honeysuckle vine since the moment they sat down. Big Verde had a weekly newspaper, but Sally Larson was the Official Town Gossip, a role she took seriously.

"Homecoming is next week," Casey said. "We're playing the Sweet Home Beavers."

"Do they still write LICK THE BEAVERS! on all the windows?"

"Now, Jess, why wouldn't they?" Casey asked, feigning innocence.

When they were in school, everyone had pretended not to know what it meant, and Jessica was pleased the tradition of playing dumb lived on.

"Lick the Beavers!" Hope cheered.

"Oh, dear," Jessica said.

Sally snorted and headed for the kitchen, where Rusty, the cook, had just hit the bell. "Order up!"

Homecoming. There was just something about the Friday night lights of the field, the announcer's voice echoing through the big speakers, the sharp drum cadence of the school fight song...

"It sure would be fun to take Hope to a game," she said.

"Why don't you come down?" Casey asked.

"I don't know. It's typically pretty hard to get away from work on a weekend."

"I'll get you a mum," Casey said, blue eyes twinkling.

"What about me?" Hope asked.

"You too. The biggest mum I can find."

Hope clapped her hands. "Yay! What's a mum?"

Sally came back to the table, balancing a huge tray. She set a short stack of pancakes in front of Hope, *huevos rancheros* in front of Casey, and scrambled eggs, sausage, and buttered grits in front of Jessica. It all smelled delicious, and for the next few minutes they ate in silence, except for the occasional groan of delight.

"Are you going to eat that last piece of bacon?" Jessica asked, pointing at Casey's plate with her fork.

"Damn, woman. You always could pack it away."

Jessica looked at her plate, which was practically licked clean. "Don't judge," she said. "I'm an emotional eater."

Casey put his hands up. "No judgment," he said. "And you're welcome to eat my bacon."

Jessica's fork stopped midway to his plate. Why had

that sounded so dirty? She glanced up and was met by a cocked eyebrow and sexy smirk. *Because he'd meant it to sound dirty.*

Suddenly, Hope snatched the bacon with her chubby little hand and hightailed it to the other side of the diner.

"Sheriff," Sally said. "We have a bacon bandit!"

* * *

Casey watched Hope settle into a corner booth with her stolen goods.

"It's not even her first offense," Jess said, standing up.

"Sit back down," Sally said. She held up a handful of crayons and a piece of paper. "She can stay in her own booth and give y'all some privacy."

Jess sat, but she bit her lip, glancing nervously at Hope in the corner.

"She'll be fine over there," Casey said. "I've got my eye on her."

The tension across Jessica's brow disappeared, and she stopped gnawing on her lip. "It's such a relief to not have to watch her like a hawk everywhere I go," she said. "Believe me. In Houston, she would not be sitting in a restaurant at her very own table. I can't let her out of my sight."

Casey couldn't imagine the stress Jessica had been under all these years, particularly the last two, where she'd been responsible for Hope by herself. "It must be hard," he said.

Carmen seemed like a good friend, but Casey couldn't help but feel that Jessica's life would be easier in a small community like Big Verde, where everyone looked out for each other. At the idea of Jessica and Hope living in Big Verde, Casey's heart thudded around his chest like a battering ram. Would the thought occur to Jessica, as well?

"You have no idea how hard," Jessica said. "The school bus used to drop her off at our apartment. But since Mom died, she goes to an after-school program. She hates it. But she can't always be at work with me, and I can't always be at home."

"You don't have any place like Hope House in Houston? A teacher walks Dalton and some other kids over after school. It's right across the street."

"Oh, there are lots of great places. But they're not near La Casa Bleu or Hope's school, and Houston traffic is horrendous. It's not like I can just get her somewhere in ten minutes."

Casey wanted to point out that you could get from one end of Big Verde to the other in under ten minutes, but he didn't want to sound as desperate as he felt.

He reached across the table and took both of Jess's hands in his. Now that they'd finished eating, and they had a modicum of privacy—Sally pretended to adjust the blinds in the booth behind them—it was time to take on the elephant in the room.

"Your mom was undocumented?"

Jessica stared at the cup of coffee in front of her. "Yes," she whispered.

"It must be hard to talk about something you'd been forbidden to speak of for so long. But there's nothing to be ashamed of, Jess."

"I didn't know her status when we lived in Big V. And I'm glad I didn't. Because at least for my childhood, I didn't live in fear. In Houston, every day was filled with dread and anxiety. I was terrified of coming home to find Mom gone and Hope all alone in the apartment."

"I wish you'd told me. Maybe my family could have helped. There's something called asylum—"

"She did ask someone from your family for help. That's how she met Wade. She naively assumed the county sheriff would know how to get her on a path to citizenship."

Wade. Casey was going to have a hard time not punching the guy the next time he saw him.

He wanted to soothe Jess with words like *what's passed is past* and *you're safe now.* But he knew from trauma training that those words were hollow. Jessica needed time. And someone to talk to.

And that led to the one burning question tumbling around inside his mouth, waiting for an opportunity to spill out. "When are you heading back to Houston?"

"We have a two o'clock checkout," Jess said. "That is, if Carmen makes it back in time."

"What the hell kind of business could she be stirring up with Gabe?"

"Oh, it could be anything, really. Somebody texted or e-mailed or called about an emergency involving rights or insurance or contracts and *whoala!* She's sitting in front of a lawyer. It happens all the time. Her life is crazy."

"I bet that means your life in Houston is also crazy."

Jess took a sip of coffee, and Sally topped it off again. "Let's just say I've enjoyed this weekend in Big Verde. I mean, we've definitely had some excitement—"

Casey laughed at the understatement.

"But it's a different kind," Jessica said. "I've missed this place."

Casey swallowed. How could this work out? "Jess, I don't want to lose you again," he whispered.

Sally, who was now pretending to clean a spotless table nearby, sniffled loudly.

"And I don't want to lose you again, either," Jess said, squeezing his hand.

"You say you missed Big Verde. That you had never wanted to leave."

"And that's all true. But there's also reality to consider."

"The reality is that you and I were torn apart by our families. We had plans, Jess. Plans to be together. And as far as I know, neither one of us intentionally changed them."

Jess took a deep breath.

Dammit. She was going to say something reasonable.

"I'm raising a Down syndrome child by myself. Thanks to Carmen, I'm able to do it on a good salary. I *do* love Big Verde. But what would I do here? Where would I work? And Casey—"

Sally stopped wiping the table, and Jessica lowered her voice to a whisper. "We don't really know each other anymore. We're not eighteen."

Casey shook his head and took a couple of seconds to gather his thoughts. She still had feelings for him, that was obvious. And he'd never stopped loving her. Letting her walk out of his life again, without even trying to pick up where they'd left off, seemed like a catastrophic mistake. "I know damn well how old we are. But we *do* know each other. Shit, you made me who I am today. How can you say you don't know me?"

Sally approached with her goddamn coffeepot.

Casey held up his hand. "Not now, Sally."

"Hope!" Jessica stood swiftly, and Casey did the same, without even knowing why.

"I got it, sweetheart," Sally said.

Hope had somehow ended up behind the counter. She was straightening the napkin holders and condiments. Putting them all in a row. Sally praised her for tidying up. "Do you like to put things in nice, neat rows?"

"Sally volunteers at Hope House," Casey assured Jess.

"These are crooked," Hope said. Then she went to work

making sure everything lined up, poking her tongue out of one corner of her mouth from the effort.

Jess sat back down with a sigh, and so did Casey.

"Listen," Casey said. "We'll work it out. There are five-star restaurants in Austin where you could work. That's not too far away. We just have to iron out some details is all."

Jess began frantically twisting a strand of her hair. "I'm not sure Carmen can live without me."

Casey leaned across the table. Kissed her on the nose and watched her blush. "I'm the one who can't live without you. I'll cancel my reelection campaign. At the end of this term, I can move to Houston, if you want me to."

Boom. He hadn't meant to say it. Hadn't even *thought* about it. But as he watched the tears build up in Jessica's sweet brown eyes, he realized that's what made it honest. Every word had come straight from the heart.

He'd follow her anywhere, because dammit, they deserved to be together.

Forever.

* * *

Jessica couldn't believe her ears. And yet, Casey gazed at her with a fierce intensity that said he meant business.

The man was serious. He was willing to leave his career and home to be with her.

Sally stood wide-eyed, clutching the coffeepot like it was a life preserver and the Corner Café was the *Titanic*. Rusty stared openly from the other side of the counter, spatula suspended in midair.

These were Casey's people. How could she live with herself if she took him away from Big Verde? But how could *she* live if she had to do it without Casey?

The little bell above the door jingled. Sally wiped her nose on the back of her hand and reached for a stack of menus. Not that anybody in Big Verde needed one.

Then she gasped at the sight of Carmen breezing in.

"I was hoping I'd still find you two here," Carmen said, yanking out a seat.

"Oh, my," Sally said. "Are you who I think you are? Well, of course you are. That's a silly question, isn't it? I'd heard you were in town. Can I get you some coffee? A Danish maybe?"

"Both of those things sound delightful," Carmen said. "And do you have anything weird for me to try?"

"Um...weird?"

"Yeah," Carmen said, shrugging her shoulders. "I'm kinky that way."

"I have some goose jerky."

"I'm down for it," Carmen said. "Bring it."

Sally hurried off.

Jessica shifted in her seat. "Listen, Carmen, Casey and I are talking. This is kind of bad timing."

"So I did a thing," Carmen said, ignoring Jessica entirely.

Jessica rolled her eyes. "Tell me there's no restraining order. Was it one of those twins?"

Carmen laughed. "This has nothing to do with them."

"Oh. Well, then maybe it can wait—"

"I bought the Village Château restaurant. Well, part of it. The chef, Frederick, is in on it too. He wanted to buy it but didn't have the resources. I'm the majority owner. We're going to call it Le Château Bleu and we plan to fuse French and German—"

The words Carmen was stringing together finally formed themselves into sentences in Jessica's mind. "Are you serious? You bought the restaurant at the Château?"

Sally came back and set a plate down in front of Carmen. It looked like dehydrated dog poop, but it was set on a fancy doily. "You've got to hold it in your mouth for a few seconds to soften it up."

"Looks delish," Carmen said.

"My son, Bubba, made it."

"Carmen!" Jessica said. "Did you hear me? Did you really buy the Village Château?"

"Not technically. Closing date is a few weeks away. But it's happening."

Jessica's brain was on overdrive. She knew where this was heading, and it was too good to be true. She glanced at Casey across the table, and he was grinning and wiggling and appeared to be about ready to pop out of his skin.

Carmen picked up a piece of jerky and eyed it curiously. "We'd like a manager on the premises as soon as possible, of course. Current owners are cool with it. It's going to be a big transition. Lots to do. Because I have *huge* plans and we're going to have a lavish and extreme grand opening. I'm talking celebrity guest list. Big Verde won't know what hit it."

"A manager? You need a manager?"

"Yep. Do you know anybody who might be interested?" Carmen's eyes twinkled, but she managed to keep a straight face as she stuffed the jerky in her mouth.

"Careful now," Casey said. "That's going to expand."

Carmen, cheek bulging, gave him a thumbs-up and mouthed *I'll miss you* to Jessica. At least Jessica thought that's what she said.

Beneath the table, a big boot rubbed against Jessica's ankle. Casey raised his eyebrows. "Well? What do you say, Jess?"

She gazed at Casey, noting the slight wrinkles around his eyes. They hadn't been there when she'd left twelve years ago. She took his hand and traced some light scars, wondering what had caused them. She'd missed parts of his life. Major parts. But the expression on his face, so hopeful and anxious, belonged to the boy she used to know.

Casey squeezed her hand. "We have our whole lives ahead of us, Jess."

He'd said the same thing on the night they'd promised to be together forever. It was true then, and it was true now.

"Oh, Casey," she said, choking back tears in disbelief. "I think I'm finally coming home."

Casey leaned over the table to kiss her, and when their lips met, applause broke out in the Corner Café.

Home was where her cowboy was, and he was in the best little town in Texas.

For more great reads by Carly, check out Big Bad Cowboy *or visit her website at carlybloombooks.com.*

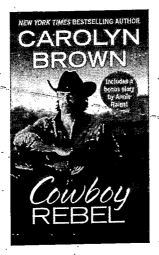

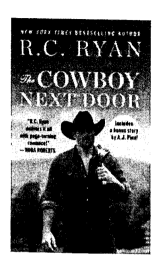

THE COWBOY NEXT DOOR
By R.C. Ryan

The last thing Penny Cash needs is a flirtation with a wild, carefree cowboy. Sure, he's funny and sexy, but they're as different as whiskey and tea. But when trouble comes calling, Penny will find out how serious Sam Monroe can be when it comes to protecting the woman he loves. Includes a bonus story by A.J. Pine!

HARD LOVING COWBOY
By A.J. Pine

Walker Everett has good and bad days—but the worst was the day that Violet Chastain started as the new sommelier at Crossroads Ranch. She knows nothing about ranch life and constantly gets under his skin. But when a heated argument leads to the hottest kiss he's ever had, Walker must decide whether he finally deserves something good. Includes a bonus story by Sara Richardson!

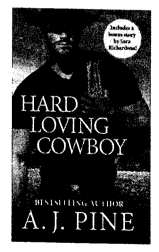

COLORADO COWBOY
By Sara Richardson

Charity Stone has learned to
hold her own in the
male-dominated rodeo world.
There's no cowboy she can't
handle...except for one.
Officer Dev Jenkins has made
it clear he doesn't look at her as
one of the guys. He's caught
her attention, but Charity
doesn't do relationships—
especially not with a cowboy.
Includes a bonus story by Jay
Crownover!

JUSTIFIED
By Jay Crownover

As the sheriff of Loveless,
Texas, Case Lawton is
determined to do everything by
the book—until he's called to
Aspen Barlow's office after a
so-called break-in. The last thing
he wants to do is help the woman
who cost him custody of his son.
But as threats against Aspen start
to escalate, it becomes clear that
Case is her last hope—and
there's nothing he wouldn't do to
keep her safe. Includes a bonus
story by Carly Bloom!

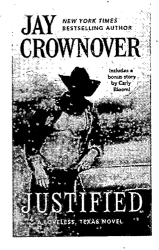